TABITHA MIN

PERDITION RISING

THE SIEGE OF AECORATH

BOOK TWO

The Ritter House Publishing name and logo are trademarks of Ritter House Publishing LLC.

www.tabithamin.com

Book and Cover design by Tabitha Min

ISBN: 979-8-9877812-5-8

First Edition : February 2025

10 9 8 7 6 5 4 3 2 1

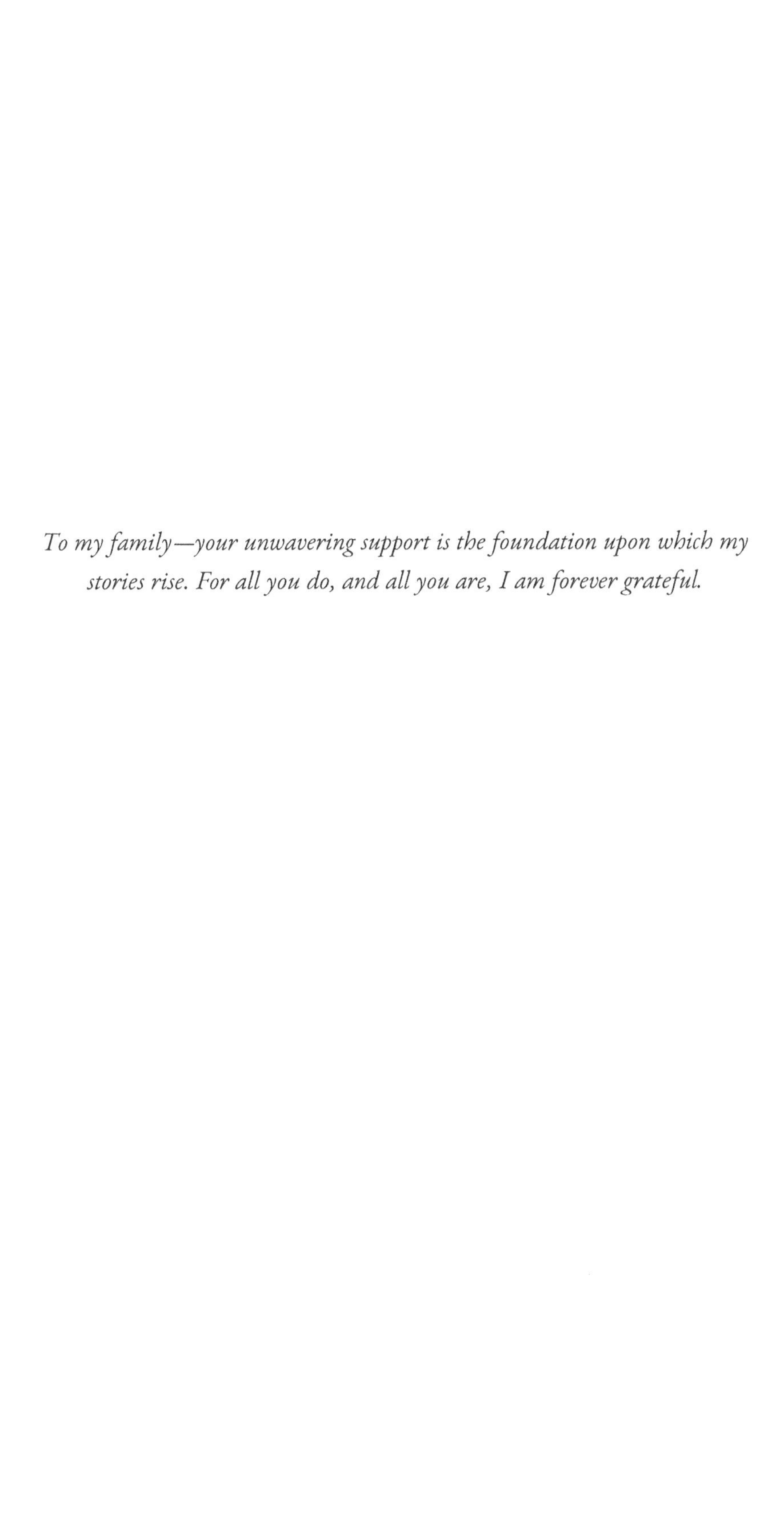

To my family—your unwavering support is the foundation upon which my stories rise. For all you do, and all you are, I am forever grateful.

SKELEG LANDS
VALENMUR
ORMSKIRK
ETHREAL RIVER
BONNORATH WOOD
EGRIN
ABENSLOH
FAERMIRE
ELSTERHEIM
WESTMEL
EVERSELT
ARMAGH
WALISBURN
DOLAM PASS
HELMERE
GRAEFELD
MISTELFELD
NANTWICH
HELMFIRTH
ERYTHEAN SEA
DUDENBE
LIMEREG
THREKELD
CAELKIRK
LINDBERG
AMMERSHOF
BEROBON
WILSDEN
CHALIS HEIGHTS
DOMAIN OF
AECORATH
SW S SE

PERDITION

RISING

ONE

KINGDOM OF FAERMIRE

Sidonis awoke with a violent gasp, his lungs burning as he sucked in the cold, damp air. The thick, swirling fog enveloped him, blurring the edges of his vision. As he struggled to lift himself from the ground, he cradled his ribs, wincing at the sharp pain that shot through his torso. Through the haze, he spotted a dark figure—Gorhan, the seer—standing with arms outstretched toward the sky, chanting in a language that reverberated with ancient power.

Desperately trying to piece together the fragmented memories of his recent past, Sidonis recalled the chaos of battle. The image of his brother, eyes wide with shock as Sidonis plunged his sword into his chest, flashed in his mind. Then, Ludica's fierce push sent him tumbling into the misty abyss where he had expected to meet his end. Instead, he was here, sprawled amongst the rubble and clinging to what life remained through the crushing pain.

Every breath was a struggle as he tried to steady himself. Each attempt at moving left him gasping all the more violently. But as Gorhan's chanting grew louder, he sensed a dark shroud enveloping his broken body, bringing with it a rising sense of terror. In his vulnerable state, he could do nothing but watch as his fractured bones suddenly began to reset themselves with a sickening crack, each movement sending waves of agony through his body. Starting from his legs and moving up into his torso, he cried out, his voice echoing eerily in the fog. Mere seconds felt like an eternity as he remained helpless against the force coursing through his body.

When it had finally come to an end, he keeled over, vomiting a foul black substance that left him trembling. Like tar, it clung to his lips as he gagged and choked on its hold over him. Finally, Gorhan lowered his arms and stepped closer, his form becoming more distinct.

"Twice I have held your life in my hands, Sidonis. The next time, I shall require it of you for myself," Gorhan said, his voice a spectral whisper that cut through the fog like a knife.

Sidonis fought to rise to his knees, his breaths ragged and shallow. "What of Ludica?" he croaked, the words scraping his throat.

"The King of Faermire has been slain by your hand. His son now rules in his stead."

"Beowyn," Sidonis muttered, the name dripping with a mixture of regret and resolve.

Gorhan's smile was cold and knowing. Sidonis took in the seer's unsettling appearance: the ashen clay covering his frail body, cracked and inscribed with deep blue runes of a forgotten tongue. Tattered pants adorned with the bones of small creatures clung to his thin frame, and an antler headdress crowned his head. His dark, hollow eyes were a stark contrast to his pale, painted skin, and the residue of black tar-like ooze marred his beard and chest.

"The day draws near, and the gods are moving. It is their blood that courses through your body, and they are calling for you. Do not betray them, Man of Aecorath," Gorhan intoned, his voice echoing as his form began to dissolve, then vanished into the mist, leaving Sidonis alone in the eerie landscape.

Sidonis forced himself to stand, his ribs still aching with every movement. He scanned his desolate surroundings, the rugged terrain and jagged rocks jutting out of the volcanic soil, adding to his disorientation. In the distance, two cloaked figures appeared, their forms shadowy and indistinct.

A chill of apprehension ran down his spine as he began to back away from their presence until a shrill, unsettling scream shattered the silence behind him. Sidonis whipped around, his heart pounding, only to be surrounded by disembodied whispers that drew near. Then, emerging from within the mist, a grotesque creature with mangled hair cascading around her face of hollow, empty eye sockets jutted toward him. Its mouth lined with jagged, needle-like teeth stretched open to devour him, only to vanish before it struck.

He cowered in terror, spinning back to face the cloaked figures—only to find that they too were gone.

His heart pounded, each beat echoing his growing dread. Surely, he was going mad... Yet amid the fear, a new purpose took root. Eventually, he caught his footing and looked toward a clearing that began to emerge from within the mist. With a determined gaze, Sidonis turned towards the path that would lead him to the land where the seer awaited him.

ORMSKIRK, KINGDOM OF VALENMUR

Tannica rode back to the capital city with her two brothers, the clatter of their horses' hooves echoing through the winding streets of Ormskirk. Her spirits were low, weighed down by Beowyn's rejection at Coventhan Ridge. Ormskirk, the heart of Valenmur, sprawled grand and imposing at the base of the fortress castle, its design echoing the formidable structure of a motte and bailey. Encircling the city was a wide, treacherous moat, breached only by a single, ancient bridge that groaned under the weight of travelers.

The city teemed with an almost palpable energy. Merchants aggressively peddled their wares to travelers, their shouts mingling with the strains of distant tavern music that floated on the breeze. The murmur of conversations interwove with the occasional outburst of a brawl in the muddy streets, adding to the chaotic symphony. Witches offered cryptic readings to passersby, one of them with a snake coiled around her forearm, its scales gleaming ominously in the pale light. On a distant hill, a large temple loomed, its presence both commanding and shrouded in mystery.

As they entered the city, the crowd instinctively parted, allowing Tannica's brothers to ride through with a callous indifference to anyone who might be injured in their path. As they entered the castle, they exuded a determined arrogance, leaving Tannica to dismount on her own. She slid from her horse, her golden hair whipping in the biting wind. The gray skies mirrored her mood, the cold air pinching her cheeks into a blushed tone.

Her brothers pushed their way through the main court doors, their heavy wooden surfaces adorned with intricate carvings that told tales of their ancestors. The stone walls of the fortress seemed to close in on Tannica as she stood in the courtyard, the weight of impending dread pressing down on her shoulders. Reluctantly, she followed her brothers into the great hall. A large rectangular fire pit dominated the center, its flames casting a warm yet eerie glow. Wooden pillars, etched with the same intricate details as the entrance doors, stretched up to the ceiling. Smoke from the fire pit drifted through a heavy grate above, creating shadows that danced like restless spirits.

At the far end of the hall, Elwin sat atop his throne, elevated on a dais. His younger children, born of other women, played freely at his feet. Servants lined the walls, heads bowed, waiting to be summoned. Tannica's brothers entered first, taking seats at a table nearest their father. Alfric, the eldest, raised his hand to signal a servant, who promptly brought tankards of ale for him and Ealric.

Elwin, still seated comfortably, snacked on a bowl of assorted nuts and fruits. Tannica could feel his eyes on her as she approached, his stern glare cutting through her like a knife. It was as if he already knew of her encounter with Beowyn. The weight of his silent scrutiny made her steps falter, but she pressed on, her heart pounding with a mix of fear and determination.

Her father's stocky frame emphasized his strength, a testament to years of command and battles. In his age, the lines of experience etched crows-feet around his keen eyes. Long strands of red and graying hair were intricately braided and tied back, the rest cascading loosely over his broad shoulders. His beard, similarly braided and adorned with ornate gold clasps, framed his weathered face. Beneath his loose red tunic, hints of a large tattoo peeked through, marking him with a warrior's history. A broad leather belt, clasped with gold, matched his tall boots snugly encasing his calves.

"Leave it to a woman to wear her heart so openly on her face," he mused. Tannica lowered her gaze, bearing the weight of his observation. He continued chewing thoughtfully, glancing over at his sons who wore expressions ranging from mild annoyance to curious anticipation, their attention fixed on their younger sister.

"Will you tell me, or must I speak for you?" he asked, his voice firm.

She hesitated briefly before relenting, her voice barely audible. "There will be no marriage," she murmured, her words carrying the weight of disappointment and resignation.

"Speak up," Elwin demanded, his gaze piercing.

"There will be no marriage, Father," she repeated more firmly, her voice tempered by apprehension. Elwin exchanged a glance with his sons, silently seeking their affirmation. He sat in contemplative silence, letting the news settle amidst the uneasy atmosphere.

"I should have gutted the bastard when I had the chance," he muttered, a grim scoff of agreement coming from Ealric.

"Why the change of heart?" Elwin's voice sliced through the tense air, his brow furrowing with curiosity.

"His father was slain—" Tannica started, her words interrupted by her father's sudden shift in attention.

"What?" His interest spiked, tinged with a hint of regret for not having taken the man's life himself.

"Beowyn believes you will use our marriage to claim his throne," Tannica continued, her voice almost drowned out by Elwin's piercing gaze now fixed on his two eldest sons nearby. His anger flared, not at his daughter, but at the realization that such critical news had reached him through her.

"Ludica is dead?" His question cut through the room sharply, demanding an immediate answer.

Alfric, the elder son, lowered his tankard slowly, exchanging a guarded look with Ealric, who took the lead in responding. "She speaks true. Ceolfrid of Abensloh sought to conquer Mistelfeld. Gwenora and Ludica allied, meeting Ceolfrid in battle. He fell, and Beowyn now reigns in his place."

Elwin's fury ignited at the belated news. He slammed a bowl of food to the ground before his sons, its contents scattering across the floor, their expressions hardened against his wrath. "The King of Faermire is dead, and I hear of this now? Where was the warning of war brewing? Their pact with Mistelfeld? While you two have been wasting away with your ale and your whores, my own kingdom stands at a loss for men of a sound mind!"

Flushed with anger, Elwin descended from his throne, seizing Alfric's cup and pouring its ale onto the floor at his feet, the liquid staining his boots. "You crave ale, boy? Then earn it."

The two men, both formidable in their own right, remained seated as their father loomed over them. Alfric, with his braided red hair and broad, muscular frame clad in leather armor studded with metal scales, exuded a presence akin to Elwin's own. His dark attire accentuated his fierce countenance, though it paled in comparison to his father's seething rage.

Ealric, slightly smaller than his elder brother but no less imposing, sat with a quiet intensity. His blond hair was neatly braided atop his head, revealing a shaved scalp adorned with an intricate tattoo. Unlike Alfric's momentary acquiescence, Ealric met their father's glare with steadfast defiance, his eyes fixed on Elwin with unwavering resolve.

As Elwin's wrath focused on his sons, Tannica felt an unexpected relief, spared momentarily from his full fury. The room fell silent, even the children paused in their play to watch their father's rage unfold.

"Get out," Elwin commanded, his voice cutting through the stillness. The sons rose, the servants ushering the children away, and Tannica turned to follow.

"Not you," Elwin added sharply, halting her retreat. Tannica's heart sank as she heard his heavy footsteps approach from behind.

Elwin waited until the room was empty, his glare fixed on Tannica. She struggled to meet his fierce gaze, her heart pounding. Being near him always felt like a test, her value weighed in cold calculation. But now, his eyes seemed to pierce through her, searching for something beyond her exterior.

Finally, he spoke, his voice slicing through the crackle of the fire behind her, the only source of warmth in the cold hall. "I have wronged you, daughter," he said, his tone unexpectedly resolute.

Tannica's breath caught in her throat. Had she heard him right? "Father?" she asked, her voice barely above a whisper as she tentatively lifted her gaze to his.

For a moment, she saw a shift in his expression, a glimmer of something almost human. It left her bewildered, uncertain of how to respond.

He continued, his voice a low rumble. "My efforts to steer you away from your fanciful and fruitless pursuits have failed. I wanted to shield you from the harsh realities that await, but I see now that my attempts were in vain. Even now, as fate deals its cruel blows, I am powerless to protect you."

Still at a loss, Tannica remained silent, grappling with the unexpected shift in her father's tone and his apparent concern for her well-being. "It's plain to see that you love the boy. And I believe that, for a time, he has loved you in return. But love is deception, and fruitless in its pursuits. If a man is worth his weight, he will always abandon love to spare his own gain. And you, Tannica, will always stand in the wake of its destruction so long as you cling to it." His words, though laced with an unusual tenderness, carried a message she refused to accept.

"No," she replied, her voice trembling with disbelief. She couldn't fathom that Beowyn, unlike every other man she had known, especially her father, could harbor such harsh sentiments. Beowyn's genuine kindness and the deep love he had once shown her had been what drew her to him in the first place. Despite his recent rejection, she couldn't shake the belief that his words were spoken in a moment of anguish rather than true conviction.

As Beowyn shattered their plans for marriage, the sting of betrayal and heartbreak reverberated through her being. Despite the anguish, she found herself unable to muster the hatred she had declared in the heat of the moment. As her father's voice echoed in the background, their love remained her sole lifeline amid the crushing despair that enveloped her world.

"You've seen it with your own eyes, Daughter. Beowyn has cast aside your love for the throne, using my name to justify his actions," Elwin said, his voice a mixture of sorrow and resignation. Tears flowed freely down Tannica's cheeks as her father approached, his hands resting gently on her arms.

"In time, you'll come to understand, as I have," he continued, his tone softer now, almost pleading. "Perhaps then, you'll see the wisdom in the path I've set for you."

"What plans?!" Tannica's voice cracked with emotion, her eyes searching his face for answers. "It's true what you've said! A man will always abandon love to protect his own interests. Even his own daughter..." Elwin bowed his head in a rare moment of defeat, and for once, Tannica couldn't contain the surge of emotions boiling inside her. Abandoned by those she loved, her value reduced to mere utility, she pulled away from her father's feigned affection, no longer willing to endure his manipulations under the guise of paternal concern.

"Then you have my blessing," Elwin declared firmly, his voice arresting her as she turned to depart, his words halting her in her tracks once more. "For now," he added, a hint of finality in his tone. She turned back slowly, wiping tears from her cheeks with a determined swipe. She berated herself inwardly for hesitating, knowing she should have walked away without looking back.

"Go to him if you wish. But when he abandons you again, then you will know the truth of what I speak," Elwin continued. "And perhaps then, you will grant me your loyalty."

Surprised by his unexpected acquiescence, Tannica hesitated, her gaze meeting his with uncertainty. She squared her shoulders, still unsure whether to trust his words. "*If* he does," she replied, her voice tinged with defiance, "then my life is yours to mold as you see fit."

For a moment, father and daughter stood in silence, the weight of unspoken promises and uncertain futures hanging between them. Finally, Elwin's voice broke the stillness, a hint of amusement lacing his words. "You are more like your father than you'd care to admit, Tannica..."

TWO

Beowyn sat uneasily on his father's throne. The high stone columns loomed above him, and the long blue banners that hung vertically behind the throne seemed to whisper reminders of his father's legacy. This was the first of many meetings where elders from all corners of the kingdom of Faermire would gather to give accounts of their governance, and more often than not, voice their complaints about the needs of their people and their lands.

Beowyn had always made a point to avoid such gatherings, dismissing them as exercises in futility. Only months ago, the thought of presiding over these disputes would have seemed laughable. Yet here he was, at the heart of their grievances, sorting through the chaff to find the wheat. As he pondered the irony, his thoughts turned to his father—the man who had once occupied this very throne. Despite their constant rivalry, Beowyn couldn't help but admire the strength in his father's posture and the unshakeable confidence in his voice. Ludica had commanded respect throughout the kingdom, earning every ounce of it.

A wave of longing and remorse washed over Beowyn. The relationship with his father, now irretrievably lost, left him with a hollow ache. He wondered if those around him could sense his attempts to project the confidence his father had embodied. The throne, adorned with gold inlay and intricate wooden carvings, bore the weight of expectation.

Ambient light from behind the throne cast a soft glow, highlighting the intricate designs, while torches lining the stone walls flickered, casting ominous shadows over the floor. The voices of the elders echoed through the great court, a constant reminder of the many eyes and ears attuned to his every move.

Beowyn hated every minute of it, gripping the armrest of the throne until his knuckles turned white, his eyes darting to avoid the frequent, scrutinizing glances cast in his direction. The weight of their judgment bore down on him, each murmur a needle pricking his nerves. Then, the guards at the end of the court pulled open the grand doors. The thick, aged wood creaked and moaned, heralding the entrance of an unexpected guest for many who were present.

His sister, Estrith stepped into the room, her presence commanding immediate attention and bringing a surge of relief to Beowyn as his grip loosened. Despite her composed exterior, he could sense her shared apprehension as she made her way down the aisle. Her steps were quick and deliberate, her shoulders squared with an air of confidence. Though she kept her gaze lowered, avoiding the probing eyes of the elders. Her long, bronze-colored hair framed a modest yet striking crown, with subtle gold twine woven into her braids. In that moment, Beowyn felt a pang of sympathy for her, coupled with a selfish relief that the spotlight had shifted for once, away from him.

Across the room stood Sgell, their father's former servant, offering a reassuring nod to them both. His presence, though distant, was a beacon of steadiness amidst the chaos. Estrith glanced up at Sgell first, then toward Beowyn, giving him an equally reassuring nod and a graceful curtsy before taking the seat closest to the throne.

Murmurs quickly rippled through the council, a symphony of suspicion and curiosity. It was unheard of for a woman to sit among the elders, an open challenge to tradition. Their hushed words were sharp and scornful, a direct rebuke of the new king's bold defiance.

The elders' chairs, arranged in two columns facing each other, seemed to close in around Beowyn and his sister, their occupants like sentinels watching their every move.

One elder's voice rose above the murmur, sharp and urgent. "My King, Ceolfrid's army has been pushed back into Abensloh, but our numbers dwindle, and we are ill-equipped should he decide to strike again."

Another elder countered, "Our alliance with Mistelfeld will bolster our defenses."

"Mistelfeld cannot be trusted," a different elder insisted, his tone as cutting as a blade.

"And what of Elwin?!" another demanded, eyes narrowing with suspicion. "It should come as no surprise that he will not take kindly to the dissolution of Beowyn's marriage to his daughter. It's only a matter of time before he brings his army upon our borders."

"The King of Valenmur must surely suspect that such a move would be anticipated," Estrith interjected, her voice steady despite the tension in the room.

The elders turned their gazes to her, eyes filled with a mix of scrutiny and disdain.

"I-I mean, he would risk too much to be so bold, especially once word has spread that we withstood the great Ceolfrid himself. And his giant..."

Her words, though brief, suddenly conjured vivid, brutal memories for Beowyn. The clamor of swords and the agonizing screams of the battlefield echoed in his mind. He could almost see the giant, Nurrock, towering over twice the size of any mighty man in Faermire, grinning callously as he held the chain-linked reins of his dragon. The fierce creature spewed molten fire from its mouth, engulfing everything in its path, the stench of burning flesh gnawing at his senses.

Beowyn's hand instinctively reached for his forearm, still wrapped in bandages that covered the painful memory of that day. Just as he was nearly lost to the memory, one elder quipped harshly in response to his sister,

"*WE*, my fair Lady Estrith, would be wise to avoid such naïve assumptions. Elwin need only a shift in the western wind to justify his actions. Bold or otherwise."

"Here, here," murmured another among the group.

"It is not naïveté, Lord Haemund, to assume that a king of Elwin's stature would employ tact in his strategy," Estrith said firmly. "On the contrary, it would be unwise to underestimate the cunning intellect of our rival."

The elderly man gripped his chair tightly as he began to rise in anger.

"Sit down, Haemund, lest you lose your head," another quipped, an amused smile playing across his face.

"My sister speaks true," Beowyn interrupted, still cradling his wound. "Elwin may be quick to anger, but he is not unwise. He knows the strength of our army and the power of our alliance with Mistelfeld. He wouldn't risk starting a war while his own enemies lie in wait for any sign of weakness."

Silence engulfed the room, and the new king stood amidst its weight. The faint whispers among the advisors threatened to break the stillness, but he swiftly subdued them, keen not to lose what little control he maintained.

"We stood united against our common enemy," Beowyn declared, his voice cutting through the quiet. "Victorious we were. Let us maintain this unity, lest our internal strife divide us. For the sake of my father, the King, and for all of Faermire."

Before another word could interrupt, Beowyn rose from his seat, adjusting his tunic with a gentle tug.

"Leave your grievances with my steward and return to your lands. You will receive word as your needs require. Until then, this council is adjourned."

As Beowyn descended the stairs, the elders and advisors rose in unison, their movements synchronized in a display of reluctant respect. He walked down the aisle, the weight of their gazes pressing against his back until he finally stepped out of the door. Once outside, he deliberately avoided further interaction, his stride purposeful as he headed straight for the upper wall overlooking the city of Elsterheim.

The winter air bit at his face, a sharp contrast to the stifling tension inside. He gripped the cold stone balustrade, exhaling a plume of breath that mingled with the frosty air. The panoramic view stretched before him, but his mind was elsewhere, consumed by the bitter realization of why his father had often sought solace in this very spot. The biting cold was a welcome reprieve from the suffocating atmosphere of the king's court, and Beowyn shook his head, the weight of his newfound understanding heavy upon him.

His countenance, marked by dark tousled hair and a furrowed brow bore an uncanny resemblance to his late father's, as he stood alone. He wore the crown of Faermire atop his head—a weighted symbol of his inherited responsibility. His leather tunic, adorned with braided designs across his chest, hinted at both practicality and regal adornment, while a thick cloak of animal skins draped heavily over his shoulders, lending an air of rugged nobility. His piercing blue eyes, sharp and calculating, scanned the landscape with a gaze that spoke of both command and deep introspection.

Eventually, the delicate footsteps of his sister approached from behind, echoing softly in the solemn stillness. She sighed audibly, a deliberate attempt to shatter the uneasy silence that enveloped them.

"I thought I might find you here," Estrith remarked, her voice carrying a hint of amusement tinged with concern. Her glassy blue eyes shimmered against the backdrop of the bleak, winter sky, reflecting the muted light filtering through the dense clouds.

Beowyn responded with a fleeting glance, acknowledging her presence without words. They stood together; siblings united in the aftermath of his coronation. For Beowyn, Estrith's familiar presence usually offered comfort, yet this time, the weight of responsibility overshadowed any solace he might have sought in her company.

"Some of the elders were eager to speak with you directly," she continued, her tone holding a hint of irony. "Most likely due to my presence in court today. They seem threatened by the idea that I might trample down their pride."

Beowyn sighed heavily, feeling the burden of her words settle upon his shoulders. "You shouldn't have spoken so quickly," he replied softly, his voice carrying the weight of weariness.

The shock flickered briefly across Estrith's face before she countered sharply, her anger palpable. "So, I should say nothing? Am I merely an 'advisor' in title alone? A token to placate your grieving sister?"

"I mean only that you should choose your words more carefully, Sister. Both of us should," Beowyn replied. "Their confidence in me as their king remains as fragile as their confidence in my decision to appoint a woman, especially my sister, to such a place of high repute."

He sensed a slight easing of tension in her expression, but the weight of his responsibility seemed to grow heavier still. Averting his gaze from her, he sought to conceal the apprehension that threatened to overwhelm him.

"I elevated you not out of mere familial duty, but because I value your insight," Beowyn continued, his voice earnest. "Now more than ever, I need you by my side."

Before Estrith could respond, Beowyn turned away, leaving her alone by the wall. The cold of the winter had already seeped into his bones, and he struggled to mask the weakness he felt consuming him.

Estrith watched her brother, Beowyn, as he walked away, the weight of his new responsibilities evident in his stride. From behind, the resemblance to their father, Ludica, was strikingly uncanny. Beowyn's gait, strong and deliberate, mirrored their father's with poignant precision. A creeping sense of sadness welled up inside her, mingled with a longing as she recalled her last conversation with Ludica before they marched off to battle.

Estrith's memories of her father were often overshadowed by his cold demeanor. His coldness was a shield, a necessity born from years of battles and betrayals. Yet, beneath that impenetrable exterior, Estrith always sensed a flicker of warmth, a hidden tenderness that surfaced in rare, precious moments. She cherished those instances when Ludica's stern facade softened, and a genuine smile broke through. Those brief glimpses of his true self were like finding rare gems in a desolate landscape, and the joy she felt when he smiled because of her was a beacon of hope in an otherwise bleak world.

In their final moments together, his declaration of love and adoration left her stunned. All she had ever yearned to hear was that he was proud of her, but instead, he bared his soul, revealing a side of him she had rarely glimpsed—a man brimming with love and tenderness. As he held her close, she felt as though the joy she had missed in her childhood flooded her heart, overflowing with the warmth of his affection. She should have considered the possibility that he might not return, but in that fleeting moment, it seemed inconceivable.

Now, as she stood silently witnessing her father vanish within the figure of her twin brother, she couldn't suppress the longing for respite from her deepening sorrow. With a heavy heart, she turned away and navigated the labyrinthine corridors of the castle.

The stone halls stretched ahead, dimly illuminated by flickering torchlight that cast dancing shadows along the walls. Echoes of distant chatter among servants and guards reverberated, punctuated by the solemn tolling of bells from the city below. Transitioning from the outer chill of the castle walls, the air inside turned damp and cool, its touch seeping into her bones even as it spared her face from the earlier bite.

Estrith's footsteps fell softly, a solitary rhythm accompanying her contemplation. The castle's architecture loomed overhead, its towering stone arches adorned with intricate carvings that seemed to converge, enclosing her in a labyrinth of reminiscence. Once familiar, these halls now echoed with the weight of memories lost, each turn a poignant reminder of what had slipped away.

Estrith stood outside Siged's door, her hand hesitating on the cold iron handle. She took a deep breath, shedding her cloak to the side.

As she entered, Siged lay reclined against the headboard of his bed, attended by a young servant woman. His eyes remained open but distant, fixated vacantly on his feet. His head tilted slightly to the right, marked by the injury inflicted weeks before, and his right arm had begun to waste away, drawn close to his chest.

The young servant woman gracefully lowered the bowl of porridge and rose to her feet, executing a curtsey to the princess with eyes respectfully averted. Estrith felt the warmth of the room envelop her, a stark contrast to the chill of the castle corridors, prompting her to gratefully shed her fur cloak at the foot of Siged's bed. Taking the bowl from the servant, who curtsied once more before briefly tending to the fire, Estrith found herself alone with her younger brother.

Maintaining a facade of cheerfulness, Estrith greeted Siged softly, "Hello, brother." His customary silence met her, unchanged as ever. She delicately inquired about his well-being, "How are you feeling today?" as she guided a spoonful of porridge to his lips. His acceptance was passive, his mind seemingly distant and unengaged.

Continuing as if speaking to herself, Estrith recounted a dream from the previous night, her voice filled with a mixture of amusement and yearning. "This morning, upon waking, I knew I had to share it. I entered your room just as I always do, but much to my surprise, there you were, rambling away as you always do, your room in disarray, trinkets scattered about as you played on the floor. I remember thinking what a mess you'd made and how I should just throw it all out, yet you had the audacity to accuse me of disrupting your order!" She chuckled softly, reminiscing about his incessant chatter that had once annoyed her. "And gods, how you wouldn't stop talking, interrupting me with your endless questions and musings." As she spoke, she couldn't help but long for those moments now lost.

Pausing in her task of feeding him, Estrith searched Siged's eyes for any hint of recognition. "Siged?" she ventured softly, her voice tinged with hope. But he remained silent, a poignant reminder of his condition. Her forced smile faded, replaced by a melancholic expression as she lowered her gaze, trying to conceal the tears welling in her eyes.

As she regained her composure, Estrith wiped a stray tear away, steeling herself against the sadness that threatened to overwhelm her. She scooped another helping of porridge into the spoon, lifting it up as another offering to Siged. Just then, a soft knock echoed through the room. "Enter," she called out, her voice gentle yet composed as she continued to feed her younger brother.

Sgell entered the room, his tall stature and dark complexion a striking contrast against the subdued light filtering through the windows. He bowed slightly upon approaching Estrith. "My Lady," he greeted respectfully, lowering his gaze with a deference that spoke of his upbringing. Sgell carried himself with an air of decorum, each movement precise and deliberate, yet tempered with a humility that set him apart.

Estrith often found solace in Sgell's presence. Hailing from the distant kingdoms of the southern desert plains and rugged wilderness of Aecorath, he embodied a steadfastness and loyalty that resonated deeply with her. As children, they had heard tales of his homeland, but now, he stood before her, a steadfast guardian of Faermire.

Once, she had asked him about his journey northward and whether he missed his homeland. His response had been simple yet profound. "This is my homeland, fair Lady. And you are my people," he had replied with a warm smile, his loyalty unwavering.

As Sgell stood before her now, Estrith couldn't help but feel a surge of gratitude for his steadfast companionship in these uncertain times.

He approached her with a grace that seemed to echo the flickering candlelight in the dimly lit room where she sat beside Siged's bed. In his outstretched hand, a letter sealed with Qereth's distinctive signet caught her attention, prompting a gentle smile to play on her lips. "Qereth remains distant, yet his hold on you, Lady Estrith, seems as firm as ever," he remarked with a hint of amusement.

Startled by her own reaction, she quickly composed herself, lowering the letter into her lap with practiced grace. Following Beowyn's ascension to the throne, Qereth had reluctantly assumed the mantle of Elder over his lands. The recent battle against Nurrock and the dragon had decimated their ranks, claiming Qereth's father and brothers among the fallen. Left with no choice but to accept his inherited responsibilities, Qereth also undertook the crucial role of Emissary to Mistelfeld, a position of diplomatic importance given his trusted status with her brother.

It was the natural choice for Beowyn to make, but that also meant much of his time was either devoted to governing his own lands or navigating the intricate politics of Mistelfeld on Faermire's behalf.

"How is he?" she asked, her voice soft with concern, as if hoping to glean more from Sgell than the mere words of the letter could convey.

"I cannot say," Sgell replied evenly, his dark eyes thoughtful. "Only that the weight of his responsibilities does little to diminish his longing for you."

Estrith's cheeks flushed slightly at his words, and she lowered her gaze to hide her reaction. Swiftly, she tucked the letter securely beneath the folds of her dress, returning her attention to Siged. With practiced gentleness, she lifted another spoonful of food to her brother's lips, the task providing a momentary refuge from the awkward tension now thickening the air in the room.

In the quiet of the chamber, the tension grew palpable as Sgell lingered, silently watching her tend to Siged.

As though defending her brother's condition, Estrith broke the silence. "His progress is slow, but we will regain his strength in due time," she murmured, though her eyes lingered on his withering hand and the tilt of his head.

Sgell, sensing the underlying doubt in her voice, stepped closer. "If I may confess," he began, his tone both gentle and resolute, "I have not come only to deliver the letter." Estrith's curiosity was piqued, her gaze lifting to meet his. "Many who travel the King's highway bring remedies and cures from their lands, things that we might not have access to ourselves."

"What sort of remedies?" Estrith asked, her interest now fully engaged.

"In my youth, my people were nomads," Sgell explained, "dwelling between the borders of Amethia and Caelkirk. We had no king and no borders, and thus no allegiance to man, only to our god. My father was a healer. Many would come to him when no other cure could be found." He hesitated briefly, then reached into his pocket and withdrew a vial, concealing it within his hand. "I've sent word to a friend who might help with the young master's plight. If you would permit, my Lady, I would like to introduce him to you."

Estrith paused, her heart torn between hope and caution. The thought of a potential cure for Siged filled her with eager anticipation, but Sgell's cryptic demeanor made her wary. She glanced at the door, noticing it was slightly ajar, and suspected that this "friend" was waiting just outside.

She nodded, her anxious gaze flickering between Sgell and the door. At her confirmation, he bowed once more and then moved to open the door fully. An elderly man stepped into the room, his complexion mirroring Sgell's, a sight that filled Estrith with unexpected surprise.

Sgell tenderly guided the elderly man by the crook of his arm. It quickly became evident that the man was blind, yet he moved with a confidence that echoed Sgell's own. His small frame shuffled cautiously along the floor, his steps deliberate to avoid stumbling in the unfamiliar terrain. His clothes, though aged, were meticulously kept, simple yet adorned with ornate details. The once vibrant colors on the collar of his white tunic had faded, and a thick fur cloak seemed almost too large for his slight build. In his other hand, a staff, worn with age, fit snugly as though it had been an extension of his body from birth. His dark complexion was etched with the deep lines of time, and his white hair, speckled with remnants of its once onyx hue, lifted slightly with the cold breeze from outside.

As they approached, Sgell whispered to him in their native tongue. Estrith, hearing the language for the first time, was entranced by its lyrical cadence. Drawn to the elderly man, she rose to her feet, an inexplicable captivation pulling her towards him. When they reached her, the man bowed with deep reverence, but she reached out, clasping his hand in both of hers, her eyes fixed on him.

The elderly man's voice, though strained with age, carried a reassuring tone. Sgell translated, "He says, 'May the god of my people, the Great Healer, be with you.'"

She smiled, turning to Sgell. "Who is your god?" she asked.

"He is called..." Sgell began, but the old man interrupted, drawing their attention back to the matter at hand. Sgell responded in their native tongue, his words flowing like a soothing melody. He then pulled a chair close for the elderly man, who lowered himself into it with deliberate care, leaning heavily on his staff. The old man reached out to Siged, cradling the boy's frail hand in his own, and began to murmur softly, his eyes closed in deep concentration. The room fell silent, save for the whispered words of the healer, as the weight of the moment settled over them.

Estrith stood beside Sgell, her heart pounding with anxious anticipation. The silence stretched on, each moment feeling interminable. She glanced up at Sgell, who remained focused on the boy and the elderly man, his brow furrowed with worry. Just as Estrith was about to speak, the old man gently lowered Siged's hand back to his side and leaned against his staff with a sigh. His expression, laden with worry, only deepened the tension in the room.

Estrith's breath hitched as she waited for his words, the hope she had dared to feel now mingling with a growing dread. The room seemed to hold its breath; every flicker of the firelight danced ominously in the hearth. Finally, the old man spoke, his voice strained yet steady, filling the silence with a weighty significance that made Estrith's heart ache with both fear and yearning.

"He says... there is a great evil that dwells within the young master..." The old man's words hung heavily in the air, casting a shadow over Estrith's hopeful heart. "Great evil? W-what do you mean?" she asked, her voice with anxious urgency.

"It has many names, but my people know it as Zemrapha. An ancient spirit that feeds on its host," Sgell explained, his tone grave and measured. The elderly healer leaned forward, placing his hand over Siged's chest, a gesture that seemed to affirm Sgell's dire assessment.

"It feeds?" Estrith's voice caught in her throat, her mind reeling with disbelief and fear. "But... Siged was brought back from the brink of death by the gods themselves. How can there be such a malevolent presence within him now?"

"Such blessings come with a cost, often more than one anticipates," Sgell replied somberly, his gaze reflecting the weight of their predicament.

Tears welled up in Estrith's eyes, despair flooding every corner of her being. She glanced desperately between Sgell and the old healer, silently pleading for a solution. Looking down at Siged, his vacant stare a cruel reminder of his fragile state, she could no longer contain her anguish.

"Please..." Her voice cracked, a desperate plea escaping her lips. "Is there nothing you can do for him? Will he not die if we do nothing?"

The old man lowered his head solemnly, as if understanding the depth of her plea. Slowly rising from his chair, he gently declined Sgell's assistance and approached Estrith, reaching out for her trembling hand. She hesitated only briefly before yielding to his touch, finding solace in his comforting grasp. Tears streamed down her cheeks unchecked.

"I cannot lose him. I beg of you," she whispered, her voice choked with emotion.

Sgell translated the healer's response, his words laden with solemnity. "The boy was appointed once to die. His fate now, cannot be certain..."

As he spoke, the old man motioned toward Sgell, who approached with the small vial in hand, its contents shimmering like opalescent oil on the healer's fingertip. With a gentle tap on Estrith's hands, he conveyed both reassurance and warning.

"My Lady, stand back," Sgell advised softly. "And whatever happens, you must not touch your brother..."

With a heavy heart, Estrith stepped away, watching with bated breath as the old healer resumed his murmuring, applying the mysterious oil with careful precision over Siged's still form.

THREE

ELSTERHEIM, KINGDOM OF FAERMIRE

The old man anointed Siged's head with opalescent oil in deliberate, solemn movements. After a moment's pause, he shifted his attention to the boy's chest, applying a small amount at its center. His murmurs intertwined with Sgell's, blending into a mysterious cadence that filled the chamber with an otherworldly aura.

Estrith watched intently, her gaze darting between the old man's focused ministrations and Siged's frail form. The boy, once vibrant, now appeared lost and vacant, his platinum blond hair streaked with oil across his forehead. His piercing blue eyes, dimmed by illness, reflected a depth of suffering that broke her heart—a faint shadow of his true self.

As their words continued, Siged's eyes suddenly rolled back, revealing the whites—a stark contrast against his pale complexion. A surge of dread washed over Estrith as the young boy began to tremble. The tremors started subtly but rapidly escalated into violent convulsions, shaking his fragile frame with alarming intensity.

"Siged!" Estrith's gasp filled the tense air, her heart lurching at the sudden agony etched across Siged's previously placid face. She took a step forward, driven by instinct to help, but Sgell's strong arm barred her path. He remained focused on the old man, their shared language continuing with an intensity that mirrored the turmoil in Siged's body.

Before she could utter another word, Siged's screams pierced the air, starting as his own voice before descending into a deep, guttural resonance that sent shivers down Estrith's spine. Gripping Sgell's arm tightly, seeking comfort and finding the restraint that kept her rooted beside him, she was unable to rush to her brother's side.

The old man's voice joined with Sgell's in an eerie, melodic cadence that reverberated off the chamber walls. The flickering candlelight seemed to falter, unable to withstand the weight of the malevolent force stirring within Siged. Estrith watched with a mixture of awe and horror, her heart wrenching with each convulsion that wracked her brother's frail form.

The room itself seemed to respond to the escalating turmoil, quivering as tremors ran through the floor. Books and small trinkets toppled from shelves, and the window glass shattered with a violent crash. Despite the chaos, the dark presence persisted, its grip tightening around Siged like an invisible vice.

Estrith felt a surge of helplessness as she listened to the ancient, ominous voice emanating from Siged. Its language was unknown to her, yet she understood its malevolent intent. The old man stood firm, his resolve evident as he confronted the otherworldly entity tormenting the young boy.

Suddenly, the chamber door burst open with a thunderous crash. Beowyn stormed in, flanked by guards whose expressions mirrored his own shock and horror. He looked at their brother, a thick, tar-like substance dribbled from Siged's mouth, staining his once-pale lips and leaving a sickly sheen on his skin.

"What are you doing?!" Beowyn's voice reverberated with anguish and desperation as he demanded the guards intervene, tearing the old man away from Siged's side.

"No, Beowyn, please!" Estrith's voice cracked with grief and desperation, her eyes pleading with him to understand the dire situation.

"Get them out of here, now!" Beowyn's command was urgent and authoritative, and the guards swiftly obeyed, ushering the old man and Sgell out of the room.

Estrith stood frozen as Beowyn, his hands trembling, rushed to Siged's side, desperately wiping the strange, tar-like substance from her brother's motionless face. Tears streamed down her cheeks as she approached, her heart heavy with fear and confusion.

"What have you done?!" Beowyn's voice thundered through the room, a potent mix of anger and disbelief. His eyes, wide with shock, bore into Estrith, who stood before him, unable to utter a single word in response. Every fiber of her being trembled under the weight of everything that had transpired just moments before.

"He came to help..." she finally managed to say. "A healer."

"What sort of healer does this?!" Beowyn's voice thundered, lifting his hand smeared with the black substance he had wiped from Siged's face. He lowered it, staring at the dark substance, his fury giving way to confusion and concern. Estrith, still reeling from the chaos, wept openly. "It wasn't their fault, Beowyn. I begged him. He... he said there's an evil spirit inside Siged, feeding on him!"

"What sort of evil?" Beowyn demanded, his tone less certain.

"He called it Zemrapha."

"Did he give this to Siged to drink?" Beowyn asked, gesturing toward the substance on his hand.

"Drink? No, the healer didn't give him anything to drink. It came from within him. Why? What is it?"

"It's nothing." Beowyn's demeanor shifted, his anger rekindling as he dropped his hand. "You had no right to do this, Estrith. He could've died."

"He was already dying, Beowyn!"

"You don't know that."

"I will do whatever it takes to save our brother—"

"And you think I would not?" Beowyn's voice seethed with rising anger. "Have I not already sacrificed much to save our brother!" He stepped forward, his fists clenched, his eyes burning into hers. Estrith saw the toll it had taken on him—the years stolen from his own life to preserve Siged's. Though they were twins, Beowyn looked older, worn by the burden he carried.

As the gravity of his words settled in, Estrith lowered her head, feeling the sting of his truth. She had always been the one to care for Siged, convinced she was his sole guardian. But now, witnessing Beowyn's anger and the pain in his eyes, she remembered how deeply he, too, loved their brother. Her heart ached with guilt for ever doubting him, and she saw, through his fury, the same desperate love that fueled her own actions.

She raised her gaze to meet her brother's once more, "Beowyn, I—"

Before she could finish, a faint yet strained voice called out from behind Beowyn.

"Estrith?"

Both siblings turned in disbelief toward the bed. Siged, still frail, was awake. They rushed to his side, their hearts pounding.

The young boy's eyes, though weary, carefully scanned his surroundings. His head remained tilted, and his arm still withered, but he was more alert than before. Despite his fragile state, the spark of awareness in his eyes was enough to fill them with a glimmer of hope

"Siged?" Estrith's voice was a gentle murmur as she tenderly brushed aside strands of blonde hair damp with sweat, revealing his tender blue eyes that flickered with a newfound alertness. With what little strength he could muster, Siged lifted his healthy hand, attempting to sit up, and Beowyn swiftly moved to support him, easing him back onto the bed. The elder siblings exchanged a glance, silently acknowledging the profound moment unfolding before them, a flicker of hope amidst the darkness that had gripped their hearts.

"Can you hear me, Siged?" Estrith's voice quivered with cautious hope, her heart pounding with anticipation. Siged moaned softly, his gaze still clouded with confusion, a reminder of the trauma he had endured. Despite his struggles to respond, a glimmer of recognition shone in his eyes, a faint echo of his former self.

"We're here, Siged," she continued, her voice filled with both relief and tears of joy that streamed down her cheeks. She marveled at the slight improvement in his condition, grateful for any sign of life after the grim prognosis they had faced. The healer's intervention, despite its uncertainties, had brought a fragile spark back to Siged's eyes.

In that moment, Estrith found solace in the small victories. Even if Siged remained fragile, even if his recovery was uncertain, the mere fact that he showed signs of consciousness was a miracle she clung to with all her heart.

Siged began to twitch ever so gently. His frail form leaned into the weakness of his right side, his head fixed in a cocked position as he surveyed his surroundings with a mix of confusion and curiosity. Beowyn settled himself beside his brother on the bed, cradling Siged tenderly in his arms.

"Fetch us some water," he commanded, and a servant promptly appeared in the doorway, bowing in acknowledgment before hurrying off to fulfill the command.

Estrith watched the scene unfold with a heart full of mixed emotions. She couldn't help but marvel at the tender display of affection Beowyn showed toward Siged, feeling a pang of regret for ever doubting the depth of his love and concern for his younger brother. In that moment, she understood the sacrifices he had made and the weight of responsibility he bore.

When the servant returned with a cup of water, Beowyn carefully guided it to Siged's lips. The boy eagerly drank, repeating "Water," in a soft, repetitive murmur as if trying to satisfy a deep, unquenchable thirst. After several sips, Siged finally relented, and Estrith gently took the cup from Beowyn's hand. Their eyes remained fixed on their brother in awe and relief. Despite nearing his ninth year, it seemed to Estrith as if her brother had been reborn, the moment marking a hopeful turn in his long struggle.

They guided Siged to the edge of the bed, helping him to sit with their support. His gaze remained fixed on the floor as he softly muttered incomprehensible words to himself. Estrith and Beowyn leaned in closer, straining to understand him, but exchanged a helpless look when his speech proved unintelligible.

Then, Siged lifted his free hand, calling out for his mother. Estrith felt a pang of guilt at his plea. Richessa, the former queen, languished in the dungeon imprisoned for treason since their father's judgment fell upon her. Estrith had tried to bury the memory of her stepmother's downfall, but now, faced with Siged's yearning for her, it resurfaced with poignant clarity.

She glanced at Beowyn, seeing the conflict mirrored on his face. Richessa was, by all accounts, a figure of disdain in Estrith's eyes, caring little for those around her, including her own son. Despite this, Siged still longed for his mother's presence, a testament to the bond that even imprisonment couldn't sever.

"It's alright," Estrith whispered, her voice a tender reassurance as she leaned over Siged, gently kissing his forehead and smoothing back his strands of golden hair.

They remained huddled together on the bed, a fragile tableau of familial devotion, when a soldier appeared at the doorway, his demeanor urgent yet tempered.

"My Lord," he addressed Beowyn respectfully.

Beowyn's gaze remained fixed on Siged, "What is it?"

"There's an urgent matter, Lord," the soldier continued cautiously. "A woman stands within the gates, and she asks for an audience with the king."

What woman?"

"She claims herself to be the Lady Tannica of Valenmur."

Beowyn's brows furrowed in disbelief, his eyes briefly flickering to Estrith, who mirrored his surprise. Questions surged through her mind about

Tannica's unexpected arrival, and she sensed her brother grappling with his own concerns.

Reluctantly, Beowyn rose from his seat, leaving Siged in Estrith's care. "Is she alone?" he asked, his voice edged with concern.

"Only her guards to serve as an escort, my Lord," the soldier confirmed.

Estrith watched as Beowyn hesitated, his mind clearly racing with decisions. With a determined nod, he took purposeful strides out of the room, disappearing down the hall. Estrith was left alone with Siged, her thoughts swirled with apprehension over Tannica's sudden presence and its implications for the kingdom.

FOUR

ELSTERHEIM, KINGDOM OF FAERMIRE

Beowyn navigated the labyrinthine corridors of the palace with purpose, his steps echoing against the cool stone walls until he emerged into the bustling courtyard. His heart thudded with nervous anticipation. Why had she come? The question reverberated in his mind, each repetition deepening his uncertainty. Amidst the swirl of emotions, doubts insidiously crept in—was she there at her father's behest? Did hidden motives lie behind her unexpected arrival? The mere thought soured his stomach, and he despised himself for doubting her.

It had been mere weeks since he had broken off their engagement, a decision that had unleashed Tannica's fury upon him. She had cursed his name, rightly so, as he struggled with conflicting desires—to embrace her and declare his undying love, or to heed his father's prescient warnings. His own selfishness had blinded him to the insurmountable obstacles they faced, the reasons why their love seemed destined for failure from the outset.

Now, as Elwin's manipulative hand seemed evident in their intended union, Beowyn chose to heed his father's cautionary counsel. He resolved to distance himself from Elwin's influence, even if it meant sacrificing any hope of a future with Tannica.

The echo of her last words had haunted Beowyn since that fateful day. The pain was vivid in her eyes, the sting of betrayal palpable. Now, as she stood unexpectedly within his own gate, the weight of guilt engulfed him once more. Was this a dream? Could it be that she hadn't truly come, despite what he'd been told? And if she had, had she found it in her heart to forgive him?

As he turned the corner, Beowyn hesitated just before she came into view. There was a part of him that dreaded facing her, afraid of the fallout from his actions and unsure of where their relationship stood now. With a deep breath, he forged ahead until, finally, there she stood. In that moment, his gut churned with a mix of longing and dread.

Her golden hair, usually left flowing, was now intricately braided, framing her delicate face and cascading down her back. Her hazel eyes, locked onto his as he approached, held a wearied apprehension—a reflection of the pain he had caused. She wore a simple, travel-worn dress that discreetly blended into the surroundings, yet still adorned with the gold necklace he had given her long ago—a cherished token from a time when their love felt unbreakable. Over her shoulders draped a thick cloak, lined with animal skins to fend off the biting winter cold.

Beowyn's heart raced as he drew closer, struggling to steady his breath. Her gaze remained steady and unwavering as he halted before her, flanked by her guards and curious onlookers.

"My Lord," she greeted calmly, her voice carrying a subtle undercurrent of tension mingled with a hint of distant familiarity.

He yearned to pull her into an embrace, to feel her close against him. Yet, despite her nearness, an insurmountable distance seemed to loom between them. Aware that her presence in Faermire could potentially ignite conflict, Beowyn felt the weight of everyone's scrutiny as he turned to the captain of the guard.

"Have the scouts bring report of our borders for any sign of Elwin's presence," he ordered, his voice betraying a mix of urgency and caution.

The captain nodded sharply and hurried away, leaving Beowyn to confront the woman before him. Her weariness from the journey was evident, yet her gaze bore into him with a mixture of familiarity and caution.

"You must be weary from your travels. My servants will attend to your needs," Beowyn offered with a polite gesture, though the air between them crackled with unspoken tension.

"Thank you, Your Grace..." Her voice, soft yet tinged with resolve, hung in the air, echoing the history between them. Her hazel eyes locked onto his, refusing to waver, a challenge that stirred a storm of emotions within him. He fought to maintain composure, to conceal the tumult that threatened to surface under her steady gaze.

The servants bustled efficiently, leading the horses towards the stables. Tannica's guards maintained a respectful distance, following closely as Beowyn escorted her towards the palace. The atmosphere remained tense, neither finding the right words to break the uneasy silence that enveloped them. Beowyn was acutely aware of her presence beside him, careful not to steal too many glances for fear of revealing the awe he felt at having her so close.

Questions clamored for attention in his mind, each vying to be the first spoken, yet he chose to maintain his silence, a choice born of uncertainty and a reluctance to disturb the fragile peace of the moment. Amidst their quiet walk, Tannica glanced up at him, her eyes betraying a mix of confidence and longing that stirred a tumult within him.

Finally reaching the base of the palace steps, Beowyn broke the silence. "The maids will ensure you are well cared for," he stated, his gaze shifting briefly to her guards—three men bearing the unmistakable crest of Valenmur emblazoned on their leather armor. Tall and formidable, they exuded the same pride and determination as Tannica's kin.

"Your guards will not be permitted beyond this point," Beowyn continued, his voice firm yet kind.

Tannica redirected her attention to her men, nodding subtly in their direction as if to reassure them, granting them a temporary respite from their duty.

Without a word, Tannica inclined her head in a respectful bow towards Beowyn, then turned to follow the maids up the grand stairwell, her figure disappearing behind the imposing stone columns of the palace.

At last, Beowyn released a sharp sigh, his frustration palpable as Elder Haemund strode purposefully across the courtyard towards him. A stern mask of disapproval marked the lines of Haemund's weathered face, signaling his intent to voice staunch opposition to harboring the daughter of Beowyn's late father's adversary within their walls.

Turning casually, Beowyn headed towards the main court as the elderly man closed the distance. "My King," Haemund addressed him matter-of-factly, bowing with forced respect.

"Lord Haemund," Beowyn responded evenly.

"I've received word that Lady Tannica has been admitted through the city gates," Haemund reported.

"You've heard correctly."

"She is the daughter of Elwin of Valenmur."

"Your observations are very astute, Lord Haemund."

"I need not remind you that her presence here can only signify she acts at her father's behest, to do his bidding."

"Perhaps," Beowyn retorted curtly. "Are you suggesting we turn her away without first ascertaining her father's intentions?"

"To be plain, my King, yes! It is no secret she wields influence over you. Would it not be clear she is here as her father's spy?"

His words struck a nerve, igniting anger within Beowyn. He turned sharply towards the elderly man beside him. Though he had entertained similar suspicions himself, hearing them voiced in such an accusatory manner was unsettling. With great effort, he held back his initial response.

"Spy or not, she is a guest in my kingdom and will be accorded the respect she deserves. If you suspect her of espionage, then question her yourself."

With that, Beowyn left Haemund standing alone and continued towards the court. The guards on either side swung open the massive doors, revealing the empty expanse of the courtroom and the throne awaiting its occupant.

Passing through, Beowyn commanded, "Send for Sgell," his footsteps resounding in the hollow silence of the room, underscoring the emptiness that surrounded him.

As Beowyn reached the top of the steps, he sank heavily into the throne, releasing a sharp sigh. He rubbed his brow, struggling to process all that had transpired. Young Siged's apparent recovery had brought a glimmer of hope, yet now the sudden resurgence of his former love threw his emotions into turmoil. Only yesterday, he had clung desperately to the fragile hope for the future. Now, he found himself face to face with what seemed to be divine favor. But distrust gnawed at him, whispering that it might all be a cruel trick on his emotions. Unable to find comfort in these seemingly fortuitous events, he withdrew, wary of embracing any semblance of joy.

The heavy doors groaned open, and Sgell strode in, his presence imposing despite his unassuming demeanor. Beowyn's gaze fell on him, and a pang of guilt struck him hard. Memories of his harsh words to Sgell replayed in his mind, the remorse settling like a weight in his chest. His initial reaction had been unjust, a misdirected outburst towards a man who had been steadfastly loyal to his family through countless trials.

Sgell approached, his unwavering loyalty evident in every step. He bowed deeply, his eyes fixed on the ground, a gesture of respect and humility that had become second nature over the years.

For a moment, Beowyn was at a loss for words. Sgell had been a cornerstone of their family, serving his father with unwavering dedication and guiding Beowyn through his own tumultuous youth. He had always been there, a steadfast presence, ready to offer advice and support. Even now, despite the recent tensions, Sgell seemed prepared to accept whatever fate Beowyn decreed.

Despite everything, Beowyn yearned to lean on Sgell once more for his counsel and comforting presence. He straightened in his seat, shifting uncomfortably before finally speaking.

"Your healer has done well to ease my brother's suffering. He speaks now, though he still struggles. His condition has markedly improved, and I believe thanks are due—"

"The young master remains at great risk from the evil that clings to him," Sgell interjected solemnly.

"What evil?" Beowyn's demeanor shifted abruptly.

"The same evil that offered an exchange on your behalf, my King. The sorcerer, Gorhan, cares not for the souls of men but for the hunger of the gods. He serves their gluttony as well as his own."

"What are you saying?" Beowyn had initially sought to break the awkward tension, but now he found himself ensnared by Sgell's cryptic words.

"Gorhan has cursed the boy, and until the curse is broken, it will continue to oppress him."

"You knew this all along?" Beowyn's voice was a mix of accusation and despair.

"I have seen it before, my King. The gods of this land take great pleasure in such suffering. You may appease them for a time, but that time is fleeting."

Beowyn's shoulders sagged under the weight of Sgell's words. He cleared his throat, attempting to stifle the knot forming in his gut. "Then what will become of him? Can your healer break the curse?"

"He came at my request to confirm my suspicions and delay the inevitable. But the boy's life was spared by ill intent, and until his destined time comes again, the evil will continue to seek him out, to feed and consume him."

Beowyn's heart sank. He glanced at the scar on his palm, a haunting reminder of his bargain with Gorhan. He remembered the black tar-like liquid he had consumed, feeling it course through his body, cementing a bond with darkness that left an indelible mark on his soul. The memory of that pain and the lingering urge to return to the darkness haunted him still. He could only imagine the toll it was taking on young Siged, and he grieved for his brother.

As emotions threatened to overwhelm him, Beowyn clenched his fist over the scar and refocused on the matter at hand. He needed Sgell's advice regarding Tannica's sudden arrival.

"Your friend, the healer, has prolonged Siged's life, and for that, I am grateful. But as you know, Tannica, the daughter of Valenmur, has come to Elsterheim... And I need your counsel, Sgell."

Sgell nodded thoughtfully, understanding the gravity of Beowyn's request.

"My King knows well what I would say."

"Yes, but I need to hear you say it."

Sgell hesitated, knowing his words would clash with Beowyn's heart. "Where there is temptation, there is folly. No matter the intent."

"Should I cast her out then?"

"Would my king do so even at my counsel?"

Just as Beowyn opened his mouth to respond, the heavy door creaked open, and a servant stepped inside, bowing deeply before speaking with measured formality.

"My Lord, the Lady of Valenmur requests an audience with the King."

A chill ran through Beowyn at the announcement. The knot in his stomach tightened once more as he glanced at Sgell, who gave a respectful bow before slipping quietly out of the chamber. Beowyn acknowledged the servant with a terse nod, then pulled himself upright in his throne, trying in vain to smooth his tunic and appear more regal. The effort felt hollow; he knew that no amount of posturing could disguise the weight of his anxieties.

The court seemed to expand endlessly as he awaited her arrival. His anticipation stretched taut, each moment amplifying his sense of apprehension. When Tannica finally appeared, her presence evoked a surge of longing that he fought to suppress. He focused instead on the reason for her visit, trying to pierce through the layers of his own emotion.

Her entrance was graceful, her steps light against the cold stone floor, each echo magnified in the silence between them. She approached with a blend of confidence and vulnerability, her hazel eyes reflecting a flicker of the same apprehension that churned within him. As she reached the base of the steps leading to the throne, she performed a deep curtsy, keeping her gaze lowered. Slowly, she raised her eyes to meet his, revealing the depth of her feelings in that simple, yet powerful gesture.

"My Lord—"

"Why are you here?... Tannica." The words tumbled out before he could restrain them, a reflection of his inner turmoil. She remained silent; her eyes locked onto his. "Does Elwin know you've come?"

Her gaze never wavered. "Does it matter?"

"In every sense. You only need to approach the gates for rumors to fly about a spy within our midst and my capitulation to your mere presence."

"Then it seems that you already have your answer, Beowyn. I needn't say a word before you've already presumed my guilt."

Beowyn's frustration flared, and he rose from his seat. The formal barriers between them crumbled as the familiar tension of past arguments resurfaced. He descended the steps, his eyes never leaving hers. Though her head reached barely to his shoulder, her demeanor was unwavering.

"The last we saw each other, you cursed my existence—"

"And you condemned me to a life you vowed to shield me from," she interjected, her voice firm. "I did curse you because I hated you for what you had done. And I hate that I see you wear that crown, knowing well the choice you made for it."

Her eyes glistened with unshed tears, the pain of their past still raw. Beowyn could see the ache in her expression, the hurt that lingered like a ghost between them.

"You know better than I, Tannica, that your father would use our marriage to seize power for himself."

"My father would exploit anything within his grasp, but you chose to abandon me when the prospect of the crown was within reach. You let your fear of my father dictate our fate. He needn't even cross your borders; he has already conquered you through your own fear."

"That's not true."

"You know it is."

Beowyn was left speechless, his heart heavy. "I never meant to hurt you," he said, his voice barely more than a whisper.

"Yet you did. And now, here we are. If you want the truth, Beowyn, I will tell you that, despite everything, a part of me still believes you love me as I do you. I cling to the hope of what might be, despite all reason."

Her confession cut deep, leaving him with nothing but the bitter sting of regret.

"Tannica—"

"Will you send me away?" she interrupted sharply, her eyes searching his with an intensity that seemed to strip him bare. "Even now, I stand here at your mercy once again."

Despite his inner conflict, Beowyn found himself unable to offer her the reassurance she sought. "And what of your father?"

Tannica's expression hardened slightly, her voice laced with bitterness. "He sends his blessing," she said simply, the words carrying the weight of their strained relationship.

FIVE

ELSTERHEIM, KINGDOM OF FAERMIRE

Estrith sat beside Siged, her eyes locked on his fragile form. Only hours ago, he had been a lifeless figure, comatose and void of any spark. Yet now, he was sitting up in bed, mumbling softly to himself, his eyes brighter, more alert. He accepted the porridge she offered, his small hands trembling as she brought the spoon to his lips. The transformation was astonishing, almost surreal. Estrith could hardly believe it, and a part of her feared that this newfound hope was too fragile to trust.

Though he wasn't entirely himself, the change was enough to make her feel as if she were witnessing a miracle. She watched him, her heart aching with a mix of joy and apprehension, afraid that if she looked away, the dream would shatter.

The servants arrived to tend to Siged, their movements efficient and gentle as they bathed him and prepared him for bed. Estrith reluctantly stepped back, allowing them to care for him. She listened to his incoherent ramblings, her heart sinking each time he called out for his mother. The mention of Richessa's name was a cruel reminder of the woman's betrayal, a wound that remained fresh in her mind.

Estrith's feelings toward Richessa were complex, a tangle of resentment and reluctant empathy. She remembered the woman's conspiracy with her uncle, the treachery that had nearly destroyed them. For a moment, Estrith wished she had let her father's wrath fall upon Richessa. Yet, seeing Siged's longing for his mother stirred something within her. She couldn't help but imagine the void she would feel in his place. Siged had no choice in who his mother was, yet the burden of her betrayal rested heavily on Estrith's shoulders.

Eventually, the servants finished their tasks, and Estrith tucked Siged in, her hands lingering on the covers as she smoothed them over him. She was hesitant to leave, her heart heavy with the weight of her dilemma. As she quietly shut the door behind her, she paused, her mind wrestling with what to do next.

The courtyard outside was bathed in the soft glow of moonlight, the air cool and crisp. Estrith stood for a moment, breathing in the night air, trying to calm her racing thoughts. Her gaze drifted to the path leading to the prison, a dark corridor that seemed to beckon her despite her instincts. The pull was undeniable, a magnetic force drawing her toward the unknown.

Before she realized it, her feet were moving, carrying her across the courtyard and down the shadowed path. The silence was almost oppressive, broken only by the soft crunch of gravel beneath her boots. Each step felt heavy with purpose, a blend of determination and dread driving her forward. The air grew colder as she approached, and the imposing entrance of the dungeon loomed before her, its dark maw seeming to swallow the feeble light. She paused, taking a deep breath, steeling herself for what lay within.

Her heart pounded as she stood before the iron gates, their cold, unyielding presence a stark contrast to her rising dread. The soldier on guard, clearly startled by her appearance, fidgeted nervously, avoiding her gaze. Estrith's eyes remained fixed on the inky darkness beyond the gates, almost as if in a trance, until she noticed the uneasy glances exchanged between the soldier and her servant standing behind her.

"Take me to Richessa," she commanded, her voice betraying a tremor of apprehension. The guard bowed quickly, unlocking the door and seizing a nearby torch to light their way. Estrith signaled for her servant to stay behind, then followed the soldier into the dank, labyrinthine depths.

As they descended, the torchlight flickered, casting eerie, dancing shadows along the stone walls. The faint drip of water echoed from unseen sources, and the occasional squeal of rats seemed to come from everywhere and nowhere at once. The corridor narrowed with each step, a suffocating tightness gripping her chest.

At last, the guard halted before a cell, its interior shrouded in darkness, save for a faint glow from a small, grated window. Estrith squinted, straining to see Richessa's form in the gloom. A coarse, yet familiar voice suddenly emanated from the shadows, making her start.

"My eyes must surely deceive me," Richessa muttered. "To what do I owe such a great honor? Or am I simply a cause for spectacle?"

Estrith stood silent, watching as Richessa slowly emerged from the shadows. She had vowed never to return, and yet here she was, face-to-face with the woman she had once spared.

Even in the depths of this prison, stripped of her title and regal trappings, Richessa exuded an air of unyielding arrogance. Her confidence wavered only slightly, her sharp features now gaunt from hunger, her fiery red hair matted and dulled by the filth of her imprisonment. The remnants of her regal gown hung in tatters, a mere shadow of its former elegance. Yet, despite her dire conditions, Richessa stood before Estrith with a defiant pride that seemed impervious to her suffering. The months of captivity had aged her cruelly, but she refused to show weakness in front of the one she deemed inferior.

Her green eyes, piercing through the dim light, locked onto Estrith with a hardened gaze. "If it were not for a cause greater than myself, I would happily leave you to rot."

"And what cause would that be?" Richessa retorted, her voice dripping with disdain.

"Your son," Estrith replied firmly, watching as the smirk vanished from Richessa's lips.

"What of him?" Richessa's tone shifted, defensive and brittle.

The last time, in a fit of spite, Estrith had refused to tell Richessa of Siged's wellbeing. Now, she wrestled with the same temptation but ultimately relented. "Siged lives. And despite everything, he calls for you."

For a moment, a flicker of humanity broke through Richessa's hardened façade. She reached for the iron bars that separated them. "How—how is he?" she asked.

"He is well. For now..." Estrith watched Richessa absorb the news, her own emotions a storm within her.

"And I suppose you want me to grovel at your mercy?" Richessa spat, her defenses snapping back into place.

"What?" Estrith recoiled, stunned by the accusation.

"My son calls out for his mother, and here you stand, holding his welfare against me. I have nothing, and yet you use him to torment me."

"That's not why I'm here."

"No, of course not. You deign to dole out information at your whim, just enough to twist the knife further. Is that it?"

Estrith rubbed her hand across her face, frustration boiling over. "Gods, Richessa, you're insufferable." She considered leaving, regretting ever descending into the dungeon. "If not for Siged, I would happily leave you here, but he is your son, nevertheless. I would like to believe that there is still some humanity left in you for his sake."

"Forgive me, dear princess, if I fail to fall for such poorly contrived manipulations."

"Manipulations?!"

"Spare me the act, Estrith. You and I both know that without your permission, I shall continue to suffer, knowing so little of my son beyond your word. You wield this power over me like salt in my wounds."

Despite her anger, Estrith couldn't dismiss Richessa's words entirely. The woman had a point. Estrith had no intention of letting her see Siged; her visit was meant to convey the boy's wellbeing out of a reluctant sense of duty. But Richessa, ever cynical, perceived it as a cruel manipulation.

Estrith found herself grappling with the purpose behind her visit. The more she considered her actions, the more she questioned whether her intentions were as genuine as she once believed.

"You're right, Richessa," Estrith admitted, her tone sharp and unyielding. The words seemed to ignite a spark of triumph in Richessa's eyes, momentarily dispelling her air of superiority. "I had no desire to let you see your son. My only aim was to inform you that he is improving. As his mother, you deserve to know this, despite the grim circumstances of your own predicament. If you choose to interpret my compassion as cruelty, then that is your misfortune."

Estrith sensed that any further exchange would be pointless. Richessa would only twist her words to suit her own needs. As she turned to signal the guard, Richessa's voice, now tinged with urgency, called out to her.

"Let me make a sacrifice," Richessa pleaded, her earlier arrogance replaced by a desperate sincerity. She pressed her face against the cold iron bars, her voice barely a whisper. "Let me offer a prayer to the gods for my son. If I am to be barred from seeing him, then allow me to at least seek a blessing for his protection…"

Estrith recalled the healer's disheartening words from just hours before and felt a shiver of doubt. The gods had seemed indifferent, if not complicit, in Siged's suffering.

She hesitated, casting a final glance over her shoulder. "The gods have played their part in Siged's fate, as have you," she said with a tone of finality. Without waiting for a response, Estrith turned and walked swiftly down the damp corridor, leaving Richessa's imploring eyes behind.

Richessa's desperation twisted her features as she clung to the iron bars of her cell, her fingers digging into the cold metal. She watched in silent fury as the torchlight from her stepdaughter's retreating form flickered away, leaving her engulfed in the suffocating darkness of her confinement.

The chill of isolation pressed in on her, its grip tightening with every moment. Her once fierce hatred for Estrith seemed trivial compared to the crushing solitude she now faced. The bruises from Ludica's wrath had healed, but his final words continued to haunt her, a daily reminder of her fall from grace. The passage of time had become a blur, the days merging into an endless night of despair.

Regret gnawed at her. She lamented her bitterness towards Estrith, realizing too late that perhaps a gentler approach might have earned her some fleeting reprieve. Now, her unyielding hatred seemed a bitter irony as she faced the relentless loneliness of her dungeon.

Collapsing to the floor, Richessa felt the weight of her circumstances settle over her, nearly suffocating. The oppressive darkness seemed to close in around her, tightening its grip on her chest as she curled into herself, knees drawn up. The small, distant window high above, a remnant of the world beyond, seemed to retreat further with every passing second, amplifying her sense of helplessness.

The remnants of the meager meal Estrith had left, which Richessa perceived as a cruel gesture, were now a feast for the rats. Their incessant squeals echoed around her, a constant reminder of her grim reality. She covered her ears, desperate to block out the sound, and shut her eyes tightly against the encroaching blackness.

In her desperation, Richessa almost called out for Estrith but stopped, knowing it would be a futile gesture. Instead, she murmured reassurances to herself, but the comfort she had once found in such words eluded her now. The strength she once relied on to combat her despair had eroded, and the fear of losing her grip on sanity grew stronger with each passing moment.

As the rats' squealing receded, it was replaced by a cacophony of voices in her mind, their whispers growing louder and more insistent. She huddled in the corner, trying to escape from them, but they seemed to close in on her, a relentless barrage that drove her to the brink of madness. Her screams echoed through the cell, a desperate cry against the encroaching darkness.

Eventually, the voices faded, leaving her with nothing but the remnants of her dwindling strength. She knew it wouldn't be enough to stave off the madness closing in on her, but she clung to the remaining fragments of dignity with fierce determination. Her life, reduced to isolation and humiliation, was a far cry from her former reign as queen. Estrith's visit had only served to remind her of her diminished state. If she were to lose her sanity, she vowed to do so clinging to the last vestiges of her self-worth, even if it was all that remained of her once formidable presence.

Richessa's resolve hardened as she faced the grim reality of her confinement. If death were to come for her, she vowed it would be on her own terms, a final act of defiance against a life of injustice.

Her gaze fell on the shabby sack of straw that served as her bed and the ragged blanket draped carelessly over it. This bleak scene, a reflection of her broken existence, had become a symbol of her suffering. Yet, as she surveyed her dismal surroundings, a sense of finality settled within her.

With a steely determination, she rose from the corner, clutching the tattered blanket. The strength she had thought lost began to return, and she felt a surge of defiant clarity. Time and despair had eroded her will, but for now, she embraced the fleeting clarity that emerged from the shadows.

Carefully, she maneuvered to a sturdy iron bar, using it to anchor one corner of the blanket. She then stepped back, her gaze fixed on the crude noose she had fashioned. The distant drips of water from the dungeon's unseen sources provided an eerie soundtrack to her solitary act.

The silence of her cell, once oppressive, now seemed a fitting witness to her final choice. Abandoned by all, even the gods, she found a dark solace in this quiet void.

Before securing the noose around her neck, she made a final, futile attempt to present herself with some dignity. She brushed the filth from her dress and attempted to smooth her tangled hair, an effort to face her end with some semblance of grace.

Climbing the iron bars with trembling hands, she adjusted the noose, feeling the cold iron bite into her skin. The makeshift hangman's knot loomed above her, a cruel reminder of her resolve. As she stood on the brink, her feet barely touching the ground, she felt a profound stillness, as if she were standing on the edge of an abyss.

Tears began to flow down her hollow cheeks as she braced herself for the inevitable. With a shuddering breath, she prepared to release her grip. Yet, just as she whispered, "Gods, embrace me," a flicker of movement in the dim cell caught her eye.

A shift in the darkness—a presence that was not her own—stirred her from her grim purpose. She was not alone...

Her voice quivered, not from the familiar apprehension of moments past, but from a deep-seated, unsettling fear. "Who's there?" she demanded, her hope dwindling that the presence was nothing more than a figment of her weary imagination. But, to her dismay, a deep and sultry voice emerged from the shadows.

"I am the answer to your groans and an offering to your plight." A faint orange glow illuminated the darkened cell, revealing the silhouette of a figure both alluring and ominous. As the form stepped into the dim light, it remained partially veiled in a swirling mist, with only its striking orange eyes and ethereal haze cutting through the gloom. Wisps of dark hair floated around it as if caught in an unseen breeze.

Richessa's breath hitched in her throat, her struggle to free herself from the noose now an almost comical battle against her own fear. She stumbled as her feet found the cold stone floor, her gaze never leaving the enigmatic figure before her. An amused smile played at the edges of the figure's shadowy form as it watched her with an unsettling calm.

"I have witnessed your suffering and heard your desperate cries, Richessa," the figure intoned, its voice resonating with a dark, seductive promise. "Your days in this dismal prison need not continue. You may indeed be freed from your torment."

"You—You would free me?" Richessa's voice trembled with a mixture of hope and disbelief. "Who are you?"

The figure chuckled softly, the sound both soothing and unsettling as it drew closer, its presence commanding yet intimate. "Have you already forgotten me? I am the one to whom you have pleaded, the one who offers solace to the forsaken. You know my name, Richessa. I am Eldra. One among many, but for you, I will be your singular salvation."

"The great goddess..." Richessa's voice trembled, the weight of her realization pressing heavily upon her. Eldra's amused smile widened in response. "You would free me from this place?"

"I would do far more than that," Eldra's voice was smooth and enticing.

"You would restore my crown?" Richessa's eyes widened, hope mingling with disbelief.

The goddess's dark silhouette moved languidly across the cell, as if weighing her words with deliberate care. "Do not mistake me for a fool. If I have answered your summons, know that my promise is bound by your own. If you seek your crown, you shall have it. But such a favor demands a commensurate offering. Would it not?"

Richessa's resolve wavered at the goddess's offer. Only moments before, she had been on the brink of ending her life, but now Eldra's presence promised a different fate. The goddess had heard her prayers, and a glimmer of hope for her future was now within reach. The cost, however, seemed worth the potential reward.

Her grip on the iron bars slackened, and she sank to her knees, ready to surrender herself entirely for the chance Eldra presented. To Richessa, reclaiming her lost crown was more than a mere symbol; it was, for Richessa, a means to an end.

Meeting Eldra's glowing orange eyes, Richessa steadied her voice, the tremor fading as she spoke. "If I find favor in your eyes, oh great goddess, I will give you whatever you desire."

Eldra's hand descended, her fingers cold and commanding as they gently rested upon Richessa's head. Her nails, sharp and dark, pressed lightly into Richessa's scalp. Though her demeanor remained authoritative, her voice carried a tone of approval.

"Say my name, Richessa. I want to hear you speak it..."

SIX

ELSTERHEIM, KINGDOM OF FAERMIRE

Tannica stood alone atop the palace wall, the city of Elsterheim unfurling below her in twilight's fading glow. She'd imagined her arrival here countless times on her journey, but nothing had prepared her for this— Faermire's capital spread wide like a jewel under a bruised sky, bustling with the distant, rhythmic sounds of its people. The hum of life echoed up the stone walls, each murmur and clink of metal strangely familiar yet distant, like half-remembered notes of a lullaby. Here, she could almost forget the weight of Valenmur, her father's schemes, the walls that had always caged her, and breathe deeply for what felt like the first time in her life.

The city's expanse was beautiful yet unfamiliar, each street and rooftop a new discovery. The wind tangled in her hair, and as she took in the distant mountains framing the horizon, she felt something shift in her chest—a glimmer of freedom, however fleeting. But her newfound solace was fragile. The moment unraveled as her mind drifted back to Beowyn's hesitant words, his guarded demeanor. She had hoped, so desperately, for his acceptance, his understanding, but even here, in a land far from her father's shadow, doubt crept in. She clung to her faith in him, in their shared past, yet felt it slipping through her fingers like sand.

A movement in the courtyard below caught her eye. Near the fortress gates, a gathering of people stood clustered in quiet reverence, with a young woman at their center—a vision of elegance and poise that seemed to draw all eyes, including her own. Tannica didn't need an introduction; she knew at once who it was. Estrith, princess of Faermire, her presence unmistakable even from this distance. Tannica had heard much about her from her brother Alfric, whose infatuation had bordered on obsession. Now, as she looked upon Estrith for the first time, she understood his fascination. Estrith exuded a serene authority, her bronze hair gleaming beneath the crown she wore with a quiet pride, every movement a testament to her lineage.

She watched as Estrith approached an elderly man among the gathering, his weathered hands held gently within her own. She bent to kiss his hands with a warmth that stunned Tannica; such reverence for a mere commoner was foreign to her. In her own world, nobility was distant, untouchable—a legacy of her father's iron rule. Yet here was the Faermire princess, defying every rule she'd known, her warmth as genuine as the lingering sunset.

A wave of envy rose unbidden within her, mingling with awe. Estrith seemed so at ease with these people, the kindness in her expression untainted by caution or fear. For a fleeting moment, Tannica felt the strain of her own guarded heart, a heart trained to see every kindness as a transaction, every smile as a weapon. What must it feel like to move so freely among others, to love without suspicion?

As the gathering dispersed, Tannica made her way down from the wall, her pulse quickening with an unfamiliar eagerness. She didn't fully understand her own intentions, but something about this woman—her quiet power, her unexpected warmth—drew her like a beacon in the dark. Navigating the winding corridors, Tannica soon found herself at the courtyard's edge, her steps faltering as Estrith's party came closer.

Tannica drew her shoulders back, schooling her expression into practiced poise even as nerves coiled in her stomach. She watched as Estrith conferred with her towering servant, a man of quiet strength whose expression softened under her words. She glimpsed a flicker of sorrow in the princess's eyes as she spoke—an echo of some grief left unspoken. Estrith's grace was undeniable, her beauty enhanced by her sorrow, and Tannica was struck by a pang of longing—for what, she could not name.

Finally, Estrith's gaze lifted, falling upon Tannica. Surprise flitted across her face, quickly followed by a cautious warmth, and Tannica felt her heart skip. She dipped into a respectful bow.

"Lady Estrith," Tannica began, her voice steadier than she felt. "It is an honor to at last greet you. I am—"

"Lady Tannica," Estrith interjected with a gentle curtsy, her voice laced with genuine welcome. "The honor is equally mine."

Estrith's unexpected warmth disarmed her, the sincerity in her smile unlike anything Tannica had ever known. She'd been raised on the belief that kindness was always laced with some hidden barb, yet here was a woman who seemed unguarded, genuine—a mystery in every sense.

"I hope your journey was well?" Estrith asked, her tone warm but perceptive.

"It has, thank you. I..." Tannica hesitated, her words faltering under the scrutiny of Estrith's calm gaze. "I am grateful for your hospitality, especially on such short notice. I realize my presence may be unsettling to some."

"To some, perhaps." Estrith's smile softened, a kindness in her eyes that seemed to see through every shield Tannica had so carefully crafted. "But to me, any friend of my brother's holds a place in my heart. He is a good judge of character, and as he cares for you, I have no reason to doubt your intentions."

Tannica's defenses wavered, her heart lifting at the sincerity of Estrith's words. She returned Estrith's smile, trying to conceal the gratitude that warmed her insides, but she knew it was in vain. For a brief moment, she felt seen—truly seen—by someone who held no ulterior motive, no scheme.

Estrith inclined her head toward the winding path leading further into the fortress. "Would you care to walk with me, Lady Tannica?"

Tannica's answer came without thought. "Yes, I would like that very much."

Together, they walked side by side, the air thick with unspoken curiosity. Tannica felt the weight of Estrith's quiet observation, her perceptive gaze noting every subtle shift in demeanor. For the first time, Tannica's carefully constructed walls felt unnecessary, and the guarded distance she'd maintained with others began to dissolve.

As they passed through the courtyard, Estrith offered hushed commentary on the various lords and noblewomen they encountered, her wit sharp yet gentle. The two shared quick smiles and laughter, an unanticipated connection blooming between them with each shared glance. For a while, Tannica forgot her apprehensions, her father's schemes, the burdens she carried. In Estrith's company, she felt for the first time a flicker of belonging.

But as they neared the doors leading to the inner halls, a glimmer of doubt returned. She couldn't afford to hope too much, couldn't let herself believe in something so fragile as friendship—not when everything in her world came at a cost. Yet, looking over at Estrith, she found herself wanting to try, to hold onto this tentative bond, if only for a moment longer.

Tannica followed Estrith through the halls of Elsterheim, marveling at the grandeur around her. The palace walls loomed high, bathed in the warm glow of sconces that cast flickering patterns over the stone. Intricately woven tapestries lined the hallways, depicting scenes of Faermire's storied past, and beneath their feet, the polished marble floors reflected the flicker of torches with a cool, ghostly shimmer. She felt as if she were walking through a story older than her own life, one that carried a weight she didn't yet understand.

They entered the grand dining hall, and Tannica's breath caught in her throat. The room stretched out vast and imposing, its vaulted ceiling supported by beams carved with symbols she didn't recognize. Golden candlelight spilled from iron chandeliers overhead, illuminating the long table set with gleaming silverware, fine crystal goblets, and platters awaiting the evening's feast. She let her gaze drift over the scene, taking in each detail—the richly colored banners of Faermire with their bold crests, the ornate high-backed chairs, the faint scent of spices and roasting meats lingering in the air.

As she took her place beside Estrith, she found herself hesitating, her fingers grazing the delicate silver utensils before her. Despite the initial warmth she had felt atop the palace wall, a sudden unease crept in. The grandeur seemed to loom, reminding her just how different this world was from the rough stone keep and loud mead halls of Valenmur. There, life had felt unrefined and brutish, like the clash of iron on iron. Here, everything was elegant and restrained, each movement a dance of etiquette. She suddenly felt out of place, aware of her every breath, her every move.

Estrith noticed her discomfort and smiled reassuringly. "Lady Tannica, are you well?" she asked softly, her tone as warm as her eyes.

"Yes, of course," Tannica replied, though her voice came out quieter than she intended. She gripped her napkin tightly in her lap, the fabric twisting between her fingers as she fought the sensation of being a stranger in a foreign land.

Estrith's expression softened as she reached across, her hand a brief, grounding presence on Tannica's arm. Just then, the heavy doors at the far end of the hall opened, and both women turned to see Beowyn enter. His gaze swept across the room, pausing briefly as he took in the sight of the two of them seated together. For a moment, Tannica thought she saw something flash across his face—a mixture of surprise and hesitation, perhaps even regret. She held her breath, feeling an inexplicable urge to look away, to shield herself from his gaze.

Beowyn's steps were slow, as if he were carefully weighing each one. He settled at the head of the table, his demeanor composed, but his expression seemed distant, preoccupied. Tannica felt the weight of his presence, heavy and unspoken, and a taut silence fell over the hall.

Estrith, however, was quick to break it, her tone as bright as it was deliberate. "I certainly hope our dinner isn't as cold as the air between us." She cast a sharp glance toward her brother, her eyes narrowing playfully, as though scolding him.

Tannica's lips curved into a small smile, grateful for the release of tension. She noted with a sense of wonder how Estrith, despite her brother's title, treated him as any sister might, offering her unfiltered thoughts without hesitation. Here, titles seemed to mean little in the face of sibling bonds, and for the first time, Tannica glimpsed a warmth and ease that felt both foreign and inviting.

Beowyn's composure softened, a faint smile tugging at the corner of his mouth. "It seems you two are getting along," he said, his voice carrying a blend of relief and something that almost sounded like surprise.

"Your sister has been very gracious to me," Tannica replied, her words carrying a subtle note of gratitude.

Estrith interjected with a knowing smile. "A conversation of common ground is often hard to find among the lords and ladies of Faermire. I find it refreshing to speak with someone who isn't, shall we say, excessively...self-assured."

Tannica stifled a laugh, nodding in agreement. For a moment, the weight of her unfamiliar surroundings faded, replaced by a sense of kinship she hadn't anticipated. She glanced at Estrith, her heart warmed by the princess's effortless kindness.

Servants arrived, placing platters of roasted meat, steaming vegetables, and baskets of warm bread upon the table, the rich aromas filling the hall. As they began to eat, the trio's conversation meandered, dipping into light-hearted remarks and shared glances that spoke of growing familiarity. Tannica found herself laughing more easily, the knot in her stomach loosening as the evening wore on.

She glanced across the table at Beowyn, catching his eye, and a thousand unspoken words seemed to linger between them. She searched his face, wondering what thoughts he concealed, what truths lay hidden behind his composed exterior. But he merely held her gaze for a moment, a flicker of warmth crossing his expression before he looked away.

As they continued their meal, Estrith kept the conversation alive, effortlessly steering it back toward lighter topics whenever a moment of awkwardness threatened to settle in. Tannica marveled at the princess's poise, her ability to ease tension with a single well-placed remark. She couldn't help but feel a pang of envy at the easy bond between Beowyn and Estrith, a sibling closeness she had never known.

But just as the hall began to fill with laughter and warmth, the doors opened once again, and a servant hurried toward Beowyn, leaning close to whisper something in his ear. Tannica watched as his face darkened, his smile fading as he nodded gravely. The servant retreated, leaving an unsettling silence in his wake.

"It's Siged," Beowyn said, his tone grim. Estrith's face blanched as she rose in an instant, the controlled ease in her demeanor vanishing. Tannica watched as Beowyn stood as well, his usual stoic expression now visibly softened with worry.

"Is...is everything alright?" Tannica asked, unable to disguise her unease

Beowyn's gaze softened, and for a brief moment, his vulnerability was visible beneath his kingly facade. "Our brother... he is unwell," he murmured, his voice heavy with worry. "I'm sorry, Tannica. The servants will see to you."

He rose swiftly, but before he could leave, Tannica instinctively reached out, her fingers brushing his arm. "Beowyn—" she whispered, a hint of desperation in her voice. He paused, his eyes meeting hers, and for a heartbeat, they lingered.

"I'll explain later," he promised, his tone gentle yet resolute. He gave her hand a reassuring squeeze, then slipped away, leaving her alone in the candlelit silence.

Tannica sat back in her chair, feeling the warmth of his touch lingering even after he had gone. The grand hall, once so full of life and laughter, now seemed empty, the shadows creeping closer in the absence of company.

The silence that followed seemed deeper, heavy with the words left unspoken. She could still hear the echo of Siged's name on Beowyn's lips, and it unsettled her like a distant rumble of thunder. Sitting idle became unbearable. Driven by curiosity and the unease winding through her, she rose, her feet carrying her out of the hall and down the corridor.

The sound of Siged's cries guided her steps, echoing down the stone walls, raw and almost otherworldly. A guard stood watch outside a door, his face drawn tight, flinching at each tortured sound that came from within. Beneath the boy's cries, there was a low, guttural sound—a voice not his own, thick and primal, the kind of sound that clawed its way into one's bones. Tannica shivered, feeling the chill of something darker than illness.

Inside, Beowyn and Estrith were fighting to hold the chaos at bay.

"Guard!" Beowyn's voice cracked with urgency as he threw himself against Siged's thrashing form, joined by two other men who strained under the unnatural force radiating from the boy. Every muscle in their bodies was taut, braced against the violent contortions that rippled through Siged, his small frame somehow bearing a strength that defied reason. Their grips slipped, fingers digging desperately back into his arms and shoulders as they struggled to keep him grounded, each movement met with a fierce resistance that seemed driven by something beyond mere fever or illness.

Around them, a cluster of servants hovered in a state of paralyzed horror, some edging forward with trembling hands, then retreating as if recoiling from a flame. A few braver souls stepped closer, drawn by loyalty and duty, only to halt, wide-eyed and pale, as they took in the full scope of the boy's frenzied struggle. The air was thick with fear, a tangible weight that pressed down on them all, and yet no one dared break the tense, terrible rhythm of that dark battle unfolding before them.

The guard at the door abandoned his post, charging into the room and leaving Tannica at the threshold, where the scene unfolding within gripped her, rooted her to the spot.

Siged lay in his bed, his small frame writhing against the sheets and twisting at unnatural angles. His limbs jerked with a rigidity that defied his frail body. His eyes were open but unseeing, clouded and dark, as though staring into some unseen abyss. Estrith was at his side, her face pale and drawn, her hands gripping his shoulders as she whispered words of comfort that trembled in the air. Beowyn knelt on the other side, holding Siged's arms with all his strength, his face twisted with determination and fear.

A strangled, guttural voice tore from Siged's mouth, uttering words that Tannica couldn't understand—a language ancient and cruel, heavy with something dark and malignant. As she watched, Siged's body lifted, hovering inches above the bed, limbs hanging, twisting in the air. Estrith's grip remained steady, but Tannica could see the strain in her sisterly resolve, her hands trembling against his shoulders.

"Fetch us some rope!" Estrith's voice held steady despite the tremble in her hands. Moments later, a young servant girl stepped forward, face ashen, clutching a coil of rope to her chest. The air thickened, oppressive, pressing down on everyone in the room, and Tannica felt it, like a shadow curling around her heart, pulling her into the darkness that seemed to engulf them all.

Without thinking, Tannica took a step into the room, her mind racing, her stomach churning with dread. The unseen weight pressed against her, urging her to flee, but she moved closer, her gaze fixed on Siged's contorted form.

Then, a familiar figure stepped into the room—a man she had noticed earlier with Estrith in the courtyard. She hadn't been introduced to him formally, but there was a quiet authority in his presence that she recognized. He was older, his face lined with age, yet there was a calm, almost otherworldly intensity in his eyes that cut through the chaos. As he approached, both Beowyn and Estrith breathed his name, "Sgell," in a tone thick with relief, their faces momentarily easing in the presence of someone they clearly trusted.

Sgell moved forward without hesitation, his gaze steady as he took the rope from the servant's grip, his eyes meeting hers briefly. There was something reassuring in that brief glance, and she felt herself ease, if only for a moment. Turning his full attention to Siged, Sgell began to murmur, his voice low and rhythmic, each word carrying a strange, melodic resonance that wrapped around the room's dark tension, like a soft current pushing back against a storm.

His voice deepened, slipping into a cadence that thrummed with an ancient, intangible power—something she felt but could not comprehend. Siged's thrashing began to still, though his small body remained suspended, as if held by some invisible force. But the dark presence within him resisted, surging back in a wave of energy that threw everyone backward. Tannica stumbled, catching herself against the wall as an unseen darkness pressed down upon her, filling her with an indescribable chill.

Yet Sgell remained unfazed, his voice unwavering, the words growing louder, threading through the oppressive silence with an unseen force. He raised his hand, commanding the darkness as though drawing it out from Siged, banishing it from the room. His final words rang out, a strong, echoing phrase that filled the space and stilled the air.

Siged's small body lowered gently onto the bed, his eyes fluttering shut as his breathing steadied, the tension in his frame easing at last. Estrith moved swiftly to his side, brushing a hand over his hair, her whispered reassurances flowing in a soothing murmur.

Tannica lingered at the room's edge, her breath shallow as the darkness receded, leaving a charged stillness in its wake. Across the room, Beowyn met her gaze, his expression unreadable yet edged with a quiet, unspoken concern. For a brief moment, she felt as though she were peering into something veiled. Neither spoke, yet in the silence, an unspoken tension passed between them—an understanding too fragile for words to capture.

For a brief moment, she felt the impulse to step forward, to close the distance and demand an answer. But the uncertainty in his expression held her back, anchoring her to the wall.

SEVEN

ELSTERHEIM, KINGDOM OF FAERMIRE

The morning light crept through the arched windows of the palace, casting muted rays that traced pale paths across the cold stone walls. Beowyn stood just beyond the threshold of Siged's chambers, watching his younger brother through the barely open door. Beside him, Estrith rested her hand lightly on the doorframe, her expression flickering between relief and worry as she observed the servants moving around Siged with solemn, careful hands.

Siged was awake, propped up in his bed with an odd stillness. His head tilted downward, and his atrophied hand lay curled against his chest, a quiet testimony to his suffering. His eyes traced invisible patterns along the chamber's high walls, as though reacquainting himself with the world. The servants moved delicately around him, their faces a mixture of guarded relief and veiled suspicion. They whispered to one another, their voices low and cautious, glancing furtively at Siged as if he were both fragile and dangerous, a soul caught between realms.

Estrith's voice broke the silence, a barely audible whisper. "I don't understand it. Just yesterday he was...," Her words drifted off as she turned to Sgell, her eyes seeking answers in his shadowed gaze.

Sgell's gaze remained steady, his dark eyes unreadable. "The healer's intervention has disturbed the spirit that clings to him, Lady Estrith. Its hold is weakened, yet it still resists. The struggle is far from over," he said, his words heavy with ominous weight.

Beowyn clenched his jaw, his eyes remaining fixed on his brother. Siged looked frail, his pale skin stretched thin over his bones, yet there was something flickering within him—a hint of awareness, a small but steady spark that refused to fade. Beowyn's heart tightened, hope and dread twisting together as he clung to that fragile reminder of the brother he once knew.

Estrith's hand tightened around the edge of the doorframe, her voice faltering as she watched Siged's slight movements, her face mirroring the ache in Beowyn's own heart. "He seems... better," she murmured, "but these attacks... I don't know how much more of this I can bear."

Sgell's eyes softened, though his voice held firm. "The boy's fate remains uncertain, Lady Estrith. Yet, it is not without reason that you are here in this time. Your presence strengthens him. In such a time as this, your intercession may be his only shield."

Beowyn shifted, his expression darkening as he looked toward Sgell. "And what of the rumors?" he asked quietly, the words slipping out like a confession. "The people will no doubt begin to talk. They will see Siged as... a bad omen."

Sgell inclined his head, meeting Beowyn's gaze with a calm that seemed to reach through the young king's unease. "Rumors are like seeds, Your Majesty. Once sown, they take root quickly, nourished by the wandering tongue. It would be wise to quench them before they grow into something larger than truth."

Beowyn's frown deepened, his gaze drifting as he pondered the weight of Sgell's words. "But how are we to quell them?" he murmured, frustration lacing his tone. "Even now, whispers are surely spreading, taking on a life of their own."

Silence hung between them, an unspoken understanding of the trial that lay ahead. Beowyn felt the weight of his responsibility settle more heavily on his shoulders. This was no battle that could be met with steel. Rumors were insidious, creeping like shadows into the hearts of those who heard them, feeding on fear and suspicion. Left unchecked, they would transform Siged into a symbol of misfortune, casting a dark shadow over Beowyn's rule before it had truly begun.

Taking a steadying breath, he forced his thoughts into stillness. He would face this as he would any foe, with unwavering resolve. But here, there were no straightforward choices, no clear path. Each decision weighed heavily, balanced between the needs of his people and the loyalty he held for his family.

"I'll take him away," Estrith said softly, her voice barely more than a whisper.

"To where?" Beowyn replied, the words carrying an edge of helplessness, as though no distance could silence the whispers already weaving through Faermire's halls.

"To Mistelfeld," she said, her tone firm yet tinged with uncertainty. "Under Gwenora's protection, perhaps he can heal in peace, away from Faermire's wary eyes. If he's no longer here, perhaps the rumors will die along with his absence." Her eyes met Beowyn's, searching for his approval, though her face showed the weight of her own doubts. She, too, felt the burden of the boy's presence, the silent threat he posed to their kingdom's stability.

Beowyn studied her, feeling the weight of her desperation. She was offering herself as much as her brother—a sacrifice born of love and loyalty, a shield for Siged against the world's creeping darkness.

With a sigh, he drew himself upright, the burden of kingship settling upon him. "Very well," he said at last, his voice softened but firm with resolve. "But Sgell will go with you."

Both he and Estrith turned to Sgell, who acknowledged the command with a solemn bow.

Estrith's expression softened, gratitude shimmering in her eyes. Beowyn knew what it meant to send Sgell away, but his duty to both Siged and Estrith demanded no less. The decision sat heavily within him, but for now, it was the only path he could take.

The palace corridors stretched before him, quiet and dim, the chill of the stone walls pressing in as Beowyn made his way toward the terrace. He had hoped for a moment to gather his thoughts, yet as he glanced toward the courtyard, his gaze caught on a cluster of figures below. Haemund was among them, his stare sharp, a silent summons that left little room for avoidance.

Beowyn turned away, setting a brisk pace down the hall, yet Haemund and two other elders fell in step behind him, their footsteps quickening until they caught up, uninvited yet persistent.

"Your Majesty," Haemund's voice cut through the silence, formal yet insistent. "A word, if we may, concerning our young prince."

Beowyn slowed, the weight of their approach pressing against his patience. He continued toward a quieter balcony, one that overlooked the city of Elsterheim, allowing the elders to fall into step beside him.

"Speak, then," Beowyn said, his tone flat, though a tension ran beneath it.

Haemund exchanged a quick glance with his companions, then inclined his head in a show of deference that felt more rehearsed than genuine. "The recent events surrounding Prince Siged have stirred... considerable unease among the people. There are whispers—rumors of ill fate, of curses that may linger upon the young prince and, by extension... upon Faermire itself."

Beowyn's jaw tightened, but he maintained his gaze over the city. "You think my brother is the cause of their unrest?"

"Not the boy himself, no," Haemund replied, his tone laced with a tempered humility that only sharpened his words. "But his affliction—the strange happenings surrounding him—have bred fear. There are... precedents, my king, ways to address such matters delicately, yet decisively. Perhaps a consultation with an oracle—an outward sign that the crown seeks the gods' guidance. A show of vigilance, if you will. Or, if it proves necessary, certain sacrifices have been made in the past to lift... spiritual afflictions."

One of the other elders, encouraged by Haemund's lead, stepped forward, his voice pitched in cautious agreement. "If the gods are displeased, Your Majesty, it may be prudent to show our acknowledgement. A token offering, to appease any... unrest they might feel."

Beowyn's mouth twisted into a wry smile, laced with sarcasm. "And tell me, which god would you have me appease? Shall we cast our offerings to the wind and hope one of them takes notice?"

The elders exchanged wary glances, and one of them, shifting uncomfortably, murmured, "Your Majesty, of course, no one would suggest such reckless offerings. But gestures have been made in the past—a show of faith. It would reassure the people, remind them that their king is vigilant, that he is taking every step to safeguard their future."

"The prince will be gone from Faermire by the day's end," Beowyn said abruptly, his tone hard and final. "He will depart for Mistelfeld, where Gwenora will see to his needs and keep him out of the public eye. With him removed from Faermire, there should be no cause for continued unrest."

The faintest flicker of surprise passed over Haemund's face, replaced almost instantly by guarded approval. "Mistelfeld," he repeated, his voice carefully neutral. "A sensible choice, Your Majesty. Removing the cause of anxiety could indeed temper the fears among your people... for now."

Beowyn's gaze remained steady. "Then let it be for now. Siged's fate will not be bound to the whims of baseless fears."

Haemund's expression softened, though a trace of discontent lingered in his eyes, as though the solution, while sufficient for the moment, fell short of his true aims. Yet he inclined his head, his tone smooth as he replied, "As you will, my king."

Beowyn watched as the elders offered stiff bows, each one measuring his response before following Haemund's lead. As their footsteps faded, the chill of their words lingered, wrapping around him like a ghostly presence, a reminder of the subtle pressures that moved unseen within the walls of his own court.

For a moment, he remained alone on the terrace, the wind tugging at his cloak, the city below sprawling in quiet indifference to the storms brewing within the palace. His gaze drifted across the rooftops and distant hills, a pang of frustration tightening in his chest. Haemund and his council were like the twisting roots of an ancient tree, tangled and stubborn, their whispers pressing in from every angle, questioning his every decision, nudging him toward choices he might never make on his own.

He observed the city unfurl below him in the pale light of the day. His gaze wandered over the expanse of Elsterheim below, feeling the weight of solitude settle around him. The city bustled with life, yet here, high above, the silence felt vast and consuming. His thoughts turned inward, to a question that lingered in the quiet corners of his mind—how would his father have managed this? Ludica had been relentless, unwavering, a force of nature Beowyn had both revered and resisted. Despite all their clashes, he now felt a hollow ache, a longing for the certainty his father's presence had once brought. So many things he'd left unsaid, questions he had foolishly believed he'd have a lifetime to ask. But that time was gone, taken in the unyielding march of life, and now, he stood alone in a seat that had never felt heavier

A flicker of movement below drew Beowyn's attention, breaking the current of his thoughts. His gaze settled on Estrith and Tannica in the courtyard, their heads bent close in quiet conversation. Tannica's hand rested gently on Estrith's shoulder, a gesture of unspoken support, a grounding presence amidst the turmoil that surrounded them. Something in the sight struck Beowyn deeply, an ache rising unbidden in his chest. He felt it—a pang of both longing and envy. In such a short span of time, Estrith had found in

Tannica a rare bond, a friendship rooted not just in shared trials but in something deeper, a trust that felt as solid and unyielding as stone. Estrith had found someone who stood beside her not as a subject or sibling, but as a friend, unflinching and true.

At last, the inevitable moment arrived, slipping past Beowyn's grasp like water through cupped hands. Almost without his noticing, the scene below transformed, the courtyard filling with motion as Estrith and Siged's entourage gathered. Slowly, they began their procession toward the docks, each step weighted with a quiet solemnity. Estrith walked beside Siged, her presence steadying his unsteady gait, her hand lightly resting near his arm as he took cautious steps. The boy's frail frame seemed almost swallowed by the cloak wrapped around him, his gaze cast downward, each stride tentative, as though the world had suddenly grown vast and uncertain. Beowyn watched, his chest tightening at the sight, realizing how swiftly the time had passed—carrying them all toward this parting.

Beowyn lingered on the terrace, his gaze following the quiet procession gathering at the docks. He hadn't expected so many—a solemn sea of figures whose silence carried a weight that seeped into his bones. A subtle disquiet coiled within him, deeper and heavier than he could shake. With a slow, steadying breath, he straightened his cloak, letting his fingers linger on the fabric for a moment before beginning his descent toward the docks. Each step felt laden with the weight of all he could not change, every footfall echoing the unspoken fears that had taken root within him.

When he reached the dock, Beowyn's eyes found Sgell already guiding Siged up the narrow plank to the ship, cradling the boy with a care that seemed to shield him from the biting air. Estrith stood nearby, her gaze drifting over the crowd until it met his. A bittersweet smile played across her face as she stepped forward, closing the distance between them. For a moment, they stood together in silence, a delicate pause holding them there, with the weight of unspoken words and all they hadn't said stretching between them like a fragile bridge.

At last, Beowyn summoned a faint, rueful smile, layering his voice with a forced lightness. "If memory serves, it was I who slipped away in haste before, leaving the kingdom in a quiet frenzy. And now, here you are, leaving me to fend for myself while you embark on your own grand escape."

Estrith's smile softened, her eyes warming with a hint of affection. "And here I was, thinking you might relish having the kingdom to yourself," she replied, her voice laced with a playful tease. Yet as the words left her lips, a flicker of concern crossed her face, her gaze settling on him with a quiet, searching intensity. "You'll manage," she murmured, her tone gentle but uncertain, as if reassuring them both. "You always have."

They stood together in silence, the weight of unspoken words stretching between them like a fragile bridge. Estrith reached out, her fingers grazing his in a touch that held all the love she couldn't voice, a promise she couldn't make.

With a soft, lingering sigh, Estrith turned toward the ship, her fingers grazing the wooden rail as she stepped onto the plank with measured grace. She paused, glancing back to where Tannica stood waiting on the dock. Their eyes met in a quiet, wordless farewell, a depth of understanding passing between them that needed no voice. Tannica stepped forward, her arms folding around Estrith in a warm, steady embrace. Beowyn couldn't catch their whispered words, but he didn't need to—their closeness was unmistakable, a connection as natural as breathing, and it stirred in him a quiet yearning, a comfort he hadn't realized he needed.

At last, Estrith joined Sgell and Siged on the deck, her figure framed against the ship's rising sails as they filled with the eager breeze, billowing outward like the wings of some majestic creature ready to take flight. Beowyn took a step back, his gaze locked on the vessel as it drifted away, carrying his sister and brother toward the horizon. A pang tightened in his chest, an ache he hadn't anticipated, as though something essential was slipping out of reach.

This was his kingdom, his legacy, yet for the first time, he felt like a stranger within it—a king without anchor, adrift in the silent, uncharted tides of fate.

Then he sensed her beside him. Tannica, steady and unwavering, had come to stand at his side. She spoke no words, offered no empty reassurances; instead, she simply looked up at him, her gaze quiet yet warm, carrying a strength that seemed to settle the unrest within him. In her silent presence, he felt an unexpected comfort, a gentle reminder that he was not as alone as he feared. Together, they stood on the dock, watching as the ship shrank into a distant speck on the water, swallowed by the boundless expanse of sea and sky.

EIGHT

HELMFIRTH, KINGDOM OF MISTELFELD

Mistelfeld's capital city loomed ahead, a waking giant rising from the mist. Estrith leaned over the rail, her breath catching as the towering spires broke through the steel-gray sky. Stone fortresses crowned the ridges like sentinels, while below, rooftops sprawled endlessly into a labyrinth of streets. The city revealed itself in fragments, each detail sharpening as they drew closer, its beauty both commanding and foreboding. Emerald and gold banners snapped sharply in the cold breeze, their colors vibrant against the somber backdrop, a proclamation of the kingdom's power and pride.

Estrith's chest tightened as she took it all in. The grandeur was undeniable, the sheer scale and symmetry of Mistelfeld's defenses unlike anything she had known in Faermire. Yet, the more she observed, the more the beauty seemed tinged with something foreboding—a magnificence that concealed as much as it revealed. The city felt alive, its towering walls and watchful spires not merely protective but withholding, as if guarding something just beyond reach. A pang of awe mixed with unease stirred within her, the vastness both intriguing and overwhelming.

A quiet presence at her side drew her attention. Sgell stood close, his gaze fixed on the approaching city. "It is remarkable," he said, his voice low, as though speaking too loudly might disturb the city itself. Then, with a gravity that made her pause, he added. "But do not be deceived by its grandeur. Mistelfeld hides its secrets well."

Estrith studied him for a moment, his words lingering in her mind like a warning she couldn't yet fully understand. She returned her gaze to the docks ahead, where the life of the city seemed to spill outward in chaotic rhythm.

The port bustled with life. Brine and smoke mingled with the sharp tang of spices, filling the air with a pungent intensity. Shouting sailors clambered over moored ships, while merchants and dockhands wove through the chaos, their movements urgent and unrelenting. As the ship moored, Estrith descended carefully, the sounds and scents enveloping her in an unfamiliar energy. Sharp glances flickered her way—curious, assessing, and lingering just a moment too long before slipping back into the crowd.

Sgell, ever watchful, moved to her side, his calm presence anchoring her amidst the chaos. "Do not mind their eyes," he said, his voice low and measured. "In Mistelfeld, everyone watches. It is their way."

Estrith gave a small nod, her attention drawn to the guards standing rigid along the perimeter. Their emerald and gold livery gleamed in the pale light, but their expressions were cold, their gazes calculating, as though they saw through her entirely. Even the practiced civility of the head servant who greeted them carried a subtle edge.

"We were pleasantly surprised to see Faermire's banners on the horizon," the man said smoothly, bowing just low enough to signal respect. "I'm certain the queen will be most pleased to hear of your arrival." His gesture toward the awaiting carriage was fluid, rehearsed, as if anticipating every step before it happened.

Estrith offered a polite smile but said little, her senses attuned to the undercurrents of the dockside. She felt the weight of scrutiny in the air, the unspoken expectations settling like a mantle around her shoulders. With Siged carefully handed into the carriage under Sgell's watchful eye, they began their ascent into the heart of Mistelfeld.

As the streets narrowed, the city rose around them in a commanding display of power and artistry. High stone buildings loomed on either side, their surfaces adorned with intricate carvings that told tales of kings and battles. Emerald and gold banners hung from archways and balconies, catching the wind in sharp bursts, but their vibrancy did little to soften the calculated coldness that seemed to emanate from the city itself. The streets twisted and climbed like veins through the capital, the enclosing walls giving Estrith an unsettling sensation of being swallowed whole.

By the time they reached the palace gates, Estrith's unease had settled into a quiet wariness. The gates themselves were massive, wrought iron woven with emerald and gold motifs that gleamed in the gray light. Above them, banners draped down like declarations of dominance, their movements subtle yet unrelenting in the breeze. Sgell glanced her way, offering a small, reassuring nod, though the tension in his shoulders betrayed his own vigilance. Taking a steadying breath, Estrith straightened her back and followed the carriage through the gates, entering the seat of Mistelfeld's power.

Inside the palace, the weight of its grandeur pressed down on her like a physical force. The walls rose impossibly high, adorned with woven tapestries depicting Mistelfeld's rulers in scenes of triumph and cunning. The emerald and gold threads gleamed with an almost lifelike vibrancy, their woven eyes seeming to follow her every step.

The towering doors of the throne room groaned open, revealing a hall both vast and commanding, its presence almost oppressive in its grandeur. Estrith stepped inside, the faint echo of her boots clicking softly against the polished stone floor. The herald had announced her arrival moments before, and now the weight of countless eyes bore down upon her—curious, calculating, and carefully indifferent. Each gaze felt like a whispered judgment, pressing against her composure as she forced her chin high and her steps deliberate.

Emerald and gold banners hung high from the vaulted ceilings, their edges rippling like silent sentinels in the draft. The air was heavy with burning resin, laced with the cold bite of stone—a weight that seemed to anchor Estrith in the gravity of the room. Around the edges of the room, nobles and advisors lined the space, their finely tailored garments gleaming with brooches and embroidery, the telltale signs of power and privilege. They bowed and curtseyed in synchronized acknowledgment, but their expressions were masks—neutral yet probing, betraying little of their true thoughts.

Estrith's gaze swept briefly over the assembly, noting the intricate balance of authority and pretense. The court of Mistelfeld was not like Faermire's; here, power danced behind veils of civility, threading itself through every glance, every pause. Yet even amidst this display of opulence, her attention was drawn to the far end of the room, where her grandmother stood.

Queen Gwenora was framed by the splendor of her court, a living embodiment of Mistelfeld's authority. Her emerald gown shimmered like molten jewels in the firelight, its edges trimmed with gold that caught every flicker of the towering hearths. Her posture was regal, commanding, but it was her eyes—keen and bright as a predator's—that captured Estrith's focus. When those eyes met hers, a flicker of warmth tempered the sharpness, a silent thread of familiarity weaving between them.

"Estrith," Gwenora called, her voice smooth and clear, carrying the weight of both affection and command across the room.

Estrith moved forward, the murmurs of the gathered courtiers brushing against her like a phantom tide. Their whispers followed her steps, and though she could not make out the words, she felt their intent: judgment, curiosity, speculation. As she approached the queen, Estrith stopped a respectful distance away, lowering into a deep bow.

"Your Grace," she said, her voice steady despite the unease stirring within her.

Gwenora's lips curved faintly, a smile that was as much an acknowledgment as it was an invitation. She extended a hand, her gesture as fluid as the sea. "Come, child, join me."

Estrith straightened and ascended the steps with measured grace, her every movement scrutinized by the court's unrelenting attention. As she took her seat beside Gwenora, she became acutely aware of the silence that followed her ascent, a palpable tension hanging in the room like the charge before a storm.

That silence was broken by a man's voice—smooth, deferential, and deliberately pitched. "Perhaps we should adjourn," he said, bowing slightly, "so that the Lady of Faermire may tend to her accommodations."

Estrith glanced toward the speaker, a tall man with a graying beard and a calculated air of authority. His suggestion, though polite, was clear: remove the unexpected guest.

Gwenora turned her gaze on him, her expression serene but laced with quiet finality. "On the contrary," she said, her voice slicing through the moment like tempered steel. "I think it would be good for the princess to observe."

The man bowed again, his acquiescence swift but laden with the unspoken displeasure of a courtier denied. He melted back into the crowd, and the meeting resumed.

Estrith settled into her seat, her spine straight as her gaze swept the room, taking in the layers of conversation and negotiation that unfolded before her. Mistelfeld's court was a symphony of subtleties—measured glances, veiled barbs, and alliances woven so delicately that even words seemed a liability. It was a far cry from the forthrightness of Faermire's council chambers, and Estrith began to understand Gwenora's earlier warnings. Here, power was not declared—it was felt, a quiet current shaping the air.

As Estrith sat beside her grandmother, her gaze swept over the court's sharp-edged exchanges, but her thoughts wandered to Siged. The image of him—so pale, so small—rose unbidden in her mind, a fragile figure dwarfed by the grandeur of Mistelfeld. The journey had drained him, his frail body seeming to shrink further with each passing day. A knot tightened in her chest, the familiar weight of guilt pressing down. She had left him in a foreign place, surrounded by unfamiliar faces, his vulnerability stark against the cold, calculated beauty of this kingdom.

For a moment, the flicker of a memory surfaced: Siged's hesitant steps as they guided him from the carriage, his wide eyes scanning the towering walls as though they might swallow him whole. The sight had clung to her, gnawing at the edges of her resolve. She reminded herself now, as she had then—this was for his protection, a necessary sacrifice. And yet, the ache lingered, a whisper of doubt she could not quite silence.

The court's gaze was like a weight pressing against her skin, pulling her sharply back to the present. The polished tones of veiled barbs and careful diplomacy filled the hall, but Estrith's shoulders remained stiff, her focus fractured. Her fingers tightened slightly on the armrest of her chair, her composure an armor against the intrusive thoughts that threatened to consume her.

Her gaze wandered across the room, sweeping over faces both familiar and unfamiliar, until she saw him.

Qereth stood near the edge of the chamber, his posture composed but unmistakable. Though his attire was far more refined than anything she'd seen him wear in Faermire, there was no mistaking the rugged confidence he carried—a trait that Mistelfeld's polish could never quite smooth away. His piercing blue eyes were fixed on her, and though he wore the stern expression expected of an emissary, she caught the faintest twitch of amusement at the corner of his lips.

Her heart leapt, a mixture of relief and elation flooding through her. Weeks had passed since his departure, and while she had anticipated their reunion, the chaos of her arrival had buried the thought beneath more pressing matters. Yet now, seeing him here—steady, composed, and very much himself—it was as though a tether she hadn't realized she'd lost had suddenly been restored.

Though she kept her expression neutral, a faint warmth spread through her chest. Qereth represented Faermire well; his bearing and demeanor had quickly adapted to Mistelfeld's protocols. But beneath the finely tailored tunic and measured stance, Estrith could still see the man she knew—rough-hewn in his charm, unyielding in his loyalty. The contrast was endearing, a reminder that even here, surrounded by veils of pretense, there was something genuine she could hold onto.

As her gaze found Qereth standing at the edge of the chamber, a quiet warmth stirred in her chest. His presence was a stark contrast to the icy precision of Mistelfeld's court—the cold civility of veiled barbs and measured glances. Here, where strength was hidden behind masks and alliances danced on knife's edges, Qereth's rugged authenticity felt like a tether to something real, something unshaken by the weight of grandeur. In a place where every word was calculated, his unspoken steadiness reminded her of home, of a simpler world where loyalty and truth had no need for embellishment.

The meeting stretched on, but Estrith's focus drifted, her thoughts anchored to the figure across the room. When Gwenora finally rose, dismissing the court with an air of practiced finality, Estrith felt a flood of both relief and anticipation.

"Come," Gwenora said, her tone softening as she turned toward Estrith, signaling the end of the formal gathering.

Estrith followed her grandmother into the adjoining chamber, where warmth from the hearth softened the edges of the evening's tensions.

"Your surprise visit is a rewarding one," Gwenora said, her voice steeped in dry wit, her sharp gaze flickering with a trace of humor. "I've grown rather weary of their endless squabbling. If half these men spent as much energy on action as they do on finding new ways to test my patience, Mistelfeld might rival the heavens themselves."

Estrith allowed a faint smile to tug at her lips, the lightness in Gwenora's tone easing some of the weight pressing down on her. But the levity was fleeting, and just as quickly, her grandmother's humor gave way to the sharper edge of her wisdom.

"But, as you will come to see," Gwenora continued, her voice low and measured, "Mistelfeld is not Faermire. Keep your wits about you, child. It would do you well."

Estrith nodded, feeling the full gravity of Gwenora's words settle over her like a mantle. Then, as though a veil had been drawn aside, the queen's stern demeanor softened. She reached for Estrith's hand, her touch unexpectedly warm, the shift from ruler to grandmother as natural as the turn of a page.

"But enough of Mistelfeld for now," Gwenora said, her tone carrying a rare gentleness. "Tell me, how are you? And Beowyn? And Faermire?"

Estrith hesitated, her throat tightening as she began to speak. "Siged... our brother... has been unwell."

A flicker of concern crossed Gwenora's face, her brows knitting together as she absorbed the words. "Unwell?" she echoed, her tone shifting to something softer, edged with worry.

"It's why we've come." The words felt heavy, dragging with them the weight of weeks of worry and sleepless nights. She lowered her gaze, her hands clenching in her lap as she forced herself to continue. "The attacks, his weakness... we didn't know where else to turn."

For a moment, Gwenora said nothing, her sharp eyes softening as they studied Estrith's face. The queen's composure remained, but her hand tightened over Estrith's, a quiet reassurance against the tide of guilt Estrith couldn't quite shake. "You did well to come here," Gwenora said at last, her voice calm yet steady. "Whatever burdens you carry, know that you are not alone. We will see to the boy's needs. All will be well."

Estrith exhaled softly, the tension in her chest easing just enough to breathe. Her grandmother's words didn't erase the ache, but they dulled its edges, offering the faintest glimmer of hope.

The assurance in her grandmother's words settled over Estrith like a balm, soothing the ache that had clung to her since their departure from Faermire. Gwenora released her hand with a faint smile, the gesture both tender and commanding. "Now, get some rest," she said. "You've traveled far, and there is much yet to do. I will check on you all later."

Estrith inclined her head in acknowledgment, her thoughts swirling with gratitude and lingering worry as she followed the servants leading her through the palace's labyrinthine halls. Their footsteps echoed softly, a rhythm that seemed to amplify the quiet grandeur of the corridors. The high ceilings and intricately carved stone walls felt imposing, their cold beauty pressing in like an unspoken warning.

Her thoughts were still tangled with Gwenora's words when the servants turned a corner, their forms disappearing into the dim light ahead. Estrith trailed behind, her pace slowing as a sudden presence emerged from the shadows. A broad figure stepped into her path with swift precision, and before she could react, a strong hand covered her mouth, silencing the gasp that rose in her throat.

She was pressed gently but firmly against the wall, her pulse thundering in her ears as her eyes searched the half-lit features of her captor. The flickering torchlight played across his face, revealing stormy blue eyes that held a familiar spark and the faintest smirk tugging at his lips. Slowly, he lowered the hand covering her mouth, the tension in his grip easing as recognition dawned.

"Qereth," Estrith whispered, her voice trembling with disbelief and relief.

His grin widened, and before she could say more, his hands cupped her face, rough and calloused but achingly familiar. He pulled her close, his lips claiming hers in a kiss that carried weeks of longing, unspoken words, and unrelenting passion. Estrith's breath caught as the world around them seemed to fade, the cold stone at her back and the looming palace melting into irrelevance.

Estrith's arms slipped around his neck, drawing him closer. Every thread of tension she'd carried since leaving Faermire unraveled, replaced by the grounding warmth of his embrace. When they finally parted, her breath hitched unevenly, her hands lingering at his shoulders, unwilling to let go of the solidity he provided.

"I thought I'd have to wait an eternity to see you," she murmured, her voice low and trembling with emotion.

Qereth chuckled softly, his hands lingering at her waist as his gaze searched hers. "Gods, I've missed you. And it seems you've taken Mistelfeld by storm already."

Estrith smiled faintly, the corners of her mouth curving despite the chaos of her thoughts. "Well, it seems you've adapted quickly enough. Though I'd know that smirk of yours anywhere."

His grin deepened, though a flicker of something softer tempered his expression. "What brings you to Mistelfeld?" he asked, his voice low, almost hesitant.

The sound of distant footsteps echoed through the hall, cutting through the intimacy of the moment. Qereth reluctantly pulled away, his hand lingering at her side for a heartbeat longer. "We shouldn't linger," he said, though his tone betrayed his reluctance. "Meet me later?"

Estrith nodded, her voice barely audible. "Please."

"I'll find you." With one last look, Qereth disappeared into the shadows, his form melting into the flickering light as if he had never been there.

Estrith stood frozen for a moment, her breath still unsteady, her hand brushing against the cool stone as she tried to collect herself. The servants had paused a few paces ahead, glancing back with questioning eyes. She straightened her posture, smoothing her features as she moved to join them.

A faint smile tugged at her lips as she followed them down the corridor, the warmth of her reunion with Qereth settling in her chest like an ember, steady and quietly burning.

NINE

HELMFIRTH, KINGDOM OF MISTELFELD

The modest chamber held an air of quiet purpose, its simplicity magnified by the soft glow of morning light spilling through high windows. Siged sat hunched in his chair, his frail form swaddled in layers of warmth, a fragile barrier against the chill that seemed to seep perpetually through Mistelfeld's ancient stone walls. As he raised the spoon in his trembling hand and brought it carefully to his lips, a flicker of hope sparked in Estrith's chest.

"Good," she murmured, her tone low and steady, a careful thread of encouragement. "Take your time, Siged."

A faint smile brightened Siged's pale face, the briefest glimpse of light breaking through the cloud of his exhaustion. His movements, though deliberate and faltering, carried a quiet determination. The slight quiver in his fingers betrayed his struggle, but the focus in his expression spoke volumes. He was fighting—against his weakness, against the weight of all that had happened.

Estrith reached across the table, gently smoothing the blanket draped over his lap, its worn folds a testament to her constant care. "It's alright to rest if you need to," she said, her voice softening with an edge of concern. "You've come so far already."

Siged set the spoon down, his hand falling lightly to his chest, the effort of even a simple task sapping his energy. Estrith watched him with quiet vigilance, noting the way his fingers twitched faintly, the faint lines of weariness etched into his ashen features. Though his recovery was visible, the fragility beneath it stirred a familiar ache in her heart. The morning light filtering through the room seemed to frame him in delicate relief, rendering him almost spectral against the imposing backdrop of Mistelfeld's stone walls.

As she adjusted the blanket again, her fingers brushed a lock of golden hair from his brow, a protective gesture she barely noticed herself making. The change in surroundings had brought some reprieve—he hadn't suffered an attack since leaving Faermire—but the peace felt tenuous, like a thread stretched too thin. The stillness unsettled her, as if it were merely the prelude to another storm. Her grip on the table's edge tightened instinctively, her gaze lingering on her brother's slight frame, as though she could shield him through sheer will.

A quiet knock broke the heavy silence, and Estrith turned her head sharply, drawn from her thoughts. The door opened with a low creak, and Sgell stepped inside, his dark robes whispering around him as he moved. The morning light played off his angular features, sharpening his already penetrating gaze as he studied the room. His eyes lingered briefly on Siged before shifting to Estrith, a faint shadow of approval in his expression.

"Good morning," Sgell said, his voice low and composed, the syllables weighted with calm authority. "It's good to see the prince awake and eating."

Estrith rose slightly from her chair, stepping aside to allow him closer. "He's stronger today," she replied, though a thread of hesitation wove through her words. "But I can't help worrying. He still feels so... fragile."

Sgell approached the table, his movements deliberate, his gaze assessing as it swept over Siged. "Perhaps," he said after a moment, his tone contemplative.

"Or perhaps his strength is returning, slowly but surely. The body and mind have ways of surprising us."

Estrith tilted her head, uncertainty flickering in her expression. "It's difficult to hope when the attacks come without warning," she admitted softly, her fingers brushing the edge of Siged's blanket.

Sgell's expression softened imperceptibly, though his voice remained measured. "You've done well, Lady Estrith. He is here, alive, and improving. That is no small victory."

Before she could respond, the door creaked open again, and Estrith's gaze snapped to the threshold. Her heart lifted at the sight of Qereth stepping into the room, his presence both familiar and grounding. He hesitated for a moment, his sharp blue eyes meeting hers in a glance that seemed to linger before turning to Sgell. A faint smile played at the corner of his mouth, and Estrith felt an unbidden warmth rising in her chest.

"Forgive the intrusion," Qereth said smoothly, inclining his head in greeting. "I thought I'd check on the young prince."

Estrith returned his smile, her tone softening instinctively. "He's doing better," she said, her voice gentle. "As you can see."

Sgell's sharp gaze shifted between them, a faint flicker of understanding crossing his features as though he could read the unspoken connection between the two. He turned his attention to Siged, his tone deliberate. "A walk through the palace would do him good," he suggested.

Estrith nodded thoughtfully, her eyes drifting momentarily to the window. "A walk does sound nice," she said, her voice carrying a quiet longing. "But... I'd like to go beyond the palace for once."

The room stilled at her words, tension creeping in like an unseen draft. Sgell's expression darkened faintly, while Qereth's posture stiffened, both men exchanging a glance heavy with caution.

"Mistelfeld is not Faermire," Sgell said carefully, his tone carrying the faint edge of warning. "Perhaps it would be wiser to remain within the palace grounds."

Estrith's chin lifted slightly, defiance flickering in her gaze. "I've been here for days and haven't seen anything beyond these walls," she countered. "Surely with an escort, it wouldn't be a problem."

Sgell's disapproval deepened, though his voice remained steady. "The streets are unpredictable, Lady Estrith."

She turned to Qereth, her gaze unyielding. "I'll have Qereth with me," she said with quiet authority. "Isn't that right?"

Qereth hesitated, caught between her expectation and Sgell's wariness. His eyes shifted briefly to the older man before he nodded, his reluctance barely concealed. "I... of course, your Grace," he said, his voice cautious but resolute.

Sgell exhaled sharply through his nose, his displeasure evident despite the veneer of composure. "As the Lady wishes," he said, his voice edged with reluctant resignation. "I will take Siged for his walk."

Estrith offered a faint smile, the tension in the room clinging to the air like mist. "Thank you, Sgell," she said, her voice steady though her thoughts lingered on the unspoken weight of his caution.

Sgell inclined his head curtly before stepping toward Siged. With careful hands, he helped the boy from his chair, draping a heavy cloak over his thin shoulders. He murmured something soft and indistinct as he adjusted the folds around Siged's frail frame, his actions efficient but gentle. Meanwhile, Qereth moved closer to Estrith, the brief brush of his hand against hers grounding her, though the touch was fleeting.

"Shall we?" he asked, his voice low and deliberate, a steady anchor amid the lingering tension.

Estrith nodded, her pulse quickening as she stepped toward the door. The thought of venturing beyond the palace walls ignited a quiet thrill within her— tinged with a flicker of apprehension she couldn't entirely dismiss.

The streets of Mistelfeld unfolded before them, vibrant and chaotic, alive with restless energy. The sharp cries of merchants clamoring for attention rang out over the din, each voice vying to be heard above the others. Fabrics of striking hues billowed in the brisk breeze, their colors weaving through the sharp angles of the market stalls. Tables spilled over with an array of exotic wares: jewels that caught the sunlight in dazzling flashes, spices that infused the air with rich, intoxicating aromas, and delicate trinkets wrought with fine craftsmanship that gleamed like fragments of starlight. Yet beneath this kaleidoscope of activity hid something darker. Estrith caught furtive glances exchanged between townsfolk, the murmur of hushed conversations that fell silent as she and Qereth passed, and the lingering sense of eyes following them from her periphery.

"It's beautiful," Estrith said, her voice soft with wonder as her gaze traced the intricate carvings on the surrounding buildings—etched stone reliefs that bore the weight of Mistelfeld's storied past. Above them, emerald-and-gold banners snapped in defiance against the cold, gray sky, the colors vivid even in the muted light.

Qereth's sharp eyes roamed over the crowd, his expression guarded, alert to the undercurrents rippling through the marketplace. "Mistelfeld is beautiful," he replied, his tone measured, though there was a shadow of caution beneath it. "But it's complicated."

They moved deeper into the heart of the city, where the noise grew sharper, the movements of the crowd more frenetic. Estrith's ears caught fragments of conversations carried on the wind—disjointed words that painted a picture of simmering unrest. One name emerged with unsettling frequency, spoken in tones that ranged from reverence to venom: Ordric. The weight of the name hung in the air, demanding her attention.

"Who is Ordric?" Estrith asked, glancing toward Qereth, her curiosity undeniable.

Qereth hesitated, his jaw tightening before he answered. "A former nobleman," he said at last, his voice clipped and wary. "He sought to overthrow the queen by aligning himself with Ceolfrid, the King of Abensloh."

Estrith slowed her steps, her brow knitting in thought. "And he's still alive?"

"For now," Qereth replied tersely, his tone leaving no room for elaboration. "But it's not my place to speak further on the matter."

Before she could press him, the atmosphere around them shifted abruptly. The steady hum of the marketplace gave way to raised voices, the sound growing sharper and more insistent with each passing moment. Around the corner, a group of protesters surged into view, their chants ricocheting throughout the streets.

"Free Lord Ordric!" they roared, their fists raised high in defiance as their numbers swelled.

Estrith froze, her breath catching as she watched the protesters advance with unrestrained fervor. The guards stationed at the edge of the market moved to intercept them, forming a wall of shields that bristled with tension. Commands were shouted, but the crowd's anger boiled over, their cries a volatile mix of desperation and fury that threatened to erupt.

"This isn't good," Qereth muttered, stepping instinctively in front of Estrith. His stance shifted, protective, as his sharp eyes darted through the throng, searching for an escape. The heat of the crowd's animosity pressed in around them, thick and suffocating.

Amid the chaos, several faces turned toward them, recognition flashing like a spark to dry tinder.

"Faermire's emissary!" a voice called out, its tone sharp and accusatory. A finger jabbed in their direction. "You've no place here!"

Another voice joined in, harsher and more biting. "Faermire doesn't belong in Mistelfeld! Traitorous dogs!"

The mob's fury shifted abruptly, honing in on Estrith and Qereth with pointed hostility. The press of bodies surged closer, their hostility like a wave threatening to break. Estrith's heart pounded in her chest, her breath coming shallow as the tension escalated.

"Stay close to me," Qereth ordered, his voice low but edged with steely resolve. He drew Estrith behind him, his frame shielding her as his gaze locked onto the crowd with unflinching intensity.

The mob's advance continued, emboldened by their own anger. Qereth's voice cut through the chaos, harder now, laced with a warning. "Get back!" he barked, his hand moving with practiced swiftness as he pulled a dagger from beneath his cloak. The blade caught the pale light, gleaming with cold menace. "I'll gut the first fool who steps closer!"

Estrith's breath hitched at the raw force of his words. The calm, diplomatic facade Qereth wore had quickly vanished, replaced by the rugged defiance of a man who would fight with everything to protect her. This was a side of him she had rarely seen, but its ferocity was unmistakable.

The protesters faltered, their momentum breaking under the weight of his command and the deadly promise of the blade in his hand. But their anger simmered, a fire still smoldering beneath the surface. Before it could reignite, another voice rang out, cutting through the din with authority.

"Clear the way!" The command was sharp, its authority unquestionable. The crowd hesitated as a squadron of soldiers marched forward, their emerald-and-gold livery gleaming even in the dim light. At their head was Aldred, the queen's trusted servant, his presence commanding.

"Get back!" Aldred bellowed, his soldiers forming a barrier as they drove the protesters back with swift efficiency. The mob's chants faltered, their resistance crumbling under the weight of the soldiers' forceful advance.

As the gates of the palace loomed ahead, Estrith cast a single glance over her shoulder. The energy of the crowd lingered, like the crackle of a storm just past. Her pulse still raced, the memory of their fury etched into her mind.

Aldred turned to them as the heavy gates groaned shut behind them, his gaze sharp and assessing. "The queen has sent for you," he said, his tone brisk yet respectful.

Estrith met Qereth's eyes briefly, the weight of the moment shared between them. The tension still clung to the air, the echoes of the crowd's chants ringing faintly in her ears as they followed Aldred into the palace, leaving the chaos of the streets behind.

Aldred led them into the palace with deliberate strides, his expression hardening as he cast a pointed glance at Qereth. "It would be wise to remain within the palace, Your Grace," he said, his tone measured but laced with quiet authority.

Estrith held back the sharp retort that rose to her lips, her fingers brushing the fabric of her skirts in a grounding motion. She allowed her composure to settle like a protective mantle, glancing at Qereth for reassurance. He met her gaze with a faint, steady nod, a silent gesture of solidarity, before they followed Aldred through the arching corridors. The unrest outside seemed to echo faintly in Estrith's mind, a dissonant undercurrent beneath the heavy quiet of the palace.

Inside, the air felt colder, weighted with the imposing stillness of stone walls steeped in history. The sound of their footsteps, sharp against the polished floors, softened as they moved deeper into the shadowed passages. A faint scent of beeswax and burning cedar mingled in the air, starkly contrasting the vibrant, chaotic spice of the city streets. Though the palace offered a veneer of calm, tension clung to the atmosphere, unshaken by the heavy doors that had shut the turmoil outside.

At last, they reached a tall door intricately carved with floral motifs entwined with the emerald-and-gold crest of Mistelfeld. The designs told a story of regal authority, the craftsmanship as deliberate and unyielding as the legacy it symbolized. Aldred rested his hand on the smooth wood for a moment before pushing it open with careful purpose, revealing the queen's private audience chamber.

Warm light poured from the hearth, spilling across walls adorned with rich tapestries that depicted battles, rulers, and triumphs of Mistelfeld's storied past. Unlike the cold splendor of the throne room, this space carried a subtle intimacy, its grandeur softened by the careful arrangement of polished wood furniture and finely woven rugs. The mingling scents of cedarwood and beeswax lingered here as well, infusing the room with a welcoming warmth that contrasted the icy streets beyond. But what immediately drew Estrith's attention was the figure standing near the hearth.

Helgisson commanded the space effortlessly. His tall, broad frame was accentuated by the fur-lined leathers he wore, each detail of his attire speaking of both practicality and status. The muted, earthy tones of his clothing framed a face weathered by countless battles, its sharp lines softened only slightly by the firelight. His pale blue eyes, as frigid and unyielding as the northern skies, swept the room with an intensity that demanded respect. He stood with his arms loosely crossed, his posture balanced between authority and ease, a man accustomed to carrying the weight of impossible burdens without faltering.

By the hearth, Gwenora sat in a high-backed chair, the emerald of her gown shimmering in the flickering firelight like molten jewels. Her keen gaze lifted the moment they entered, locking onto Estrith with the same sharp focus that had been used to command armies and outmaneuver enemies. "Come in," she said, her voice blending warmth and steel, an authority that brooked no refusal.

Helgisson turned at her words, his piercing eyes narrowing as they settled on Estrith and Qereth. Though his expression softened slightly, there was no mistaking the weight of his scrutiny.

"Estrith," Gwenora said, gesturing for her to step forward, "allow me to introduce Helgisson, elder of Graefeld and a steadfast ally in these uncertain times."

Helgisson inclined his head, a faint smile easing the harshness of his features. "Lady Estrith," he greeted, his voice low and resonant, like the distant roll of thunder. "It is an honor to meet you. Though I knew your father only briefly, I held great respect for him—as both a warrior and a king."

Estrith blinked, momentarily caught off guard by the sincerity in his tone. Praise for her father outside of Faermire was rare, often dulled by political rivalry or enmity. Hearing such respect from Helgisson stirred an unexpected mix of pride and grief within her. "Thank you," she replied softly, bowing her head. "The honor is mine, my lord."

Helgisson's faint smile deepened before he turned his attention back to Gwenora. She gestured for Estrith to sit, her expression sharpening with purpose as her focus shifted to the matters at hand. Estrith lowered herself into the chair opposite her grandmother, her posture straight but tense. Behind her, Qereth remained standing, his quiet presence a steadying force amid the room's charged atmosphere.

"Lord Ordric's imprisonment has stirred unrest in the city," Gwenora began, her voice steady, though a current of frustration underpinned her words. "Despite his treason, his supporters grow bolder—a rallying cry for the disenfranchised and disillusioned."

Estrith's frown deepened as she gripped her hands tightly in her lap. "He allied with Ceolfrid to overthrow you," she said, disbelief threading her voice. "How can anyone support a man like that?"

"Because power," Gwenora replied, her tone sharp with pragmatic insight, "is rarely about truth. It is about perception. Ordric has mastered the art of shaping his image. To those who feel overlooked, he is not a traitor but a savior—a man who would risk everything for their cause."

Estrith's thoughts churned as her grandmother's words sank in. She met Gwenora's gaze, her voice quieter but no less certain. "And if you execute him," she said slowly, realization dawning like a storm gathering on the horizon, "he becomes a martyr."

Gwenora inclined her head slightly, a flicker of approval in her sharp eyes. "Precisely. His death would cement his supporters' narrative and ignite the unrest into full rebellion. Mistelfeld's alliances are already fragile enough without inviting further division."

Estrith's stomach churned as the weight of the conversation settled over her, each word from her grandmother drawing the intricate web of Mistelfeld's fragile balance into sharper focus. This was no simple matter of justice or retribution; it was a precarious dance on a razor-thin edge, every decision tipping the scales closer to ruin or stability.

"Someone continues to stoke the flames, Your Grace," Qereth said, breaking the silence. His voice was low, deliberate, the meaning behind his words heavy with unspoken implications. "Even as Ordric sits behind bars."

Helgisson nodded, his expression hardening like stone. "The unrest itself is proof," he said, his tone carrying the weight of grim certainty. "Such agitation doesn't sustain itself."

Gwenora's lips pressed into a firm line, her gaze turning inward as though tracing an invisible thread through the chaos. Her voice, edged with steel, cut through the stillness. "I have my suspicions," she admitted, her words careful and deliberate. "But without proof, any accusation would only deepen the divide."

The conversation wound on, circling the same dilemmas with no resolution in sight. At last, Helgisson shifted slightly, a subtle movement that hinted at his desire to draw the discussion to a close.

A weighty pause followed, heavy with unspoken thoughts and lingering tension. Helgisson straightened, his imposing frame easing as his piercing pale eyes softened, their intensity giving way to something gentler as he turned toward Estrith. "Your grandmother's wisdom is the reason Mistelfeld still stands," he said, his voice low and deliberate, carrying a reverence that hung in the air like a benediction. "Graefeld owes her much, and for that, she has my loyalty."

Gwenora inclined her head, her sharp gaze mellowing as the corners of her lips curved into a faint but genuine smile. The usual steel in her demeanor softened, giving way to a flicker of warmth. "Graefeld's strength has been a steadfast ally in these turbulent times," she replied, her tone carrying both gravity and sincerity.

Helgisson dipped his head in acknowledgment, the faintest curve of a smile gracing his otherwise stoic expression. "Nevertheless, Your Grace," he continued, his voice steady and resolute, "it is your leadership that has given my people hope."

The words settled over the room like the echo of a bell, their weight lingering in the charged silence that followed. For a moment, no one spoke, the air between them heavy with the gravity of what had been said. Helgisson was the first to break the stillness, stepping back with measured composure. His expression remained firm, though there was a hint of finality in his tone as he said, "But if you'll excuse me, I have preparations to attend to."

Qereth, who had stood silently at Estrith's side throughout the exchange, inclined his head slightly, his movement fluid and deferential. "I too must see to other matters, Your Grace," he added, his tone polite yet firm, his piercing gaze flicking briefly to Estrith before settling back on Gwenora.

Both men offered final bows, the smooth synchronicity of their gestures underscoring the weight of their respect. Their retreat was quiet but deliberate, their footsteps fading down the corridor like whispers lost in the vastness of the stone walls.

Estrith's gaze lingered on the doorway long after it had closed, the heavy wooden barrier now separating her from their composed departures. The tension of their exit left a palpable void, replaced only by a quiet unease that seeped into the chamber, clinging to the edges of the room.

Gwenora's shoulders seemed to ease, but only slightly, her regal composure faltering in the flickering firelight. Her voice, barely above a whisper, slipped into the stillness. "I've grown tired of these games," she murmured, as though the admission itself could strip away her resolve.

Estrith hesitated before speaking, her voice cautious yet probing. "Why do so many favor Ceolfrid?" she asked, her tone carrying the weight of genuine curiosity. "It's no secret his rule stifles those beneath him."

Gwenora's gaze drifted toward the hearth, her sharp features softened by the firelight's shifting glow. "Because Ceolfrid offers stability," she replied, her tone cutting with pragmatic finality. Her fingers tightened ever so slightly on the armrest, betraying the strain beneath her composed exterior. "Consistency can be more enticing than freedom. For many, that is enough—even if it comes at a cost they can't afford." The flickering flames cast shadows across her face, deepening the faint bitterness in her expression.

Leaning back in her chair, Gwenora's eyes grew distant, her thoughts stretching beyond the room's confines. "My people have always valued security above autonomy," she continued, her voice carrying a quiet disdain that cut sharper than anger. "They'll gladly surrender their freedoms if it means their comforts are preserved—whether by the promise of luxury or the distraction of spectacle."

Estrith said nothing, letting the weight of her grandmother's words settle over her. Her gaze followed the flames as they danced, their restless movements a mirror of the turmoil swirling in her mind.

After a long pause, she broke the silence, her voice soft but searching. "And what do you offer them, Grandmother?"

A dry chuckle escaped Gwenora's lips, low and tinged with wry amusement. "I offer them purpose," she said, her voice sharp yet resigned. "But purpose is a far less alluring prize than the illusion of ease."

The room fell quiet again, the fire crackling softly in the hearth as the air thickened with contemplation. Gwenora's expression shifted, her tone softening into something almost wistful. "That Helgisson..." she murmured, her eyes narrowing slightly as if peering into a memory. "He reminds me of his father."

Estrith tilted her head, curiosity sparking in her gaze. "You knew his father?" she asked, her voice light but inquisitive.

A faint, fond smile tugged at Gwenora's lips. "We crossed paths many years ago," she said, her voice dropping into an almost nostalgic cadence. "Let's just say he left an impression."

Her sharp eyes shifted to Estrith then, amusement flickering to life in their depths. "And that Qereth of yours," she added, her lips curving into a knowing smile, "he's quite the sight."

Estrith felt a warmth rise to her cheeks, though she kept her expression measured, determined not to betray her reaction. "He's... been a loyal friend," she said simply, her tone even and guarded.

"A friend," Gwenora echoed, her voice lilting with quiet mirth. Her smile widened, sly and knowing. "Of course. You'd do well to keep him close. I like that one."

Estrith lowered her gaze, her thoughts churning as she searched for a response that refused to form. The weight of her grandmother's words hung between them, heavy and undeniable, even as the conversation drifted to quieter tones.

When Gwenora finally offered a subtle nod of dismissal, Estrith rose with careful composure, her movements measured but deliberate. The unspoken gravity of their exchange followed her, lingering in the air as she stepped away from the room, her thoughts tangled in the echoes of their conversation.

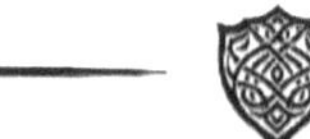

The chamber was cloaked in quiet, the low crackle of the hearth the only sound as its amber light painted shifting shadows across the stone walls. Estrith leaned back in her chair, her fingers tracing absent patterns over the carved armrest. Her gaze followed the flames, their slow, hypnotic dance both comforting and restless. Across from her, Qereth perched on the edge of his chair, his posture taut despite the room's warmth. The firelight caught the contours of his jaw, casting his features in stark relief. The flickering glow lent him an intensity that Estrith found difficult to ignore.

The weight of the day lingered between them, unspoken yet palpable. The tension of the protest, the crowd's angry voices still ringing in her mind, mingled with her own simmering doubts. The silence that stretched between her and Qereth was heavy but not unwelcome, a space filled with all the things left unsaid.

Finally, Qereth broke the stillness, his voice low and roughened with a depth that caught Estrith's attention. "I miss it," he said, his eyes fixed on the fire as though searching its depths for something lost. "Home." A faint, self-deprecating smile curved his lips. "Even your brother—though I'd never admit that to him."

Estrith's lips twitched into a small smile of her own, though the vulnerability in his tone settled uneasily in her chest. "You'll return," she murmured, her voice weaving through the quiet with a steadiness she didn't entirely feel.

For a moment, Qereth said nothing, his gaze distant. The firelight softened the sharp lines of his face, its glow catching a flicker of wistfulness in his expression. When he finally spoke again, his voice carried a thread of caution. "How is it?" he asked, his eyes flicking briefly to hers before dropping back to the flames. "How is Beowyn?"

Estrith's fingers stilled against the armrest, her thoughts turning inward. Her gaze fell to the fire, its restless movements echoing her own uncertainty. "He's... trying," she said at last, her voice tinged with both pride and doubt.

"But the people—they still compare him to our father. They expect him to command the same authority, the same presence. It's a weight that never seems to lift."

Her words lingered in the air, heavy with unspoken emotion, as the fire's quiet crackle filled the void.

Qereth's jaw tightened, his brows furrowing as frustration carved itself into his features. "He's stronger than they know," he said, his voice steady but edged with conviction. "He'll find his way. He always does."

Estrith nodded faintly, though her thoughts lingered on her brother's struggles. After a moment, she hesitated, her voice soft as she said, "Tannica came to Elsterheim."

Qereth's brow arched, his surprise flashing briefly before giving way to a more guarded expression. "Tannica?" he repeated, leaning back slightly in his chair. "What's she doing there?"

Estrith offered a faint smile, though uncertainty flickered in her eyes. "At first, I thought she had some hidden motive," she admitted, her voice low. "But... she's been good for Beowyn. And for me."

"For you?" Qereth's curiosity sharpened, his head tilting as his gaze locked on hers.

Estrith nodded again, her tone softening as she spoke. "She's kind. And steady. I didn't realize how much I needed someone like her until she was there."

Qereth leaned back further, his arms crossing as he weighed her words. The firelight played over his features, deepening the thoughtful crease in his brow. "Her father must have his reasons for sending her," he murmured, his voice carrying a note of unease. "I just hope, for Faermire's sake, that they're genuine."

Estrith didn't reply immediately. The tension between them thickened. She wanted to defend Tannica, to push back against Qereth's skepticism, but a part of her understood his caution. Trust, after all, was as fragile as it was precious.

The lines of tension in Qereth's shoulders gradually eased, his expression softening as he leaned forward. His gaze sought hers, unguarded now, the firelight lending a quiet intensity to his eyes. "Still," he said, his voice low and warm, carrying the weight of unspoken feelings, "I'm glad you're here with me now. Faermire can manage without us for a little while."

Estrith's lips curved into a genuine smile, the heaviness in her chest easing. His words, simple and sincere, chased away the storm of her thoughts. "You make it easier," she admitted, her voice barely above a whisper. "Everything feels... less overwhelming when you're here."

The fire's flickering glow seemed to draw them closer, narrowing the space between them. The warmth it radiated mirrored the quiet intimacy growing in the air, a connection undeniable. Qereth's gaze lingered on hers, the raw openness in his expression causing her breath to catch.

"Estrith," he murmured, his voice steady but laced with something unshakable, "I'd follow you anywhere. You know that, don't you?"

Her breath caught, his words sinking into her like a tether. Steadying, grounding—but overwhelming all the same. Instinctively, her fingers brushed his, a featherlight touch that sent a shiver racing through her. Her heart quickened, her voice trembling as she whispered, "It's a thought I hold onto more often than I care to admit."

The space between them dissolved as Estrith leaned forward, her chest tightening with anticipation as her gaze flickered to his lips before lifting to meet his eyes once more. A quiet pause lingered between them before their lips finally met. The kiss was soft, tentative, like the first notes of a song unsure of its melody. But as the moment stretched, it deepened, a surge of intensity sweeping through them like a wave crashing against the shore.

Qereth's hands found her waist, his touch firm yet steady, grounding her even as her heart raced. Her fingers curled into the fabric of his tunic, clutching him as if to anchor herself in the swirling tide of emotions. The warmth of his embrace melted away the weight she had carried for so long, leaving only the crackle of the hearth and the beating of her heart to fill the quiet chamber.

In his arms, the world outside ceased to exist. The distant protests, the strain of political games, the endless questions pulling her in different directions—all of it faded into irrelevance. Here, in the golden glow of firelight and the strength of Qereth's presence, Estrith found a fleeting sense of certainty.

But just as their emotions threatened to carry them further, the sound of small, shuffling footsteps broke through the quiet.

"Estrith?" Siged's soft, sleepy voice cut through the stillness.

Estrith and Qereth pulled apart abruptly, their breaths shallow and uneven as they turned toward the doorway. There, framed by the flickering firelight, stood Siged, his wide eyes blinking sleepily as he leaned against the doorframe.

Estrith recovered first, her pulse still racing as she rose to greet her brother. She softened her expression, brushing a hand gently through his disheveled hair. "Siged," she said, her voice warm and soothing. "You should be asleep."

He mumbled something unintelligible, his words slurred by exhaustion as he rubbed his eyes with his good hand. The sight of him—so small and vulnerable—stirred a deep ache in Estrith's chest. She placed a steadying hand on his shoulder, her fingers brushing the edge of his blanket as she guided him closer.

Behind her, Qereth stood awkwardly, smoothing his tunic as though the motion could erase the moment that had just unfolded. "I should leave you to tend to him," he said softly, his tone tinged with reluctance. He hesitated for a brief moment, his gaze lingering on Estrith before stepping closer.

His hand brushed lightly against her shoulder, a fleeting touch that sent a warm shiver down her spine. "Goodnight, my lady," he murmured, his voice low and sincere.

Then, taking her hand in his, Qereth bent to press a kiss to her knuckles. His lips lingered against her skin, a quiet gesture of affection that carried far more weight than words could. When he finally released her hand, his gaze held hers for a heartbeat longer before he turned and slipped from the room. His footsteps echoed faintly down the corridor, each one pulling him further away until the silence of the chamber reclaimed its hold.

Estrith let out a soft breath, kneeling before Siged and wrapping an arm around him. She guided him toward a chair by the hearth, smoothing the blanket around his shoulders as he blinked sleepily at the flickering flames. The fire's embers pulsed, warmth radiating as Estrith settled beside her brother. Yet, even as she focused on him, the memory of Qereth's touch lingered, a quiet warmth that refused to fade.

TEN

The cobbled streets of Elsterheim stretched before Tannica, winding through the city like a living maze of sound and color. The air was alive with the clamor of voices and the ceaseless rhythm of commerce. Stalls brimmed with brightly hued fabrics that rippled in the breeze, while carts overflowed with ripe fruit and fragrant spices, their aromas mingling with the tang of leather and iron. Somewhere, a blacksmith's hammer struck with steady precision, its metallic ring a distant but persistent backdrop.

Flanking her on either side, her personal guards moved with practiced vigilance, their imposing figures cutting through the crowd. The leather armor they wore bore the bold crest of Valenmur, its intricate design gleaming under the midday sun. Their presence was unmistakable, and as they wove through the narrow streets, heads turned and conversations faltered. The bold markings of a rival kingdom carried weight, stirring a blend of curiosity and unease that followed them like a shadow.

For a fleeting moment, Tannica allowed herself to be swept up in the market's chaos. It felt liberating to walk amidst the lively hum, to step outside the suffocating confines of courtly life. She lingered by a woodcarver's stall, her fingers brushing over the fine details of a figurine shaped like a soaring hawk. She traced the edges of bolts of fabric dyed in rich shades of blue, marveling at the way the colors mirrored the deep lakes that dotted Valenmur. Even the uneven stones beneath her boots felt grounding, a connection to something real and tangible.

Yet, the guards' silent watchfulness trailed her every step, their shadows long and heavy. Their vigilance, though intended to protect, only magnified the unease rippling through the crowd. Glances—fleeting and sharp—flickered like sparks of suspicion. At first, they were easy to ignore, mere flickers at the edges of her awareness. But as she moved deeper into the market, the whispers began, faint and insidious.

"Spy," someone murmured, the word barely audible over the market's din.

"Whore," came another, louder, slicing through the air with chilling clarity.

Tannica's spine straightened instinctively, her chin lifting as though she could will away the weight of their accusations. She forced her gaze ahead, refusing to meet the eyes of her detractors, but the words lingered, curling around her like smoke. They seeped into her composure, a slow and relentless erosion. Her guards, sensing the shift in the air, edged closer, each keeping a hand near the hilt of their sword. The tension between protection and threat coiled tighter with each step.

She stopped at a jeweler's stall, drawn more by a need to collect herself than genuine interest. The display was dazzling, sunlight catching on polished metals and gemstones that seemed to shimmer with their own light. Rings etched with intricate patterns rested beside delicate necklaces, their designs as bold as they were elegant. A silver cuff set with sapphire caught her eye, the deep blue stones reminiscent of the glacial waters that bordered her home-land—cold, untouchable, and impossibly beautiful.

"It's beautiful," she said softly, her voice tinged with a longing she hadn't intended to betray.

The vendor froze, his hands hovering over a necklace he had been adjusting. For a brief moment, his gaze met hers. In his eyes, she saw the clash of instinctive politeness and the oppressive weight of the crowd's silent judgment. His glance darted toward the nearby merchants, their expressions hard and unyielding, before he quickly looked away. With shaky hands, he resumed rearranging the jewelry, a nervous attempt to busy himself.

"Thank you, my lady," he murmured, his voice strained but polite. The words felt hollow, stripped of sincerity, and his trembling fingers betrayed the unease he could no longer hide.

The guards stepped closer, their imposing forms casting long shadows that stretched across the stall. The crowd had thickened at the market's edges, their stares sharp and unrelenting. Tannica could feel the weight of their hostility pressing down, a suffocating force that stole the air from her lungs. She lingered a moment longer, her fingers brushing the cool metal of the bracelet as though its beauty might anchor her. But the judgment in the air was too thick, the whispers too loud, and she knew she could not stay.

Straightening, she let her hands fall to her sides and turned away. The vibrant market, so alive moments before, now felt oppressive, its colors muted and its sounds tinged with malice. Her guards flanked her like silent sentinels, their imposing forms a protective wall against the sea of hostility. Their heavy footsteps echoed against the uneven cobblestones, a steady rhythm that contrasted sharply with the disjointed thoughts swirling in her mind. Yet even their presence failed to dispel the unease that trailed her, shadowing her every step. The marketplace, once a haven of life and energy, felt stifling now—a stage where she stood exposed, every gaze and murmur a harsh spotlight.

The venom of their accusations gnawed at her, replaying in her thoughts with relentless clarity. *Spy. Whore.* The words, sharp and cutting, stung despite their baselessness, their malice burrowing deep beneath her composed exterior. Her hands tightened into fists at her sides, nails pressing crescents into her palms. *What had she done, besides exist?* The questions churned, unbidden, feeding the fire of her frustration.

The narrow street leading to the palace stretched out, lined with aging stone buildings that leaned together like weary companions. Their cracked facades and sagging eaves seemed to bear the weight of time, much as she bore the weight of the crowd's judgment. The faint roar of laughter spilled from the open doors of a nearby tavern, mingling with the pungent tang of ale and the stale musk of unwashed bodies. The noise grated against her already frayed nerves, and for a fleeting moment, she considered taking a different route, avoiding the growing chaos altogether. But she dismissed the thought with a sharp shake of her head.

Her pace quickened, as if she could escape the tightening knot in her chest. The tension mounted with every step, her breaths shallow and uneven. She was almost past the tavern when the door burst open with a resounding creak.

A man stumbled into the street, his unsteady movements erratic, and the acrid stench of ale clung to him like a second skin. He staggered, colliding with a cart before stumbling backward. Tannica barely registered the shout from one of her guards before the drunkard barreled into her path. The impact jolted her, forcing her to catch herself as the world seemed to tilt for a breathless moment.

The chaos that followed came swiftly, like a wave crashing against the fragile calm she had tried to hold.

Her guards reacted before she could even gather her breath. One shoved the man with brutal precision, sending him sprawling into the mud with a heavy thud. The drunkard groaned, his hands clawing at the ground as he struggled to right himself. Another guard stepped forward, fist raised, his intent clear.

"That's enough!" Tannica's voice shattered the growing tension, sharp and commanding, carrying an authority that silenced the growing tension. Her hand shot out, catching the arm of the nearest guard before his blow could land.

The drunkard lay sprawled in the muck, moaning softly, his humiliation soaking into the earth beneath him. Around them, the murmurs of the crowd swelled into a crescendo, a tide of judgment and speculation. All eyes were on her now—piercing, scrutinizing, condemning.

Her cheeks burned under the weight of their collective gaze. The tension in the air was thick, oppressive, pressing down on her like a vice. "Let's go," she said tightly, her voice strained but steady. Without waiting for a response, she turned away, the guards hesitating only a moment before falling into step behind her.

The walk back toward the palace was heavy with unspoken tension. Her guards loomed closer than before, their leather armor creaking faintly with each step. Their faces were grim, their posture stiff with suppressed frustration. One muttered something under his breath, his voice low but unmistakable—a venomous sneer about Faermire, laced with disdain.

Tannica halted abruptly, her sharp gaze cutting to the offending soldier. Though she spoke no words, the weight of her glare said everything. His defiance melted under her unyielding stare, and he bowed his head in grudging acknowledgment, his lips pressed into a thin line. Without a word, she turned and continued forward, her steps deliberate, each one heavier than the last.

The remainder of the journey passed in tense silence. The city's noise faded behind them, replaced by the distant rustle of wind through the trees and the rhythmic clatter of boots on stone. The weight of the day pressed down on Tannica, a stone in her chest that seemed to grow heavier with every step.

When the palace gates came into view, her relief was fleeting. She dismissed the guards with a curt wave of her hand, their presence now more an irritation than a comfort. They hesitated for a moment before dispersing, their movements stiff with barely concealed frustration. Tannica climbed the winding stone stairs alone, her footsteps echoing in the stillness. The cool air of the palace interior offered little solace, and her thoughts churned with the events of the day, each moment replaying with a bitter edge.

As she turned a corner, lost in her thoughts, she nearly collided with someone. Her breath caught as she looked up to find Beowyn standing before her, his familiar figure an unwelcome reminder of her isolation. His expression was guarded, his presence both a comfort and a wound she wasn't ready to confront. She stepped back, straightening as she braced herself for whatever came next.

"Tannica," Beowyn said softly, his voice low but threaded with concern. His eyes darkened as they studied her, searching for answers in her guarded expression. Usually steady, his tone carried a rare uncertainty that made her pause. "Is something wrong?"

"It's nothing," she replied briskly, her words clipped as she tried to step around him. But Beowyn shifted, blocking her path. His broad frame was an unmoving barrier, his presence calm yet unyielding.

"Tannica, please." His voice softened further, a gentle plea that lingered in the quiet air between them. "What troubles you?"

She stopped abruptly, her posture rigid and her fists trembling at her sides. The storm that had churned within her all day surged closer to the surface, threatening to spill over. Her breath hitched as the silence between them stretched taut, electric with tension. For a moment, she couldn't speak, couldn't trust herself to shape the emotions clawing their way to her throat.

Finally, her voice broke the quiet, low and trembling with pain barely held in check. "Do you think I don't notice?" she asked, her words sharp and bitter, cutting through the fragile stillness. "The way they look at me. The things they whisper."

Beowyn frowned, his brows knitting tightly as he stepped closer, the movement hesitant yet instinctive. "Tannica—"

"I'm not blind, Beowyn. Nor am I deaf," she interrupted, her voice rising like the wind before a storm's breaking point. Her gaze burned as she met his eyes, no longer able to contain the tide of emotions welling inside her. "Your people hate me. They think I'm a spy, a harlot, someone who's unworthy to even stand within your gates."

He flinched, his expression tightening at her words, but his voice remained steady, even as he seemed to brace himself. "That's not true."

"Isn't it?" she snapped, her tone like a blade striking stone. She took a step closer, her movements deliberate, the space between them charged and suffocating. Her voice dropped to a trembling whisper, raw with vulnerability. "Even your court looks at me like I'm some kind of invader. And you—" Her voice caught, breaking under the weight of what she needed to say. "You hesitate. Every time you look at me, every time you speak, there's doubt. So, tell me, Beowyn—do you trust me?"

Beowyn opened his mouth as though to respond, but the silence that followed was heavier than words could ever be. His hesitation, fleeting yet undeniable, cut through her like a knife. She watched as his gaze faltered, dropping to the cold stone floor, his hand lifting slightly as if to reach for her. But it hung there, suspended in uncertainty, before falling back to his side.

That hesitation was enough.

Tannica's breath hitched, her composure fracturing as she took an unsteady step back. The air between them felt unbearable, too thick to breathe. Her lips parted, but the words that slipped out were broken, her voice raw with hurt.

"That's all I needed to know."

"Tannica, wait—" Beowyn's voice followed her, tinged with regret, but she turned sharply and fled before he could say anything more. Her footsteps echoed through the stone corridors, each one striking harder than the last. She didn't look back, couldn't look back. Tears blurred her vision, the walls around her seeming to close in as the weight of everything bore down on her.

When she reached her chambers, she slammed the heavy door shut behind her, the sound reverberating through the empty halls like the final toll of a bell.

Alone at last, the last of her strength crumbled. She sank onto the edge of her bed, her face falling into her hands.

The sobs came in waves—deep, unrelenting, and raw. They wracked her body as the isolation, the doubt, and the overwhelming pain consumed her, leaving no space for anything else.

Beowyn's thoughts lingered on Tannica long after their brief exchange earlier that morning. Her words had carried both gratitude and frustration, a subtle mix that hinted at her recognition of the precariousness of her presence in Elsterheim. Despite her strength, he could see the strain in her eyes—a reflection of the weight they both bore. The way she had held his gaze, unflinching and vulnerable, lingered with him now, even as the drone of the council surrounded him.

Seated at the head of the council chamber, his fingers drummed absently against the polished wood of the high-backed chair. The murmurs of his advisors and elders faded to a dull hum, their words slipping through the cracks of his focus as his mind replayed her parting glance. It was only when Haemund's sharp voice broke through the din, accompanied by the pointed mention of Lady Tannica's name, that Beowyn's wandering thoughts snapped back to the present.

"Your Grace, the people are growing restless. Rumors spread like wildfire—this court cannot ignore them." Haemund, his graying hair lending him a severity that matched his tone, leaned forward, his fingers drumming impatiently against the table. "It is said that Lady Tannica's continued presence here undermines not only our alliances but your authority. The longer she stays, the more they question your priorities."

Beowyn's jaw tightened, the words cutting deeper than he cared to admit. He swept his gaze over the room, taking in the councilors' expressions—some wary, others openly judgmental. The eldest among them exchanged subtle nods, their silence more damning than words. Banners of Faermire's crest hung limply, their once-proud sigils seeming to accuse him with their silent presence.

"Rumors," Beowyn said, his voice low, though a touch of irritation seeped through. "Rumors are nothing new in Faermire. What, exactly, do they whisper now?"

Haemund leaned forward, his graying hair catching the pale light filtering through the narrow windows. "They say your priorities have shifted," he said plainly, his gaze unyielding. "That Lady Tannica's continued presence in Elsterheim undermines not only our alliances but your authority. They question your focus, Your Grace."

A ripple of murmurs spread among the elders, each hushed exchange biting into the heavy air. Beowyn's jaw tightened, the accusation sinking deeper than he cared to admit. He straightened in his seat, his fingers curling around the armrest as his gaze swept over the councilors' faces. Wary expressions, veiled judgment, and the faintest traces of pity. It was always pity that stung the most.

"There is truth in what Haemund says," another advisor ventured, his voice calmer but no less insidious. "The longer Lady Tannica remains, the greater the tension with Valenmur. Her father will not sit idle forever. And the people... they fear you keep her here for your own pleasure rather than for the kingdom's good. If her father–"

The sharp crack of Beowyn's hand striking the table cut the man off mid-sentence. The sound echoed against the stone walls, silencing the murmurs and forcing all eyes on him. Slowly, Beowyn stood, his height casting a long shadow over the gathered council.

"Tannica is no prisoner," he said, his voice carrying a steely authority that dared them to challenge him. "She is our guest—my guest. Her presence here is no insult to Valenmur, but a testament to our efforts for peace."

Haemund's brows furrowed, his disbelief evident. "Peace? Is that what you call this? Valenmur will not see it that way, nor do the people of Faermire."

"Let them talk," Beowyn snapped, his patience worn thin. He stepped away from the table, his boots heavy against the cold stone floor. "Let them spread their rumors and whisper their lies. I will not send her away simply to appease cowardice."

"Cowardice?" Haemund retorted, rising to meet him. "This is not cowardice—it is strategy. If Valenmur perceives her presence as defiance—"

"They already do," Beowyn interrupted, his voice a cutting edge. He turned sharply to face the council, his gaze blazing. "Do you think Elwin hasn't already planned for this?"

A heavy silence fell over the room, the weight of his words settling into the cold stone. Beowyn's chest heaved, the frustration and isolation he carried boiling to the surface. He turned away from the council, his eyes fixed on the hearth at the far end of the chamber. The flames leaped and danced, their light flickering against the shadows, but they offered no warmth.

"Understand this," he said, his voice quieter but no less firm. "I will not be ruled by fear, nor will I abandon someone to placate the doubts of those who refuse to trust me."

The councilors shifted uneasily, exchanging glances that spoke of their uncertainty. Even Haemund hesitated, his usually sharp tongue subdued by the finality in Beowyn's tone.

At last, Haemund sighed, his shoulders sagging with reluctant acceptance. "Very well, Your Grace," he said, his voice tight. "The council is, as always, here to advise you. But I must caution you—patience, both ours and the people's, has its limits."

As the councilors filed out, their whispers faded into the silence, leaving only the crackle of the hearth. Beowyn remained still, his gaze fixed on the flames as they licked at the edges of shadow. The weight of their doubts pressed heavily against him, but his mind drifted—to Tannica. He exhaled sharply, drawing strength from the thought of her, even as the cost of his choice loomed.

For now, it would have to be.

The fire burned low in Beowyn's chambers, its embers casting shadows that flickered like ghosts on the walls. The warmth of the hearth barely reached him, its flickering light a poor companion to the chill that coiled deep in his chest. He sat slumped in his chair, one hand gripping the carved armrest while the other pressed against his forehead. His thoughts churned like a storm at sea, each crashing wave a reminder of the impossible choices he faced.

The council's voices still echoed in his mind, their words heavy with criticism and veiled accusation. And yet, amidst their rebukes, his own voice had risen, clear and unyielding, defending Tannica.

His defense had felt like the only truth he could cling to in a tide of doubt. But even now, he could see their disapproving glances, hear the murmur of dissent that had followed. The burden of their judgment weighed on him as he sat alone, his thoughts spiraling toward the edges of despair.

Beowyn exhaled sharply, the sound brittle in the quiet. He dragged his fingers through his hair, as though the action might unravel the tension knotting in his chest. But the stillness only deepened, pressing against him like an invisible force.

A soft knock broke through his thoughts, startling him. His gaze flicked to the door, his voice heavy with weariness. "Enter."

The door creaked open, and his breath caught at the sight of Tannica standing in the doorway. Her silhouette was framed by the faint light of the hallway, but it was the expression on her face—hesitant, searching—that sent a fresh wave of unease through him.

"Tannica," he said, her name weighted with surprise and concern. He rose from his chair, his movements slow, deliberate, as though trying to read the reason for her presence.

"I didn't mean to disturb you," she began, her voice low, carrying a tremor that betrayed the effort it took to speak. She stepped into the room and closed the door softly behind her. "But I needed to see you."

"You're never a disturbance," he replied, his voice softening. He gestured to the chair opposite his. "Please, sit."

She hesitated, her gaze searching his as though trying to find the truth hidden in his eyes. Instead of sitting, she took a tentative step closer, her hands clasped tightly in front of her. "I was ready to give up," she admitted, her words raw, trembling. "Ready to believe that nothing I did would change the course the fates had set for me. For us."

Beowyn's brow furrowed, a flicker of pain crossing his face. "Tannica—"

"No," she interrupted, shaking her head. "Let me finish." Her voice steadied, even as her hands tightened their clasp. "Then I overheard two of your servants speaking. They mentioned your council meeting. They spoke of what you said... about me."

Her words hung in the air, and Beowyn's chest tightened. He lowered himself back into his chair, unable to hold her gaze for a moment longer. "I couldn't let them blame you for what they fear," he said, his voice low but resolute. "I know what your father is doing. I know the position he's put me in. But none of this is your fault."

A breath escaped her, somewhere between relief and disbelief. Slowly, she moved to the chair opposite him, lowering herself into it with a grace that belied the storm behind her eyes. "You have no idea what that means to me," she murmured, her voice trembling with emotion. "To know you see it. To know you're willing to stand by me."

Beowyn leaned forward, resting his forearms on his knees. His voice softened, but the weight of his words remained. "Despite what they say, despite everything, it doesn't change how I feel for you."

Tannica's breath hitched, her hands unclasping as she leaned closer. "I'm scared, Beowyn," she admitted, her voice breaking just enough for him to hear the vulnerability beneath. "I don't know how far my father will go. If I return to Valenmur, I'll lose myself again. I become nothing more than a pawn in his endless game. He won't stop until he's taken everything—everything—from me. From us."

Reaching across the small space between them, Beowyn took her hand in his. His grip was firm but gentle, his thumb brushing over her knuckles in a gesture both steadying and intimate. "He won't take you from me," he said, his tone low and unshakable. "Not as long as I have the strength to fight."

The ember's glow pulsed faintly, casting fleeting shapes that moved like whispers across the walls, its warm glow flickering between them like a silent witness to the storm of emotions swirling in the quiet. Tannica's gaze lingered on Beowyn, and in that fragile moment, something within her seemed to break free. Rising from her chair, she closed the space between them with careful steps, her hands settling lightly on his shoulders. Her touch trembled, hesitant and laden with unspoken emotion.

Beowyn looked up, his eyes meeting hers, and the resolve in her expression deepened. "I love you, Beowyn," she whispered, her voice carrying the weight of a truth too long held back.

Slowly, he rose to his feet, his hands finding her waist with a reverence that steadied them both. "And I love you, Tannica," he replied, his voice quiet but unyielding, as though the words themselves could anchor them amidst the chaos of their world.

Her breath shuddered as her lips brushed his, soft at first but growing bolder as the barriers between them crumbled. The kiss deepened, their fears and uncertainties dissolving in the heat of the moment until only the raw, unguarded truth remained. His arms encircled her, pulling her closer as her hands gripped his tunic, anchoring herself to him with a fervor that spoke louder than words.

"Tannica," he murmured against her lips, his voice thick with emotion.

She silenced him with another kiss, her fingers tangling in his hair as if afraid to let him go. The walls he had so carefully built around himself shattered beneath her touch, leaving only the vulnerable man who had dared to love her despite everything.

Their movements toward the bed were instinctive, unspoken, their urgency tempered by a deep reverence for the moment they shared. Beowyn's hands instinctively traced the edges of her gown, peeling away the layers that had kept them apart. The firelight bathed her skin in a golden glow, rendering her almost otherworldly.

Tannica's touch mirrored his reverence, her fingers exploring the contours of his chest, the strength in his shoulders, as if to memorize every inch of him. When their eyes met, hers brimmed with an intensity that stole the breath from his lungs, an unspoken promise that transcended the chaos around them.

Words became unnecessary, their connection unfolding in the language of touch and whispered breaths. Beowyn's lips trailed along her skin, his kisses a silent vow to convey what he struggled to say. Together, they moved with a rhythm that felt timeless, a testament to the love they had carried for so long.

In her arms, Beowyn found a rare and fleeting peace, a reprieve from the weight of his doubts and the burdens of the crown. And though the world outside this chamber would demand more from them than either could bear, for this one night, they belonged wholly and only to each other.

ELEVEN

ELSTERHEIM, KINGDOM OF FAERMIRE

The days that followed unfolded in a fragile, gilded haze, each moment between Beowyn and Tannica slipping through the cracks of his burdens like stolen treasures. Their shared laughter began as whispers, hesitant and cautious, but soon grew unguarded, echoing softly in shadowed corners and secluded alcoves. Glances once fleeting now lingered like unspoken confessions, and every touch, however fleeting, carried the weight of something undeniable.

But in the halls of Elsterheim, the air grew heavy with scrutiny. Whispers slithered through the corridors like smoke, curling around pillars and seeping beneath closed doors. Accusations sharpened with each passing day, their venom leaving no corner untouched. The king, they murmured, was faltering—his heart tethered to Tannica rather than Faermire. Beowyn bore their judgment in silence, his posture unyielding even as their words festered. Yet, their discontent pressed harder with each step he took, a relentless reminder that kingship afforded no room for indulgence.

One brisk morning, frost clung to the grass like a silken veil, crackling softly beneath Beowyn's boots as he made his way through the palace gardens.

The cold air stung his cheeks, but his thoughts were fixed on the promise of a brief reprieve. Tannica had asked to meet him before the day's deliberations, and he welcomed the thought of her presence—a fleeting sanctuary from the demands threatening to consume him.

As he approached the carved stone bench where they often sat, his pace slowed, anticipation building. But just as he rounded the corner, a servant emerged from the path ahead, breathless and pale-faced, blocking his way.

"Your Grace," the young man stammered, bowing low, his voice trembling with urgency. "I bring urgent news."

Beowyn's brow furrowed, unease unfurling in his chest. "Speak," he commanded, his tone calm but edged with the tension now tightening his gut.

The servant straightened, fumbling with a rolled parchment clutched tightly in his hands. "King Elwin of Valenmur has been sighted, Your Grace. He crosses the border with a sizable entourage. Scouts anticipate his arrival at Elsterheim by tomorrow's end."

The words struck like a physical blow, stealing the breath from Beowyn's lungs. For a moment, the crisp morning air seemed colder, its bite sharper against his skin. His jaw clenched, and he forced himself to swallow the surge of emotions clawing at his composure.

"Gather the elders," Beowyn ordered, his voice steady but laced with a gravity that left no room for hesitation. The servant bowed swiftly, retreating down the frosted path as Beowyn stood motionless, his thoughts a storm of realization and dread.

The carved bench where Tannica waited now felt worlds away, a fleeting warmth he could no longer afford to seek. Beowyn turned sharply, his strides purposeful as he retraced his steps toward the council chambers. The sunlight that filtered through the garden seemed harsher now, its pale brilliance stripped of comfort, illuminating the stark reality of what awaited. Elwin's arrival loomed like a shadow over the horizon, and Beowyn felt the weight of his every choice pressing heavier on his shoulders.

The council chamber buzzed with tense voices by the time Beowyn entered. Advisors and nobles gathered in tight knots around the long oak table, their words a tangled storm of overlapping opinions. The scent of burning tallow from the sconces mixed with the cold bite of damp stone, amplifying the heavy atmosphere. At the sound of the door, their frantic deliberations stilled, every gaze snapping toward the young king.

Beowyn strode to the head of the table with measured steps, his expression carved from stone, though his clenched fists betrayed the storm within. He paused, letting the silence settle over the room like a shroud before speaking. "What has been decided?"

An advisor stepped forward, his face pale with unease. "Your Grace, the situation grows more dire by the hour. Elwin approaches with an armed retinue. This is no simple grievance—it reeks of provocation. If he intends to force our hand, we must tread carefully."

Low murmurs swept through the chamber, subdued but laden with agreement. Haemund, one of the elder councilors, leaned forward, the lines on his weathered face deepened by flickering torchlight. "This," he said gravely, his voice cutting through the murmurs, "is precisely the outcome we feared. If Elwin demands her return and we refuse, the consequences could be disastrous."

Beowyn's jaw tightened, the weight of the room pressing down on him. "And if we send her back?" he demanded, his tone sharp, yet unable to mask the raw edge beneath it.

Haemund hesitated, his gaze shifting uneasily. "It may placate Elwin for the moment," he admitted, his words deliberate, "but it will cast Faermire as a kingdom that bows to Valenmur's will. That would not go unnoticed, nor unpunished, by our enemies."

The tension thickened, heavy and suffocating. Beowyn swept his gaze across the chamber, meeting the apprehensive eyes of each council member. Their fear wasn't just for the kingdom—it was for his faltering rule. He could feel their doubts circling him like vultures.

"Strengthen the river defenses," he ordered abruptly, his voice commanding but clipped. "If Elwin seeks conflict, we will meet him prepared."

Haemund leaned forward, unrelenting. "And what of Tannica, Your Grace? The hour of decision is upon us."

"I need more time to consider," Beowyn snapped, though the admission stung. The weight of indecision coiled around him like a vice.

"But, Your Grace—" another advisor began, his voice high and taut with anxiety.

"Enough!" Beowyn's voice lashed through the chamber like a whip, silencing the room. He fixed his gaze on a random spot on the table, unwilling to meet their stares, which carried both expectation and judgment. "Leave me."

The council hesitated, glancing between one another before reluctantly filing out. The scrape of their boots against the floor faded, leaving Beowyn alone in the cavernous chamber. The sudden quiet was deafening.

He sank into his chair at the head of the table, his composure unraveling as his head bowed into his hands. The table, once a symbol of authority and counsel, now felt like an empty stage for his failure. Every decision seemed to lead to ruin—sending Tannica back would solidify his people's perception of his weakness, while keeping her risked the kingdom itself.

Beowyn closed his eyes, his chest tight as he wrestled with the impossible weight of his choice. The cold stone beneath his boots felt grounding, yet it offered no solace. How much more could he sacrifice for a crown that demanded everything and offered nothing in return?

Time seemed to dissolve, the minutes bleeding into hours as Beowyn navigated the halls, each step carving deeper into the storm of indecision swirling within him. The choice loomed before him, stark and unforgiving, demanding he sever the fragile tether that held him to her. The promise he had made echoed in his mind, a vow he now knew he could not keep. He had always known this moment might come, but he had clung to the illusion that it wouldn't. Now, the weight of his reluctance threatened to crush him, and he feared it had cost him everything.

The cold air of the courtyard wrapped around him like a vice as he strode briskly through its expanse, his gaze fixed forward, avoiding the curious or accusatory eyes that lingered on him. The whispers of passing courtiers seemed louder than the crunch of his boots on the cobblestones, each murmured word another stone in the growing pile of doubts pressing on his shoulders. He didn't pause until she appeared before him.

Tannica intercepted him with a quiet urgency, stepping into his path with a resolve that belied the tremor in her hands. Her pale face was set, her lips pressed tightly as if to steady the storm within her. Her fingers clasped before her, knuckles white with tension, but her voice, when it came, was steady.

"I know why he's here," she said, her words sharp and without preamble. "My father is here to manipulate you, Beowyn. He'll twist this into something that suits his ambitions. He always does."

Beowyn stopped short, his breath clouding in the crisp air. Her words struck with precision, cutting through the tumult in his mind. He met her gaze, the strain in his own composure impossible to mask. "I know," he admitted quietly, his voice a hollow echo of resignation. "But knowing doesn't make the choice any easier."

She stepped closer, her eyes searching his, their intensity unrelenting. "Don't let him win," she pleaded, her voice trembling, though her resolve did not falter. "You know the truth. You know his lies. Don't let him use this to destroy what we've built."

Her words hung in the air, charged and raw. Beowyn's throat tightened as he reached for her hand, his touch a careful balance of firmness and gentleness. "Tannica," he began, but his voice faltered, the weight of his own hesitation dragging the words down. "My people—"

Her fingers tightened around his, grounding him in the moment even as the stares of the passing courtiers bore into them like daggers. Her voice softened, but it carried a fierce urgency that refused to be ignored. "Please, Beowyn," she said, her plea cutting through the din of doubts in his mind. "Please don't send me back to him."

For a moment, silence stretched between them, heavy and suffocating. The world seemed to narrow, the distant hum of the castle fading into the background. Beowyn couldn't bring himself to meet her gaze again, afraid she would see the uncertainty festering within him. He let the silence linger, let it fill the space between them like a chasm neither could cross.

Finally, Tannica pulled her hand from his, the warmth of her touch replaced by a chill that sank deep into his chest. Her expression hardened, resolve replacing the vulnerability that had laced her words. "You've already made your choice," she said quietly, her voice carrying the weight of finality.

The truth settled over them, cold and unrelenting. No matter what he decided, Beowyn knew he had already lost. The battle was unwinnable, and the cost—her trust, her love—was a price he could scarcely bear.

Tannica turned from him without another word, her steps purposeful but laced with an unspoken pain that cut deeper than any blade. Beowyn watched her retreat, her final words lingering in the air like a shadow, heavy and unshakable. Alone once more, the young king stood in the courtyard, the weight of his crown pressing harder than ever.

The tension in Elsterheim was almost suffocating the following day as Elwin's entourage arrived, their approach a spectacle that drew every gaze. The black and orange banners of Valenmur rippled boldly in the biting winter wind, their sharp contrast a herald of looming conflict. From the walls, Beowyn could see them clearly—Elwin astride a formidable steed, his figure imposing and unmoving, flanked by his sons like living statues. Behind them stretched rows of soldiers, their armor reflecting the pale sun in dazzling flashes that seemed almost mocking. The rhythmic clang of hooves and the creak of leather saddles filled the crisp air, adding to the oppressive atmosphere.

A murmur spread through the assembled crowd below like a restless tide, their unease a living, breathing entity. Elwin's entourage halted a field's length from the gates, a deliberate and calculated show of force. The people of Elsterheim had gathered instinctively, drawn to the spectacle by both dread and curiosity. Even from this distance, Beowyn could feel the weight of their collective gaze boring into him, expectant and questioning.

His eyes lingered on Elwin, the man's features set in a mask of cordial civility that barely concealed the predatory gleam in his eyes. The sight struck a bitter chord within Beowyn, dragging him unwillingly into the shadows of his memories. He could almost feel the iron shackles against his wrists, as he was paraded before his father and all of Elsterheim as Elwin's hostage. Elwin's voice rang in his ears, the taunting barbs and accusations when Beowyn had been caught with Tannica the first time. The humiliation of his captivity, the shame of bringing his father to such a precarious position—it all came flooding back, as vivid and cutting as the day it happened.

And now, here he stood, facing the same man, the same banners, the same pointed accusations—but this time, the throne of Faermire rested on his shoulders.

Beowyn tightened his grip on the parapet, his knuckles blanching as his thoughts churned. The gathered nobles and courtiers clustered behind him on the wall, their hushed conversations a sharp contrast to the shouts of soldiers below preparing the gate. From the corner of his eye, he noticed an elderly councilor approach, his movements deliberate and steady against the chaos of the scene.

It was Lord Theric—one of the quieter voices in Beowyn's court. The old man rarely spoke in council meetings, his sharp but understated presence often mistaken for indifference. His hands, knotted with age, usually rested folded before him as he listened to the debates with an air of patience. But today, his expression carried something new: resolve.

Theric stepped to Beowyn's side, his gray eyes fixed on the spectacle beyond the gates. He said nothing at first, allowing the moment to settle between them. His gaze seemed to pierce through the tension, as though he were examining the very fabric of the choices that lay before Beowyn.

"You know what must be done," Theric said finally, his voice low but steady. There was no admonishment in his tone, only quiet understanding. "This is no longer a matter of who is right or wrong. It is simply the way things are now. What you decide next will shape far more than this moment."

Beowyn braced himself for the usual barrage of counsel urging him to send Tannica out, to choose peace for Faermire's sake. But Theric surprised him. He did not press for a specific course of action, only gestured faintly toward the gates as if to say the decision was already Beowyn's alone to bear.

"Logic, Your Grace," Theric continued after a pause, his eyes never leaving the banners of Valenmur. "It may feel cold, even heartless, but it has a way of enduring where emotions falter. You've already endured so much. Now is the time to decide what will endure beyond you."

The weight of the words pressed into Beowyn, but there was no rebuke in them—only a quiet gravity that felt strangely grounding. When Theric's hand came to rest on Beowyn's shoulder, its weathered touch brought an unexpected steadiness to his chaotic thoughts. The turmoil that had dogged Beowyn since Elwin's arrival ebbed slightly, replaced by a fleeting, fragile calm.

Theric offered a faint smile, his presence a balm against the unrelenting pressure of the moment. "You will do what must be done. And Faermire will endure because of it."

For a moment, Beowyn let himself breathe, drawing strength from the old man's quiet confidence. Below them, the crowd stirred, their tension palpable in the air. Beyond the gates, Elwin waited, his calculated patience as unnerving as the soldiers at his back. Beowyn's grip on the parapet loosened slightly, his gaze hardening as he allowed Theric's words to take root.

The riders emerged from the horizon, their approach deliberate and unrelenting, their horses' hooves drumming a rhythm that reverberated through the tense air. Dust billowed in muted plumes behind them, tracing their path like a warning as every eye on Elsterheim's walls turned to watch. Clad in the vibrant orange of Valenmur, the two messengers cut stark figures against the pale expanse of the open field, their presence a sharp intrusion into Faermire's territory.

From the gates of Elsterheim, two of Beowyn's riders rode out to meet them, their deep blue cloaks snapping in the brisk wind like banners of defiance. The colors of the two kingdoms collided in the middle of the plain, where words began to flow—low and clipped, carried off by the breeze before they could reach the gathered onlookers. Still, the exchange spoke volumes. The Valenmurians gestured with barely restrained force, their urgency palpable even from a distance. Beowyn's men remained stiff-backed and deliberate, their composure like a wall against the emissaries' fervor.

On the battlements above, Beowyn stood motionless, his silhouette sharp against the pale sky, his gaze fixed on the distant figures. Though the details were impossible to discern, the tension in their movements told him everything. His stomach churned with a familiar unease, that nagging sense of inevitability tightening around him. The distant negotiations dragged on, stretching time until it felt unbearable. Finally, the two parties broke apart, each retreating toward their respective camps, their messages carried like invisible burdens.

Beowyn's eyes followed his own riders as they galloped back toward the gates, the wind catching their cloaks and tossing them like storm-tossed waves. The moment they reached the courtyard below, one of the messengers dismounted with urgency, his movements stiff with unease. He crossed the stone yard at a brisk pace, his helm gleaming in the midday sun, but his face beneath was pale and strained.

"Your Grace," the messenger said, bowing quickly before meeting Beowyn's gaze. His voice, though steady, held a tautness that betrayed the weight of his words. "King Elwin demands the immediate return of his daughter. And he insists upon an audience with you and the elders of Faermire."

The words struck like a hammer's blow, even though Beowyn had braced himself for them. His chest tightened as a wave of cold unease washed over him. On his right, Haemund's sharp gaze cut into him like a blade, the elder's unspoken *I told you so* evident in the grim downturn of his mouth. The same quiet reproach simmered in the faces of the other advisors, their expressions heavy with vindication.

Beowyn's jaw clenched as he nodded sharply, refusing to let their doubt unnerve him. "Prepare the field," he ordered, his tone clipped and resolute. His words carried across the battlements, dismissing the messenger with a wave of his hand. "We will hear him."

As the messenger turned and hastened away, Beowyn's gaze returned to the horizon. The plain seemed to stretch endlessly, the dust of the riders still faintly lingering in the distance. He drew a slow breath, steadying himself against the storm that had long been gathering, its clouds now heavy and imminent. The pit in his stomach remained, but he stood unmoving, the weight of the moment settling heavily on his shoulders.

The meeting took place in the open plain between the two armies, a neutral ground steeped in tension. On one side sat King Elwin, flanked by his two sons and a retinue of advisors. His imposing frame loomed large over his gilded saddle, his braided red hair and beard streaked with white, adorned with golden clasps and leather wraps. The ornate markings of Valenmur's kingship gleamed over his chest, etched into his worn but meticulously maintained leather armor. His crown—a heavy, simple band engraved with intricate designs—rested with unmistakable authority on his brow.

To his right was Alfric, his eldest son. A brute of a man, Alfric's broad shoulders and perpetually scowling face radiated disdain. His red hair fell in thick braids over his armored chest, and his every movement seemed to seethe with restrained aggression. His glare never left Beowyn, a silent declaration of his desire to kill the young king.

Beside him sat Ealric, leaner but no less intimidating. His blond hair was partially shaved, revealing intricate tattoos carved along the sides of his scalp. His sharp beard framed a face marked by intelligence and cold calculation. Though his expression lacked Alfric's open hatred, the way his eyes swept over Beowyn betrayed a similar disdain.

Opposite them, Beowyn sat astride his own mount, his advisors arrayed behind him. The elders of Faermire whispered among themselves, their glances heavy with judgment. Beowyn kept his gaze fixed on Elwin, his back straight, though the weight of their stares pressed heavily on him.

Elwin let the silence stretch, his smirk cutting deeper into the moment with every passing second. At last, he spoke, his voice rich with condescension.

"The boy king," he said, his grin widening.

Beowyn met his gaze without flinching, his voice steady. "Elwin"

Elwin's smirk faded, replaced by a cold, assessing expression. "Where is my daughter?"

"She is safe," Beowyn replied evenly.

"In your bed, no doubt," Elwin snapped, his lips pressing into a hard line. "She was sent to you as a gesture of peace, and yet I receive no word of her welfare. Am I to believe you've kept her here to suit your own whims?"

Beowyn stiffened, but before he could respond, Elwin pressed on, his voice rising to carry across the field.

"You claim to honor peace, yet you dishonor Valenmur by keeping Tannica in Elsterheim after breaking your engagement. You shame her and my kingdom with your actions, and you dare to hold her against my will?"

Murmurs rippled through the gathered advisors. Elwin's tone shifted, sharp and cutting. "You took advantage of my good will, boy, and now you defile my daughter and all of Valenmur."

Beowyn's jaw clenched, and he raised his voice to counter. "Tannica came to Elsterheim of her own accord. I have treated her with the utmost respect."

Elwin sneered, his expression hardening. "Do not take me for a fool. You broke the treaty I brokered with Ludica, and you spit on Valenmur's good graces. And now, you shame me before my sons."

He gestured broadly to Alfric and Ealric, who glowered at Beowyn. "By all rights, I should kill you where you sit. But instead, I offer you a chance to salvage what little honor you have left. I owe that much to your late father."

Elwin leaned forward, his eyes blazing with triumph. "Bring me my daughter, and we will speak no further of this… indignity."

One of Faermire's elders stepped forward, his voice calm but strained, as though every word bore the weight of the kingdom's unease. "King Elwin, surely there is a path to peace here."

Elwin's gaze snapped to the elder, sharp and unyielding, like a blade drawn from its scabbard. His lips curved into something resembling a smile, though it carried no warmth. "Peace?" he repeated, his tone dripping with scorn. "There is only one path to peace—my daughter's return. Anything less would be war."

The murmurs among Beowyn's advisors swelled, rippling like a tide of unease through the gathered court. Their whispers, urgent and biting, carried questions they dared not speak aloud: Could Beowyn lead them through this? Would his choice bring ruin to Faermire? Beowyn felt their stares boring into him, each glance like a stone added to the growing burden on his shoulders.

Before he could muster a response, Elwin seized the moment, his voice cutting through the noise with chilling clarity. "But perhaps," he said, his tone suddenly smooth, almost conversational, "we settle this matter like men. A duel, boy king. You and me. Let us resolve this personally, without the bloodshed of our armies."

The air grew thick, the weight of the challenge suffocating. A stunned silence fell over the assembly as Elwin's words hung in the air like a noose waiting to tighten. The faintest smirk tugged at his lips, mocking and deliberate, as he added, "Unless, of course, you lack the spine for it."

The elder flinched, his conciliatory demeanor faltering as Elwin's eldest son shot a startled glance toward his father, clearly blindsided by the sudden proposal. The air crackled with tension, and Beowyn's stomach twisted into knots. He gripped the reins tightly, the leather creaking under his fingers. The idea of facing Elwin—a seasoned warrior with decades of experience—was a daunting prospect. Yet to refuse would confirm every doubt his advisors, his people, and even he himself harbored about his ability to lead.

Slowly, Beowyn squared his shoulders, drawing himself up with a steadiness he didn't feel. There was no escaping this moment. The eyes of Faermire rested on him, their hopes and fears intertwining in the silent pressure of expectation.

"I accept," Beowyn said, his voice firm despite the chaos roiling within. The words felt heavier than any weapon, their finality sealing his fate. "Name your terms."

Elwin's grin widened, his triumph barely concealed. "We'll settle this at the border, by the next full moon. That should give you ample time to prepare yourself... and to settle your affairs."

The insult was deliberate, meant to unnerve him. Beowyn met Elwin's gaze, his own steady and unflinching. "Then I will require a witness from each court to oversee the terms," he added, his tone calm but edged with resolve. "To ensure this duel ends as agreed."

For the briefest moment, Elwin's eyes narrowed, but he inclined his head, the flicker of surprise quickly masked. "Agreed," he said smoothly. "I'm sure we'll both find suitable witnesses."

Elwin waved his hand with a flourish, signaling for his horse. As the steed was led forward, the king mounted with a practiced ease that exuded both victory and disdain. The tense silence was broken by the sharp rhythm of the horse's stamping hooves, each impact echoing in the still air like a challenge. His sons and advisors followed, their gleaming armor catching the fading light, a cold procession of power and authority as they rode away with deliberate purpose. The retreating figures moved with the precision of a blade, leaving an air of finality in their wake.

Beowyn remained motionless in his seat, his fingers gripping the armrests of his chair so tightly that his knuckles blanched. The ache in his hands barely registered, a muted sensation beneath the roiling tempest within him. The storm in his chest was relentless, swirling with anger, doubt, and the crushing weight of decisions yet to be made. He could feel the eyes of his advisors flickering toward him, their whispered conversations punctuating the heavy silence that had descended over the room.

The distant sound of Elwin's retinue faded into nothingness, swallowed by the wind and the stretch of land beyond the gates. The quiet that followed was oppressive, pressing down on Beowyn like a physical weight. He exhaled, slow and measured, as if to keep the turmoil within from spilling out.

The border. The full moon. The clash that would determine honor, peace, and perhaps more than he dared to contemplate. The words Elwin had left behind reverberated in his mind, each syllable striking like a hammer. The challenge wasn't just a duel—it was a statement, a test, a line drawn in blood and pride. Beowyn's gaze remained fixed on the path Elwin had taken, his jaw tightening as the weight of expectation settled squarely on his shoulders.

For now, he sat in the suffocating stillness, his thoughts racing ahead to the battlefield that loomed on the horizon. The storm gathered strength within him, a prelude to the trials that would soon come crashing down. Yet despite the tempest, Beowyn stayed rooted, his breath steadying as he braced himself for the coming weeks.

The ride back to Elsterheim was a haze of cold winds and heavy silence, the wintry landscape blurring into a smudged canvas of white and gray. Each hoofbeat felt like a drumbeat against Beowyn's chest, echoing the sick churn of his stomach. The weight of his decision, inevitable as it had seemed, pressed down on him, suffocating. Everything he feared—everything he had tried to hold together—had unraveled in the span of a single meeting. The world around him felt distant, muted, as if he were already witnessing his failure from afar.

As they passed through the gates, a subtle shift rippled through the air. The tension on the faces of the guards and townsfolk softened, their collective relief at news of a resolution evident. But to Beowyn, it felt hollow. The words "resolution" and "peace" rang bitter in his mind. A nearby steward's voice cut through the stillness, calling for preparations to escort the Lady of Valenmur back to her father's camp.

The words struck him like a blade. His gaze shifted to Tannica, her form stiff and unyielding as servants surrounded her, making ready for her departure. Her face was a mask, cold and unreadable, but it was her refusal to meet his eyes that stung the most.

Desperation flared in his chest. "Wait," he commanded, his voice sharp with urgency. The servants paused, startled by his tone. "I need a moment."

The nearby guards exchanged glances, hesitant, but eventually stepped aside. Tannica followed without protest, though her movements were deliberate, her silence heavy with unspoken judgment. Once inside a private chamber, she remained standing, arms crossed tightly, her eyes fixed on a distant point over his shoulder.

"Tannica..." Beowyn began, his voice cracking under the strain. He stepped closer, but she didn't flinch or turn to him. "I met with your father. He—" His breath caught, the words feeling like splinters in his throat. "He threatened war. If I didn't—if I didn't send you back..."

Her gaze finally met his, sharp and unrelenting, her eyes glinting like ice under firelight. "And so, you don't hesitate," she said softly, her tone devoid of warmth. "You've given me back to him."

"It's not what I wanted!" he protested, his hands clenched into fists at his sides. "You have to understand—I had no choice! The kingdom—"

"The kingdom," she interrupted, her voice rising, though it remained eerily calm. "Always... the kingdom. Your people. Your throne. And yet, where does that leave me, Beowyn?" Her words cut through him like a whip, the edges raw and unforgiving. "You promised me freedom from him. Safety. But when it mattered most, you proved no different. You bowed, just like everyone else."

"Tannica," he pleaded, stepping closer, his hand outstretched, "I am not your enemy. I've fought for you—"

She let out a soft, bitter laugh, shaking her head as she stepped back, evading his touch. "What's done is done," she said, her voice trembling but resolute. "I've never escaped my father's control. Not truly. And now, not even you—" She faltered for a moment, her breath catching. Then she straightened, her expression hardening. "Not even you could protect me."

He opened his mouth to respond, to offer some defense, some assurance that she wasn't entirely right—but the words died in his throat. She turned to the door, her movements deliberate and regal, as if she were determined to mask her heartbreak with formality. She paused only briefly, her hand resting on the doorframe.

"I didn't lose you today, Beowyn. I lost the man I believed you were." With a faint tilt of her head, she added, "Your Grace," she said, her tone cutting with finality before she left the room.

Beowyn stood frozen, her absence like a physical blow. Her words lingered in the air, sharper than any blade. After a long moment, he forced himself to move, trailing her outside. His boots echoed faintly against the stone as he reached the courtyard.

The air was heavy with the muted hum of the gathered crowd, their voices hushed but charged with unspoken judgment. Beowyn stood at the gates of Elsterheim, his fingers curling into fists at his sides as he watched Tannica mount the dapple-gray horse that Elwin's entourage had brought for her. The reins slipped through her hands as though she, too, was reluctant to hold them, her gaze lingering on him one final time. Her personal guard surrounded her, their armor glinting as they prepared to escort her to her father's camp.

His throat closed around the words that would never come, leaving only silence between them. Around him, the air was crisp and bitter, the chill biting through the warmth of his cloak. The banners overhead snapped against the gray sky, their blue and gold crests a stark reminder of the kingdom he had chosen over her.

As Tannica turned her horse, her movements sharp and deliberate, the world seemed to narrow. The steady rhythm of the horse's hooves echoed hollowly against the cobblestones, each strike hammering the weight of his decision deeper into his chest. The sound grew fainter with every step, until it blended with the distant murmur of the crowd, leaving only the cold, hollow ache of her absence.

Beowyn's eyes remained fixed on her retreating figure, her golden hair over the fur-lined cloak she wore. The gates swung shut behind her with a groan of iron, the sound reverberating through the stillness like a sentence passed. The murmurs of the onlookers swelled in his ears—low, discontented, but far away, as though they belonged to another world.

He stayed rooted where he stood, his breath misting in the cold air, until the last echo of her departure faded into silence. Only then did he realize the unbearable emptiness that had settled over him.

The crowd began to disperse, their whispers trailing off into the streets, but Beowyn remained motionless, his gaze locked on the closed gates. The stillness around him was deafening, broken only by the faint rustle of the wind against the walls. He had done what was necessary—what was expected of him. But as he turned and walked back toward the castle, his steps heavy and slow, the hollow ache in his chest spread, heavier than the wintry sky that loomed overhead. This time, he knew, the loss was final. And it was entirely his own.

TWELVE

HELMFIRTH, KINGDOM OF MISTELFELD

The quiet hum of activity outside her chamber filtered through the heavy wooden door, muffled yet unrelenting. Estrith sat by the wide windowsill, Beowyn's letter cradled in her hands, the paper soft and worn from where her fingers had smoothed it countless times. She had read it the day before, devouring its words in haste, but now, with the preparation for departure unfolding beyond her door, she found herself reading it again, more slowly this time, savoring and dissecting every line.

The tone of the letter was measured, even diplomatic, but Estrith could see through its careful construction. Beowyn's words spoke of duty and the weight of decisions made for the good of Faermire, but Estrith could feel the turmoil that lurked beneath the surface. He hadn't written of Tannica explicitly, yet the traces of her presence were everywhere in the lines. There was guilt there—unspoken, buried deep—and something else that tugged at Estrith's heart. Regret, perhaps, or the loneliness of a man who was beginning to understand the isolation that came with power.

She exhaled, her breath clouding faintly against the cool glass of the window. The implications of his words lingered in her mind. Beowyn was navigating a treacherous sea, balancing the trust of his people with his own personal desires, and the toll was evident. He had made choices he could not undo, and she could only guess at the full weight of them. As much as he tried to shield her from his burdens, she knew the cost he had paid. She folded the letter carefully and set it on the windowsill, her fingers lingering on the parchment as though touching it might bridge the growing chasm between them.

The soft creak of the door drew her attention. Sgell entered with his usual composed air, his dark robes whispering faintly as he moved. His keen eyes flicked to the letter before settling on her, a faint shadow of understanding crossing his features.

"You've read it again," he observed, his tone even.

Estrith nodded, her gaze returning to the window. "I can't help but feel there's more he's not saying."

Sgell tilted his head slightly, considering her words. "That's the nature of Beowyn. He has always been careful with his emotions, even as a boy. He bears the weight of his choices alone, or so he believes."

Estrith glanced at him, searching his face. "And what do you make of it? Of what's happened in Elsterheim while we've been away?"

Sgell's expression darkened faintly, his voice dipping into a thoughtful cadence. "Elwin's arrival was calculated, as all his actions are. And the king was forced to make a choice that would be perceived as weakness regardless of intent."

Estrith sighed, the weight of Sgell's words sinking into her. "And now, we return to Faermire, leaving this behind. But I can't help but feel that Mistelfeld—my grandmother—needs me still.

As if summoned by her words, a knock sounded at the door, and Gwenora entered. She swept into the room with her usual commanding presence, the rich emerald of her gown catching the light as she approached. Her sharp eyes scanned the chamber before settling on Estrith, softening slightly.

"I've come to see you off," Gwenora said, her tone firm but laced with something warmer. She stepped closer, her hands brushing a stray lock of hair from Estrith's face. "I would have you know, granddaughter, that Mistelfeld is not merely a passing duty for you. It is part of who you are."

Estrith looked up at her, uncertain. "You mean for me to take a more active role."

Gwenora inclined her head, her gaze steady. "Mistelfeld needs strength, Estrith, and a vision for the future. You have both, even if you doubt it now. When the time comes, remember what you've seen here—what you've learned. This is your heritage, and your voice carries weight, more than you realize."

Estrith swallowed hard, feeling the gravity of Gwenora's words. "I understand," she said softly, though the quiver in her voice betrayed the depth of her emotions.

Gwenora's lips curved into a faint smile. "Good." She replied.

Her gaze lingered on her grandmother, studying the sharp lines of her face, the glimmer of resolve in her eyes that spoke of battles fought long before Estrith's time.

They remained in the chamber for a moment longer, silence filling the space like the lingering warmth of the hearth. Estrith hesitated, unwilling to break the fragile connection that had formed between them during their exchange. Gwenora's gaze softened, her features easing as if she, too, felt the strain of unspoken goodbyes.

Finally, the Queen relented, "Now go, before I change my mind and keep you here."

Estrith's chest tightened, torn between duty and the rare vulnerability she had glimpsed in her grandmother. She dipped her head in a gesture of respect, forcing herself to move despite the pull to linger. Each step toward the door felt heavier than the last, as if the shadows of Gwenora's words clung to her like a second skin.

As she reached the threshold, Estrith glanced back, her fingers brushing the carved frame of the door. Gwenora was already turning toward the hearth, her profile illuminated by the hearth's steady glow. The image etched itself into Estrith's mind. She swallowed the lump in her throat and stepped into the corridor, the door clicking shut behind her like a final note in an unfinished melody.

The queen's parting words clung to Estrith like a veil as she made her way to the docks. The crisp sea air kissed her cheeks, carrying the tang of salt and the faint musk of damp wood. Around her, the harbor buzzed with life—sailors barked commands, merchants haggled over wares, and the rhythmic creak of ropes and masts wove a chaotic symphony. Yet Estrith felt apart from it all, her focus narrowing to the fragile figure of Siged as he leaned heavily on Sgell's arm. The boy's cloak billowed slightly in the breeze, masking his frailty but not the quiet determination as he boarded the waiting ship.

Estrith lingered at the gangplank, her fingers brushing the edge of the railing. Her gaze swept over the busy docks, the faces of strangers passing like blurs—until it rested on Qereth.

He stood slightly apart, his tall frame a still point amid the frenetic motion. The light caught his golden hair, and for a moment, he seemed a part of the sun-drenched harbor itself, something timeless and steady. When their eyes met, he moved toward her, the crowd parting as if recognizing his quiet authority. His expression was warm but shadowed with regret.

"Estrith," he said softly, inclining his head. His voice, low and familiar, carried easily over the noise, wrapping around her like a thread of solace. "It seems our time together is always too short."

She mustered a faint smile, "It always is," she replied, her voice barely above a whisper.

Qereth hesitated, his hand brushing against the hilt of his sword as if grounding himself. "I wish I could go with you," he said at last, his tone quieter, almost vulnerable. "Especially now, after everything. But Mistelfeld—"

"Needs you," Estrith finished for him, her heart sinking even as she spoke the truth. "And Faermire needs me."

Qereth stepped closer, the space shrinking until she could see the faint lines of worry etched at the corners of his eyes.

"We always seem to be caught between desire and obligation," he murmured, his gaze steady, searching hers for an answer neither of them could give.

Estrith nodded, her throat tightening. "But we'll see each other again. Soon."

A faint smile ghosted across his lips, tempered with a sadness that mirrored her own. "I'll hold you to that."

His hand found hers, rough and warm, and she held onto the moment as tightly as she dared. He bent over her fingers, his lips brushing her knuckles in a gesture both tender and restrained. The kiss lingered just long enough to send a shiver through her, filling the space between them with an aching intimacy. When he straightened and released her, the absence of his touch left her cold, but she forced herself to take a step back.

The ship's sails snapped sharply overhead, the wind filling them with restless purpose. As Estrith moved to board, she cast one last look over her shoulder. Qereth remained where she had left him, a solitary figure framed by the bustling harbor. His gaze held hers, unwavering, as though trying to bridge the distance already stretching between them.

Estrith raised a hand in farewell, her fingers trembling as she fought to maintain her composure. The ship groaned and lurched as it pulled away from the dock, each wave carrying her farther into the endless horizon. The sun glinted off the water, dazzling and cold, but her thoughts remained anchored to the shore.

Qereth stood motionless, his figure shrinking with the growing distance, but his presence burned vividly in her mind. As the wind carried the briny scent of the sea and the promise of the unknown ahead, Estrith closed her eyes, clinging to the memory of what she was leaving behind.

Their arrival in Elsterheim was a bitter distortion of the homecoming she had once envisioned. The city that had always pulsed with life now languished in an oppressive stillness, as though its very soul had been siphoned away. The streets, usually teeming with merchants peddling their wares and townsfolk exchanging lively chatter, were subdued, heavy with unspoken tension. Conversations died into whispers as she passed, wary glances darting toward her like shadows. The banners of Faermire, once proud emblems of its strength, hung limp against a sky the color of tarnished steel, their faded colors muted as though mourning the vibrancy they once held. Even the air felt wrong—thick and stagnant, charged with a quiet dread that hinted at an unseen storm gathering on the horizon.

As the gates creaked open to admit them, Estrith felt a shiver crawl along her spine. The city felt watchful, alive in its silence. Eyes, both hidden and overt, seemed to track her every movement. Even the guards stationed at the entrance seemed unnerved; their rigid postures and tightened grips on their spears betrayed an anxiety that no amount of discipline could mask. They wore Faermire's livery, but there was no pride in the way they held themselves—only a guarded apprehension, as though the very walls they defended had turned against them.

The castle loomed ahead, its stone façade stark and unyielding, a grim monument to duty and endurance. The familiar structure, once a place of fleeting warmth amid Faermire's harsh winters, now bore a foreboding presence. Shadows gathered beneath its towering battlements, stretching long and thin as the overcast sky dimmed the daylight further. Estrith's heart sank as they entered, the once-inviting corridors now dim and hollow. The air inside was colder than she remembered, and the faint echoes of their footsteps were devoured by the heavy silence, leaving an almost suffocating emptiness in their wake.

Servants greeted them with measured haste, their heads bowed as they approached. They moved quickly to tend to Siged, their hands deft but their gazes avoiding hers. Estrith lingered as they fussed over her brother, tucking his blanket tighter around him and murmuring soft reassurances. Her gaze followed them as they led Siged away toward his chambers, the thought of his fragile form hidden behind closed doors stirring an ache in her chest.

Another servant appeared, his demeanor brisk but not unkind as he gestured for Estrith and Sgell to follow. She exchanged a glance with the older man, his expression unreadable yet steady, before turning to trail after the servant. The deeper they ventured into the castle, the more the atmosphere seemed to constrict around her, its once-familiar halls now foreign and steeped in unease. The flicker of torches cast fleeting shadows against the stone walls, their faint light doing little to chase away the pervasive gloom.

Estrith's steps faltered briefly as they reached the threshold of a chamber. Beyond it lay one of Beowyn's advisors, waiting with what she could only assume would be news or demands. A faint echo of her father's voice stirred in her mind—a memory of his expectations, his unrelenting weight of duty. Steeling herself, she straightened her shoulders and stepped inside, her breath shallow as the reality of Elsterheim's transformation sank deeper into her bones.

The man Estrith was brought to—a lean, hawk-eyed figure with an air of perpetual vigilance—looked like a specter of sleepless nights. His sharp features were carved with fatigue, his hollowed eyes shadowed by deep circles that spoke of relentless toil. Before him, a weathered table groaned under the weight of scattered parchments and maps, their surfaces covered in frantic scrawls and hastily drawn notations, a chaotic testament to a mind consumed by crisis.

At her arrival, he straightened abruptly, his bony hands gripping the table's edge as though it were the only thing anchoring him. Relief flickered briefly in his gaze, only to be overshadowed by resignation.

"Lady Estrith," he said, his voice clipped but heavy with weariness. "Your return is timely. The situation here has become... delicate."

He wasted no breath on pleasantries, launching immediately into an unrelenting torrent of grim revelations. His words hit like hammer blows: Elwin's schemes, the duel that had unsettled the court, and the tenuous grip Beowyn now held on his kingdom. Each detail unfolded with increasing urgency, the air in the chamber thickening as the gravity of the situation settled around Estrith. Her composure faltered, her breath catching as the enormity of it all sank in. Beowyn's struggle, no longer a distant burden, became a crushing reality bearing down on her.

When the advisor finally fell silent, Estrith turned to Sgell, her mind a whirlwind of anger, dread, and fear.

"The king will need you," Sgell said gently, his steady voice a rare island of calm in the storm. His words held no judgment, only an understanding of the responsibility she now carried.

Estrith nodded, though her heart felt heavy with doubt. Without another word, they began their journey through the labyrinthine corridors of the castle. The walls seemed to close in around her as her thoughts churned. The flicker of torchlight illuminated somber tapestries that had once spoken of glory but now felt like hollow echoes of better days. Servants bowed as she passed, their gestures subdued, as if the air itself demanded silence.

As they reached the heavy oak door of Beowyn's chambers, Sgell paused, placing a firm yet reassuring hand on her shoulder. His expression, though impassive, carried a quiet confidence.

"He'll draw strength from you," he said quietly, his tone weighted with conviction. With that, he excused himself, his measured footsteps fading into the distant murmur of the castle.

Estrith stood alone before the door, the stillness amplifying the storm within her. She closed her eyes, inhaling deeply as she steadied herself. The cool metal of the handle felt grounding beneath her fingers as she pushed it open, the hinges groaning softly in protest.

Inside, a dim, pale light filtered through the narrow windows, casting the room in muted tones of gray and silver. The air was thick, almost tangible, pressing against her as her gaze fell on her brother. Beowyn stood near the far wall, his back to her, his broad shoulders silhouetted against the overcast sky beyond the glass. The faint light caught the edges of his form, highlighting the tension etched into every line of his posture. His hands, clasped behind him, betrayed a tremor of unease.

The silence between them was heavy, but Estrith could sense the turmoil radiating from him. He didn't turn at her entrance, his focus seemingly locked on the stormy horizon, as if seeking answers from the bleak expanse of the sky. For a moment, she lingered in the doorway, her heart aching at the sight of him. Then, quietly, she stepped inside, the door clicking shut behind her like the closing of a sanctuary.

"Beowyn," Estrith said softly, her voice a fragile thread of sound that barely carried across the chamber.

He turned slowly, his face etched with exhaustion. For a fleeting moment, his expression softened when his eyes met hers, but the weariness returned almost immediately, carving deep lines of pain and doubt into his features.

"I wondered when you'd come," he said, his voice low and rough, the words laden with sleepless nights.

Estrith stepped closer, her heart clenching at the sight of him. The proud, unyielding brother she had known seemed hollow now, his strength sapped by a storm of guilt and uncertainty. She reached for words, any words, but found nothing. "We came as soon as we could," she managed. "Beowyn... I'm so sorry."

He exhaled sharply, a sound filled with bitterness and resignation, and turned back toward the window. The pale light filtering through cast his silhouette in sharp relief, emphasizing the tension in his shoulders as he stared out over the expanse of Elsterheim. "They see me as weak," he muttered, the words heavy with frustration and self-loathing. "Elwin played his hand perfectly. I sent Tannica back to protect Faermire, and yet it feels as if I've only brought us closer to ruin."

Estrith stepped nearer, the distance between them a yawning chasm she longed to close. "You were trying to do the right thing," she said, her voice quiet but insistent. "You acted for the good of the kingdom, for all of us."

Beowyn let out a mirthless laugh, sharp and cutting. "The right thing?" he echoed bitterly, his tone laced with scorn—though it was unclear whether it was directed at her or himself. "Elwin's demand wasn't just about Tannica. It was a trap, Estrith—and I walked into it as if blindfolded. Sending her back has only made things worse. Now, the duel will decide more than just my honor. It will decide whether I live long enough to see this kingdom fall."

Estrith flinched at the raw pain in his voice but refused to look away. Taking another step, she placed a hand gently on his arm. The tension beneath her touch was rigid, unyielding, but she held on. "You mustn't speak like that," she said firmly, though her voice softened with the emotion threatening to break through. "If you fight, Beowyn, fight for more than duty. Fight for the people who need you. Fight for Faermire. Fight for the brother I refuse to lose."

He turned then, and for the first time, a flicker of vulnerability broke through his hardened exterior. "I'm not our father, Estrith," he said, his voice barely above a whisper, weighted with an ache that seemed to stretch beyond the walls of the room. "And I'm not sure I ever will be."

Estrith's grip on his arm tightened, her expression resolute. "No," she replied, her tone resolute. "You're not him. But Faermire doesn't need another Ludica. It needs you."

The room fell into a fragile stillness, her words hanging openly in the air. The soft light from the window painted them in muted hues, illuminating the fears etched into his face and the fierce determination in hers.

For a moment, neither of them moved, the silence wrapping around them like a shroud. But within that quiet, something stirred—a fragile hope that briefly passed between them.

The soft patter of rain against the windows cast a mournful rhythm through the halls of Elsterheim. Estrith moved through the corridors, her steps measured, her mind heavy with the weight of what lay ahead. The days had stretched thin between her and Beowyn, his turmoil an ever-present shadow that she could neither dispel nor fully comprehend. His words had grown fewer, his silences longer, and though she ached to ease his burden, the walls around him felt impenetrable.

She had resolved, quietly but firmly, to remain by his side no matter the outcome of the coming duel. Whether it ended in victory or bloodshed, her loyalty would not waver. But the thought of Beowyn facing Elwin—his strength tested not only by a blade but by the crushing expectations of his people—gnawed at her like a silent storm. The tension coiled within her as she turned a corner, the dim light of a single lantern casting long shadows that flickered with the breath of the wind.

The castle felt unnaturally still, as if holding its breath. The scent of damp stone mingled with the faint tang of wax from the candles that struggled to keep the darkness at bay. Estrith's footsteps echoed faintly as she neared Siged's chamber, her heart stirring with the familiar ache of concern for her youngest brother. The faint murmur of a dream escaped his door—soft, unintelligible sounds that marked his restless sleep. She hesitated, her hand brushing the rough wood of the doorframe.

Then, she saw it.

A dark figure, faintly luminous, stood at Siged's bedside. Its form was shrouded in indistinct, shifting movements, like smoke illuminated by the moon– a figure both alluring and ominous. It remained partially veiled in a swirling mist, with only its striking orange eyes and ethereal haze cutting through.

Wisps of dark hair drifted around the figure, stirred by an invisible breeze that seemed to ripple through the air. Its outline shimmered with an otherworldly glow, undeniably female in form. Estrith's breath hitched, frozen in her throat as an icy chill cascaded over her, raising the hairs along her arms and anchoring her in place. The apparition leaned forward, its translucent hand lingering above Siged's frail body, poised as though to touch him—but the contact never came, the space between them charged with an eerie, unfulfilled intent.

The air grew oppressive, and a faint, almost imperceptible whisper curled through the room. It was neither a voice nor a sound, but a feeling—a presence so ancient and cold it seemed to seep into her bones.

The figure's head tilted slightly, as though sensing her, and Estrith's heart thundered in her chest. Her instinct was to step forward, to demand an answer or drive the entity away, but her limbs refused to obey. Fear gripped her like iron chains.

Then, as suddenly as it had appeared, the figure dissolved into nothingness, leaving the room bathed in its former stillness. The oppression lifted, but Estrith's breathing remained shallow, her pulse hammering in her ears. She swallowed hard, her trembling fingers brushing the frame of the door as she finally willed herself to move.

Inside, Siged stirred faintly, his head turning on the pillow. His face was pale, and his breathing shallow, but there was no sign of distress beyond what already lingered in his fragile form. The room seemed as it always had, save for the stagnant cold that clung to the air, unnatural and biting. Estrith stepped closer, her gaze scanning the chamber for any trace of what she had seen. There was nothing.

"Siged?" she whispered, her voice trembling as she knelt beside him. He did not wake, his breathing even but faint. A lump rose in her throat, the fear she had suppressed threatening to break loose. She brushed a lock of hair from his brow, her touch featherlight. "I'm here," she murmured, though the words felt as much for herself as for him.

For several moments, she remained at his side, her fingers gripping the edge of his blanket as she fought to steady herself. What had she seen? Was it a specter of her own imagination, a trick of her restless mind? Or was her presence a harbinger of something darker, something she could not yet name?

When she finally rose, her legs felt unsteady, her resolve shaken. She cast one last glance at Siged, ensuring he remained undisturbed, before stepping back into the corridor. The shadows seemed deeper now, the flickering light of the lanterns less certain. As she walked, her hand trailed along the cold stone wall, a tether to reality as her thoughts swirled with questions she dared not voice.

Estrith resolved not to speak of what she had seen, not yet. The strain on Beowyn was already unbearable, and the court was rife with tension. She could not add to the weight pressing down on her brother's shoulders—not when the duel loomed so near. But in the solitude of her own thoughts, the image of what she had seen lingered, a spectral warning that refused to fade.

When Estrith finally reached her own chamber, she stood in the doorway for a long moment, staring into the familiar space that now felt distant and foreign. She closed the door behind her with a soft click and leaned against it, her eyes falling shut. For the first time since she returned, her resolve wavered. A shiver coursed through her as she whispered into the silence, "gods help us?"

The room offered no answer. Only the faint patter of rain against the windows remained, a mournful echo of her own unease.

The first rays of dawn broke weakly through the heavy clouds over Elsterheim. The castle, usually cloaked in stillness at this hour, stirred with activity as soldiers and courtiers prepared for the journey ahead. The clatter of armor echoed faintly through the corridors, mingling with the murmurs of hushed voices and the occasional barked command. Outside, horses snorted and pawed at the damp earth, their breath steaming in the cold morning air. The atmosphere was thick with anticipation.

Estrith stood near the main gates, the chill seeping through her cloak as she waited. Her gaze drifted toward the horizon, where the mist clung stubbornly to the rolling hills, obscuring the path Beowyn and his men would soon take. The unease from the night before lingered in her mind and refused to fade. The apparition she had seen by Siged's bedside haunted her thoughts, its glowing eyes a silent omen she couldn't ignore. Was it a warning? A prelude to what awaited the days to come? The questions gnawed at her, but she forced them aside as the sound of boots crunching on gravel drew her attention.

Beowyn emerged from the castle, his armor gleaming faintly in the dim light. His face was set in a mask of stoic determination, but Estrith knew him too well to be deceived. His shoulders carried the weight of more than his sword and shield; the expectations of the people, the memory of their father's legacy, and the uncertain outcome of the duel all pressed down upon him. She stepped forward, her fingers instinctively brushing against the edge of his cloak as he approached.

"You look the part of a king today," Estrith murmured, her voice steady though a lump rose painfully in her throat, threatening to break her composure. The words carried a quiet reverence, laced with the fragile hope she clung to.

Beowyn halted at her words, turning to meet her gaze. His storm-gray eyes held hers, "If I am to wear the part," he replied, his tone low and resolute, "I must play it well."

Estrith's fingers tightened on the fabric of his cloak, the coarse weave grounding her in the moment. "Then I will await your swift return, Brother," she said, her voice soft but laced with quiet determination. Her grip lingered, as though she could anchor him to her by will alone, even as the world seemed to conspire to pull him away.

He studied her for a moment, his expression unreadable, before reaching up to clasp her hand. "I'll do what I can," he said, his voice low. "For Faermire. For you."

Estrith's heart ached at his words, and she fought to keep her composure. She wanted to tell him everything—about the figure in Siged's room, about her growing dread—but now was not the time. Instead, she leaned closer, her voice dropping to a whisper. "No matter what happens, Beowyn, you have my faith—and you always will."

Beowyn nodded once, a small but deliberate gesture, before stepping back. Estrith's fingers lingered on his cloak for a heartbeat longer, reluctant to let go. She watched him turn toward the assembled army, his broad shoulders squared against the weight of what was to come. The courtyard was alive with muted chaos—soldiers tightening straps, adjusting swords, and mounting restless horses. The banners of Faermire, deep blue and silver, snapped sharply in the cold morning breeze, their colors stark against the ashen sky.

The sound of soft footsteps drew her attention, and she turned to see Sgell approaching with Siged at his side. The boy's steps were slow but steady, his frail frame shrouded in a thick woolen cloak that dwarfed him. Estrith felt a pang in her chest as she watched Beowyn pause mid-step, his stoic mask faltering at the sight of their youngest sibling. For a moment, the weight on his shoulders seemed to lift.

Beowyn knelt carefully, his armor creaking softly, as he met Siged's gaze. The boy mumbled quietly to himself, his words incoherent but his eyes bright with recognition. A tear glistened in Beowyn's eye as he smiled warmly, brushing a stray wisp of hair from Siged's pale forehead.

"You're looking stronger than ever," Beowyn said softly, his voice steady despite the raw emotion that brimmed beneath it.

Estrith averted her gaze, blinking rapidly to hold back her own tears. The tenderness in her brother's voice, the unspoken promise in his touch—it was almost too much to bear.

From beneath his armor, Beowyn withdrew a small, wooden trinket. The carving, a snake coiled in a simple design, was worn. Siged had made it for him before his injuries, a token of simpler, happier days. Beowyn held it up, his fingers tracing its familiar grooves.

"I'll keep it safe," he said, his smile soft and reassuring. "And I'll bring it back to you. I promise."

Siged's thin fingers reached out, grasping weakly for the wooden snake. Beowyn took his hand gently, enfolding it within his own, and held it tightly for a moment that felt suspended in time. When at last he rose to his feet, he leaned down and pressed a kiss to Siged's head, lingering as if to draw strength from the boy's presence.

Estrith stiffened as Beowyn turned to her. He didn't need to speak, the weight of his farewell was etched into his expression. She managed a small, strained smile, reaching out to touch his arm. "Ride safely," she whispered. "Come back to us."

Beowyn's gaze softened, his lips curving into the faintest of smiles. "Always."

He stepped back, offering a final nod to Sgell before turning toward his waiting horse. The courtyard grew quieter as he mounted, his figure tall and unyielding in the saddle. A ripple of motion moved through the army as the men prepared to follow their lord, their breaths clouding the frigid air.

Estrith stood rooted to the spot, her hands clasped tightly together as she watched him ride toward the gate. Siged shifted closer to her, his small hand slipping into hers for comfort. She squeezed it gently, her heart aching with the knowledge that this moment might be their last as a family.

As the banners of Faermire disappeared into the mist, Estrith let out a slow, unsteady breath. The courtyard fell still, the echoes of hooves and armor fading into the distance. For a long moment, she and Siged remained there, staring at the empty gate, as if willing Beowyn to return even before he had truly left.

Finally, she turned, her hand resting lightly on Siged's shoulder as they made their way back inside. The castle loomed around them, cold and silent, but Estrith couldn't shake the lingering warmth of Beowyn's smile. It was a fragile hope she clung to as the chill of the day settled in her bones.

THIRTEEN

DONNORATH WOOD

The Donnorath Wood loomed ahead, a dense maze of gnarled trees and thick underbrush that swallowed the sunlight whole. Shapes moved unnaturally beneath the canopy, their edges jagged and imbued with a silent, watching menace. Sidonis urged his horse forward, though the beast's ears flicked nervously, and its hooves hesitated on the uneven ground. He had heard the tales as a boy—stories of the cursed forest where outcasts and the broken of the world vanished, leaving no trace. It was a place whispered about with dread, a refuge for the forgotten and forsaken.

Sidonis did not believe in curses, but the wood felt wrong, its oppressive silence gnawing at the edges of his composure. Every creak of the trees, every rustle of unseen movement in the brush, seemed amplified by the stillness. His hand brushed the hilt of his sword, though he doubted it would offer much protection against whatever lurked here.

As the hours stretched, the path narrowed, forcing him to dismount and lead his horse through the tangled foliage. The air grew thick with the scent of damp earth and decay, and the occasional glimpse of movement at the edges of his vision kept his hand near his weapon. He knew better than to look too closely—here, the mind played cruel tricks.

The forest began to climb, the ground sloping upward into a steep hill. At its peak, half-hidden by the twisted limbs of ancient trees, stood the ruins of a temple. It was a decrepit thing, its stone walls cracked and consumed by moss and creeping vines. Time had battered it, yet it exuded a sense of defiance, as though it refused to be forgotten by the world. The sight of it stirred unease in Sidonis that had nothing to do with the forest.

At the temple's base, figures emerged from the undergrowth. They moved with an animalistic grace, bodies painted in ashen gray clay and clothing stitched together from animal skins. Their eyes held no fear, only the quiet, unsettling devotion of those who had forsaken the civilized world. They did not speak as they surrounded Sidonis, their silence more unnerving than any threat. He let go of his horse's reins, allowing the beast to bolt, and strode forward with feigned indifference.

The figures parted as he approached the temple's entrance, revealing the interior in all its eerie glory. The room was dimly lit by torches, their flames casting jagged shadows over walls carved with ancient symbols. The air smelled of ash and something metallic, sharp enough to sting his nostrils.

At the center of the chamber, seated atop a throne crafted from bones and twisted wood, was Gorhan. His frail frame was painted in the same grey clay as his followers, though blue symbols and letters in the old language adorned his skin, glowing faintly in the flickering light. A tattered cloak hung from his shoulders, and small animal skulls dangled from a crude belt at his waist. He was shirtless, his long, stringy hair and beard falling over his chest like a shroud. The antler headdress he wore seemed almost a part of him, its jagged points giving him a presence both regal and monstrous.

Gorhan's eyes, dark and hollow as pits, fixed on Sidonis. His lips, smeared with a black residue that had dried into his beard, twisted into a knowing smile.

"Man of Aecorath," Gorhan intoned, his voice low and rasping. "The gods are pleased you heeded their call."

Sidonis halted before him, his jaw tightening. "It was not their call I heeded. I came for answers."

Gorhan tilted his head, the antlers casting long, spindly shadows across the chamber. "Answers you shall have. But first, the gods must be heard."

Gorhan gestured, and his followers moved with unnerving precision. They encircled the chamber, their ashen-painted bodies blending with the dim, flickering shadows. As one, they began to sway, their movements subtle but hypnotic, like leaves stirred by an invisible wind. A low hum rose among them, vibrating through the chamber like the echo of distant thunder.

"Aran etar ionos..." the chant began, soft and rhythmic, each syllable deliberate and haunting.

Their voices grew louder, weaving together in an unholy harmony that reverberated off the stone walls. The words were indecipherable to Sidonis, but their weight pressed down on him. The symbols carved into the walls seemed to shimmer faintly in response, as if awakening to the chant's call.

"Aran etar ionos... Kael ithron velor..."

The chanting quickened as two followers stepped forward, carrying a shallow bowl etched with ancient runes. They placed it reverently at Gorhan's feet, their heads bowed low in submission before retreating into the circle. Gorhan extended a hand to Sidonis, his blackened fingers curling expectantly.

"Your blood, Sidonis. The gods demand it."

Sidonis hesitated, his resentment flaring. He had given so much—his loyalty, his family, his humanity. Now they demanded his blood? He drew his blade without a word, slicing a shallow line across his palm. The blood dripped into the bowl, hissing faintly as it touched the surface. The liquid darkened unnaturally, swirling as if alive.

Gorhan began to chant, his voice rising and falling in guttural tones. The symbols painted on his skin began to glow brighter, and the air thickened, pressing down on Sidonis like an invisible weight. The flames of the torches turned blue, casting an otherworldly light over the chamber. The blood in the bowl bubbled violently, releasing tendrils of smoke that coiled like serpents toward the ceiling.

Then came the voice—not Gorhan's, but something deeper, ancient and unknowable. It reverberated through the chamber, a sound that bypassed the ears and sank directly into the bones.

"Sidonis," the voice intoned, neither male nor female. "You live by our will. You walk because *We* spared you."

Sidonis clenched his fists, his jaw tightening under the crushing weight of the voice. Defiance radiated from his rigid stance, but deep within, a gnawing fear clawed at him. Men he could fight, swords and steel he could meet head-on—but this? This was something else entirely. Here, in this oppressive, otherworldly presence, he felt like a fragile creature standing at the edge of an abyss, teetering on the brink of being swallowed whole.

"Your survival was ordained," the voice intoned, its words slithering through the air like a serpent.

The declaration twisted in his gut, sharp as the blade he had used to kill Ludica. He had fought to escape his brother's shadow, spilling blood to claim the throne and forge a legacy of his own. Yet now, the gods declared his survival to be their doing—a gift unearned, a fate handed down like a cruel joke. It was an insult, a mockery of every sacrifice he had made, every act of rebellion to shape his own destiny.

Sidonis's gaze darted to Gorhan, who stood like a statue, his frail body caught in a trance. His hollow, blackened eyes stared unblinking into the void, consumed by the force that filled the chamber. Around them, Gorhan's followers pressed their faces into the dirt in reverence, their bodies trembling as though in worship. The sight only deepened the churning turmoil in Sidonis's mind.

"What is your will?" Sidonis forced out, his voice hoarse and tight, barely audible against the suffocating presence that lingered.

"The Purging Fire comes to consume the land," the voice replied, cold and measured. *"To devour all of Aecorath."*

The words sent a chill down Sidonis's spine, colder than the air in the ruined temple. There was something vast, something unknowable in their warning, and for the first time, he felt a flicker of something beyond anger—something close to dread.

"The Purging Fire?" he repeated, his throat tightening. "What sort of fire?"

The voice did not answer immediately, but the oppressive weight in the air thickened. He could feel it pressing against his skin, against his very soul. Finally, the reply came, slow and deliberate, each word like a tolling bell.

"Unite the kingdoms, Man of Aecorath. Before it overtakes the land..."

The cryptic command rattled Sidonis's thoughts. His mind raced, struggling to piece together the fragments of the gods' message. Darkness? A threat to Aecorath? What could they mean? What was this menace, and why did they speak in riddles? The flurry of unanswered questions stoked his frustration.

"Wait!" he shouted, his voice sharp with desperation as the oppressive presence began to ebb. "What is this fire? Tell me more—what must I do?"

The air lightened, the torches lining the walls flickering back to their normal, golden hue. The otherworldly power that had filled the chamber dissipated like smoke on the wind, leaving a void in its wake. Gorhan blinked slowly, as if waking from a dream, the faint glow fading from the symbols painted on his frail body.

When the silence finally fell, it was deafening. Gorhan's eyes gleamed with a strange satisfaction, but Sidonis's expression darkened, frustration etched into every line of his face.

"The gods spared me," Sidonis spat, his voice low and sharp, each word dripping with venom, "but for what? To play a pawn in their game? I killed my brother to escape the shadows, not to trade them for chains." His gaze burned into Gorhan as he continued. "They speak of fire, a threat to all of Aecorath, yet they leave me with nothing but riddles. How am I to unite the kingdoms when I have not even secured my own?"

Gorhan tilted his head, his thin lips curling into a knowing smile. "You made an oath with Ceolfrid, did you not?"

Sidonis's mouth tightened, his silence betraying the unease that stirred within him. The thought of rekindling an alliance with the king of Abensloh seemed laughable. After their failure, Ceolfrid would hardly incline his ear to Sidonis, let alone trust him again. But as if reading his thoughts, Gorhan leaned forward, his blackened fingers curling over the arms of his throne.

"The king will require a sign," Gorhan said, his voice a low murmur, thick with implication.

Sidonis frowned, his jaw tightening. "What sort of sign?"

With deliberate slowness, Gorhan rose from his throne, his skeletal frame casting long, spindly shadows against the walls. The faint rattle of the skulls at his waist echoed in the stillness as he approached Sidonis. His black-stained teeth glinted in the dim light as his smile widened.

"When the time comes, I will come calling," Gorhan rasped, his voice a jagged whisper that echoed unnervingly in the chamber. The words hung in the air like a specter, both a promise and a warning. "The gods' debts are not so easily paid."

Sidonis stood his ground, though every fiber of his being urged him to recoil. Gorhan raised a skeletal hand, his blackened fingers curling as they reached toward Sidonis's chest. The movement was deliberate, almost ritualistic, and Sidonis fought the instinct to pull away as the seer's touch met his armor. The fingers pressed firmly, and Gorhan began to mutter in a language Sidonis barely recognized, the guttural incantation dripping with ancient power.

A sudden heat flared beneath the cold steel of his armor, blooming like fire but without pain. It spread outward, threading through his body in tendrils of energy, searing yet oddly weightless. Sidonis felt his chest tighten, his breath hitching as a strange weight settled over him—a presence, a mark that did not belong to him. It was as though something unseen had latched onto his very soul, its grip unyielding.

Gorhan's hollow eyes burned with an unnatural light, their emptiness somehow filled with knowledge that Sidonis could not fathom. The seer pulled back slowly, his fingers leaving behind an invisible imprint that Sidonis felt more than he saw.

"It will come as the dawn comes, unyielding, unrelenting, a force written into the very fabric of existence," Gorhan intoned, his voice a rasping echo of finality. He sank into the gnarled seat as if it had been waiting to reclaim him, the flickering torchlight casting his skeletal form against the wall. His antlered headdress seemed to stretch impossibly high, its points scraping the edges of the gloom. "You bear their mark now, Sidonis. The gods will not be ignored."

Sidonis scowled, his lips curling in defiance. The weight of the mark bore down on him, and the heat still lingered beneath his skin, a constant reminder of what had just transpired. His thoughts churned with resentment. He hated the feeling of being beholden to this man—to the gods. Their favor felt more like a chain than a gift, and the very thought of it filled him with fury. But for now, he had no choice. He would carry their mark. He would endure their game.

For now.

Without a word, Sidonis turned on his heel, his boots striking the stone with sharp, echoing finality. The chamber's oppressive air seemed to cling to him, even as he made his way toward the exit.

Near the archway, two cloaked figures stood motionless, their forms half-swallowed by the shadows. Their presence was unnerving, their outlines indistinct and wavering, as if they existed only halfway in this realm. Sidonis froze for a heartbeat, his eyes narrowing. He had seen them before—after Gorhan had healed him on the battlefield. They had been watching him then, and now, here they were again, silent sentinels who offered no explanation.

The figures made no move to stop him. They simply stood, their faces obscured by the darkness of their hoods, their stillness more unnerving than any threat. Sidonis drew in a breath, his resolve hardening. He stepped forward, his boots crunching faintly against the loose gravel beneath him. As he passed between them, he braced himself for some reaction, some movement—but none came. Instead, their forms dissolved into the shadows, vanishing as if they had never been there.

He emerged into the night, the temple's oppressive gloom giving way to the twisted, foreboding embrace of the Donnorath Wood. The forest felt darker now, its silence deeper and more hostile, stretching toward him like grasping hands. The chill in the air seeped into his bones, but Sidonis pushed forward, his steps steady as the temple receded behind him.

The farther he walked, the more his thoughts churned. The gods wanted him to unite the kingdoms. They claimed it was his destiny, their grand design for him. But Sidonis did not care for their divine plans. He would not do this for them. He would do it for himself—for his name, for his legacy, for the freedom to write his own story.

The gods had given him this second chance, but he would not remain their pawn forever. When the time came, he vowed, he would find a way to sever their grasp. No matter the cost.

The glow of the temple faded completely behind him, swallowed by the shadows of the forest, and Sidonis disappeared into the night.

The great doors of Ceolfrid's hall groaned as they opened, the sound reverberating through the stone corridors like the growl of an ancient beast. Sidonis stepped into the threshold, his boots sinking into the plush crimson carpet that stretched toward the throne. Behind him, the heavy doors swung shut with a hollow thud, cutting him off from the cold night air and plunging him into the warmth of the court.

It had taken cunning to reach this point. He had disguised himself among traveling merchants, slipping past the outer gates with the flow of commerce. By the time Ceolfrid's guards at the inner sanctum caught sight of him, his mere presence had done the work—whispers of his name, disbelief, and hesitation among the ranks allowed him to push forward unchallenged.

Now, standing under the vaulted arches of Ceolfrid's court, Sidonis moved with measured steps, his expression calm, though a storm brewed beneath. His eyes swept over the scene before him, taking in the revelry. Dancers twirled in elegant patterns, their silk-clad forms catching the golden glow of the chandeliers. Musicians played lively tunes, their melodies mingling with the hum of conversation. All eyes turned to him as he strode forward, his dark figure cutting through the light like a shadow come to life.

The whispers began as ripples of disbelief. Gasps punctuated the air, and the room seemed to hold its breath. The man presumed dead had returned, walking among the living with the confidence of a king.

Ceolfrid sat atop his massive throne of carved ebony, its high back crowned with spiked adornments. The king's heavy brow furrowed as his sharp eyes locked onto Sidonis. He raised a hand abruptly, the gesture freezing the dancers mid-step and silencing the music. The hall fell into a suffocating stillness, broken only by the faint hiss of torchlight.

Sidonis stopped several paces from the throne, standing tall despite the wave of hostility emanating from Ceolfrid and his court. His dark hair framed his face, and the faint shadows under his eyes made him look more spectral than human. Yet he stood firm, his poise masking the bitterness festering within. He had not come to beg but to take what was owed.

"Sidonis," Ceolfrid said at last, his voice cutting through the silence like a blade. "I should have you cut down where you stand." His knuckles whitened as he gripped the armrests of his throne. "You've come back to beg for scraps after leaving my armies to rot in the mud?"

Sidonis did not flinch under Ceolfrid's glare. He met the king's fury with steady eyes, his voice calm yet edged. "Ludica is dead by my hand, as you demanded."

Ceolfrid surged to his feet, his crimson cloak flaring as he descended the steps of his dais. "And what of the throne you promised to deliver? What of the kingdom you left in chaos?" His tone dripped with venom. "You speak of your deeds as though they mean anything. Ludica is dead, yet you've done nothing but turn his throne into a graveyard for your ambitions."

The court murmured in approval, the sound like a low growl echoing through the hall. Sidonis absorbed the fury, his expression unchanging as Ceolfrid's words struck like lashes. He let the older man exhaust himself, each accusation fueling the fire smoldering in his chest.

Finally, Ceolfrid paused, his chest heaving from the fury of his tirade. The air in the hall was thick with tension, the gathered courtiers frozen as if caught between breaths. Sidonis let the silence stretch for a beat longer, his gaze unflinching as he absorbed the king's scorn. Then, with a voice as sharp and unyielding as forged steel, he replied, "I upheld my end of the bargain. If Helgisson betrayed us, that shame is his alone, not mine. I returned to finish what we began."

Ceolfrid barked out a short, mirthless laugh, the sound echoing off the stone walls like a derisive whip. "Finish what we began?" he sneered, stepping down from his throne with deliberate menace. "You crawled back to me to salvage your failure, nothing more."

Sidonis advanced a step, his movements deliberate, his presence growing with every inch he claimed. "I returned because the gods demand it," he said, his voice steady yet charged with restrained power. "They spared me, Ceolfrid, because I am chosen for a purpose greater than any of us."

The temperature in the hall seemed to drop, an unnatural chill settling over the court as Sidonis stopped at the base of the dais. His eyes burned with a calm intensity as they met Ceolfrid's. "They spared me to unite the kingdoms, to claim Faermire's throne, and to fulfill the destiny they have decreed. Your name will stand alongside mine, Ceolfrid—but only if you stand with me."

Ceolfrid's disdain deepened, his laugh this time slower, laced with genuine disgust. "You? Chosen by the gods?" His words dripped with ridicule, each syllable a blade meant to cut deep. "You insult me with such absurdity. A weakling who failed his own ambitions now dares to speak of destiny?"

The king's scorn spilled over as he waved dismissively at Sidonis. "You've wasted enough of my time with your delusions. But rest assured, I will relish every moment of your death."

As the guards began to move, Sidonis remained rooted, his calm unbroken. Slowly, deliberately, he raised a hand to his chest, pulling back the fabric to reveal the faint etching beneath his skin. The lines of the ancient symbol glimmered faintly in the dim light, intricate and otherworldly. His fingers traced the mark, each movement deliberate, as though awakening something hidden within.

Ceolfrid's derisive smile faltered, his gaze narrowing in suspicion. Though unconvinced, a flicker of unease crossed his face as he regarded the mark.

"Enough of this charade," Ceolfrid growled, his voice bitter and low. "Seize him."

As the guards reached Sidonis, their hands closing on his arms, he spoke— his voice a low, commanding cadence that carried through the hall like a ripple in still water. "Aran etar ionos."

The ancient words rolled from his tongue with the gravity of an incantation, each syllable resonating with a power that seemed to awaken the air itself. The hall darkened in an instant, the torches along the walls dimming as if choked by an unseen force. Their flames flickered weakly, retreating into trembling embers.

Dark tendrils writhed and twisted from the mark on Sidonis's chest, coalescing into a shifting, enigmatic form. A figure emerged, its edges blurring as if it hovered between realms, tethered to this world by sheer force of will. The figure was tall, cloaked in an impenetrable darkness that rippled like smoke. Its edges blurred and flickered, defying the eye's attempts to capture its true shape. Where its eyes should have been, two orbs of piercing light burned with a brilliance so stark it seemed to sear the air, casting faint, flickering reflections on the stone walls.

The apparition moved, its presence oppressive and suffocating. A wave of unease rippled through the court as the entity glided forward, silent yet commanding. Its steps did not touch the ground, but each movement reverberated within the minds of those who dared to look upon it. Ceolfrid's warriors, hardened by years of battle, faltered. Their grips on their weapons slackened, the steel suddenly feeling like feeble trinkets against the overwhelming power now in the room. Gasps echoed through the hall, the sound mingling with the silence that followed, like the muted crash of distant waves.

The entity stopped before Ceolfrid's throne, its towering form casting long, writhing shadows across the chamber. Its gaze—or whatever force emanated from those burning orbs—bore down on the king, pinning him in place. The room seemed to constrict, stifling any movement and stole the breath from every chest.

For a moment, the court remained frozen, trapped in an unnatural silence. Then, with a chilling inevitability, the entity moved once more, stepping directly through Ceolfrid.

The king's body stiffened as the shadow passed through him, his eyes widening in shock. A faint, otherworldly glow lit his chest for a fleeting instant, pulsing like a dying ember. He gasped, clutching the armrests of his throne as though they were the only anchor in a sea of chaos. The light faded, leaving behind a chill that seeped into his bones and lingered in the room like an unspoken warning.

The entity continued its silent march, its form unraveling into wisps of light and shadow as it moved. Like smoke caught in an unseen breeze, it dissolved, fading into nothingness. The torches lining the walls flared back to life, their flames trembling as though recoiling from the recent darkness. Sidonis stood tall in the aftermath, his chest rising and falling with deliberate calm. The incandescent mark on his chest dimmed, retreating into faint, lifeless etchings beneath his skin. His voice sliced through the silence, low and unyielding. "The gods have spoken. They demand unity."

Ceolfrid remained seated, his face pale, his breaths uneven. Slowly, he pushed himself to his feet, his gaze locked on Sidonis. The fire of defiance that usually burned in the king's eyes was dimmed, replaced by a wary respect laced with unease. "I do not doubt what I have seen," he said, his voice uneven but steady. "But the gods' favor alone will not bring kingdoms to their knees."

Sidonis stepped closer, his movements deliberate and precise, each step an unspoken acknowledgment of Ceolfrid's authority. His voice, measured and resonant, carried both deference and conviction. "The gods may have set the path," he began, "but even their will requires the strength of great men to shape the world. Men like you, Ceolfrid."

He paused, letting his words settle, his eyes meeting the king's with unwavering confidence. "Your name is already spoken in fear and respect across Aecorath. Your blade has carved a legacy that rulers envy and bards dare not embellish. But this—this is an opportunity to elevate that legacy beyond mortal bounds."

Ceolfrid's expression remained guarded, though the faintest flicker of intrigue passed through his eyes. The room still seemed to echo with the apparition's presence, its otherworldly gravity lingering like a shadow.

Sidonis continued, his tone softening slightly, becoming almost reverent. "I do not come as a beggar, but as one who recognizes greatness and seeks to amplify it. Faermire's throne is the keystone in this destiny. Together, we can unite the kingdoms, not just under my rule, but under a legacy that bears both our names. When the kingdoms bow, they will do so to the vision we forged."

Ceolfrid's lips pressed into a thin line, his skepticism flickering as he glanced toward the place where the apparition had vanished. The weight of what he had seen warred with his natural distrust. Slowly, he leaned forward, his tone edged with caution. "You speak of greatness, Sidonis, but greatness is not gifted—it is earned. If I lend my blade to your cause, it is because I will see this path forged through strength, not feigned promises."

Sidonis inclined his head, his faint smile one of calculated humility. "Strength is what brought me here, Ceolfrid, and it is what will see us prevail. Your hand, your vision, is indispensable to this alliance. The gods may guide, but it is men like you who command the world."

For a long moment, Ceolfrid studied Sidonis, the silence heavy with the weight of unspoken deliberation. Finally, he inclined his head, his voice sharp with warning. "Then let the gods witness our pact. But hear this—if you falter, no divine favor will shield you from my wrath."

Sidonis straightened, his smile deepening ever so slightly, tempered with ambition and resolve. "A king does not forget the hand that lifts him to his throne. Together, Ceolfrid, we will not merely rule—we will redefine this land."

FOURTEEN

HELMFIRTH, KINGDOM OF MISTELFELD

The marketplace in Mistelfeld thrummed with life, a sea of voices rising and falling in a chaotic symphony. Helgisson moved through the throng, his shoulders brushing against strangers as the sea of humanity shifted and swelled around him. Vendors called out their wares, their voices blending into a medley of accents and dialects—some sharp and clipped, others lilting and musical. The air was thick with competing aromas: freshly baked bread, sizzling meats, and the acrid tang of dye vats bubbling in the sun.

Helgisson moved with a deliberate, measured pace, his gaze sweeping over the bustling marketplace. Each calculated step revealed a man accustomed to navigating precarious terrain, his every glance and gesture steeped in purpose. He was in Mistelfeld to strengthen Graefeld's hold, not for conquest but for survival—to secure vital supplies, forge crucial alliances, and bolster his people against the hardships that pressed upon their borders. Every deal struck here would ripple back to Graefeld, fortifying the lives of those who depended on him to ensure their future.

The worn leather of his cloak shifted with his steps, its edges frayed and weathered. It bore the scars of practicality, a testament to its owner's rugged life.

Helgisson's hand drifted to the pouch at his belt, his fingers brushing the sturdy fabric with a confidence born of routine. Each action was deliberate, as though even this small movement played a role in the larger game he orchestrated.

Wooden stalls sagged under the weight of their goods, their surfaces piled high with everything from bright bolts of cloth to glinting trinkets and dull iron tools. Children darted between legs, their laughter rising above the hum of conversation, while merchants haggled in sharp tones that teetered between friendliness and hostility. Above it all, the sun burned white-hot in a cloudless sky, casting harsh shadows that pooled under carts and crept along the cobblestones.

Helgisson paused beside a fruit vendor, eyeing a crate of plump, waxy apples. He handed over a coin without a word, pocketing an apple before moving on. His path was purposeful, winding deeper into the heart of the marketplace where the press of bodies grew tighter and the smells more pungent.

A brief lull in the noise caught his attention—a momentary ripple as heads turned, conversations faltering. He followed the shift in energy, his instincts prickling. The marketplace returned to life just as quickly, but the sensation lingered, a whisper of warning too faint to grasp.

Helgisson passed a cart laden with copper pots, his reflection distorted and fragmented in the polished surface of a pot. He glanced over his shoulder, the movement casual, but his expression tightened. Someone was watching him.

He turned sharply down a narrow lane where the market's chaos seemed to thin. The stalls here were quieter, the goods less luxurious, and the crowd more subdued. The din of the main thoroughfare dulled to a murmur, distant yet constant.

That was when he felt it—a sharp, searing pain plunging into his side. Helgisson's breath caught as his hand shot out, seizing the assassin's wrist with a grip born of desperation. His gaze locked onto the shadowed figure, and for the briefest moment, something flickered in his eyes—a recognition that sharpened the pain twisting through his body.

His lips parted as though to speak, but the words faltered, drowned in the blood pooling at the corners of his mouth. The assassin yanked back, wrenching free from Helgisson's grip, but not before Helgisson's fingers brushed against the fabric of the killer's cloak—an almost imperceptible pause in the movement, as if he had grasped a fleeting memory.

Around him, panic rippled through the crowd. Vendors shouted, their voices sharp with fear, as bystanders stumbled over one another to flee the scene. The once-bustling marketplace erupted into disorder, leaving Helgisson alone in the rapidly emptying square.

He fell to his knees, the cobblestones unrelenting beneath him, his vision blurring as the blood pooled beneath him. His trembling hand brushed the cold stone before he crumpled fully, his strength fading. The marketplace, now devoid of its life and vitality, seemed to echo his final moments—a world indifferent to the man who lay dying in its midst.

The damp air of the dungeons clung to Gwenora like an unwelcome shroud as she descended the spiraling stone steps. The faint torchlight above grew dimmer with each step, the flickering flames casting jagged shadows on the walls. The faint scent of mildew mixed with something sharper—blood, sweat, and the pungent tang of desperation.

She tightened her grip on the hem of her emerald gown to keep it from brushing the grimy floor. Her footsteps echoed faintly, sharp against the low murmurs and occasional grunts rising from below. Two guards flanked the heavy oak door, their posture stiffening as she approached. With a curt nod from Gwenora, one of them pushed the door open, revealing the grim scene within.

The room was dimly lit, the flickering light of a single torch dancing across the rough-hewn walls. Aldred stood at the center, his broad shoulders tense as he loomed over the assassin, who was bound to a heavy wooden chair. Two guards flanked the prisoner, their expressions stoic but alert. The assassin's face was a mask of defiance beneath the swelling and dried blood. His lip was split, and one eye was nearly swollen shut, but his gaze burned with disdain as it locked onto Gwenora.

The queen entered with deliberate grace, her every movement a study in restrained power. Her cloak swept behind her as she stepped closer, the faint rustle of the fabric the only sound in the tense chamber. She paused a few paces from the prisoner, her sharp eyes taking in his battered form. His chest heaved with labored breaths, but even in his broken state, he held himself with silent resolve.

Aldred turned to her, his voice low but taut. "Your Majesty, he's refused to speak. Even under duress."

Gwenora's gaze didn't waver from the assassin. "He attempted to take his own life when he was captured, did he not?"

Aldred nodded, his lips pressed into a thin line. "We stopped him before he could finish the job. But since then, he's been silent. No name, no motive, no allegiance."

She stepped closer, her presence a suffocating weight that seemed to fill the room. The assassin's eyes followed her, defiant but wary. His hands, bound tightly with coarse rope, twitched slightly, the only betrayal of his discomfort.

"You killed a man of considerable importance to me," Gwenora said, her voice measured and cold. "Helgisson's death will not go unanswered. You understand that, don't you?"

The assassin said nothing. The defiance in his gaze did not falter, but Gwenora caught the faintest twitch at the corner of his mouth—an almost imperceptible smile. It was not fear that drove him, she realized, but conviction.

Her eyes narrowed. "You believe in whatever cause brought you here, that much is clear. But convictions can break. They break under pain. They break under time." Her voice dropped, each word deliberate and sharp. "And I have both to spare."

The man remained silent, his jaw tightening as he stared past her, refusing to give her the satisfaction of a response.

Gwenora's patience wavered, a flicker of frustration creeping into her tone. "Your resistance serves no one. Speak now, and I might grant you a quick death. Continue this charade, and I will let my men take their time with you."

The assassin's lips parted slightly, and for a fleeting moment, Gwenora thought he might speak. But the words never came. Instead, he spat at her feet, the defiance in his gaze burning brighter than ever.

The room stilled, the tension thick as Aldred and the guards exchanged uneasy glances. Gwenora's expression hardened, her anger icy rather than explosive. She took a single step back, her voice cutting through the air like steel.

"Do whatever is necessary to make him talk," she said, her tone devoid of emotion. "I want answers, Aldred. No matter the cost."

Aldred inclined his head, his features set in grim determination. "As you command, Your Majesty."

Without another word, Gwenora turned on her heel, the heavy skirts of her gown swishing as she strode toward the door. The assassin's muffled laughter followed her, low and guttural, though it faltered under a sharp blow from one of the guards.

The door slammed shut behind her, sealing the chamber's grim purpose. As Gwenora ascended the stairs, her mind churned with questions. Who had sent the assassin? Why had Helgisson been targeted in the heart of Mistelfeld? And why did the assassin's defiance feel so calculated, so deliberate?

The assassin's resolve had unsettled her—not because he had refused to break, but because his conviction was unwavering. What kind of man would give his life so readily? And for whom?

She tightened her grip on the folds of her gown, her knuckles whitening as her mind turned to Helgisson. His death was a loss, not just to his people, but to the delicate balance of power in Mistelfeld. Someone had wanted him silenced, and they had sent a man willing to die for the cause.

The morning light filtered through the narrow panes of Gwenora's private chambers, casting faint streaks of gold across the polished floor. The fire in the hearth had burned low, its embers glowing faintly, and the air was tinged with the sharp scent of smoldering ash. Gwenora sat at a carved wooden desk, a map of Mistelfeld unfurled before her. Her emerald cloak pooled around her shoulders as she leaned forward, tracing potential supply routes with the tip of her finger.

The knock on the door was soft but deliberate. Gwenora straightened, her sharp gaze flicking toward the entrance. "Enter," she called, her voice calm yet laced with authority.

Aldred stepped in, his broad frame filling the doorway before he crossed the room. His expression was grim, the faint lines of sleeplessness etched around his eyes. Gwenora's stomach tightened—whatever news he brought, it would not be good.

"My queen," Aldred began, bowing his head briefly. "The assassin is dead."

Gwenora's breath hesitated though unsurprised by the news, she kept her composure. "Were you able to glean any good information?"

Aldred exhaled heavily, his voice taut with frustration. "He succumbed to his injuries during the night. Despite our efforts, he gave us little—save a name."

Gwenora arched a brow, her tone sharp. "What name?"

"Sidonis," Aldred said, the weight of the word lingering between them like a palpable force.

For a moment, Gwenora froze, the name hung in the air, thick and suffocating, dredging up memories she had thought buried alongside him months ago. Her breath faltered, her lips parting slightly as though to form words, but none came. Sidonis was dead—slain on the battlefield, struck down by his brother's own hand. Yet the unshakable truth of that moment now wavered like a shadow in her mind.

Her fingers tightened against the edge of the desk, the polished wood biting into her palms as her thoughts churned. A whisper of disbelief escaped her lips, the name trembling as she spoke it aloud. "Sidonis?" Her voice wavered, the word tinged with equal parts doubt and dread. She hesitated before adding, her tone sharper, more urgent, "That's all?"

Aldred shifted, the tension in his posture betraying his unease. "There wasn't much more, Your Majesty," he said cautiously, the words deliberate. "The man's mind was failing toward the end—ramblings, most of it. But this... this name was clear. As clear as day."

The finality in his voice hung heavy between them, but for Gwenora, the room seemed to blur at the edges, her focus narrowing on that single thread of possibility: Sidonis, alive. It was unthinkable—and yet the absence of his body now echoed like a haunting refrain in her mind.

Gwenora rose from her seat, the folds of her gown sweeping around her ankles as she paced to the window. The cold glass pressed against her fingertips as she gazed out at the snow-dusted rooftops of Mistelfeld. Her reflection in the glass was pale, her brows furrowed in thought.

"If Sidonis lives..." she began, her voice trailing off. Her mind raced, piecing together fragments of the past months: the unrest among her nobles, the whispers of rebellion, the growing shadow of Ceolfrid's influence. "Ceolfrid may still be working with him."

Aldred stepped closer, his tone careful but resolute. "It would explain much, Your Majesty. The instability, the precision of Helgisson's assassination—it bears the mark of a calculated move."

Gwenora turned to face him, her green eyes sharp with determination. "And yet, it is only speculation. We need confirmation." Her voice hardened. "If Sidonis lives, he must be advancing Ceolfrid's ambitions. This cannot be ignored."

Aldred inclined his head. "What would you have me do?"

She hesitated for a moment, then her gaze flickered toward the door. "Prepare a messenger for Faermire. I will write to Estrith and Beowyn. If Sidonis is alive, they need to know."

As Aldred left to fulfill her command, Gwenora paced a moment longer consider the recent revelations that now stood at her front door. For a moment, she regretted not killing Ordric as soon as his treachery was revealed. It would have saved her the strife she now faced and it was only growing as the days carried on. In hindsight, she did it to spare the upheaval, and now worried that she only contributed further to it.

She couldn't help but feel like Ordric was still playing his games, tugging on the strings while he remained behind bars and she hated him even more for it. Though she couldn't help but feel a glimmer of admiration (however faint) for his ability to do so, even from prison.

Still, with the possibility of Sidonis alive and working with Ceolfrid, she needed more answers, and the only man she knew that she might get them from, was from the traitor himself.

The dungeon corridors seemed to breathe their own misery, the dim, flickering light of torches casting long shadows that clung to the damp walls. The air was heavy, thick with the stench of mildew, decay, and despair. Gwenora's steps echoed softly as she descended, each one a steady beat against the oppressive silence. She caught a faint gleam ahead, a single, stubborn sliver of daylight spilling through a narrow window high in the stone wall. It pierced the gloom like a defiant whisper of the world above.

She paused at the threshold, her emerald gown trailing over the cold stone as her eyes flicked over the man she had come to see. Lord Ordric sat with the calculated poise of a man who refused to bow to his circumstances. His back was straight, his shoulders relaxed, and his hands moved with an elegance that defied the grim setting of the cell. He was a man in his mid-sixties, his salt-and-pepper hair now a near-unbroken silver, meticulously combed to gleam faintly in the soft daylight filtering through the narrow window. A neatly trimmed goatee framed his thin, pale lips, lending his sharp features an air of studied authority. Though slender, his figure bore the unmistakable marks of privilege—a body unweathered by toil, shaped by a life steeped in indulgence and ease.

Even in the damp, oppressive confines of the dungeon, Ordric presented himself as if he were still seated in the halls of power. There was not a speck of dirt on his clean, fitted tunic, no sign of disarray in his groomed appearance. Every detail of his presentation seemed a deliberate declaration that the dungeon walls were no more than a temporary inconvenience, a stage he used to project an unbroken sense of command.

In his hands, a crude fork and knife moved methodically over a modest plate of bread and cheese. Somehow, he wielded the utensils with such practiced ease that they seemed almost transformed, elevated by the deliberate grace of his movements. The sunlight caught the faint lines of his face, accentuating the sharpness of his cheekbones and the deep-set wisdom—or cunning—in his dark eyes.

He looked up as she entered, his gaze sharp and unyielding, and the faintest smile curved his lips. It was a smile that held layers: arrogance, calculation, and just enough warmth to feign civility.

"Your Majesty," he said, his voice smooth and rich, each word weighted with a tone of mockery so subtle it could almost be missed. He inclined his head slightly, as though she were a guest in his private quarters rather than the ruler who had sentenced him to rot in the dungeons. "To what do I owe this rare honor? Surely, my modest accommodations have not piqued your curiosity."

His words lingered in the air, and Gwenora's expression hardened. She stepped forward, the rustle of her gown the only sound in the tense moment that followed. Even in this prison, he held himself with the arrogance of a man who believed he still had the upper hand, and the thought both infuriated and unsettled her.

Gwenora's expression remained cold as she stepped closer, her gaze sweeping over the pristine cell. "I see you've wasted no time making this dungeon your own," she remarked dryly, her tone laced with faint disdain.

Ordric inclined his head slightly, as if accepting a compliment. "One must adapt, Your Majesty. After all, a man can do little about his surroundings, but he can always maintain his dignity."

Her eyes narrowed, a flicker of disgust barely masked in her otherwise composed demeanor. "I doubt dignity was a factor in the choices that brought you here."

Ordric took another measured bite of his meal, chewing thoughtfully before responding. "Ah, but choices, like perceptions, are so often subjective, aren't they? Much like power. A throne can be a gilded cage just as easily as a cell can be an extension of one's influence."

Gwenora stepped closer, folding her hands in front of her as she studied him carefully. "Tell me, Lord Ordric, how far does your influence reach these days? Does it extend beyond these walls?"

He set his fork down, wiping his fingers on the edge of a clean cloth. His smile widened, his tone light but edged. "Why, Your Majesty, I wouldn't know. These walls are quite sturdy, as you intended. How could a humble prisoner like myself possibly know what transpires beyond them?"

She tilted her head slightly, her voice soft but firm. "You underestimate yourself, Ordric. Influence is like a seed—it grows in even the harshest conditions if nurtured properly. Surely you've heard whispers of the unrest beyond these walls."

Ordric chuckled softly, leaning back in his chair. "Oh, I've heard the guards' grumblings. The usual discontent, rumors of alliances, of power shifting hands. But I am just a man confined to these walls, cut off from the world. What could I possibly know of matters that trouble a queen?"

Gwenora's gaze didn't waver. "And yet you speak of shifting power as though you've been briefed on the latest developments."

He leaned forward slightly, resting his elbows on the table. "Power is a game, Your Majesty, and the rules don't change, no matter who plays it. The strong take from the weak; alliances rise and fall. If there's a storm brewing beyond these walls, I suspect you would be the first to feel its chill. Tell me, my queen... is there something I should know? Something that has you uneasy?"

Gwenora's jaw tightened at the subtle jab, but she didn't rise to it. "You are quick to deflect," she said coolly. "But it matters little. If you are so removed from current events, then you are of no use to me." The conversation seemed to produce little fruit and for a moment, Gwenora resented having even tried to coax anything meaningful out of the conversation.

Ordric smirked faintly, leaning back once more. "If I am of no use, then why are you here, my queen? Surely not to indulge a curiosity about my welfare."

She turned to leave, her voice cutting the air like a blade. "Perhaps I came to confirm your irrelevance."

As Gwenora turned to leave, her fingers tightening around the cold iron latch, Ordric's voice drifted after her—smooth, almost absentminded, yet with a practiced undertone of cunning.

"Your Majesty," he began, the faintest hint of mockery lacing his tone, "do you ever wonder why certain men fall... and yet others rise again?"

She froze, her back still to him, the words settling uncomfortably in the air. Slowly, she glanced over her shoulder, her expression calm but her sharp gaze narrowing. "Speak plainly, Ordric," she said, her tone cool and unyielding.

Ordric leaned back in his chair, his movements deliberate as he set the crude fork down on the plate with an almost regal precision. His fingers intertwined, resting lightly on the edge of the table, and his dark eyes glinted with something unreadable.

"Merely an observation," he said, his tone conversational, almost bored. "Some men—those with ambition—have a way of surviving... even when the world thinks them gone. A talent, really, wouldn't you agree?"

Her expression didn't shift, but the tension in the air thickened. "If this is your idea of wit, I suggest you choose a more useful way to waste my time."

He tilted his head, a faint smile ghosting his lips, calculated and maddeningly composed. "Of course, Your Grace. I wouldn't dream of wasting your valuable time." He leaned forward slightly, his voice lowering into a conspiratorial whisper. "But perhaps I've heard whispers—mere fragments—of a name you might recognize. An old acquaintance, one presumed buried in recent days. Sidonis, I believe it was. Or am I mistaken?"

The name fell with casual precision, yet its weight struck like a blade. Gwenora's face remained an impassive mask, but something shifted in her gaze—a glimmer of recognition she carefully concealed. Without dignifying his words with a response, she turned back to the door, her hand steady as she pushed it open and stepped into the dim corridor.

Behind her, Ordric's chuckle echoed softly, low and guttural, trailing her like the smoke of a dying fire.

As she ascended the damp stone steps, her disgust swirled beneath the icy knot tightening in her chest. Ordric's veiled revelation—delivered with such sinister amusement—confirmed her darkest fears. Sidonis was alive. The realization churned in her mind, relentless and unyielding. If he still drew breath, then Ceolfrid's machinations were no longer idle whispers. They were tangible, dangerous, and already in motion.

When Gwenora reached her chambers, the familiar warmth of the hearth did little to thaw the cold resolve hardening within her. Summoning a scribe with a single, clipped command, she seated herself at her desk. Her hand moved with deliberate purpose as the flickering candlelight illuminated her features, shadowing the fire of determination burning in her eyes.

Faermire had to be warned, as time was not her ally.

The early evening sunlight slanted through the windows of Gwenora's study, painting the room in hues of amber and gold. The faint crackle of the hearth filled the quiet space, its warmth doing little to ease the tension coiled in her chest. The air carried the faint scent of old parchment and ink, mingling with the subtle tang of smoke from the fire. She sat at her desk, her quill poised above the parchment.

The letter was almost complete, its ink glistening as it dried. Her elegant handwriting outlined the dire situation with deliberate precision, but as Gwenora reread her words, her lips tightened. The weight of her thoughts pressed down on her, a relentless reminder of the instability spreading through Mistelfeld like a rising tide. She hesitated, her quill hovering over the page, before adding one final line: *Faermire must not ignore this threat. Time is against us.*

A knock at the door broke her concentration. "Enter," she called, her voice even, though a flicker of relief crossed her features. She knew who it would be.

The door creaked open, and Qereth stepped inside, his broad frame illuminated briefly by the fading light. The contrast of his rugged build and youthful features caught her attention as it often did. Blonde hair fell loosely around his temples, framing striking blue eyes that gleamed with both determination and concern. His presence was unassuming yet purposeful, a mix of humility and the quiet confidence that came from a life spent in service to Faermire.

"My queen," he greeted, bowing his head briefly. His voice was steady, but she detected the faint undertone of urgency. "You sent for me?"

Gwenora nodded, folding the letter and sealing it with the wax stamp of Mistelfeld's crest. She pressed the seal firmly, letting the wax harden as she regarded Qereth. She extended it toward Qereth, her gaze fixed on his as he stepped forward to take it. His large hand closed over the letter with care, and for a moment, their eyes met.

"This must reach the king," she said, her voice low but firm. "It cannot fall into the wrong hands."

Qereth nodded, slipping the letter into the inner pocket of his tunic with practiced ease. "You have my word, Your Grace."

For a brief moment, Gwenora hesitated, letting her sharp gaze linger on Qereth. The silence between them deepened, filled only by the faint crackle of the hearth. Slowly, she straightened, her movements deliberate, and drew her cloak tighter around her shoulders as though bracing herself for what came next.

"Beowyn's uncle lives," she said, her voice low and grave. Qereth's breath caught, his blue eyes widening in shock. For a moment, he simply stared at her, the weight of her words crashing over him like a wave. "Sidonis?" he repeated, his voice barely above a whisper. "The same Sidonis who betrayed Ludica? The same man who—"

"Yes," Gwenora interrupted, her tone clipped but not unkind. And if my suspicions are correct, he is still working with Ceolfrid."

Qereth took a step back, his expression clouded with a mix of disbelief and anger. He ran a hand through his blonde hair, pacing briefly before turning back to face her. "How could this be?" he asked, his voice rising slightly. "Sidonis fell in battle. Beowyn said it himself—"

"Yet he lives," Gwenora said, her words cutting through his rising panic like a blade. "And I fear that his survival was not by chance. There are forces at work, forces that may have ensured he lived for a purpose—one that serves Ceolfrid's ambitions and threatens us all."

The weight of her revelation settled heavily in the room, each word a stone that Qereth silently turned over in his mind. His sharp blue eyes darkened as the implications unfurled. He lifted his gaze to Gwenora, whose steady composure only seemed to magnify the urgency of the task.

"His ambitions won't end with an alliance with Ceolfrid," Qereth said at last, his voice low but resolute. Gwenora inclined her head, her expression a mask of calm authority. "Precisely why the message cannot be delayed," she said, her tone clipped but laced with a hint of gratitude. "The sooner they know, the better prepared they'll be for whatever schemes he may have set in motion."

Qereth hesitated, the faint lines of worry creasing his brow. "And Mistelfeld, Your Majesty? With tensions rising here, I—" He paused, searching her expression. "I fear for your safety."

A faint smile touched Gwenora's lips, but it didn't reach her eyes. "You needn't concern yourself with me, Qereth. I've spent years fending off threats. Mistelfeld has endured, and so have I." Her gaze softened slightly, and for a moment, the steel in her voice gave way to something warmer. "But it's good to know I have people I can trust. That, too, is a rare gift."

Qereth nodded, the shadow of his worry lingering.

"Go, then," Gwenora said, her tone firm as she rose to her feet, the rich fabric of her gown smoothing under her hands. The sunlight filtering through the window painted her figure in warm hues, casting an almost regal glow. "We cannot delay."

Qereth bowed deeply, his blonde hair catching the last rays of light as they flickered across the room. "I'll leave at once, Your Majesty," he said, his voice underscored by unwavering loyalty. Without another word, he turned and strode toward the door, his steps sure and purposeful.

Their conversation lingered in the silence after Qereth's departure, leaving Gwenora alone with her thoughts in the dim quiet of her chambers. She returned to the desk, her hands resting on the edge of the map spread before her. The fire had burned low, its embers glowing faintly, casting flickering light across the room. Outside, the twilight deepened, painting the world in muted shades of blue and gray.

Her reflection in the window caught her eye—pale and tired, yet resolute. Mistelfeld felt more fragile than it had in years, its fractures evident in every corner of her kingdom. The nobles schemed in whispers, the common folk voiced their discontent, and threats from old enemies loomed ever closer, pressing in like the tightening grip of a noose.

For a moment, doubt stirred—a quiet voice at the edge of her mind, questioning whether she had the strength to hold her kingdom together. But Gwenora silenced it swiftly. She could not afford hesitation, not now. Mistelfeld's survival depended on action, and she had no choice but to act.

Her fingers traced the contours of the map, pausing over the borders of Faermire. Beowyn and Estrith were her last, tenuous hope. Their support might not guarantee victory, but it would be a foothold—a chance to resist the forces threatening to engulf her kingdom. And in these dark times, even the faintest glimmer of hope was a lifeline.

Straightening her shoulders, Gwenora breathed deeply, a quiet resolve hardening within her. She would fight for her kingdom, for its people. Even if the storm raged and the odds seemed insurmountable, she would stand her ground. Because if no one else could, she would bear the burden alone.

FIFTEEN

The iron gates of Elsterheim loomed ahead, their darkened bars wreathed in frost, a silent sentinel to the winter's chill. Qereth reined in his horse, its flanks heaving with exhaustion, steam rising from its nostrils and curling into the icy morning air. Though his body screamed for rest after the grueling journey, he pressed onward.

The guards stationed at the gate straightened at his approach, their hands instinctively tightening on their spears. Recognition flickered in their eyes, and one stepped forward, bowing briskly.

"My lord," the guard said, his tone both respectful and edged with curiosity.

"Open the gates," Qereth commanded, his voice firm. "I bear news from Mistelfeld."

The guard's face tightened, and with a sharp nod, he turned to bark orders to the others. The gates groaned in protest, the ancient iron creaking as it swung inward, granting him passage. Without hesitation, Qereth spurred his weary mount forward, its hooves striking the frost-laden cobblestones with sharp, deliberate echoes.

The city unfolded before him, its streets cloaked in the muted hues of winter. Merchants huddled near shuttered stalls, their faces pale and drawn, while tendrils of smoke rose languidly from scattered hearths. Qereth barely registered the signs of life around him as his eyes fixed on the palace rising in the distance. Its high stone walls jutted against the pale sky, an unyielding bastion in the heart of the kingdom.

He urged his horse forward, the guards stationed there recognizing him instantly and stepping aside without hesitation. His position in Faermire afforded him swift passage, and he acknowledged them with a brief nod.

As the courtyard opened before him, Qereth pulled sharply on the reins, his horse skidding to a halt, breath billowing in white clouds as it shifted beneath him. He dismounted with practiced efficiency, his boots striking the ground with purposeful force. A stable hand rushed forward, and without a word, Qereth handed over the reins.

Then he saw her.

Estrith stood atop the palace walls, her bronze hair gleaming as it caught the pale light of the sun. A fur-lined cloak draped over her shoulders, its edges stirring in the crisp breeze, while her figure remained motionless against the stark backdrop of the winter sky. She gazed out over the city, her posture rigid, but as her eyes landed on him, they widened in surprise.

For a fleeting moment, the exhaustion that had gripped Qereth's every muscle seemed to fade. The sight of her—her steady presence, the faint glimmer of recognition softening her features—ignited a flicker of warmth amidst the cold.

"Qereth!" she called down, her voice carrying with a mix of elation and disbelief. Without hesitation, she turned and disappeared from the parapet, the sound of her hurried footsteps echoing down the stone stairs.

Qereth barely had time to collect himself before she emerged from the palace entrance. She stopped short, her green eyes searching his face, a mixture of joy and worry playing across her features.

"Qereth," she said again, her voice softer now, as though confirming it was really him. She reached out, gripping his arms tightly. "You're here. I wasn't expecting you."

He clasped her hands briefly, his touch firm but fleeting. "Estrith," he said, his voice low and urgent. "Where is Beowyn? I need to speak with him immediately."

Estrith hesitated, her brow furrowing. "He's not here," she admitted cautiously. "He left this morning—he's gone to duel Elwin on Coventhan Ridge."

The words struck Qereth like a blow. He stiffened, his breath catching. "Coventhan Ridge?" he repeated, his tone sharp with disbelief. Turning away, he ran a hand through his disheveled blonde hair, muttering a curse under his breath.

"Qereth, what is it?" Estrith pressed, stepping closer. "What's wrong?"

He spun back to face her, his expression grim. "Your uncle, Estrith," he said, each word heavy with urgency. "Sidonis lives."

Her expression shifted from confusion to shock, her lips parting as though to refute him. "No," she whispered, shaking her head. "That's impossible. Beowyn, he—he said—"

Qereth shook his head, his frustration barely restrained. "Gwenora sent word. She believes he's alive and working with Ceolfrid. If he's planning an attack, it will be soon—perhaps even now. And with Beowyn riding straight into a duel with Elwin..." He trailed off, his jaw tightening as the weight of the situation settled between them.

Estrith's hand flew to her mouth, her hazel eyes wide with fear. "What are we to do?"

"Prepare the city," Qereth said firmly, gripping her shoulders. "If Sidonis strikes, Faermire will be his first target. Evacuate the people if necessary—get them to safety."

Her eyes searched his face, wide with worry but resolute. She nodded slowly, stepping back. "Go," she said, her voice steady despite the tremor in her hands. "Find him."

He paused, glancing back at her with a faint smile that carried the weight of reassurance, though it never quite reached his eyes. "I'll come back for you," he said, his voice quieter now, edged with a softness that did little to mask the resolve beneath. For a moment, the unspoken gravity of his promise hung between them before he turned away.

With practiced ease, he swung himself onto his horse, the leather saddle creaking under his weight. The animal shifted beneath him, sensing his urgency, and with a swift kick, Qereth spurred it into motion. The sharp ring of hooves on stone filled the courtyard as he galloped toward the gates, the winter wind cutting through the air with biting ferocity.

The path to Coventhan Ridge was unforgiving, a serpentine road that twisted through icy terrain and jagged outcroppings. Frost-laden branches overhung the narrow track, their skeletal forms clawing at the sky like sentinels of the cold. The ground beneath his horse's hooves was slick and treacherous, threatening to give way with every stride, but Qereth urged the beast onward, his cloak snapping violently behind him in the wind's relentless grip.

The howling gale roared in his ears, drowning out all but the pounding of hooves against the frozen earth—a relentless rhythm that matched the quickening pace of his thoughts. The growing dread in his chest swelled with each passing mile, the fear of Beowyn walking blindly into an ambush gnawing at his resolve. He leaned forward in the saddle, his breath clouding in the icy air as determination burned fiercely in his veins.

The ridge loomed somewhere ahead, shrouded in the haze of winter's chill, and Qereth's grip on the reins tightened. There would be no faltering, no slowing—not while the weight of Gwenora's warning and the lives of his people spurred him forward.

The icy wind screamed across the ridge, tearing through Beowyn's cloak and biting into his skin with a cold ferocity. His fingers tightened around the hilt of his sword, the leather-wrapped grip stiff from the cold. Snow crunched beneath his boots as he stepped forward, each movement deliberate, measured, despite the storm of tension building inside him. His breath spilled in pale clouds into the frozen air, mingling with the sharp tang of metal and frost.

Ahead, Elwin waited, a dark silhouette against the stark, unbroken white of the ridge. The faint glint of steel in his hand mirrored the gleam of his cold, calculating eyes. His heavy fur-lined coat billowed in the gusts, the faint clink of armor beneath it betraying the predator's readiness. The ridge sloped steadily on either side, setting a stage for the world to watch.

Behind them, two armies faced each other in a frigid, unyielding standoff. The colors of Faermire—deep blue and silver—snapped sharply in the wind, defiant against the burnt orange and black banners of Valenmur. The soldiers stood motionless, shields braced and spears steady, their breath a quiet rhythm in the stillness. The ridge became a frozen theater, the outcome of this duel a judgment that would ripple across nations.

Beowyn's eyes locked onto Elwin, studying every detail of the man before him. The older king held his sword with a deceptive ease, his stance relaxed but poised. Elwin's reputation for cruelty and cunning preceded him, and Beowyn knew the older king had little interest in honor or fairness.

Behind Elwin, his sons stood in a tight cluster, their postures tense, their expressions dark with barely concealed frustration. They looked as if they itched to stand where their father stood, to carry his sword, to spill Beowyn's blood themselves.

Elwin's lips curled into a sneer, his voice cutting through the wind with ease. "This is it, boy. I expected more steel in your spine. At least some fire—like your father had."

The insult landed like a spark on dry tinder, but Beowyn kept his face impassive, the anger simmering beneath the surface held tightly in check. He lifted his sword, the weight of the blade familiar, grounding. "Just pick up your sword," he replied, his voice calm, though the edge of warning in his tone cut through the wind.

Elwin's smirk deepened, his teeth flashing like a wolf's in the pale light. He shifted his stance, the sword rising in his grasp as if to test the air. "That's a good start," he said, his voice dripping with condescension.

The two men squared off, their gazes locked in a clash of wills as fierce as the battle their blades were about to wage. The ridge seemed to hold its breath, the howl of the wind falling into the background as the world narrowed to the space between them.

The duel began with a clash of steel, the sound sharp and piercing as it echoed across the desolate ridge. Elwin moved with startling speed for his size, each swing of his blade heavy and deliberate, designed to overpower and crush. Beowyn countered with precision, his movements quick and controlled, sidestepping the older king's sweeping strikes with an almost instinctive grace. The snow beneath their boots sprayed with every step, creating a chaotic dance of slashed patterns in the pristine white.

Beowyn feinted left, his blade darting toward Elwin's exposed side, but the older man was ready. With a sharp twist, he parried the strike, the force of the clash nearly unbalancing Beowyn. Elwin grinned, a wolfish gleam in his eyes, and surged forward with a brutal overhead swing. Beowyn raised his sword just in time, the impact reverberating down his arm and sending a jolt of pain through his shoulder.

"You've got fight in you," Elwin said, his voice strained as their swords locked, steel grinding against steel. "But not enough to walk away."

Beowyn pushed back with a grunt, breaking the lock and forcing Elwin to retreat a step. He circled cautiously, his eyes never leaving his opponent. The snow at their feet was streaked with thin lines of blood from near-misses, a grim reminder of how close each man had come to landing a fatal blow. His breaths came sharp and ragged, the cold biting at his lungs, but he steadied himself, refusing to falter.

Elwin lunged again, this time feinting high before slashing low. Beowyn dodged, but not fast enough; the blade nicked the edge of his boot, throwing him off balance. He stumbled, and Elwin seized the opening with a vicious kick to Beowyn's chest.

The impact sent him sprawling backward, the air ripped from his lungs as he hit the frozen ground. Snow closed in around him, cold and suffocating, as he struggled to regain his breath.

"Yield, boy," Elwin growled, towering over him with his blade raised to deliver the killing blow. "Or die like your father."

Beowyn's vision blurred, his chest heaving as he gasped for air. His hand groped desperately for his sword, which lay just out of reach. His heart thundered in his ears as Elwin's blade descended.

In a desperate move, Beowyn rolled to the side, the blade striking snow where he had been moments before. Seizing his sword, he swung upward with a wild, instinctive strike, the edge biting into Elwin's side.

Elwin staggered back, clutching at the fresh wound. Blood seeped through his fingers, staining the snow beneath him. A snarl twisted his features, but he muted any sound of pain.

Beyond him, Beowyn caught a flicker of movement—Elwin's eldest son, Alfric, gripping the hilt of his blade, his face taut with fury. He nearly surged forward, only to be held back by his brother Ealric, whose hand rested firmly on his arm.

Beowyn pressed his advantage, rising to his feet and charging forward. Their swords clashed again, the sound sharp and grating. Elwin struck out with renewed ferocity, his blade finding Beowyn's arm in a shallow but painful cut. Beowyn hissed through his teeth, retreating a step as Elwin's grin widened, the glint of satisfaction in his eyes unmistakable.

The duel grew more savage, Elwin's blows heavier, each one a calculated attempt to drive Beowyn to his knees. Beowyn countered with all the speed and precision he could muster, but the older king's strength began to press him back. A heavy strike knocked Beowyn off balance, forcing him to stumble. He barely caught himself before Elwin advanced again, his sword raised high.

And then it happened.

A single flaming arrow struck the ground between them, its fiery light casting flickering shadows across the snow. Both men froze, their gazes snapping to the arrow lodged in the ground.

A moment later, the sky was alight.

A volley of flaming arrows arced overhead, their fiery trails cutting through the cold, gray air. They rained down on the ridge, hissing as they struck snow and embedding themselves in wooden shields and the frozen earth. The ridge erupted into chaos, soldiers from both armies shouting in confusion and scrambling to defend themselves.

Beowyn rolled to the side, his guard rushing to shield him from the onslaught. Elwin cursed loudly, his eyes darting toward the source of the attack. Beowyn scrambled to his feet, his breath catching as his gaze followed Elwin's.

Beyond the ridge, past the line of opposing armies, a dark mass emerged from the forest. At first, it was shapeless, a shadow against the trees. But as it drew closer, the distinct shapes of men and weapons became clear.

An army.

Beowyn's heart thundered in his chest as he strained to make out the advancing banners. The figures remained blurred, shrouded by the smoke of flaming arrows and the hazy winter air. Confusion rippled through the ranks of both Faermire and Valenmur, soldiers breaking formation to turn toward the oncoming threat, their weapons raised in defensive instinct.

"What is this treachery?" Elwin's voice cut through the clamor, sharp with accusation. His eyes burned into Beowyn, his grip tightening on his sword. "A coward's ploy!"

Beowyn whirled to face him, his voice ringing clear above the chaos. "Look to yourself, Elwin! If there's treachery here, it's not mine!"

For a moment, Elwin faltered, his confusion as raw as Beowyn's. The third army continued its steady march forward, the shapes of their warriors growing sharper with every passing second. The indistinct banners swayed in the wind, their designs obscured, but the numbers were undeniable—a force large enough to shift the tide of any battle.

The tension snapped as Elwin thrust his sword toward Beowyn and his army. "Attack!" he bellowed, spurring his soldiers into action.

Beowyn didn't hesitate, his own voice cutting through the growing chaos. "Stand your ground!"

The two sides surged forward, colliding with a brutal ferocity. The clash of steel against steel echoed across the ridge, mingling with the cries of battle and the howl of the wind. The pristine snow churned beneath their feet, stained with blood and trampled into mud as the armies of Faermire and Valenmur met in a storm of violence.

In the midst of the turmoil, Beowyn struggled to maintain his focus, the weight of the battle pressing in on all sides. He parried blow after blow, each strike sapping his strength as he fought to push forward. For a fleeting moment, he found a brief reprieve to catch his breath, but his gaze was inexorably drawn to the line of advancing soldiers on the horizon.

And then, he saw him.

A figure astride a black horse emerged from the ranks of the third army. His cloak billowed in the icy wind, and the air around him seemed to shift as if the world itself bent to his presence. Beowyn blinked, his breath catching in his throat. It couldn't be.

Yet as the figure drew nearer, his features became unmistakable.

Sidonis.

The name seared through Beowyn's mind like a brand. His uncle. The traitor. The man he thought slain on the battlefield now rode at the head of an army, alive and commanding the bedlam around him.

Time seemed to slow as Beowyn locked eyes with Sidonis, his mind struggling to reconcile the impossibility of what he was seeing. The cold grip of shock rooted him in place, his chest tightening with a mix of disbelief and fury. Sidonis's gaze bore into him, unyielding and cold, his expression betraying nothing but resolve.

The ridge erupted into greater disarray as the third army descended upon the battlefield. Both Faermire and Valenmur turned against one another, shouts of betrayal rising from their ranks as confusion gave way to violence. Swords clashed and arrows flew, and the snow-covered ground transformed into a scene of utter carnage.

Beowyn shook himself free of his stupor, his instincts roaring to life. He surged forward, his sword raised, his focus narrowing to a single, burning goal—to reach Sidonis, to confront the man who had torn his family apart. He fought with reckless determination, cutting through the pandemonium, but no matter how hard he pushed, his uncle seemed to remain just out of reach.

The battlefield was a storm of noise and movement, the cries of the wounded and the clash of weapons filling the air. Beowyn's breath came in short, ragged bursts, his muscles screaming in protest as he pressed on. For a moment, he lost sight of Sidonis amidst the upheaval, but then their eyes met once more.

Sidonis was watching him.

The older man's expression remained unreadable, his presence almost otherworldly as he stood amidst the bloodshed, unmoving, like a ghost risen from Beowyn's darkest memories. The sight sent a shiver down Beowyn's spine, a flood of anger and grief threatening to overwhelm him.

"Beowyn!"

The sound of his name cut through the mayhem. He turned sharply to see Qereth, his hair disheveled and his face streaked with sweat and grime, standing just behind him. Qereth's sword flashed as he deflected an incoming blow, his voice filled with urgency.

"We have to move!" Qereth shouted, his eyes locking with Beowyn's. "We cannot stay here!"

"No!" Beowyn's voice tore from his throat, raw and defiant, as he yanked his arm free from Qereth's grasp. His chest heaved with exhaustion, but the fire in his eyes burned undiminished.

"There's no time!" Qereth snapped, his blue eyes fierce with urgency. "Our forces are crumbling. We need to regroup now. Follow me!"

Beowyn faltered, his gaze locking onto the distant figure of Sidonis. His uncle remained a haunting silhouette amidst the carnage, an ever-present specter in the chaos. The urge to charge forward, to confront him, gripped Beowyn like a vice. But then his focus shifted—to the encroaching Valenmur soldiers, their armor gleaming like predators closing in for the kill. Among them, Alfric and Ealric moved with fierce determination, their faces set with a singular goal: to finish what their father had started.

Beowyn's jaw clenched as he tore his gaze from the battlefield, taking in the brutal reality around him. The ground was littered with the bodies of Faermire and Valenmur alike, blood staining the snow in crimson streaks. The clash of steel and anguished cries filled the air, a cacophony of desperation. Men fought like cornered animals, driven by little more than survival, and the lines between friend and foe blurred in the melee. Beowyn felt the weight of Qereth's words sinking in—the battle was lost.

He gave a terse nod, his grip tightening on his sword as he fell in beside Qereth. The remnants of his guard surged around them, their swords flashing as they cut a desperate path through the melee. Beowyn fought with grim resolve, his every swing driven by the need to protect those who still stood at his side. Yet the chaos pressed in relentlessly, and with each step, the carnage seemed endless.

At last, an opening appeared—a narrow corridor through the chaos—and Qereth seized the opportunity. "This way!" he shouted, his voice slicing through the din as he waved the group forward. Beowyn's guards rallied, closing ranks as they formed a shield around their king, their movements disciplined despite the relentless assault.

"There!" Qereth pointed toward the dark line of trees on the horizon, the shadowy expanse of Donnorath Wood looming like a foreboding refuge. The forest offered the cover they needed, but its haunting presence carried the weight of past horrors—memories that Beowyn and Qereth shared all too well.

Beowyn's gaze flicked to Qereth, his expression a mix of hesitation and objection. The woods were no place of safety; they knew that better than anyone. But the open terrain offered even less hope, with Valenmur's soldiers closing in fast.

Qereth met his gaze, understanding the unspoken protest. "We can't risk the open terrain!" he said firmly, his voice edged with a quiet resolve. "The forest is our only chance."

Before Beowyn could respond, one of his officers stepped forward, blood streaking his face but determination burning in his eyes. "Go, my lord!" the man bellowed. "We'll hold them here!"

Beowyn hesitated, the weight of the decision pressing down on him like a leaden chain. The officer gave a final nod, resolute. "You are the king. Faermire needs you alive."

Beowyn's shoulders stiffened, his gaze lingering on the men who stood ready to sacrifice themselves for him. Then, with a sharp exhale, he relented. "Let's go," he said, his voice low but steady as he turned to Qereth.

Without another word, Qereth led the way, and Beowyn followed, his grip on his sword unyielding as they made their way toward the shadowy edge of Donnorath Wood. The cries of battle faded behind them, replaced by the eerie silence of the forest waiting ahead.

Beowyn hesitated at the edge of the forest, his boots sinking into the brittle snow that clung to the undergrowth. The shadows of Donnorath Wood stretched out before him, dark and foreboding, their skeletal branches clawing at the pale sky. Each step forward felt like a betrayal of the men he left behind on the ridge. Their shouts and cries still echoed faintly in the distance, mingling with the distant clash of steel—a haunting symphony of sacrifice.

His chest tightened as he glanced over his shoulder. The ridge was now a blur of chaos and bloodshed, his men holding the line with a desperate resolve that made his retreat feel like cowardice. Beowyn's grip on his sword tightened until his knuckles whitened. He wanted to turn back, to charge once more into the fray, but Qereth's voice cut through his doubt.

"They're buying us time," Qereth said, his tone heavy with understanding but unyielding. "Don't waste their sacrifice."

SIXTEEN

DONNORATH WOOD

The trees of Donnorath Wood stretched upward like skeletal fingers, their gnarled branches clawing at a pale, indifferent sky. The deeper Beowyn and Qereth ventured, the more the forest seemed to tighten its grip, the world shrinking into a labyrinth. Snow muffled their footsteps, the faint crunch beneath their boots was the only sound in the oppressive stillness. Even the air was heavier here, thick with the cloying scent of damp earth and the bitter tang of decaying leaves. Around them, the shadows seemed alive, shifting and pulsing as if they watched with a malevolent awareness.

"We need to keep moving," Qereth muttered, his voice barely louder than a whisper. Even that felt too loud, as though the forest might hear and punish their intrusion.

Beowyn cast a glance at his companion but remained silent, his jaw set in grim determination. He didn't need to reply—Qereth was right, and they both knew it. Every instinct screamed for him to turn back, to flee this cursed place, but retreat was not an option. Somewhere behind them, the soldiers of Valenmur pursued with relentless precision, driving the two men further into the wood's suffocating depths.

The ground underfoot became treacherous, the snow concealing tangled roots and uneven terrain. Beowyn stumbled for the third time, his knee slamming into the frozen earth as he barely managed to catch himself against the rough bark of a tree. The cold bit through his gloves, and he hissed in frustration. Beside him, Qereth was no better. His breathing came in ragged bursts, each exhale forming faint clouds in the icy air.

Beowyn scanned the trees ahead, but the view was the same in every direction—an endless tangle of skeletal trunks and shifting shadows. His heart sank as his gaze fell on a fallen tree lying just ahead. Its jagged branches were unmistakable. They had passed it before, not ten minutes ago.

"We're doubling back," Qereth said, his voice tight with unease. "The forest is playing tricks on us."

Beowyn's hands tightened into fists at his sides, frustration bubbling dangerously close to the surface. He exhaled sharply, forcing the tension from his body as he stared into the endless dark. The forest was a maze, its paths looping back on themselves as though it bent reality to its will. Every step forward felt like sinking deeper into a trap they couldn't escape.

"Stay close," Beowyn said at last, his voice hard with resolve. He knelt and grabbed a sturdy stick from the ground. "A torch."

Qereth struck flint against steel, the faint spark catching on the stick's dry bark. Flames flickered to life, casting a weak circle of light around them. It was a meager defense against the encroaching darkness, but it was better than nothing.

The torchlight revealed the dense network of trees around them, their bark slick with frost and damp patches of moss. The air seemed colder now, the stillness more oppressive. Beowyn gripped the hilt of his sword, the familiar weight grounding him. The blade gleamed faintly in the flickering firelight, a small comfort in a place that seemed determined to rob them of hope.

"Let's keep moving," Beowyn said, his tone steady despite the unease in his eyes.

Qereth nodded, and the two pressed on, their steps cautious as the forest pressed in closer. The torchlight danced against the trees, casting long shadows that twisted unnaturally, as though mocking their feeble attempt at illumination. The scent of damp earth grew stronger, almost suffocating, and the faint rustle of unseen movement echoed just beyond the edge of their light.

The path ahead was a void, an unbroken stretch of darkness that seemed to stretch into eternity. Beowyn forced himself to focus on each step, each breath, refusing to let the growing sense of dread take hold. Yet with every passing moment, the forest seemed to push back harder, its presence heavy and suffocating.

It felt alive.

And it was calling for him.

Then the wind came.

It began as a low murmur, rising quickly into a howling gale that screamed through the skeletal trees. The gust ripped through them, extinguishing the fragile flame of Beowyn's torch with a sharp hiss. In an instant, the forest plunged into absolute darkness, a void so complete it felt tangible.

"Damn," Beowyn hissed, his voice taut with frustration as he fumbled for the flint. His hands trembled against the biting cold, the steel striking uselessly against the rock. Sparks danced and fizzled, but the flame refused to take hold. The damp air seemed to swallow the sparks whole, as if the forest itself had rejected their light.

Beside him, Qereth's breathing quickened, each ragged inhale far too loud in the suffocating stillness. The darkness pressed in, a weight that seemed to creep into their lungs and minds alike.

"Hurry," Qereth urged, his whisper carrying the fear of something worse than the cold.

Beowyn struck the flint again, harder this time, his teeth clenched. Still, the flame refused to come. "It's no use," he muttered, shoving the useless torch back into his belt. His tone was steadier than he felt, his own unease curling around his chest like a vice.

"Forget it," he added, though he didn't dare admit how much he hated the thought of moving forward blind.

They pressed on, each step an act of trust in touch and instinct. The cold seemed sharper in the dark, cutting through their cloaks as if it sought to strip them bare. The world around them transformed, becoming an endless sea of shadow and silence where nothing felt solid. Beowyn kept one hand on the hilt of his sword, the familiar weight his only anchor in this twisting void.

Then the sounds began.

At first, it was barely a whisper—a faint rustle, a murmur on the edge of perception. But soon it grew louder, more distinct: faint laughter, distant and haunting, followed by soft, almost musical whispers. They seemed to come from nowhere and everywhere at once, threading through the trees like phantoms. Beowyn's breath caught, a chill racing down his spine as the sound seemed to shift, teasingly close.

"Do you hear that?" Qereth whispered, his voice taut with fear.

Beowyn nodded stiffly, his eyes straining to pierce the oppressive dark. "I hear it," he replied, gripping his sword so tightly his knuckles ached.

The sounds grew bolder. The whispers gained words, the laughter an edge of cruelty. Beowyn's blood turned to ice as he realized the voices weren't disembodied. They were human. Mocking tones floated through the trees, distorted by the wind but unmistakable in their intent—taunting, cruel, and far too close.

"It's them," Qereth said, his hand gripping Beowyn's arm. "Elwin's sons."

Beowyn's pulse thundered in his ears, his heart hammering against his ribs. He turned his head, scanning the void for any sign of movement. The voices warped in the air, bouncing from tree to tree, making it impossible to tell where Alfric and Ealric might be—or how near.

"They're hunting us," Beowyn murmured, his voice low, edged with barely contained fury.

Qereth tightened his grip. "Then we move. Now."

They pressed forward, their steps quick and careful. The forest seemed to conspire against them, its uneven ground hidden beneath layers of frost and shadow. Beowyn's boots caught on roots he couldn't see, and his breath came in shallow bursts as he fought to steady himself. Beside him, Qereth stumbled, catching himself on a low-hanging branch. His breathing had grown heavier, each rasping exhale betraying the toll the forest's oppressive weight was taking.

The voices followed, closer now, their sharp laughter cutting through the dark like blades. Beowyn's stomach twisted as he fought the urge to whirl around, to charge at shadows and silence. Instead, he pushed forward, leading Qereth deeper into the abyss of the wood, their path uncertain and their hope dimming with every step.

Qereth stumbled again, his boots catching on an unseen root. He cursed under his breath, the sound swallowed by the oppressive stillness of the forest. Beowyn moved quickly to his side, gripping his arm to steady him.

"Leave me," Qereth rasped, his voice a harsh whisper that cut through the air like a blade. "You'll move faster without me."

"No," Beowyn snapped, his tone sharper than he intended, his own fear twisting into defiance. "We're getting out of here together."

Qereth shook his head, his expression hard and resolute, even as his breathing came in ragged gasps. "If they catch us both, it's over," he said, his voice steady despite the exhaustion that etched deep lines into his face.

Beowyn opened his mouth to argue, to refuse, but the sound of voices in the distance froze the words on his tongue. The brothers' mocking taunts sliced through the trees, each word a cruel reminder of their relentless pursuit.

Qereth's hand clamped down on Beowyn's shoulder, his grip firm despite his trembling fingers. "There's no time," he said, his eyes searching Beowyn's with a quiet intensity. "I'll draw them off. You have to go."

Beowyn hesitated, his chest tightening as his gaze locked on his friend. "I can't just leave you."

"You can, and you must," Qereth said firmly, cutting him off with a tone that brooked no argument.

Beowyn's breath caught in his throat, his heart twisting painfully as Qereth stepped back. Before he could form another protest, Qereth turned and disappeared into the shadows, moving deliberately, his boots crunching loudly through the snow. The sharp crack of branches echoed in his wake, a calculated noise to lure their pursuers away.

"Qereth!" Beowyn called after him, his voice raw with desperation, but his friend didn't stop. He didn't even look back.

The forest swallowed Qereth whole, the dark shapes of its trees closing around him like a living thing. Beowyn stood rooted to the spot, his sword feeling impossibly heavy in his hand as the sounds of pursuit shifted, veering away in the direction of Qereth's retreat.

For a moment, Beowyn could only stare into the void where his friend had vanished, the weight of his sacrifice pressing down on him like a physical force. The distant sound of laughter and snapping branches pulled him back to the present, and with a heavy breath, he forced himself to move.

Each step into the deeper darkness felt like a betrayal, his boots crunching softly on the snow as he pushed forward. The silence around him was deafening now, broken only by his own breath and the pounding of his heart.

Shadows writhed in the corners of Beowyn's vision, their shifting shapes like whispers of unseen things lurking just beyond the veil of perception. He shook his head, trying to focus, but the image of Qereth disappearing into the trees clung to his thoughts like a curse. The echo of his friend's voice urging him to go, to survive, seemed as much a part of the forest as the creaking branches overhead.

He halted, straining his ears against the oppressive silence. His breath hung in the air, visible and shallow, as he listened for any sign of Qereth—

snapping branches, hurried footsteps, anything. The forest answered with cruel deceit, the faintest rustling of movement seeming to emanate from everywhere and nowhere at once. Each sound pulled him deeper into the labyrinth, every step twisting his sense of direction until he no longer knew if he was following Qereth's trail or circling endlessly on his own.

His fingers tightened around the hilt of his sword, the leather-wrapped grip grounding him against the rising tide of disorientation. Focus, he commanded himself. Keep moving. Survive. But guilt gnawed at his resolve, a relentless ache that only grew sharper with each passing moment.

And then the voices returned, threading through the trees like a venomous chant.

"Run, little king," one of the brothers jeered, his voice slick with mockery, carried unnaturally by the cold wind. "We're coming for you."

Laughter followed—a sharp, biting sound that sent an involuntary shudder through Beowyn's frame. It felt closer this time, far too close. His chest tightened as adrenaline surged through him, spurring him forward. He weaved through the skeletal trees, their gnarled branches clawing at him like skeletal hands.

His breath came quick and shallow, clouding the air as he pressed on, the ground crunching loudly beneath his boots.

Then, through the oppressive silence and the taunting voices, another sound reached his ears—a faint whimper.

Beowyn froze mid-step, his pulse pounding. He strained to discern the source, at first believing it to be another of the forest's cruel tricks, another phantom sound designed to unnerve him. But the noise came again, soft and plaintive, undeniably real. His brow furrowed as he turned toward it, his movements deliberate, his boots making slow, muffled crunches in the snow.

What he saw brought him to a halt.

Huddled at the base of a gnarled tree, a girl no older than ten struggled against the grip of a rusted snare. The trap's jagged teeth bit cruelly into her leg, blood staining the snow beneath her. Her form was small, almost impossibly delicate, her long white hair spilling over her shoulders in silken waves that caught the pale light like strands of moonlight itself. Her skin bore an ethereal grayish hue, so faint it seemed she might fade into the shadows if not for her wide, tear-filled eyes.

Those eyes—silver and luminous, reflecting a world beyond human understanding—locked onto Beowyn, pleading silently for help. They shimmered with a mix of fear and fragile hope, anchoring him where he stood.

An elf.

Beowyn's breath caught as the realization struck. The tales of his youth—of rare, otherworldly beings, hauntingly beautiful and elusive—paled in comparison to the reality before him. For a moment, all thought of his own survival slipped away, replaced by a stunned awe that left him rooted to the spot.

The girl tugged at the trap, her movements frantic but futile. Her lips moved, forming silent words, while her gaze flickered between him and the encroaching darkness. She looked ready to cry out, but no sound escaped her trembling form.

Beowyn's instincts screamed at him to move, to turn away and keep running. The brothers were near—he could hear their voices threading ever closer, their taunts taking on a sharper edge. He had no time to waste.

And yet, he didn't move.

Her frightened eyes held him in place, the raw desperation in them pulling at something deep within him. For all her otherworldly beauty, she looked so small, so helpless.

A sudden snap of a branch somewhere behind him broke his trance. The voices of Alfric and Ealric cut through the forest again, sharp and cruel, their pursuit relentless. Time was running out.

Beowyn's heart raced, the weight of the moment pressing down on him. He tightened his grip on his sword, his mind warring with itself. You don't have time for this. Leave her. Save yourself.

But his feet refused to move away.

The crunch of snow shattered Beowyn's fleeting hesitation, dragging him back to the present. A voice rang out, sharp and taunting, slicing through the cold like a blade.

"He's close. I can smell the coward," Alfric sneered, his words laced with dark satisfaction.

Beowyn's jaw tightened, his teeth grinding as he wrestled with the choice before him—survival or conscience. His eyes met the girl's once more, her silvery gaze trembling with a fragile hope that seemed to pierce straight through him.

"Damn it," he muttered under his breath, the decision made before his mind could argue otherwise.

He dropped to one knee beside her, the icy ground biting through his cloak. "Stay still," he whispered, his voice rough but steady. His fingers went to work, prying at the rusted metal teeth of the snare. The ancient trap groaned in protest, its metallic wail unnaturally loud against the suffocating stillness of the forest.

The girl winced, her delicate features contorted in pain as the snare bit deeper into her pale skin. Her lips trembled, but she held back a cry, her small body rigid with fear. Beowyn's hands moved faster, each tug and twist fueled by desperation.

The trap resisted stubbornly, each groan of its rusted joints slicing through the suffocating silence like a warning bell. Waves of dread rolled over Beowyn with every creak, the sound too loud, too damning.

The crunch of approaching boots grew louder, deliberate and menacing. Beowyn's heart thundered as the brothers' voices cut through the icy air.

"Wait," Ealric said, his tone sharp and tense. "I hear something."

"He's here," Alfric growled, his voice low and brimming with malice.

Beowyn's heart hammered as sweat beaded on his brow despite the freezing air. "Come on," he hissed, his voice a desperate whisper. His fingers ached against the cold metal, but he didn't stop. The girl's wide eyes darted toward the shadows, her breaths shallow and fast.

With a final, deafening snap, the snare gave way, its grip on the girl's leg released. Beowyn grabbed her arm to steady her, his voice urgent and low. "Go. Run."

But she didn't move. She flinched at his touch, her ethereal gaze darting back toward the trees. The voices were so close now, their cruel intent unmistakable. For a moment, she looked poised to flee, her small frame trembling, but then her gaze snapped back to his.

Her hands rose, delicate and trembling, and she grasped his arm tightly. Her touch was impossibly light, yet the command in her eyes was unyielding.

"Quiet," she whispered, her voice like the faintest breath of wind rustling through leaves.

Before Beowyn could respond, the air around them shifted. A tingling sensation coursed over his skin, a strange, electric warmth that made his breath hitch. The world around him blurred, the shadows deepening and twisting, as if the forest itself bent to her will. His surroundings dimmed, the familiar shapes of trees and snow refracting into something intangible.

"What—?" Beowyn began, but the girl pulled him closer, her fingers tightening on his sleeve. Her head tilted toward the approaching voices, her expression filled with quiet urgency.

The sound of Alfric and Ealric's footsteps grew louder, breaking through the eerie silence. Beowyn's pulse roared in his ears as the brothers' figures emerged from the darkness, their swords gleaming faintly in the fractured light. They were so close he could see the steam of their breath mingling with the forest's cold mist.

Alfric's sharp gaze swept the shadows, his frustration evident in every tense line of his posture. "Damn this cursed forest," he muttered, his voice low and dangerous. "He couldn't have gotten far."

Ealric slowed, his steps hesitant as his eyes darted to the twisting shadows that seemed to close in around them. The jagged branches overhead swayed cautiously, casting fleeting shapes across the snow. His expression was taut with unease, and his voice came low and unsteady. "This place... it feels wrong," he murmured, the words barely carrying over the icy wind. "We should turn back."

Alfric's jaw tightened, a snarl escaping his lips as his frustration flared. But even he couldn't fully mask the tension etched in his face. His piercing gaze swept the trees one last time, as though daring the forest to reveal its secrets. Finally, he growled, the sound low and bitter. "Fine," he spat, his voice dripping with reluctance. "But if he's here, he won't last long."

For a moment, they lingered, their heavy presence pressing against the stillness. Beowyn held his breath, his pulse pounding as their silhouettes loomed dangerously close, the air thick with the threat of discovery.

Then, with a sharp pivot, Alfric turned. Their footsteps crunched against the snow, the sound fading slowly into the depths of the woods. The shifting darkness swallowed them whole, their retreat leaving an eerie stillness in their wake.

Beowyn didn't dare move, his breath caught in his throat. He stared at the girl in disbelief, her pale features calm despite the faint tremble in her hands. Slowly, the tingling warmth around them faded, the forest settling back into its unnatural quiet.

"What did you—" he began, but her silver eyes silenced him, their soft glow reflecting both fear and something deeper—an unspoken bond that had formed in those tense moments. She let go of his arm and stepped back, her gaze fixed on the spot where the brothers had vanished.

Beowyn turned to the girl, his voice barely above a whisper, trembling with awe. "How...?"

She didn't answer. Her luminous, silvery eyes studied him with a mixture of curiosity and lingering fear. For a moment, the world seemed to hold its breath as Beowyn stared back, transfixed by her ethereal presence. Her grayish skin shimmered faintly in the dim light, her features impossibly delicate yet hauntingly fierce.

Before he could form another word, the shadows stirred, and a new figure emerged from the trees. A taller elf woman stepped into view, her movements impossibly fluid yet laced with urgency. Her silver hair was swept back in a tight braid, and her sharp, angular features carried an expression of barely concealed panic. Her piercing eyes immediately sought out the girl, relief flickering across her face before her gaze hardened as it shifted to Beowyn.

The girl rose unsteadily to her feet, her small frame leaning toward the older woman as she spoke rapidly in a language Beowyn couldn't decipher. The words were melodic yet clipped, flowing like a stream over stones, but their tone carried urgency and pleading. The older elf's gaze shifted to Beowyn, narrowing with unspoken judgment. Her presence was commanding, her distrust palpable, and Beowyn instinctively lowered his sword, his palms open in a gesture of surrender.

"I mean no harm," he said softly, though he doubted she believed him.

The woman remained unmoved, her rigid posture a shield of defiance. For a long, tense moment, her gaze bore into him, as if searching for any trace of deception. Beowyn held still, the weight of her scrutiny pressing against him like the forest itself.

The girl's small hand reached up, tugging insistently at the woman's arm. Her voice rose, pleading now, the musical cadence of her words striking a contrast against the grim silence of the forest. The older elf's jaw tightened, her expression flickering with conflict. At last, she exhaled sharply through her nose and gave a reluctant nod, her stiff shoulders signaling surrender rather than agreement.

Her hand moved in a quick, dismissive gesture, motioning for Beowyn to follow. Her gaze, cold and unyielding, made it clear this was no act of trust but one of reluctant necessity.

The girl glanced back at Beowyn as they began to move, her wide eyes softening with something like gratitude. A faint, fleeting smile curved her lips before she turned away, her white hair catching the dim light as she fell into step beside the older elf.

Beowyn hesitated, his heart pounding with a mixture of relief and apprehension. Every instinct screamed to tread carefully, but the thought of the brothers hunting him—and the forest's growing malevolence—left him little choice. With a deep breath, he stepped forward, his boots crunching softly against the snow as he followed the elves further into the forest.

SEVENTEEN

COVENTHAN RIDGE

The battlefield was a desolate expanse of death and ruin, its once-pristine snow trampled into a gory morass of blood and mud. Coventhan Ridge sprawled with the dead and dying, bodies strewn like discarded game pieces across the ravaged landscape. The crimson-streaked snow bore witness to violence and desperation, the air thick with the metallic tang of blood and the stench of decay. Scavenger birds circled above in grim patience, their shrill cries piercing the eerie stillness, a macabre symphony to the day's slaughter.

At the edge of a makeshift camp, Elwin sat bound, his posture rigid despite the ropes biting into his wrists. His officers, battered and subdued, huddled in grim silence nearby, their faces pale and hollowed by exhaustion. The firelight flickered over their dented armor, its glow highlighting the cracks in their remaining pride. Around them, Sidonis's soldiers moved with a precision that was unnervingly silent, their eyes cold and their expressions unreadable.

The camp radiated a tension that crawled under the skin. Occasionally, a soldier would glance at Elwin with thinly veiled contempt, their scorn cutting deeper than any blade. The clink of metal punctuated the heavy stillness as they cleaned weapons or adjusted armor, their movements efficient and mechanical, as if guided by some unspoken rhythm.

Elwin's gaze swept over the camp, noting every detail with the practiced eye of a man accustomed to survival. There was no chaos here, no disorderly shouting or frantic scrambling that so often marked the aftermath of a bloody conflict.

The banners standing tall around the camp bore no emblem, no sigil to mark allegiance, but their starkness made them more ominous. Elwin's brow furrowed as he studied them, a prickle of discomfort spreading through his thoughts. These weren't mercenaries or simple raiders; their discipline was too sharp, their tactics too coordinated. This was the work of a benefactor—a powerful one.

The faint rustle of movement broke through his thoughts, and his spine stiffened. The soldiers began parting, their precise movements unsettling in their uniformity. As the crowd separated, a single figure emerged, stepping into the glow of the central campfire.

Sidonis.

He moved with an eerie calm, his polished armor gleaming under the flickering firelight. Not a speck of mud or blood marred its dark surface, a stark contrast to the carnage surrounding him. His neatly cropped black hair and close-trimmed beard gave him an air of calculated precision, his every detail meticulously maintained.

The firelight played cruel tricks across Sidonis's angular features, emphasizing their sharpness. He carried himself like a man who had already won, and the air around him seemed to thicken, weighted with his unspoken authority.

Elwin's lips curled into a bitter smile. "The ghost of Faermire," he drawled, his voice low and biting. "I see you've traded honor for cheap victories. How fitting."

Sidonis stopped a few paces away, his hands clasped loosely behind his back. His expression remained impassive, though his eyes glittered faintly with amusement. Tilting his head slightly, he regarded Elwin as though he were observing a curiosity, not a man.

"Honor," Sidonis said softly, his tone laced with quiet menace, "is a luxury afforded to those who lose. Tell me, Elwin—what does honor taste like to the defeated?"

Elwin's jaw tightened, but he forced a scoff. "It tastes better than the rot of cowardice," he shot back, his words sharp enough to draw blood.

A faint twitch at the corner of Sidonis's mouth betrayed something close to amusement. He took a slow, deliberate step forward. "Cowardice, you say?" he murmured, his voice smooth and deliberate. "Tell me, then—did your honor win you this battle? Or did it leave you bound and broken at my feet?"

The words struck like a blow, but Elwin masked his reaction with practiced ease. He leaned forward, his bound hands digging into the cold earth. "Bold words from a man who cowers behind another's armies," he said, his tone seething with disdain. "Tell me, Sidonis—who holds your leash this time?"

For the first time, a flicker of emotion crossed Sidonis's face—something sharp and fleeting, gone before Elwin could place it. When he spoke again, his voice was colder, quieter.

"I do not concern myself with the opinions of men who have already lost," Sidonis said, his words clipped. "Fairness, honor—these are the comforts of the powerless. They cling to them like talismans, hoping they will shield them from the inevitable."

Elwin studied him in silence. There was no rage in Sidonis, no gloating. His composure was unbroken, his control absolute, and that control unsettled Elwin far more than any outburst could have.

After a long pause, Elwin finally spoke, his voice low and probing. "Where are my sons?"

Sidonis's gaze didn't waver. "I couldn't say," he replied smoothly. "Perhaps they've abandoned you like the rest of your army."

The remark landed with a faint sting, but Elwin refused to let it show. He straightened his back, his bound wrists pressing against the ropes. "If you're going to kill me, do it now," he said, his tone steady despite the bitterness beneath. "I tire of this dreary conversation."

Sidonis tilted his head again, his dark eyes glinting with something unreadable. "In due time," he said simply.

Elwin's gaze sharpened, studying Sidonis as if he could peel back the layers of the man's composure to reveal whatever twisted truth lay beneath. Silence stretched taut between them, a tension neither seemed inclined to break.

At last, Elwin leaned forward, testing the limits of his bonds. His lips curled into a faint, sardonic smirk. "You know," he began, his voice deceptively light, the tone of a man toying with a blade, "I hear they sang songs about your death. Ballads, even. The tragic tale of a king's brother, buried beneath his own folly."

Sidonis's expression remained impassive, but a flicker of something colder lit his eyes.

"But here you are," Elwin continued, letting the mockery curl like smoke through his words, "not just alive, but playing the part of some untouchable warlord. So, tell me, Sidonis—how did you survive?"

Sidonis took a measured step forward, his boots crunching softly against the snow-dappled ground. He spoke with the calm precision of a man who knew the exact weight of his words. "Does it trouble you?" he asked, his tone smooth and low, carrying the faintest edge of amusement.

"Trouble me?" Elwin snorted, leaning back as though the question were beneath him. "No, I find it fascinating. Call it curiosity, if you will. Surviving what you did—that's the kind of tale that grows in the telling. Unless, of course, you simply crawled out of the dirt and found yourself an army to cower behind."

"You've always had a gift for spinning tales, Elwin," he said softly. "Perhaps one day, you'll write one about this."

It was a deft deflection, but Elwin caught it, his smirk deepening. "Ah, but every story needs a kernel of truth at its heart. Was it Ceolfrid who plucked you from death's door? Or," he leaned closer, his voice dropping to a conspiratorial whisper, "did you sell your soul to the gods themselves?"

The faintest shadow of a smile curved Sidonis's lips. "The gods," he said, his voice soft and measured, "do not bargain, Elwin. They command."

Elwin's smirk faltered, his sharp tongue momentarily stilled. He searched Sidonis's face, seeking a crack in the mask, a hint of duplicity, but found nothing. Only his confidence.

"You expect me to believe that?" Elwin said at last, his voice quieter now, tinged with disbelief. "That the gods spared you for some grand purpose? Convenient, don't you think?"

Sidonis remained, unmoving. "Convenience has nothing to do with it," he replied, his tone carrying the weight of finality. "You can doubt all you like, Elwin, but the truth doesn't bend to your skepticism. The gods have a plan for this land. I am merely the instrument through which it will be realized."

For the first time, unease curled in Elwin's gut, a flicker of something he couldn't quite name. Was Sidonis mad, or worse—did he truly believe what he was saying? Either possibility was dangerous. And yet, the certainty in Sidonis's words was a weapon sharper than any blade, an unshakable resolve that made Elwin feel, for the briefest moment, small.

Elwin forced a laugh, though it sounded thin even to his own ears. "And what a plan it must be. Soon enough, I suppose, you'll have that crown of yours, and the world will finally be as it should."

Sidonis's smile widened ever so slightly, the glint in his eyes turning predatory. "This isn't about crowns, Elwin," he said, his voice dropping an octave, rich with quiet intensity. "It's about unity. The fractured kingdoms of this land are a weakness—a poison that has festered for too long. My ambition isn't conquest; it's order."

Elwin raised an eyebrow, his skepticism flaring anew. "Order," he repeated, his tone dripping with disdain. "And I suppose Ceolfrid shares your noble vision, does he? The man whose sword is stained with the blood of kings?"

"Ceolfrid and I," Sidonis said smoothly, "share an understanding. He sees the chaos for what it is—a disease that must be purged. Together, we will bring stability to this land, but only if the remaining pieces fall into place."

"And that's where I come in," Elwin said, his voice a blade unsheathed.

Sidonis inclined his head, acknowledging the truth without hesitation. "You are a pragmatist, Elwin. You understand better than most that alliances are born of necessity, not sentiment. What I'm offering you isn't subjugation; it's opportunity."

Elwin's eyes narrowed, suspicion coiling tightly around his thoughts. "Opportunity," he echoed, tasting the word as though it might be poisoned.

"Freedom," Sidonis continued, his tone deliberate and unwavering. "Your army restored. Your honor intact. And a stake in Faermire once Elsterheim falls. Together, we can carve a new order from the ruins of the old."

The words hung in the air, laden with both temptation and menace. Elwin's breath hitched, though he hid it well behind a mask of practiced indifference. The audacity of the offer was staggering, and its boldness gave him pause.

"A stake in Faermire," he repeated slowly, rolling the words over in his mind. "How generous. Almost too generous. Why should I trust a man whose entire empire is built on betrayal?"

Sidonis's smile didn't falter, but his eyes gleamed with something dark and unreadable. "Because, Elwin," he said softly, his voice carrying a thinly veiled threat, "even betrayal is a kind of loyalty—to oneself. But think carefully before you dismiss my offer. Refuse, and what then? Your men, executed. Your legacy, forgotten. Your kingdom, swallowed by the chaos you've spent your life fighting to contain."

Elwin's jaw clenched, his thoughts spinning in tight, suffocating circles. Sidonis had cornered him, the logic of his words a vice that tightened with each passing second. Every instinct screamed of a trap, but the alternative—a swift and unceremonious end—was no less damning.

"What are your terms?" Elwin asked at last, his voice low, stripped of pretense.

Sidonis inclined his head, the motion almost imperceptible, like a predator acknowledging worthy prey. "Terms imply negotiation," he replied smoothly. "I deal only in expectations."

The answer landed like a stone in Elwin's gut, heavy with implications he couldn't yet parse. He studied Sidonis carefully, his sharp eyes searching for any crack in the man's impenetrable composure. But Sidonis stood steady.

The fire between them crackled softly, its glow painting their faces in shifting hues of amber and crimson. Elwin's bound hands rested on his knees, his fingers curling and uncurling as his mind churned. Refusing meant death—not just for him, but for his men, the officers who had followed him to this ruinous point. Accepting, though, felt no less like a death sentence. The terms Sidonis hadn't spoken were louder than the ones he had.

Still, the offer was undeniable in its appeal: freedom, restoration, the chance to rebuild what had been lost. Yet Sidonis himself was the very embodiment of risk.

As if sensing Elwin's turmoil, Sidonis finally began to outline the deal, his voice low and deliberate. The words—whatever they were—remained obscured, hidden from the world beyond their circle of firelight. Elwin sat motionless, his gaze fixed on the flames, his mind a tumult of conflicting instincts.

When Sidonis finished, silence enveloped the camp once more, broken only by the faint rustle of scavenger birds overhead. Elwin lifted his head, his sharp eyes meeting Sidonis's with a cold, unwavering intensity.

"You'll forgive me," Elwin said at last, his voice edged with bitterness, "if I don't leap at the chance to align myself with a man whose ambitions could devour the world."

Sidonis's smile widened, though it was devoid of warmth. "Ambition," he said evenly, "is merely the courage to see what others refuse to. You speak of betrayal, Elwin, but tell me—how many alliances have you forged on the foundations of necessity, opportunity, and survival? What I'm offering you isn't destruction. It's salvation."

Elwin leaned back slightly, the faint groan of the ropes binding him barely audible over the fire's crackle. His hands curled into fists against his knees. "And what happens when salvation hides chains behind its promises?"

Sidonis stepped closer, his shadow stretching long behind him, the cold gleam in his eyes catching the firelight like a blade. His voice dropped to a near-whisper, its tone almost conspiratorial. "You're a king," he said softly. "You already know the answer. Every choice you make is a gamble, every alliance a risk. But this choice, Elwin, is the only one that offers you a future. The question isn't about trusting me. It's whether you have the courage to trust your own judgment."

Elwin's lips pressed into a thin, bloodless line. Pride and pragmatism battled within him, the weight of the decision settling like a stone in his chest. Sidonis's words rang with unnerving clarity, a mirror reflecting truths Elwin didn't want to face.

Finally, Elwin raised his head, his gaze piercing as it locked onto Sidonis. "You'll damn us both," he said, his voice low and resolute.

Sidonis inclined his head, his expression unreadable but his presence unyielding. "We're already damned."

EIGHTEEN

DONNORATH WOOD

The air in Donnorath Wood wrapped around Beowyn like a damp shroud, heavy and unmoving. It carried an unnatural stillness, as if the forest itself held its breath, watching. The dense canopy overhead swallowed the moonlight, leaving only the faint luminescence of the elvish woman and child ahead to light his way. Their glow was subtle, not bright enough to banish the shadows, but enough to outline their otherworldly grace.

They moved like wraiths through the underbrush, their steps so light they left no trace, no sound. In contrast, Beowyn stumbled with every few steps. Roots snaked out of the earth as though determined to trip him, and patches of sodden moss clung to his boots, pulling at his footing. His breath rasped in the cold air, each exhale a visible puff that dissolved quickly into the oppressive darkness.

"Where are we going?" he asked, his voice breaking the silence like a crack in glass. It sounded foreign in the stillness, hoarse from disuse and the chill that had settled deep into his bones.

The woman didn't turn. Her sharp profile, carved by fleeting threads of light that filtered through the trees, remained impassive. When she finally glanced over her shoulder, it was with a look that silenced further questions. Her dark eyes carried a warning—stern and unyielding, as though the forest itself had chosen her to deliver its message. She murmured a response in her native tongue, the words soft and clipped, their meaning as unreachable as the stars.

The girl at her side glanced back, her wide, curious eyes a stark contrast to the woman's guarded demeanor. She seemed untouched by the forest's oppressive energy, humming a melody that slipped through the air like a ghostly thread. The tune was haunting, its notes neither mournful nor joyful, but something in between—something ancient. The sound wove itself into the fabric of the forest, as though the trees themselves swayed in rhythm to her unearthly song.

Beowyn felt the melody settle into his chest, resonating in a way that left him spellbound. It filled the silence with a sense of timelessness that defied his understanding. He shook his head, desperate to resist its pull. "Do you at least have names?" he asked, his frustration breaking through the spell.

The woman offered no reply, only quickened her pace. Her cloak brushed against the brambles lining the narrow path, the faint rustle the only indication she was even real. Beowyn clenched his fists, swallowing a curse as he pushed forward. His legs ached with every step, but pride kept him moving. He wouldn't fall behind—not now.

Time unraveled the deeper they went. Minutes stretched into what felt like hours, and yet nothing seemed to change. The paths twisted unnaturally, looping back on themselves to familiar landmarks—an ancient tree hollow, a weathered stone carved with incomprehensible runes. It was as though the forest were alive, shifting its bones to toy with him. His pulse quickened, a flicker of panic gnawing at the edges of his resolve.

And yet the elves remained undeterred. They moved with purpose, weaving through the labyrinthine woods as though guided by an invisible thread. Each step they took seemed to defy the forest's twisting chaos, their movements as fluid and deliberate as a stream carving its way through rock. Beowyn struggled to keep up, his every stumble a stark reminder that he did not belong in this place.

Eventually, the oppressive weight of the forest began to loosen its grip, the air growing lighter with each tentative step forward. The tangled canopy above, once a smothering veil of darkness, began to thin, allowing faint shards of moonlight to pierce through the shadows. The trees, their gnarled limbs twisted like the hands of ancient sentinels, now stood farther apart, as if retreating to make way for the world beyond. Beowyn caught the faint murmur of wind brushing across unseen fields, a sound so foreign after the suffocating silence that it tugged at his frayed nerves with a bittersweet promise of freedom.

When they finally emerged from the forest's grasp, the change was stark, almost overwhelming. The impenetrable gloom gave way to a wide expanse of rolling hills, their undulating forms bathed in the cool silver glow of the moon. The sharp, cold scent of pine was replaced by the earthy aroma of damp soil and the faint, woodsmoke-laden breeze that whispered of distant hearths.

Beowyn paused at the forest's edge, blinking as his eyes adjusted to the openness. The scene before him unfurled like a quiet revelation. Nestled in the valley below lay a small village, its cottages clustered like whispered secrets against the landscape. Thatched roofs sparkled with a thin veil of frost, their sharp angles softened by the moonlight. Thin trails of smoke spiraled upward from stone chimneys, mingling with the crisp night air. Somewhere nearby, a river babbled softly, its gentle voice weaving a lullaby that stood in stark contrast to the chaos he had left behind.

The elves moved without hesitation, leading him down a narrow, winding path that descended toward the village. Their steps were light and purposeful, their forms blending almost seamlessly into the muted tones of the hills. Beowyn stumbled, his legs heavy from the relentless tension of the forest, but he forced himself to keep pace. The strange melody the girl had hummed earlier still lingered in his mind, haunting in its simplicity.

At the outskirts of the village stood a single cottage, set apart from the others like a lone sentinel. Its weathered wooden beams bore the marks of years of wind and rain, yet it stood sturdy and proud. The golden flicker of firelight escaped through the gaps in the shutters, a beacon of warmth against the night's chill.

The elvish woman approached the door and knocked softly, her movements as deliberate as ever. Within moments, the door creaked open to reveal an older woman with graying hair braided neatly over one shoulder. Her face was lined but kind, her sharp eyes surveying the visitors with a mixture of surprise and recognition. Her gaze lingered on Beowyn, and a flicker of shock crossed her features before she bowed deeply, her voice a hushed reverence.

"My King," she said, her words carrying the weight of unspoken loyalty.

A tall man appeared behind her, his broad shoulders filling the doorway. His weathered face spoke of quiet endurance, though his watchful eyes betrayed a hint of wariness as they flicked between the elves and Beowyn. Without a word, the couple stepped aside, beckoning them inside.

Moira, as the woman introduced herself, moved with quiet efficiency. She disappeared into a back room and returned moments later, her arms laden with supplies—bread wrapped in linen, a flask of water, and a heavy woolen shawl. She handed them to the elvish woman with a nod of understanding, and the two exchanged a few hurried words in the lilting, musical language of the elves. Though their tones were soft, there was an urgency beneath their quiet exchange, a meaning Beowyn couldn't hope to decipher.

The girl clung to the woman's cloak, her wide eyes darting back to Beowyn. Slowly, she stepped forward, her small hand outstretched as though reaching for him. She hesitated just before her fingers could brush against him, her expression shifting to a fleeting smile before she retreated to her companion's side.

With no further ceremony, the elves turned and vanished into the night. Their departure was swift, their forms dissolving into the shadows at the forest's edge until it was as though they had never been there at all.

Beowyn watched their retreat with an unexpected heaviness in his chest, a hollow ache he couldn't quite name. For all the unease they had stirred within him, their departure felt like the closing of a door to something far older and more profound than his understanding. He exhaled slowly, grounding himself in the present as the warmth of firelight spilled over him once again.

"Come, please," Moira said gently, her voice firm but kind. She gestured toward the hearth, where the flames crackled softly, their light casting flickering shadows across the modest room.

Her husband, after a moment's hesitation, lowered his head in a respectful bow, silently acknowledging the reality of the man standing before him. Beowyn hesitated, his pride warring with his exhaustion, before he finally stepped over the threshold. The cottage welcomed him with the scent of woodsmoke and herbs, the heat of the fire easing the cold that had settled deep in his bones. For the first time in what felt like days, he allowed himself to breathe.

The warmth of the cottage readily embraced Beowyn, banishing the lingering chill that had clung to him since leaving Donnorath Wood. The air inside was thick with the comforting scent of herbs and woodsmoke, a balm to his raw nerves. The crackling fire in the hearth dominated the modest room, its golden glow chasing shadows into corners. Shelves lined the walls, sagging beneath jars of dried plants and faded books. Tapestries depicting rolling hills and grazing livestock hung beside the shelves, their colors dulled by time but no less inviting. At the center of the room stood a sturdy wooden table, its surface scored with the marks of countless meals and conversations yet polished to a soft sheen that spoke of care.

The woman, who introduced herself as Moira, gestured toward a low bench by the fire. Her sharp eyes softened as she guided him forward, her movements brisk yet unflinchingly gentle. "Sit," she instructed, her tone brooking no argument. "You look half-dead, and no king has the luxury of such carelessness."

Beowyn stiffened at her words, the title grating against him like an old wound reopened. But Moira's voice carried no malice, only practical concern, and her expression remained calm. She exchanged a glance with her husband, Halvar, who lingered near the doorway. His broad shoulders leaned against the frame, his arms crossed, his quiet watchfulness tempered by an air of unspoken respect.

"You've no need to fret, my lord," Halvar said, his deep voice steady. "We are no enemies to the crown."

Beowyn hesitated, then sank onto the bench, the tension in his legs giving way to exhaustion. Moira disappeared briefly and returned with a steaming bowl of stew balanced in one hand and a soft cloth in the other. She set the bowl on the table before him, the rich aroma of meat and root vegetables rising to meet him, before kneeling to examine his face.

She dabbed carefully at the dried blood crusted along his forehead, her movements sure but tender. Her brow furrowed in concentration as she worked, and she muttered under her breath, half to herself and half for him to hear. "Men and their stubbornness," she said, her tone exasperated yet warm. "Wandering through Donnorath Wood, as if it's no more dangerous than a stroll through a meadow."

Beowyn flinched as she pressed against a particularly raw scrape. "Was not by choice," he said, his voice low and rasping from disuse.

Moira huffed but didn't look up. "That place twists the mind," she said sharply. "Bends time and spirit alike. Do you even know how long you were in there?"

Beowyn frowned, searching his memories, though they felt disjointed, fragments slipping through his grasp. "A few hours, maybe," he said, unsure.

Moira froze for a moment, her gaze flicking to Halvar before she spoke again, her voice clipped with disbelief. "Two days," she said. "Two whole days since we heard of the battle o'er yonder."

The words landed like a blow. Beowyn stared at her, his exhaustion momentarily giving way to a creeping unease. Two days? His mind reeled, the forest's sinister grip on him suddenly more real and far-reaching than he had comprehended. He pressed his palms against the rough edge of the bench, grounding himself as the weight of her revelation settled over him.

Moira pushed the bowl of stew closer, the motion snapping him from his spiraling thoughts. "Eat," she said, her tone firm but not unkind. "We'll talk once you've regained some strength."

The rich scent of the food filled the space between them, and Beowyn reached for the spoon, his hands trembling with fatigue. Moira rose, dusting her skirts as she returned to her husband's side. They exchanged a quiet, knowing glance as Beowyn took his first bite, the warmth of the stew spreading through his body like an anchor pulling him back from the edges of despair.

The broth was simple but rich, its warmth spreading through Beowyn's chest with every bite. Hunger, long ignored, clawed its way to the surface, and he found himself immersed in the simple act of eating, each spoonful a small reprieve from the chaos that had engulfed his life. Across the table, Halvar sat with a wooden cup of tea cradled in his weathered hands, his steady gaze fixed on the firelight. His voice, low and measured, broke the silence.

"There's talk of skirmishes," Halvar began, his tone heavy with unease. "A foreign army moving through Faermire, clashing with what's left of your forces. They're retreating, it seems—heading for the capital, trying to regroup." He paused, his sharp eyes meeting Beowyn's. "Word's spreading, my lord. Patrols are out—they're looking for ya."

Beowyn set his spoon down, his grip tightening around it. The weight of Halvar's words settled over him like a shroud. He nodded, his voice steady despite the turmoil inside. "I'll leave as soon as I've finished," he said, resolute.

"Nonsense," Moira interjected, sweeping past with her usual briskness and refilling his bowl before he could protest. "You'll stay until you've regained your strength. Running headlong into danger helps no one, least of all your kingdom."

The conversation settled into a fragile quiet, broken only by the soft clink of bowls and the crackle of the fire. Beowyn hesitated, his thoughts circling back to the enigmatic figures who had led him out of Donnorath Wood. Finally, he ventured, his tone almost passive, "The elves... Who were they?"

Halvar lowered his cup slowly, placing it gently on the table. His eyes grew distant, his words deliberate, as if drawing from some deep well of memory. "They are ghosts now, my lord," he said. "Once, they were revered—guardians of this land. Their magic wove through the rivers, the trees, even the stones beneath our feet. But power invites envy."

Beowyn leaned forward, the steady cadence of Halvar's voice drawing him in.

"Humans betrayed them," Halvar continued, his voice tinged with quiet regret. "Hunted them, drove them from their homes. They retreated into the shadows, taking the old magic with them. Donnorath Wood is one of the last places still touched by their power, but it's... changed. Twisted by loss and centuries of neglect."

"The forest remembers," Moira added softly, her expression somber. "And the elves... they're always moving. They're a people on the edge of extinction."

Beowyn listened, his thoughts swirling with the weight of their words. He'd heard the legends, of course, but hearing them here, in this modest home, after seeing the elves himself, made them feel like truths etched into the fabric of the world.

"I've heard the stories," he murmured, his voice quieter now. "But seeing them... It was something else entirely."

The conversation drifted into silence, the fire filling the void with its soft crackle. Beowyn's exhaustion settled over him like a heavy cloak, dragging him deeper into his seat. Moira, ever observant, noticed his weariness and rose to her feet, bustling about to prepare a place for him to rest. Despite her deference, there was a quiet determination in her movements, a blend of reverence and maternal care.

Beowyn, too drained to argue, allowed himself to be guided to the humble bed Moira had set up near the hearth. The sheets smelled of fresh herbs and woodsmoke, a comforting contrast to the damp earth and cold steel that had filled his senses for days.

As he lay down, the crackle of the fire and the faint murmurs of Halvar and Moira faded into the background. Yet sleep didn't come easily. The couple's stories weighed heavily on him, mingling with the guilt and doubt already rooted in his chest. He stared into the flickering glow of the fire, its shifting light painting shades that danced over the walls. The faces of his people, the cries of his soldiers, the ruin of his kingdom—they haunted him.

"You mustn't fret, Your Grace," Moira said quietly, her voice cutting through his restless thoughts. She stood nearby, her hands folded, her presence calm but firm. "You still draw breath. And in times like these, that's no small act of defiance."

Beowyn's gaze shifted to her, his expression grim. "Breathing isn't enough," he said, his voice low. "Not when my people are dying. Not when everything I've sworn to protect is falling apart."

Moira stepped closer, her tone steady. "As long as you're alive, there's still hope. Don't underestimate what that means to those who look to you."

Her words lingered long after she left him to his solitude. Finally, exhaustion claimed him, pulling him into a restless sleep. The crackle of the fire faded, and the warmth of the hearth became a fragile barrier against the weight of the world pressing down on him.

Beowyn jolted awake, a hand gripping his shoulder and shaking him with urgent force. His reflexes took over, his hand darting toward the knife he kept at his side. But as his vision cleared, the blur of sleep fading, he saw Halvar standing over him, his face tense, eyes shadowed with urgency.

"They're coming, my lord," Halvar said, his voice low but firm. "A patrol rides toward the village as we speak. I can't say if they're Faermire's or another's, but you must hide."

The air seemed to thicken with his words. Beowyn's jaw tightened, his mind churning. He swung his legs off the bed, gathering his gear in a practiced, silent motion. The weight of Halvar's warning pressed on his chest like iron, though he gave no voice to his rising dread.

Before the gravity of the situation could fully settle, a shout rang out from beyond the cottage walls. Raised voices pierced the still night, followed by the ominous clink of armor and the thud of boots on frozen earth. The sound carried with it an inevitability, like thunder heralding a storm.

Halvar's expression darkened, his features hardening. Moira, standing near the hearth, gasped softly and brought a trembling hand to her mouth. "They're here," she whispered, her voice thin and laced with fear.

Halvar crossed the room in swift, purposeful strides and flung back a worn rug to reveal a hidden trapdoor. The edges were rough, the wood warped with age, but it opened easily, revealing a yawning blackness beneath.

"In," Halvar ordered, his voice low and commanding. "Quickly."

Beowyn hesitated, his instincts flaring at the idea. But one look at Halvar's determined gaze silenced his protest. Gripping the edge of the trapdoor, Beowyn lowered himself into the cramped cellar. The air was cold and damp, the scent of earth thick and choking. Above him, Halvar carefully shut the trapdoor, the faint light of the fire disappearing as the rug was replaced.

The voices outside grew louder, harsh and demanding, until a sharp knock rattled the door on its hinges. Beowyn's breath stilled.

Halvar moved to the door with deliberate calm, his broad frame blocking the flicker of firelight. As the door creaked open, the harsh, guttural voices of soldiers spilled into the cottage, sharp and biting despite the muffling walls. The cold air carried the clank of armor and the scrape of boots as more men entered unbidden, their presence an intrusion as heavy as the metal they bore.

Beowyn strained to hear from his hiding place. The floor above groaned under their heavy boots, each step sending a fresh jolt of tension through his body. Moira's voice suddenly rose, sharp and indignant, as she protested their intrusion. The soldiers' retorts were sharp and dismissive, their tone thick with authority.

For what felt like an eternity, the chaos swirled above him—the scrape of furniture, the heavy stomp of boots, Moira's heated protests. One set of footsteps creaked closer, pausing directly overhead. Beowyn froze, his hand instinctively tightening around the hilt of his knife. The air was so still he could hear his heartbeat thundering in his ears.

Then, just as suddenly as it had begun, the commotion ebbed. The voices moved away, retreating toward the door. The hinges groaned, followed by the heavy slam of the door closing. Silence fell, oppressive and lingering, broken only by the faint crackle of the fire and the soft creaks of the house settling.

The trapdoor opened with a faint scrape, and Halvar's face appeared above. His expression was pale but steady. "They've gone," he said, his voice barely above a whisper. "For now."

Beowyn climbed out slowly, his muscles taut with lingering tension. Moira stood beside Halvar, her hands shaking as she pressed a small bundle into his arms. It was heavy with supplies—bread, water, and a cloak for the cold.

"There's a path through the hills," she said hurriedly, her voice trembling but resolute. "It'll take you out of the valley. You must go, Your Grace."

Halvar placed a firm hand on Beowyn's shoulder, his voice gruff but sincere. "You'll be safe for a time if you're swift. But they'll be back, and they'll bring more."

Beowyn nodded, his jaw tightening. "I won't forget this," he said, his voice steady despite the weight of exhaustion and guilt pressing down on him.

Halvar clasped Beowyn's shoulder, his grip firm. "Remember us when you reclaim your throne," he said.

Beowyn nodded, swallowing the lump in his throat and turned toward the door. The path through the hills was steep and uneven, the rocky terrain illuminated only by the pale light of the moon. The chill bit at his skin, but he pushed forward, his mind focused on the road ahead.

With a final glance at the couple, he slipped out into the cold night, the dark hills stretching before him like an endless abyss. Behind him, the cottage stood quiet and resolute, its light flickering faintly against the encroaching darkness.

The path through the hills stretched ahead, steep and uneven, its jagged rocks lit faintly by the pale glow of the moon. The chill gnawed at his skin, but he pressed forward, his focus narrowing to the treacherous road ahead.

The silence of the night was broken by the crunch of his boots on loose gravel. Then a shadow shifted in the distance. Beowyn's hand flew to his sword, the cold steel rasping as he drew it. His body, still aching from days of battle and flight, protested as he braced himself, muscles taut and ready to fight. His breath clouded in the frigid air as more shadows emerged, figures closing in from the darkness.

Before he could strike, the lead figure raised an arm, halting the others. Slowly, the shadow stepped into the moonlight, resolving into a familiar form. The man's clothes were torn, his face marred by bruises, but his eyes burned with a fierce determination.

"Beowyn?" The voice was hoarse but unmistakable.

Beowyn froze, disbelief washing over him before relief took hold. Lowering his sword, he stepped forward, gripping the man in a fierce embrace. "Qereth," he said, his voice steadying for the first time in days. "You're alive."

"Barely," Qereth replied, a wry smile tugging at his lips. His exhaustion was evident, but his relief was palpable. "I searched for you in the wood, praying you'd make it out. The fact we're standing here together? That's nothing short of providence."

Beowyn stepped back, his smile tinged with amazement at the reunion. "What are you doing here?" he asked, the disbelief clear in his tone.

"I've been dodging patrols, gathering what's left of our people," Qereth said, his voice growing serious. "I hoped we'd find each other again before reaching Elsterheim."

Beowyn's expression darkened at the mention of the city. "What news do you have?" he asked, his grip tightening on the hilt of his sword.

Qereth shook his head. "Little, but enough to know your uncle's forces are moving swiftly. We don't have much time. If we're to make it back before the siege begins, we need to move now."

Beowyn nodded, his resolve hardened, the uncertainty and weariness of the past days giving way to a simmering determination. Together, they pressed onward, the rugged terrain testing every step. Loose rocks shifted underfoot, and the cold air bit at their exposed skin, but neither faltered. The silence between them was not one of emptiness but of purpose.

As the night yielded to the pale, tentative light of dawn, the gnarled trees gave way to a clearing where a hidden camp nestled against the rise of a hill, almost camouflaged by the thick brush surrounding it. Smoke rose in thin, spiraling tendrils from a few scattered fires, the scent of ash lingering in the crisp morning air.

The camp was small, its inhabitants huddled in quiet clusters. They were a battered remnant, their faces etched with exhaustion and loss. Clothes hung loose on bodies thinned by hardship, and their movements were slow, heavy with the burden of survival. As Beowyn entered, the sun's first rays broke over the horizon, painting the scene in soft hues of gold and amber.

Heads turned at his approach, eyes lifting from the ground or the small fires where hands worked absentmindedly. For a moment, silence hung over the camp, broken only by the crackle of flames and the distant rustle of leaves. Then recognition dawned, spreading across the faces of Faermire's survivors like ripples over water. Their hollowed eyes widened in disbelief, then slowly filled with a cautious, fragile hope.

One by one, they rose to their feet. Their postures straightened despite the burden of fatigue that clung to them, and an air of quiet reverence settled over the clearing. They looked to Beowyn, not with the blind devotion of unquestioning loyalty, but with the desperate trust of people grasping for something to anchor them in a sea of despair.

Beowyn stood motionless for a moment, his gaze sweeping over the crowd. The sight of their worn faces, the hollow hunger in their eyes, and the faint tremor in their hands struck him deeply. The weight of his failures pressed heavily against his chest, each face a reminder of the lives he had been unable to protect. Yet amidst that weight, he felt something stir—something small but fierce.

Beside him, Qereth stepped forward, his steady presence a quiet reassurance. He placed a hand on Beowyn's shoulder, his voice calm but resolute as he spoke. "Your men await your orders, my King."

The words settled like an anchor, grounding Beowyn in the moment. He straightened his back, the exhaustion that had dogged him for days pushed aside by a rising tide of determination. The flicker of hope in his people's eyes, fragile though it was, ignited a spark within him.

NINETEEN

ARMAGH, KINGDOM OF HELMERE

The stench of excess permeated in the air, cloying and inescapable, as though the room itself was complicit in the debauchery that had unfolded within. Nurrock, the Giant King of Helmere, strode barefoot over the remnants of the night's revelry, his massive form casting long shadows against the sputtering light of dying torches. The chamber bore the evidence of his hedonism: overturned tankards spilled stale ale across the floor. Shattered platters lay among the debris, and the twisted forms of his worshippers were strewn like discarded offerings. Some clung to each other in drunken stupor, their limbs tangled and bare, while others lay motionless, caught in the grip of restless dreams.

Nurrock's steps were deliberate, crushing shards of pottery and discarded bones underfoot. He paid no heed to the detritus or the people, his shaven head gleaming under the dim light. Tattoos, intricate and savage, coiled across his scalp, twisting as his muscles moved. They spilled down his thick neck and broad shoulders, a tapestry of ink etched into his flesh, each line telling stories of conquest, slaughter, and divine devotion. His ears bore iron gauges, thick and heavy, the weight a badge of his indomitable power.

No crown adorned his head; Nurrock needed no fragile circlet to proclaim his sovereignty. Instead, an ornate belt encircled his waist, a masterpiece of craftsmanship that spoke of his reign. Forged with intertwining dragons and blades, it glinted with a dull menace, a stark declaration that his rule was forged not by birthright but by might. His massive frame, bare save for the belt and a draped cloth over his hips, radiated raw, primal dominance. The average man, should he dare to stand before Nurrock, would find himself dwarfed, barely reaching the giant's thigh.

The heavy thud of Nurrock's steps echoed as he left his chambers and entered his throne room, a vast hall hewn from the stone of Helmere's marshy cliffs. The dampness of the swamps seeped into the air, mingling with the faint glow of the torches that lined the walls. The low croak of marsh frogs filtered through the chamber, their chorus an unsettling counterpoint to the hushed murmurs of Nurrock's attendants, who watched his approach with a mixture of fear and reverence.

At the far end of the room loomed his throne, a towering monolith carved from blackened stone. Its crude engravings depicted dragons writhing in flight, battles waged in blood, and the carnage of his many conquests. The throne seemed to amplify his presence, its hulking size matched only by the king who now lowered himself into it. The stone groaned beneath his immense weight, as if protesting its burden.

A servant scurried forward with trembling hands, carrying a tankard nearly as large as himself and a platter piled high with glistening, smoked meat. Nurrock snatched the tankard from him, raising it to his lips and draining its contents in one long, careless gulp. The servant had barely backed away when Nurrock slammed the empty vessel against the arm of the throne, the sound reverberating through the chamber like a drum.

He reached for the platter, seizing a thick bone and biting into it with a sickening crunch. The marrow oozed as he gnawed, the sound of his teeth grinding against the bone echoing in the uneasy silence.

"Bored," Nurrock growled, his voice a deep rumble that seemed to resonate in the very stone around him. He tossed the mangled bone aside, the gnawed remains skittering across the floor. Wiping his mouth with the back of his hand, he leaned forward, his gaze sweeping over the room, his attendants shrinking beneath the weight of his stare. "Is this all my reign has become? Feasts and fools?"

The words lingered in the air, an unspoken indictment against the very gods Nurrock claimed dominion under, as if even they had failed to provide him with a challenge worthy of his might.

The oppressive silence of the throne room fractured as the massive stone doors groaned open, their hinges wailing under the strain. A lone figure stepped through, cloaked in the crimson and black of Abensloh, his polished demeanor an uneasy contrast to the raw brutality of the chamber. The flickering torchlight danced across his cloak's edges, but even the sharpness of its colors seemed muted, dwarfed by the enormity of the space and the colossal figure at its heart.

The ambassador moved with calculated precision, his footsteps echoing faintly through the cavernous hall. Though tall by human standards and cloaked in the authority of Abensloh, he appeared almost diminutive against the towering stone walls and the imposing bulk of Nurrock seated upon his throne. The faint arrogance etched into his movements softened as he advanced, worn thin by the palpable weight of the giant's gaze.

As he neared the throne, the ambassador's confidence wavered under the scrutiny of those piercing eyes, and by the time he halted at a respectful distance, he had been stripped of all pretenses. Bowing deeply, he moved with the practiced humility of one well-versed in the peril of missteps before powerful rulers, his polished form now shaped by caution rather than pride.

"Great Nurrock," the ambassador began, his voice steady but cautious, each word measured as though walking a blade's edge. "I bring word from my lord of Abensloh. Ceolfrid bids you a message."

Nurrock barely stirred, his massive frame sprawled across his throne. His expression remained unmoved, save for the faintest narrowing of his cold, pale eyes. "What message?" he asked, his deep voice rumbling like distant thunder, devoid of interest.

The ambassador straightened, rising from his bow as confidence flickered back into his posture. He met Nurrock's gaze and delivered the words with simplicity yet weight, his voice reverberating faintly in the vast chamber. "It's time."

For a moment, it seemed as though even the torches hesitated to flicker. Nurrock's lips curled into a deliberate grin, his teeth glinting faintly in the dim light.

"My lord awaits your arrival near Dolam Pass," the ambassador added, his tone now more subdued, as if aware of the shift in the atmosphere.

Nurrock leaned forward, the colossal muscles of his shoulders and chest coiling like a great beast preparing to rise. Slowly, he stood, his full, staggering height dominating the hall. The ambassador, already diminutive in the giant's presence, shrank further under the weight of his gaze.

Nurrock's grin stretched into something primal, a feral hunger gleaming in his eyes as he descended the dais with deliberate, thunderous steps. Each footfall sent faint tremors through the stone floor, the weight of his presence reverberating through the vast hall. A goblet, abandoned in his path, crumpled beneath his bare foot with a sharp, jarring crunch that shattered the oppressive silence. He halted before the ambassador, his massive form towering over the messenger. Without sparing the man a glance, he growled to the servants hovering nearby, his voice low and commanding. "Signal the beast."

The ambassador dipped into a deep bow, his duty fulfilled. With measured steps, he excused himself, the soft rustle of his cloak trailing behind him as he retreated from the giant's presence.

Nurrock turned his attention to an attendant crouched near the base of the throne, a wiry man who trembled visibly under the giant's scrutiny. With a flick of Nurrock's hand, the attendant scrambled to his feet, bowing hastily before disappearing into the shadows.

The giant king lingered for a moment, his predatory grin still fixed in place. His gaze shifted to the open doors, where the faint sounds of the marsh beyond filtered into the hall. The promise of destruction loomed in the air, the hall itself seeming to hum with the anticipation of chaos.

Outside, the capital of Armagh pulsed with dark, primal energy, a living reflection of the brute who ruled it. From the highest tower, the mournful bellow of a ram's horn shattered the swamp's oppressive stillness. The sound rolled like a thunderclap through the marshlands, low and resonant, stirring the stagnant air and cutting through the dense fog. Its haunting note seemed to vibrate in the bones of those who heard it, carrying its message far beyond the city's edge.

The horn's call set the landscape into motion. In its heart, colossal drums—each taller than a man—began to beat. The first strike was slow and deliberate. The second, louder, sent a deep tremor through the earth. The rhythm grew, steady and unrelenting, each booming note shaking the precarious stilt-houses that hovered above the marshes. Shutters banged against walls, and ripples formed in the stagnant pools below, as though the swamp itself recoiled from the sound.

Warriors emerged from their homes, drawn toward the call like moths to flame. Their armor was a patchwork of scavenged pieces, bone and metal, yet their movements carried a practiced unity born of survival and bloodshed. Some were hastily fastening belts or clutching weapons; others stood already armed, their faces painted with crude war symbols, their expressions grim with purpose. The streets filled with the clatter of boots on wood and the guttural growls of orders barked over the relentless drumbeats.

At the city's edge, an ancient mechanism groaned to life. A colossal iron weight, blackened with age and wear, was painstakingly hoisted into the air. Chains strained and creaked, their echoes swallowed by the steady thrum of the drums. Servants, their muscles taut and faces drenched with sweat, worked in unison, their breaths sharp and labored. When the weight reached its apex, there was a brief, charged silence before the chains were released.

The iron monolith plummeted, striking the ground with a deafening crash that shook the city to its core. The earth beneath Armagh seemed to convulse, the impact rippling outward like a stone dropped into water. Birds erupted from their nests in a cacophony of startled cries, their silhouettes darting through the swamp's heavy mist. The stagnant pools rippled violently, muddy water spilling over the marshy banks.

From his vantage point on a stone balcony overlooking the chaos, Nurrock stood unmoving, his massive hands gripping the rough railing as if to anchor himself to the moment. The ram's horn still groaned in the background, its relentless cry mingling with the pounding drums and the rising clamor of his warriors below. His city was alive. Its chaos a reflection of his will, its pulse an echo of his power.

The faint light of dawn struggled to pierce the murky skies, casting Armagh in a dim, unearthly glow. From his elevated perch, Nurrock surveyed the scene with a mix of satisfaction and hunger. This was his domain—a kingdom of mud and blood, bound together by fear and worship. Below, his warriors roared their readiness, their voices rising in a discordant hymn of violence.

The horn's cry faded, but the drums carried on. Their steady rhythm reverberated through the city, a heartbeat of war that called for destruction and conquest. Nurrock's piercing gaze turned toward the horizon, where the distant outlines of mist-shrouded peaks loomed like sleeping giants.

Suddenly, the air trembled as a roar erupted from the distance, a sound so ferocious it seemed to tear the heavens apart. It began as a guttural rumble, low and menacing, building into a crescendo that echoed across the land. The dragon's cry reverberated through the mountains and swamps alike, a primal declaration of fury and dominion that sent creatures scattering from their dens and caused the swamp's stagnant pools to ripple in fear.

In the heart of Armagh, Nurrock stood motionless on his balcony, his colossal hands gripping the weathered railing. Below him, his city roared to life, a maelstrom of movement and sound set in motion by his will alone. Satisfaction carved itself onto Nurrock's scarred face as the distant echoes of the dragon's roar gave way to the rising clamor of his soldiers. Their cries blended with the thunderous drum beats, a symphony of chaos and fervor that vibrated through the swamp.

He did not need to speak, did not need to command. Armagh moved to his rhythm, its pulse a reflection of his raw power and ambition. He stood above it all, not merely as its king but as its god, his presence woven into every echoing beat.

The air inside the council chamber was heavy with tension, each breath steeped in dread. Gwenora stood at the head of the long oak table, her sharp gaze fixed on the sprawling map of Mistelfeld spread before her. Lines of ink and clusters of crimson markers carved a brutal narrative across the parchment, tracing the relentless march of Ceolfrid's army. Every marker spoke of ruin—villages burned to cinders, strongholds crushed, and countless lives scattered like ash on the wind.

The chamber itself was somber and unadorned, its austerity amplifying the gravity of their discussion. A single iron chandelier hung overhead, its flickering candles casting restless shadows on the walls. The light danced across the drawn faces of her advisors, their worry etched into every furrow and frown. At Gwenora's side stood her captain of the guard, Aldred. His battered armor bore the scars of countless battles, yet the polished steel gleamed faintly—a testament to his unyielding discipline. His broad frame and weathered face exuded the quiet strength of a soldier who had seen kingdoms rise and fall.

Edmar, the royal steward, broke the oppressive silence. His voice, low and steady, carried the grim tidings as he leaned over the map, a thick finger tracing a jagged path southward. "The reports from the border are dire, Your Majesty," he began. "Nurrock's dragon has left nothing but smoldering ruins in its wake. Entire towns have been reduced to ash. Survivors are fleeing south in desperation. Ceolfrid's army is advancing upon Helmfirth swiftly."

A ripple of unease spread through the room, councilors exchanging glances heavy with apprehension. One, a wiry man with streaks of gray in his hair, leaned forward. His voice, edged with desperation, cut through the tense silence. "Perhaps we can negotiate," he suggested, the words tumbling out like a plea. "Ceolfrid's demands are clear—land, allegiance, subjugation. If we offer him terms, something he finds acceptable, we might spare the city."

A sharp scoff broke the fragile calm. The voice belonged to Lord Eanric, a man whose rigid posture and cold eyes mirrored his disdain. "Negotiate? With Ceolfrid?" He spat the name as though it tasted foul. "The man sees our kingdom as an affront to his ambitions. What terms do you think will satisfy him? Our complete capitulation? Our dignity? If you believe he'll stop there, you're a fool."

"Better our dignity than our lives!" another councilor snapped, his face flushed with anger. "Do you think our people will thank us for clinging to pride while they burn in the streets?"

The argument erupted like a storm, voices clashing in a chaotic chorus of fear and frustration. Some clamored for retreat, others for surrender, their words filling the chamber with a rising cacophony. Gwenora stood silent, her jaw tightening as the bickering reached a fever pitch. Then, with a sharp motion, she raised her hand.

"Enough," she commanded, her voice cutting through the din like steel through cloth. The room fell silent, the councilors freezing under the weight of her authority. Gwenora straightened, the emerald folds of her cloak shifting with her movement. Her gaze swept the room, cool and unyielding. "We will not negotiate."

Her words landed with the force of a hammer. A few councilors opened their mouths to protest, but Gwenora pressed on, her tone brooking no argument. "Ceolfrid's ambition is insatiable. To offer him anything is to invite him to take everything. He will not stop until Mistelfeld is broken and its people enslaved."

"But Your Majesty," another advisor ventured, his voice measured but insistent, "surely there's wisdom in preserving what we can. If we retreat to the southern mountains, we can regroup, fortify, and mount a more effective resistance."

Gwenora's gaze hardened, her eyes flashing with defiance. "And what of the people we leave behind?" she demanded, her voice rising with barely contained fury. "What of the thousands who will have no choice but to kneel before Ceolfrid or perish under Nurrock's boot? Retreat is not a strategy—it's surrender under cheap disguise."

Her voice softened, but only slightly, as she continued. "Mistelfeld will not bow. Not to Ceolfrid, not to Nurrock, and certainly not to fear." She turned her gaze to Aldred. "Begin the evacuation of the city. Ensure the safe passage of as many as you can to the southern reaches. Bolster the defenses. If Ceolfrid and Nurrock think Helmfirth will be an easy prize, they will learn the price of underestimating us."

The captain of the guard bowed his head. "It will be done, Your Majesty."

Her declaration had cut through the simmering apprehension among her advisors, but not all were swayed. She could feel the icy disapproval radiating from several councilors, their restrained anger palpable. Among them were Ordric's supporters, their feigned loyalty teetering on the edge of rebellion.

"Pride will be our undoing, Your Majesty," one councilor said, his voice firm but laced with a restrained fury. "If you refuse to listen to reason, you doom us all."

Gwenora's gaze sharpened, "If survival demands submission, then I'd sooner we face extinction. Mistelfeld's freedom is not a prize for Ceolfrid's taking, nor a matter for this council's debate."

A ripple of tension coursed through the chamber as the councilors exchanged wary glances. Before any could muster a response, a low, resonant toll shattered the uneasy quiet. The war bells.

The mournful sound reverberated through the chamber. The councilors froze, their faces draining of color as the echo seemed to press against the very walls. Aldred stepped back instinctively, his hand falling to the hilt of his sword. "They're here," he murmured, his voice barely audible.

Gwenora didn't wait for further confirmation. Her movements were swift and deliberate as she swept past the stunned councilors. She reached the balcony doors, flinging them open with a force that sent a gust of icy wind rushing into the chamber. The cold bit at her skin, but she didn't flinch.

She stepped onto the balcony, her gaze fixed on the horizon. Smoke smudged the northern sky, rising in thick, dark plumes that smeared the early evening light. The faint, flickering glow of flames danced beneath the haze—a harbinger of destruction and death, marching closer with each passing moment.

Behind her, the councilors and Aldred followed hesitantly, their expressions pale and drawn. The decisions they had debated mere moments ago felt like distant echoes, rendered meaningless by the chilling reality now laid bare before them. The sound of distant war drums began to creep into the air, faint but unmistakable, their steady rhythm like a countdown to devastation.

Gwenora's voice, steady and commanding, broke the silence. "Sound the alarms. Call every soldier to their post. We fight."

Her words carried a finality that left no room for doubt, no space for argument. Without hesitation, Aldred turned and barked orders to the guards stationed nearby. The clatter of boots on stone echoed down the corridor as messengers rushed to relay the queen's command.

"You've doomed us all!" one councilor hissed, his voice thick with venom, before storming off the balcony, his footsteps fading into the cacophony of the city below.

The bells continued to toll, their mournful cry stirring Helmfirth into motion. The hurried shouts of soldiers mingled with the frightened wails of children and the frantic steps of evacuees gathering their belongings. The city trembled under the weight of impending battle, its people scrambling to prepare for the storm that loomed on the horizon.

Gwenora stood motionless, her hands gripping the cold stone railing. Her eyes remained fixed on the northern sky, her resolve unbroken even as the distant glow of flames painted the horizon a sinister red. The rhythmic beat of Nurrock's war drums grew louder, the sound vibrating in her chest, each thud a challenge she silently accepted.

"Let them come," she whispered, her voice steady and quiet but sharp enough to cut through the rising chaos.

As the shadows of war marched ever closer, Gwenora remained unmoving, her figure silhouetted against the darkening sky, a beacon of defiance for the city she had vowed to protect.

TWENTY

KINGDOM OF MISTELFELD

Ceolfrid sat astride his black warhorse on the crest of the ridge, the creature's dark coat glistening with sweat despite the crisp chill in the air. His gloved hands rested lightly on the reins, an image of composure in the midst of unfolding chaos. His angular features, framed by the golden hair that fell just past his collar, betrayed no emotion, though his eyes—a piercing gray flecked with steel—burned with cold calculation. A neatly trimmed beard outlined his jaw, lending him an air of sharp, deliberate authority, while the rich black and crimson of his armor gleamed faintly in the low light.

His warhorse shifted beneath him, hooves clinking against frost-laden stone, its breath rising in wispy plumes that caught the muted glow of the dying sun. Ceolfrid, unmoved by the beast's restless energy, kept his gaze fixed on the battlefield below. His expression, equal parts satisfaction and calculation, drank in the scene like a tactician admiring the final strokes of a long-antici-pated masterpiece.

The gods had finally summoned him to fulfill his divine purpose, and every moment was a symphony of exultation. It was as if the very fabric of destiny had aligned, and Ceolfrid stood at the epicenter, basking in the weight of his ordained role. The call he had awaited with bated breath, through years of ambition and calculated patience, now thundered in his ears like the roar of a tempest. Every heartbeat resonated with the intoxicating clarity of triumph, each second stretching into an eternity of vindication. This was not mere conquest—it was the fulfillment of a mandate written in the stars, and he would savor every breathless instant of its unfolding.

The sprawling walls of Helmfirth rose defiantly against the darkening sky, their weathered stones bearing the scars of previous sieges. The defenses were formidable, but even stone could crumble under the right pressure, and Ceolfrid intended to apply it in devastating fashion. Smoke billowed from within the city, mingling with the bitter wind, a harbinger of destruction and despair that spread like a stain across the landscape.

Below, his siege units advanced, their silhouettes casting monstrous shadows against the flickering fires. Defensive trebuchets stationed atop Helmfirth's battlements answered their advance with brutal efficiency. Massive boulders arced through the air, their descent marked by a heavy, ominous whistle before smashing into his forces. One siege tower splintered under a direct hit, its wooden frame collapsing in a cacophony of shattering timber and screams. Undeterred, Ceolfrid's own catapults roared to life, launching fiery projectiles in response. The flaming orbs streaked across the sky like falling stars, raining destruction upon the city as defenders scrambled to extinguish the inferno.

A faint smile tugged at the corner of Ceolfrid's mouth, laden with quiet resolve. The siege played out like a symphony of war, and Ceolfrid its masterful conductor. He had waited years for this moment, biding his time with the patience of a spider weaving its web. Mistelfeld had always been his by right, stolen from him by the cunning of a woman who had no claim to its throne. Now, at last, its walls would fall, and its crown would rest upon his brow.

Further down the ridge, a figure of raw, barbaric might approached with deliberate, thunderous strides. Nurrock, the Giant King of Helmere, towered over his warriors, his bald head glinting in the weak light like polished steel. Tattoos spiraled across his scalp and down his thick neck, jagged and angular, telling stories of bloodshed and conquest in a language as old as the marshlands he ruled. His muscular frame, clad in scraps of armor scavenged from conquered foes, seemed to ripple with barely restrained energy, each step shaking the frozen earth beneath him.

The war drums of Nurrock's barbarian horde boomed with relentless rhythm, their sound reverberating through the ground like the heartbeat of a god. Beside the pounding drums, the haunting wail of a war horn—a twisted, metallic carnyx—split the air, announcing Helmere's arrival.

In his right hand, Nurrock held a thick iron chain, its links groaning under the strain of the monstrous beast tethered to the other end. The dragon moved with a predatory grace, its long, muscular body slithering across the uneven ground like a monstrous skink. Its scales, dark as obsidian, gleamed with the faint sheen of healing scars, souvenirs from the fiery clash it had endured during the last battle against Mistelfeld and Faermire.

The dragon's wings, once proud instruments of flight, hung in ruin, their skeletal frames jutting through shredded membranes like the remains of a forgotten banner. Its bearded maw twitched, exhaling a low, guttural growl that reverberated through the air. Every step it took was deliberate, its claws digging into the frozen soil with a purpose that mirrored its master's.

Nurrock tugged sharply on the chain, the beast's head snapping toward him as it snarled, exposing rows of jagged teeth. He grinned, a feral gleam lighting his eyes. "Steady, beast," he growled, his voice a thunderclap that carried across the ridge. Turning to his warriors, he raised his free hand, his fingers curling into a fist. "Prepare yourselves!" he bellowed. "The walls won't hold for long. Tonight, we feast on their bones!"

The barbarians roared in response, a guttural cry of bloodlust and fury. Nurrock's grin widened as his gaze returned to the city, his nostrils flaring as though he could already taste the slaughter awaiting him. "I can smell their blood calling to me!" he roared.

From his elevated perch, Ceolfrid watched the giant and his forces with detached interest. He had no love for Nurrock or his savagery, but he recognized the value of such raw brutality. Nurrock was chaos given form, a blunt instrument to batter down the city's defenses and sow terror among its people. Ceolfrid had no intention of wasting his own disciplined troops on the first wave of bloodshed. Let Nurrock and his dragon tear down the walls and expend their fury on Helmfirth's defenders. When the city's spirit was broken, Ceolfrid would step in and claim the prize.

As the dragon reared its head and unleashed a deafening roar, Ceolfrid's faint smile returned. Mistelfeld's fall was inevitable, and tonight, the kingdom's fate would be sealed.

He shifted his focus back to the siege, his piercing gaze narrowing as his troops surged forward. The siege towers, monstrosities of timber and iron, crept toward the walls like mechanical leviathans, their groaning wheels churning the earth into a mire of mud and blood. Below, Nurrock's dragon thrashed, the thick chain pulled taut as it strained with primal fury against its restraint. A guttural, thunderous roar tore from its gullet, reverberating through the battlefield like a storm unleashed.

With a guttural command, Nurrock released the chain. The dragon sprang forward with terrifying speed, a blur of primal muscle and power. The ground trembled beneath its charge as it closed the distance to the walls with terrifying speed. Its bearded jaw parted, revealing rows of jagged teeth, and a reverberating hiss escaped its throat, a sound that sent shivers through even Ceolfrid's seasoned warriors.

The creature's climb was unnervingly swift, its claws finding purchase in every crevice and groove of the fortifications. The defenders atop the walls redoubled their efforts, their voices sharp with urgency as they called for flaming arrows. A volley of fire streaked through the dusk, their blazing heads illuminating the battlefield below. Some arrows struck true, embedding into the beast's flesh and eliciting guttural growls, but they did little to deter its advance.

The dragon crested the parapet, its bulk dwarfing the defenders as it unleashed a torrent of fire. The flames roared as though they carried a life of their own, engulfing soldiers in a hellish inferno. Screams pierced the air as men were consumed, their silhouettes vanishing into the blaze. The dragon's tail lashed out, a whip of muscle and bone that sent defenders hurtling from the walls, their cries lost in the tumult of destruction.

Below, Nurrock roared with savage delight, his booming voice cutting through the chaos. "More! Push forward!" He raised his massive arms, rallying his barbarian warriors. They surged ahead, a frenzied tide of flesh and steel, clustering around the siege towers as they neared the walls. The wooden behemoths groaned under their own weight, ropes and gangplanks prepared as they crept closer. Ceolfrid's archers provided covering fire, their arrows a relentless rain that kept the defenders pinned.

The defenders retaliated with desperation. Boiling tar cascaded down from the walls, splashing over soldiers and siege towers alike. One tower burst into flames, devouring its wooden frames with ferocious intensity. Within moments, the structure buckled, sending men tumbling from its blazing heights. Their screams pierced the air, lost amid the roar of the fire that consumed them. Thick, acrid smoke coiled upward, carrying the stench of burning flesh. Yet the remaining towers pressed on, their heavy frames grinding inexorably forward under the relentless push of Ceolfrid's war machine.

Ceolfrid observed from the ridge, his expression one of cold detachment. His troops fought with the precision of a well-oiled mechanism, each piece of his strategy unfolding as planned. The defenders were stretched thin, their resistance fragmented by the ferocity of Nurrock's assault and the dragon's unrelenting onslaught.

The battle raged on, hours slipping by as the tide of war began to turn. The walls of Helmfirth were engulfed in chaos, defenders falling back as Ceolfrid's forces gained ground. The dragon roared again, its fiery breath illuminating the darkened battlefield, casting long shadows over the carnage below.

Ceolfrid then raised a gauntleted hand with practiced ease, signaling to his commanders nearby. "Prepare the cavalry," he ordered, his voice even and measured. "When the gates fall, we take the city."

He turned his gaze back to the battlefield, watching as the dragon reared atop the walls, its flames a beacon of destruction. The defenders' screams mingled with the clash of steel and the roar of war drums. Smoke and ash filled the air, obscuring the stars above. Victory was at hand, and he intended to savor every moment of it.

The stench of smoke and charred flesh clawed at Gwenora's lungs as she stood resolute on the battlements, her emerald cloak snapping violently in the chaos of wind and fire. The fur-lined collar of her cloak brushed against her weathered cheeks, offering little comfort against the bitter chill of the night air that mingled with the scorching heat of the flames below. Her sharp eyes, lit with both fury and determination, scanned the pandemonium unfolding around her, standing as an unyielding beacon amid the storm.

The defenders of Helmfirth fought with grim tenacity, their swords clashing against the relentless tide of invaders surging up the walls. The parapets shuddered under the force of the onslaught, each battering ram's blow threatening to fracture the ancient stones beneath their feet. Officers' voices pierced through the clamor, barking commands that sought to bring some semblance of order to the chaos. "Hold the line!" they shouted, their tones sharp and unwavering, but their desperation seeped through nonetheless.

Below, Nurrock's barbarian horde swarmed the siege towers like insects over a carcass, their guttural war cries rising to meet the howling wind. The dragon loomed above them, prowling the parapets with a terrifying grace. Its jagged claws carved deep gouges into the stone as it unleashed torrents of fire, each blaze illuminating the night in a hellish glow and leaving charred corpses in its wake. Screams of the dying punctuated the air as defenders scrambled to fend off the advancing tide, their courage tested with every roar of the beast.

Nearby, Aldred fought like a man possessed. His dented armor reflected the flickering firelight, casting an aura of defiance around him as his sword flashed in relentless arcs. His hoarse voice rose above the din, barking orders to those around him. "Archers! Aim for the siege towers! Don't let them reach the walls!" His words spurring the weary defenders to fight on.

Gwenora's gaze shifted beyond the walls, where Ceolfrid sat atop his warhorse on the ridge, his figure an ominous silhouette against the darkened sky. Even at this distance, she could feel his cold, calculating gaze bearing down on the city like a predator watching its prey. Though separated by the battlefield, their silent war raged, their unspoken challenge locked in the tension between them.

For a brief moment, Helmfirth's defenses seemed to hold. The trebuchets atop the walls found their marks, crushing advancing siege towers and scattering their crews. The defenders managed to repel one wave of attackers, their efforts kindling a faint flicker of hope amid the despair. Yet that hope was fleeting. The dragon's relentless onslaught left devastation in its wake, while Nurrock's barbarians, driven by bloodlust, pushed forward with unrelenting ferocity.

Gwenora's sharp eyes narrowed as she caught sight of movement near the western gate. A group of Mistelfeld soldiers lingered in the shadows, their behavior starkly out of place amid the chaos. They exchanged furtive glances, their hands gripping their weapons with a tension that spoke of something far darker than fear. Suspicion twisted in her gut, its weight heavy and nauseating.

"Why aren't they reinforcing the defenses?" Gwenora muttered, her voice low and tense. "Aldred!" she called, gesturing toward the group.

Before her warning could take shape, the soldiers sprang into action. With shocking precision, they forced their way toward the mechanisms controlling the drawbridge. Aldred, catching sight of their treachery, bellowed a curse and rallied a group of men to intercept them. Steel clashed as loyalists engaged the traitors, but their divided focus left them vulnerable. Gwenora's personal guard moved quickly, ushering her away from the scene despite her protests.

"No!" she screamed, her voice raw with disbelief and fury. The defenders around her froze in shock, their morale cracking under the weight of betrayal. The realization spread like wildfire: their own had turned against them. Gwenora watched, helpless, as the traitors slaughtered their comrades, cutting through the remaining resistance with brutal efficiency.

The sound of creaking wood filled the air, low and ominous. The fortified western gates strained audibly as their chains slackened. For a moment, time seemed to suspend, the world holding its breath. Then, with a deafening crash, the gates gave way, lowering to reveal the flood of enemies waiting beyond.

Nurrock's barbarians surged forward with savage glee, their war cries blending with the thunder of Ceolfrid's cavalry charging into the breach. The giant himself wielded a battering ram like a weapon, clearing a path for his forces as boiling tar rained down from the parapets. Despite the defenders' desperate retaliation, their efforts faltered under the sheer force of the invading tide.

The cavalry poured through the open gates, their polished armor gleaming in the infernal light. They moved as a merciless wave, cutting down disoriented defenders with ruthless precision. The cries of the wounded and dying filled the air, drowning out the commands of officers and the clash of steel. The western wall, once the city's strongest line of defense, was now its greatest vulnerability.

Gwenora turned, her heart a storm of rage and despair as the enemy forces flooded Helmfirth. The betrayal stung deeper than any blade, its wound festering even as she forced herself to focus on the battle ahead.

The walls inner walls dissolved into further dissonance, the unity of the defenders fracturing under the unrelenting assault. Soldiers who had moments ago stood shoulder to shoulder now faltered, their resolve wavering as the invaders pressed their advantage.

Aldred spun toward Gwenora's guard, his voice cutting through the pandemonium. "Fall back to the council chambers!" he commanded, his tone sharp and unyielding.

A guard nodded grimly, rallying the scattered remnants of their loyal soldiers. "With me! Protect the queen!" he bellowed, slicing through a barbarian who lunged toward them with a feral snarl. Gwenora moved swiftly, her cloak whipping around her as she strode through the chaos. Each step was firm, deliberate, a testament to her resolve even as the city crumbled around her.

Gwenora's gaze caught a fleeting yet jarring sight. In the distance, a white flag unfurled, its stark pallor cutting through the smoke and carnage. It rose hastily above the melee, trembling against the acrid wind, a symbol not of peace but of betrayal. The fabric fluttered erratically, as if the very air recoiled from the treacherous plan it heralded. Her breath hitched, a cold realization settling in her chest. Whatever was unfolding, it had been set in motion with deliberate intent, and the tide of the battle was about to turn.

The council chamber was a sanctuary of desperation, its heavy oak doors hastily barred with furniture and debris scavenged by the soldiers. Candlelight flickered against the walls, its soft glow indifferent to the peril that loomed around it. Gwenora stood at the heart of the room, her breath coming fast and shallow as the muffled roar of the siege filled the air. Around her, her loyal guards formed a circle, their faces etched with the weariness of battle but alight with a fierce determination.

"We'll hold them here," Aldred said, his voice steady despite the thunderous impacts reverberating through the door. Each crash sent splinters flying, a brutal testament to the inevitable.

Gwenora's jaw tightened as she swept her gaze over the men who had sworn to protect her. Their armor bore the scars of countless clashes, their swords slick with blood. The weight of their loyalty was suffocating. "Treason," she spat, the word heavy with venom. "We could have held them if not for him." Her voice cracked, but her anger burned undiminished.

Aldred stepped closer, his sword hanging loosely at his side, his expression steady and resolute. "Your Majesty, we do not fight for a victory beyond our reach—but to uphold the honor that cannot be taken from us."

Before she could reply, a deafening crash split the air as the doors buckled under the rebels' relentless assault. Each impact was a hammer blow to their fleeting hope.

Gwenora turned to Aldred, her voice trembling but firm. "You don't have to do this. None of you do. If you surrender—"

"No, Your Majesty," Aldred interrupted, his gaze unflinching as he met hers. "To surrender would be a betrayal of all we've fought for. If we must die, let it be a worthy death."

Her throat tightened as his words pierced through her. For a brief moment, Aldred's hardened expression softened. "It has been an honor," he said quietly, his voice heavy with finality. Turning to his men, he raised his sword high. "For Mistelfeld!" he roared.

The guards echoed his cry, their voices rising in a defiant crescendo that reverberated through the chamber. The barricades gave way, and the doors exploded inward as the rebels surged through. Aldred and his men met them head-on, the clash of steel and the roar of battle filling the room with a violent symphony.

Gwenora stood frozen, her heart pounding as the carnage unfolded before her. Aldred fought with unmatched ferocity, his sword a blur of lethal precision as he cut down rebel after rebel. But the tide was insurmountable. One by one, her loyal guards fell, their bodies crumpling beneath the weight of overwhelming numbers.

Tears stung her eyes as she watched Aldred fall last. His final cry was a rallying call for the dying embers of loyalty in the room, but his strength could not outlast the fury of betrayal. A rebel's blade pierced his chest, and he sank to the floor, his lifeless eyes fixed on Gwenora in unspoken apology.

The room fell silent, save for the labored breathing of the victors. Gwenora stood alone now, her posture unyielding. The rebels advanced cautiously, their weapons still drawn, as if her defiance alone was a force to be reckoned with.

"Take her," one of the rebels snarled. Shackles were snapped onto her wrists, the cold metal biting into her skin. They dragged her from the chamber, but her gaze lingered on Aldred's fallen form. Grief and fury warred within her, the weight of loss crushing but tempered by the iron will she refused to relinquish.

Outside, the city burned. Smoke rose in dark plumes, twisting and curling into the night sky. The barricades of Helmfirth lay broken, their twisted hinges and splintered wood scattered across the cobblestone streets.

Ceolfrid rode through the shattered gates of Helmfirth, his black warhorse stepping delicately over the rubble and corpses littering the streets.

Crimson banners fluttered behind him, stark against the fiery backdrop of destruction. His expression was calm, almost serene, a conqueror surveying the spoils of his triumph.

As Gwenora was dragged into the open, her eyes locked onto Ceolfrid. His sharp features betrayed a faint smile, one of cold satisfaction. He reined in his horse, his piercing gaze meeting hers.

"I've missed you dearly, Gwenora" Ceolfrid said, his tone mocking, the faint lilt of victory curling his words.

Gwenora said nothing, her silence a note of disdain against his greeting.

Ceolfrid's smile widened. "Ah, that fire in your eyes. Still as bright as ever."

Gwenora remained still, and pulled her shoulders back as the man dismounted his horse. His boots crunched against the broken cobblestones as he approached her.

Gwenora's chin rose slightly, her defiance a sharp contrast to the devastation surrounding her. When she finally spoke, her voice cut through the smoke-choked air with precision. "Your ambition reeks of desperation, Ceolfrid. Mistelfeld may burn, but the legacy you build will be nothing more than ash in the wind."

He chuckled, the sound low and devoid of warmth, like the rumble of distant thunder. His steps slowed as he circled her, his sharp eyes studying the elderly queen. "Is that the best barb you can muster?" he asked, his tone dripping with condescension. "You always were a stubborn one, Gwenora. Even Ascferth could see that. It's why he drowned himself in his ale every night."

Her jaw tightened, but she refused to flinch, her emerald eyes steady. "My husband's failings are no reflection of my rule," she replied. "Though I imagine your reliance on betrayal and brute force says plenty about yours."

A shadow of insult flickered across Ceolfrid's gaze, but his smile never faltered. Instead, he leaned closer, his voice dropping to a chilling whisper. "I've waited years for this moment," he said, his tone coiling with restrained triumph.

"Mistelfeld was always meant to be mine. You were nothing but a usurper playing queen. Now, you'll serve as a lesson to all who dare defy me."

Their eyes locked, the air between them charged with silent enmity. Her defiance clashed against his arrogance, a battle of wills played out in the space of a heartbeat.

Before either could speak again, the heavy clatter of chains and the echo of approaching footfalls shattered the tension. Both turned their heads, their battle momentarily paused.

From the far side of the square, a contingent of Ceolfrid's guards emerged, their measured steps escorting a man whose bearing defied the weariness etched into the faces of those around him. Lord Ordric strode forward with the confidence of a man who had played his hand to perfection. The faint smirk tugging at the corner of his mouth betrayed the triumph simmering beneath his composed exterior. Though the bindings on his wrists signaled captivity, there was no mistaking the victory in his proud, deliberate stride.

As the guards brought him before Ceolfrid, Ordric's expression shifted to one of feigned humility. A quick, dismissive glance in Gwenora's direction revealed a flicker of arrogance—a sly grin that cut through the air like a blade, carrying with it an unspoken declaration of his ascendancy.

Ceolfrid motioned to his men with a curt nod, and the bindings were removed with a metallic clink. Freed from his shackles, Ordric sank to one knee, bowing deeply. His voice rang steady, "My lord," he began, the words laced with calculated deference. "Mistelfeld is yours, as it was always meant to be. My loyalty is to you and you alone."

Gwenora stood rigid as she watched the scene unfold. Her face remained a stoic mask, but her eyes betrayed the storm roiling within—a volatile mix of fury, regret, and cold resignation. Silence became her armor, shielding her against the bitter humiliation that surged through her veins.

Ceolfrid studied Ordric with a calculating gaze. After a deliberate pause, he extended a hand, gesturing for the man to rise. "Mistelfeld will rise anew," he said, his tone carrying the weight of absolute authority, "under your stewardship. Of course, it will remain under my command. Serve me well, and you shall be rewarded well."

Ordric bowed once more, his gratitude oozing with contrived sincerity. "I will not fail you, my lord."

Ceolfrid turned to his assembled soldiers, raising a gauntleted hand to silence the murmurs among them. His voice carried over the chaos, firm and resolute. "Let it be known that Lord Ordric is the new ruler of Mistelfeld, by my decree!"

A ripple of murmurs spread through the crowd, a subdued undercurrent of discontent and resignation. The proclamation solidified the city's subjugation, stamping Ceolfrid's dominion onto the ashes of Gwenora's rule.

From her place amid the rubble of her kingdom, Gwenora's gaze locked briefly with Ordric's. His eyes gleamed with the unspoken triumph of a man who had orchestrated every moment of this betrayal. His expression—a mixture of vindication and mockery—was a blade twisting in her chest. She despised herself for misjudging him, for underestimating his cunning. In his machinations, she had become little more than a pawn.

Ceolfrid stepped closer, his voice dropping to a low murmur meant for her ears alone. "Your time as queen is over, Gwenora," he said, his tone smooth, almost mocking. "But you will live to see Mistelfeld thrive under my rule. A fitting punishment, don't you think?"

She did not answer. Instead, her gaze drifted past him, falling on the broken forms of the men who had fought and died for her. Their sacrifice burned in her heart like a brand, each fallen soldier a testament to her failure to protect them. A pang of regret lanced through her, sharp and unrelenting, but she held her ground, refusing to yield her dignity.

Even as the crushing weight of defeat settled over her, a fragile thread of hope glimmered faintly in the depths of Gwenora's heart. It was a tenuous light, flickering like a lone candle struggling against an encroaching storm. She clung to the thought of her grandchildren, to the desperate message she had sent, now a prayer whispered into the void. If the winds of fate carried it swiftly enough, perhaps they would receive her warning in time.

Her legacy, tarnished and battered as it was, might yet endure. The embers of all she had fought for—of the kingdom she had ruled and the people she had sworn to protect—could still spark to life in their hands. If there was any justice left in this broken world, they would rise from the ashes where she had fallen, igniting a flame that even Ceolfrid's tyranny could not extinguish.

TWENTY ONE

KINGDOM OF FAERMIRE

The ridge was a cruel vantage point, offering Beowyn, Qereth, and their ragged band of stragglers an unyielding view of Elsterheim's descent into chaos. Below them, the once-proud city sprawled like a wounded beast, its towering walls framed by the fading light of dusk. Smoke curled upward in thick, twisting plumes, casting the sky in hues of ash and despair. The dying embers of the setting sun glinted off the distant flames, lending a sinister glow to the city's agony. The rumble of siege engines reverberated through the chilling evening air, punctuated by the sharp cries of battle carried on the wind.

Beowyn stood motionless, his jaw clenched tight as he absorbed the scene. The weight of his failure settled heavily on his chest. His fists curled at his sides, the leather of his gloves creaking softly as his grip tightened. This was the city he had fought for, bled for, and now it lay under siege, its people trapped behind burning walls.

Elwin's fleet choked the Ethreal River, its sails emblazoned with the sigils of Valenmur, which glowed faintly in the fading light. The blockade was impenetrable, snuffing out any hope of escape by water. Beneath the ships, the river shimmered deceptively, its ripples catching the last traces of sunlight. To the west, Sidonis's forces encircled the city in a tightening noose. Their torches burned like a sea of unholy stars, and the fires along the outer defenses cast cruel shadows that mocked the desperation within.

Beowyn shifted his weight, the frost-laden grass crunching beneath his boots. "It's already begun," he said, his voice low, every word taut with tension.

Qereth crouched beside him, his sharp blue eyes scanning the enemy lines with the focus of a predator. His face was streaked with grime, the lines of exhaustion carved deep into his rugged features. "We can't flank them," he muttered, shaking his head. "Not with these numbers."

Beowyn turned to survey the small band of men gathered behind him, their number scarcely reaching twenty. They were a haggard sight—exhausted, bloodied, and worn thin by endless hardship. Some leaned heavily on their spears, their breaths forming faint clouds in the frigid air. Others crouched low, their weary eyes locked on the burning city below, their expressions shadowed by the weight of despair.

"We'll need reinforcements," Beowyn said, his voice hard with forced conviction. "Pray Mistelfeld and Graefeld heed our call."

He said the words with the weight of command, but they rang hollow in his ears. Even as he spoke, doubt gnawed at him. If their allies did not arrive soon, the city—and everyone within it—would be lost. He lifted his gaze to the horizon as if willing the messengers he had sent days ago to appear. But the horizon remained empty, a barren expanse offering no relief.

"What about your sister? Siged?" Qereth's voice broke through the tense silence, his tone heavy with unspoken implications.

"I know," Beowyn replied, his voice low and strained. His thoughts churned with fear for Estrith and Siged, trapped within the besieged city. The image of them being dragged before Sidonis or Elwin as trophies gnawed at his resolve. Below, the defenders of Faermire fought valiantly, their catapults trading brutal blows with the enemy's trebuchets. Yet Beowyn knew it was a losing battle. It was only a matter of time before the walls fell, and starvation would succeed where swords and engines failed.

"I know a way in," Beowyn said abruptly, breaking the silence.

Qereth turned to him, his grim expression giving way to a flicker of curiosity. "What?"

"There's a tunnel," Beowyn said, his voice gaining a sharp edge. "I've used it before. It leads into the city. We can evacuate whoever we can, maybe even strike back once the reinforcements arrive."

Qereth's eyes narrowed, disbelief etched into his features. "A tunnel? And you're just telling me this now?"

Beowyn ignored the jab, glancing over his shoulder once more at the barren horizon. His stomach twisted at the absence of their allies, but he pushed the thought aside. "If we wait too long, we won't get the chance to use it. We need to move, now."

Qereth studied him for a long moment, then nodded, his expression hardening with resolve. "Show me."

Beowyn led Qereth and the others into a forest, weaving through the dense undergrowth that concealed the remnants of an ancient, abandoned village. Nearly consumed by time, the ruins lay hidden near the base of a small mountain, overgrown with tangled roots and creeping foliage.

The group followed him in silence, their breaths forming faint clouds in the crisp air as they climbed over crumbling stone outcroppings and avoided false footings that threatened to collapse beneath their weight. Rotting wood and loose vegetation made their progress treacherous, but Beowyn pressed on, his memory guiding him through the haunting ruins.

The others, clearly awestruck, cast fleeting glances at the overgrown remnants of structures that dotted the valley. The skeletal outlines of crumbled foundations and moss-covered walls peeked through the dense foliage, faint echoes of a past long buried. The location, once a cleared valley, now lay shrouded in mystery, the forest reclaiming what civilization had abandoned. But there was no time for curiosity or wonder; urgency drove Beowyn forward, his mind racing to recall the location of the hidden entrance Estrith had once revealed to him.

Finally, he paused, his eyes narrowing as the memory of Estrith's words clicked into place. Beowyn pushed aside a curtain of vines, revealing a dilapidated stone well, its opening concealed by a heavy slate slab that had weathered the elements. He knelt, brushing away the foliage and moss that clung to its surface. "Here," he said, his voice low but commanding, as he hacked away the remaining vines with his blade.

Qereth approached, his gaze shifting from the well to the ruins around them, still bewildered by the discovery. "How did you know of this place?" he asked, his tone a mix of curiosity and suspicion.

Beowyn placed a hand on the heavy slate cover, his expression softening for a fleeting moment. "Estrith told me about it," he said quietly. "When I fled from Father's punishment. This tunnel—" he paused, glancing at Qereth— "it leads directly into the palace."

With Qereth's help, Beowyn heaved the heavy stone aside, the grinding sound of slate against stone shattered the forest's eerie quiet. The dark, yawning mouth of the well-like tunnel revealed itself, a shadowy portal into the unknown. "Quickly," Beowyn urged as he began to position himself for the descent.

But before he could lower himself into the tunnel, Qereth's firm hand gripped his shoulder, stopping him mid-motion. Beowyn turned, his brow furrowing in confusion. "What is it?"

"You should stay," Qereth said cautiously, his tone measured but insistent.

Beowyn's jaw tightened, his frustration evident. "Don't be absurd," he shot back, attempting once more to descend. Yet again, Qereth's hand restrained him.

"Beowyn, wait," Qereth said, his voice steady despite the tension between them. "If you're caught within the city—"

"I won't be," Beowyn snapped, his voice cutting through the quiet as his temper flared.

The two men exchanged heated words, their argument escalating as Beowyn resisted Qereth's reasoning. But despite his reluctance, the weight of Qereth's argument settled on him like a stone.

"If your uncle takes Elsterheim, there will be nothing left," Qereth pressed. "But if you're here, there's still a chance."

Beowyn studied his friend for a long moment as he weighed the risk against the necessity. Finally, he relented, though the decision burned in his chest. "Fine," he said at last, his voice thick with reluctance. "If anything goes wrong—"

"We'll make it," Qereth interrupted, his tone resolute. "I swear it."

Beowyn gave a curt nod, his hand falling to the hilt of his sword as he turned to the small group of men behind him. Selecting several of the fittest and most capable among them, he pointed toward the tunnel. "Go with him," he ordered, his tone brooking no argument.

The chosen soldiers nodded grimly, their expressions hard with resolve. Qereth clasped Beowyn's forearm in a firm grip, his blue eyes meeting his friend's. "Hold fast," he said, his voice low. "We'll be back before you know it."

Beowyn stood motionless as Qereth and the others descended into the tunnel, their forms swallowed by the shadows. The heavy silence of the forest pressed in around him, broken only by the distant echoes of battle from Elsterheim. The knot of unease in his stomach tightened, but he forced himself to remain outwardly calm, his focus shifting to guarding the tunnel entrance.

Time dragged on, the light of dusk fading into the deeper blues of night. Beowyn's patience wore thin, his thoughts racing as he paced near the concealed entrance. Then, the uneasy quiet was shattered by the hurried footfalls of returning scouts. Beowyn spun toward them, his heart leaping with a flicker of hope, but the grim expressions on their faces extinguished it almost instantly.

His stomach sank as he stepped forward, dread coiling in his chest. "What news?" he demanded, though part of him already knew the answer would not be the one he hoped for.

"Your Grace," one of the messengers began, his voice roughened by the cold and exhaustion etched into every line of his face. "Mistelfeld has fallen."

Beowyn's chest tightened, the weight of those words crushing the air from his lungs. "What?!" he demanded, the disbelief raw in his voice.

"There was a battle..." The messenger hesitated, his eyes shadowed with guilt. "The banners of Abensloh now fly above the city."

Beowyn's thoughts immediately turned to his grandmother, Gwenora. Despite the short span of their relationship, she had become a steadying presence in his turbulent reign—a beacon of wisdom and resilience. The image of her standing defiant now felt like a knife twisting in his heart.

"And Graefeld?" he asked, his voice trembling despite his effort to maintain composure.

The messenger hesitated, swallowing hard. "Helgisson is dead, my lord. The clans... they war amongst themselves for dominance. There is no leader, no unity."

Beowyn staggered back a step, as if struck by the very words. The implications cut through him, leaving a hollow ache that pierced deeper than any wound. He turned away from the group, his fists clenched so tightly his knuckles burned. He forced himself to breathe, struggling to steady the rage and despair bubbling within him, but it was a losing battle.

"Damn it!" he roared, the word tearing free like a primal cry of anguish.

The truth crashed down over him. Every plan, every fragile hope he had clung to, shattered into fragments too fine to grasp. Reinforcements were not coming. They had been abandoned, left to face their fate alone. Beowyn pressed his hands to his face, his breath shallow and ragged as the edges of panic clawed at him, threatening to consume his reason.

He began pacing, his boots crunching against the frost-laden ground as if movement could somehow silence the storm in his head. Around him, the world remained indifferent to his anguish. The distant rumble of the siege continued—a constant reminder of the precarious reality closing in from all sides.

"Your Grace!" one of his men shouted, breaking through his spiraling thoughts. Beowyn spun toward the voice, his heart lurching in his chest.

The soldier was pointing toward the horizon. In the faint moonlight, a small contingent of Sidonis's forces could be seen moving in their direction. Their armor glinted ominously as they advanced, deliberate and focused.

"They're coming this way," the soldier said, his voice taut with urgency. "They'll find the tunnel if—"

"They won't," Beowyn cut in sharply, his mind snapping back into focus. The fog of doubt cleared, replaced by a sharp resolve.

Beowyn turned to his men. "We need to draw them away from here," he said, his tone sharp and unyielding.

He scanned the faces before him, quickly dividing the group into smaller contingents. "You'll take the western flank with me," he added, pointing toward a cluster of men. His voice was steady, carrying the weight of both command and urgency. "If they come from that direction, we can intercept and redirect them before they get too close to the tunnel."

A flicker of hesitation rippled through the group, concern etched on their weary faces, but Beowyn's piercing gaze quelled any resistance. "Stay sharp, and don't engage unless absolutely necessary," he continued, his voice firm. "Your only job is to lead them away. Draw them as far as you can."

The men nodded, their resolve hardening under the weight of their king's command. Without further delay, they dispersed, their hurried footsteps fading into the darkness as the ridge fell silent once more.

Beowyn turned to the small contingent that remained by his side, their expressions a mixture of fear and steadfast loyalty. He gestured toward the dense forest to the west, the faint sounds of approaching enemies growing louder. "With me," he ordered, his tone low but resolute.

The group moved swiftly, their steps careful but urgent, muffled by the frost-laden earth beneath their boots. Beowyn's heart thundered in his chest, but he forced the panic to the back of his mind. Each moment felt precarious, every second critical. Behind them, the faint silhouette of the tunnel entrance vanished into the shadowed embrace of the ridge.

As they weaved through the dense underbrush, tangled roots and jagged branches clawed at their cloaks, a cruel reminder of the burning city and all they risked losing.

Beowyn's fingers flexed around the hilt of his sword, the chill of the steel seeping into his skin. Somewhere in the inferno of battle were Estrith and Siged. The thought gripped his chest, but he refused to yield. Elsterheim had not fallen yet, and neither would he.

TWENTY TWO

KINGDOM OF FAERMIRE

The tunnel stretched into an abyss, its damp, narrow walls closing in as Qereth led the group deeper beneath the earth. The flickering light of their torches painted restless shapes on the stone, shadows shifting like dancing spirits against the age-worn carvings. Symbols were illuminated in the unsteady glow—intricate swirls and angular runes etched with a precision that defied time. They gleamed faintly, as if imbued with a life of their own, whispering secrets too ancient to decipher.

Qereth's steps slowed, his sharp gaze lingering on the markings. His fingers brushed the cool, damp stone, the carvings biting cold against his skin. "This tunnel is older than Elstcrhcim itself," he murmured, his voice barely more than a breath. Awe flickered in his tone, momentarily distracting him from the urgency of their descent.

Behind him, the soldiers exchanged wary glances. The young man at the rear, his face pale and taut with fatigue, swallowed hard. "It's the old language," he muttered, the words laced with unease, as if speaking them might summon something best left undisturbed.

Qereth shook his head, the faintest hint of a frown on his brow. "Let us hope it's an omen worth following," he replied, his voice distant, as though the ancient past pressed down on him more heavily than the siege above.

As they pressed further, the air thickened, laced with the scent of damp earth and a sharp, metallic tang that clung to their senses like rusted iron. The walls seemed to get closer, the oppressive atmosphere dragging at their steps as if the stones themselves resisted their passage. Distant, muffled tremors rolled through the earth, a grim reminder of the chaos unfolding above.

Qereth adjusted his grip on his sword, his knuckles whitening as the faint, skittering squeals of rats echoed through the tunnel. The sound was a warning—this was no place for hesitation. There was no turning back.

The tunnel finally ended, giving way to a weathered ladder that rose toward a hatch above. One by one, they climbed into a forgotten storeroom buried deep beneath the palace. The air was stifling, thick with the weight of disuse and the musty scent of decay. Dust hung like a veil over everything, clinging to their skin and clothes, while cobwebs draped the corners in ghostly shrouds. The faint tang of old wood and mildew mingled in the stagnant air, each breath carrying a taste of abandonment.

Qereth's gaze swept the dimly lit space, sharp and searching. His eyes lingered on the piles of neglected crates and sacks, probing for the hidden exit that would lead them forward. Every detail seemed to whisper of a time long past, but his focus remained unshaken, attuned to the present and the task at hand.

Pushing aside crates and sacks, he found the lock disguised by a low, unassuming wall. With a practiced motion, he unlatched it and slipped into the open air. The courtyard beyond was a study in disarray: the upper towers loomed above, their once-proud silhouettes fractured by the onslaught of the siege.

He turned back, motioning the others forward. They emerged in silence, their forms slipping through the storeroom like phantoms. The sudden movement startled a group of female servants rushing supplies across the courtyard. Frightened cries rang out, sharp and fleeting, as they scattered like birds startled into flight.

"Go! Find shelter!" Qereth commanded, his voice steady yet urgent. His raised hand cut through their panic, and they fled into the night without hesitation.

Turning back to his men, his expression sharpened, all reverence replaced by resolve. "You three," he barked, pointing to a cluster of soldiers, "find the captain of the guard. I want word on the defenses immediately."

The men nodded and disappeared into the labyrinth of corridors. To the rest, he gestured sharply. "With me."

The bombardments above swelled, each impact sending tremors through the ground, shaking loose dust and debris that rained down from the ceilings. The fine mist of grit hung in the air, choking their breaths as they moved with purpose. Qereth's boots struck the stone floor in a measured rhythm, each step reverberating through the empty halls like the beat of a war drum. The palace, once a bastion of power, felt hollow now—its grandeur overshadowed by the weight of impending ruin.

When Qereth found Estrith, she was kneeling beside her brother, her hands trembling as she adjusted the fur skin blankets draped over him. The glow from the hearth cast a fragile warmth over the scene, but the room was heavy with unspoken tension. Siged sat slumped in a worn chair, mumbling softly to himself, his words a jumble of incoherence that tugged at the heart. Estrith moved with a forced calm, as though her meticulous care could shield the boy from the chaos outside.

Beside her stood Eohric, his hand resting on the hilt of his sword, his expression grim and watchful. The weight of his presence only deepened the oppressive silence.

Qereth's hurried breaths broke the stillness, drawing Estrith's attention. Her head snapped up, and for a fleeting moment, disbelief clouded her face before she leapt to her feet, rushing into his arms. She clung to him with an intensity born of fear and relief, her tears soaking into his tunic as their lips met in a desperate kiss.

"Qereth," she whispered, her voice calm but heavy with exhaustion. "I feared you wouldn't make it."

"Are you alright?" he asked, his hands trembling as they brushed back her hair, his touch almost frantic, as though he needed to confirm she was real and not some cruel trick of his imagination.

She shook her head, her gaze softening. "Yes."

His eyes moved to Siged, lingering on the boy's fragile frame, before shifting to Eohric, whose silent nod conveyed a shared understanding.

"Beowyn," Estrith began, her voice catching. "Is he—?"

"He lives," Qereth interjected quickly, watching the relief ripple across Estrith's face.

"Thank the gods," she breathed, pressing a trembling hand to her lips.

"But there's no time," Qereth said, his tone urgent. "We have to leave. Now."

Estrith straightened, her eyes shifting to young Siged in his chair. "And go where?" she asked, her voice steady but laced with hesitation.

"Beowyn is waiting for you both outside the city," he explained, his words quick but firm. "There's a tunnel. It'll lead us to safety."

Estrith's brow furrowed, her gaze darting to Eohric and then back to her brother. "And the city? The people?"

"We've sent for aid from Mistelfeld and Graefeld," Qereth replied, his voice a mix of determination and regret. "They'll come. All will be well."

Estrith's lips pressed into a thin line, her skepticism evident. "Help is coming?" she asked, her voice tinged with cautious hope.

"It is," he assured her. "But we must move now, before it's too late."

As if to emphasize his words, a distant rumble echoed in the palace, the vibrations trembling the walls like the forewarning of a storm. Dust sifted down from the rafters, and the faint, anguished cries of soldiers pierced the oppressive silence.

Estrith hesitated, her fingers brushing against Siged's pale cheek. Her expression was a tempest of conflicting emotions as she straightened her shoulders.

She nodded and stepped aside, allowing Qereth to approach the chair. He knelt beside Siged, his hands moving toward the boy with the instinctive care of someone desperate to shield what little remained.

He began to slip his arms beneath Siged's frail frame when he felt Estrith's hand on his wrist—a gentle but firm restraint.

"It's alright," she said, her voice calm yet laced with quiet resolve. Her eyes met his. "We'll tend to Siged and join you at the tunnel. Gather who you can. I could never forgive myself if we left without trying to save as many as possible."

Qereth hesitated, his hand lingering on Siged's arm. The thought of leaving her behind, even briefly, twisted his gut. His instincts screamed to keep her close, to shield her from the chaos consuming the city. But in her gaze, he saw the same determination that had drawn him to her.

He exhaled slowly, the tension in his shoulders softening as he relented. "Very well," he said quietly, his words carrying both resignation and trust.

Qereth turned to Eohric, whose stoic expression mirrored his own inner conflict. With a slight bow, Eohric offered his silent reassurance, a subtle promise to protect her.

Straightening, Qereth cast one last glance at Estrith, "Be swift," he murmured, his voice barely audible.

Estrith nodded.

With a sharp breath, Qereth strode toward the door. He paused briefly in the frame, his silhouette outlined by the faint light from the corridor beyond. For a moment, he lingered, his hand gripping the frame of the door as though it anchored him to the present. Then, without another word, he disappeared into the corridor, his footsteps fading into the din of the distant siege.

Estrith pressed a trembling hand against the cold wall, her fingers splayed as she steadied herself against the vibrations that rippled through the palace. The muffled roar of bombardments outside was unrelenting, each explosion a reminder of the siege wearing down Elsterheim's defenses. The ancient walls, once a symbol of power, now felt fragile—ready to collapse under the siege's weight.

Estrith's throat tightened as she took in the scene. The palace, her childhood sanctuary, had become a cage. Her eyes darted toward the doorway, where Qereth and the soldiers were coordinating the nobles' evacuation. Their movements were brisk, their voices clipped with urgency, but her thoughts were far from their plans.

The realization hit her like a blade to the chest, stealing her breath. She stared at her brother, her mind spiraling through the possibilities, the risks. His body was too fragile, his spirit too broken. The tunnel—long, dark, and cold—would destroy him. She imagined him faltering in the damp shadows, his body giving out as they stumbled helplessly forward. The thought twisted her stomach into knots.

She turned toward Eohric, who was busy gathering supplies for the journey. The sight of his steady movements gave her a fleeting moment of comfort, but it wasn't enough to silence the dread clawing at her.

"Siged won't make the journey," she said, her voice soft but firm.

Eohric froze mid-motion, his back to her. Slowly, he straightened and turned, his eyes searching her face. She braced herself, expecting disappointment, or worse, disapproval.

"We're staying," she added, the weight of her words settling in the silence.

"My lady—"

"I've made up my mind, Eohric," she interrupted, her tone unwavering. "You should go. While there's still time."

Eohric studied her for a long moment, his expression unreadable. Then, to her surprise, a faint, reassuring smile tugged at his lips.

"I've devoted my service to this house," he said evenly. "But today, I believe I'll take pride in refusing such an order."

"Eohric—"

"I've made up my mind," he said softly, cutting her off with a gentle finality.

Before she could respond, Qereth's voice rang out from the hall. "Estrith!"

She turned to see him striding toward her, his brow furrowed with urgency. Behind him, a small group of nobles clustered together, clutching what few belongings they could carry.

"We're ready to move," he said, glancing around the room as though assessing their readiness.

Estrith swallowed hard, forcing a calm facade over the storm raging within her. "You go on ahead," she said, her voice measured. "We'll follow after you."

Qereth's eyes narrowed, suspicion flickering across his face. "Then we'll wait," he replied firmly, stepping into the room to help gather supplies.

"No—" Estrith began, searching for an excuse when Eohric stepped in smoothly.

"My lord, it would be wise to let the nobles clear the tunnel ahead of us. The space is narrow, and moving all at once could slow us down or cause confusion. I'll finish preparing the boy to ensure he can be carried safely through the passage."

Qereth hesitated, his gaze shifting between Estrith and Eohric. Before he could argue further, a thunderous rumble shook the room, dust and debris raining from the rafters. Estrith instinctively shielded Siged, her arms tightening around him as the walls trembled.

"We haven't much time," she said sharply, her voice steady despite the fear gnawing at her. "We'll be right behind you."

Qereth searched her face, doubt lingering in his eyes. He stepped closer, lowering his voice. "Promise me."

Estrith's heart twisted, but she forced a soft smile, her hand rising to caress his cheek. She pressed a lingering kiss to his lips, her touch as tender as it was desperate.

"I promise," she whispered, her voice steady despite the lie.

For a moment, Qereth seemed to waver, but finally, he relented. With a last glance, he turned and ushered the others out of the room, disappearing into the corridor.

As soon as his footsteps faded, Estrith exhaled sharply, the act she had maintained crumbling under the weight of reality. Her knees nearly buckled as the dread she had suppressed surged to the surface. She had sent away the only person who might have saved them, knowing there was no way out of this for them.

For a moment, doubt threatened to consume her. But as her eyes fell on her brother, so small and fragile, and then to Eohric, standing steady and resolute, she knew there was no other choice. This was the only decision left to make.

TWENTY THREE

KINGDOM OF FAERMIRE

The blade sliced cleanly through the soldier's neck, and Beowyn spun back toward the tunnel entrance, blood hot on his hands despite the icy air. Behind him, the muffled cries of Sidonis's men were snuffed out one by one as his warriors finished their grim work. The night's stillness was shattered by the sharp clash of steel and the guttural sounds of battle, but the skirmish was brief. Beowyn's men moved with practiced efficiency, silencing the threat before it could spread.

But there was no time to revel in their victory. A scout had already reported the advance of Sidonis's forces, encroaching on their position like wolves encircling prey.

Beowyn paced near the tunnel's entrance, his breath clouding in the chill as he surveyed the forest around him. The haunting scent of smoke mingled with the damp earth, a cruel reminder of the city burning behind them. His men stood in a tight circle, their faces pale with apprehension, eyes darting toward the faint glow on the horizon where the enemy loomed. The woods offered concealment for now, but it wouldn't last.

A rustling sound broke the fragile silence, and Beowyn froze mid-step, his hand instinctively tightening around his sword. The sound deepened, an echo from the tunnel, and his pulse thundered in his ears as he turned toward the concealed entrance. The seconds stretched, each heartbeat feeling like an eternity, until Qereth emerged from the shadows.

Qereth's face was drawn and streaked with grime, his shoulders sagging with exhaustion. Behind him, the first of the evacuees began to file out, their faces hollow and ashen. Women clung tightly to their children, shielding them from the biting air and the horrors left behind. The elderly leaned heavily on younger companions, their steps uncertain, as though every stride carried the weight of the siege itself. The quiet sobs of the displaced hung in the air like a haunting refrain.

Beowyn strode forward, his movements tense and purposeful. "We have to move," he said, his voice firm, though it cracked slightly under the strain. His sharp eyes swept the crowd, counting heads as if that alone could reassure him. "Sidonis's forces are closing in. They'll cut us off if we don't leave now."

Qereth nodded wearily, wiping his brow with the back of his hand. "We'll be ready," he replied, though his tone lacked the conviction Beowyn wanted to hear. Without pausing, Qereth turned to assist an elderly woman struggling up the last step of the tunnel, his movements quick but strained.

The stream of evacuees thickened before thinning, replaced by soldiers emerging from the tunnel, their armor smeared with blood and dirt. Beowyn's heart raced as his gaze flickered from face to face. Each figure who stepped into the open brought a fresh surge of hope, only to snuff it out moments later.

"Where are they?" he asked sharply, his voice tight with desperation. His eyes snapped to Qereth, searching his expression for reassurance, for anything to silence the gnawing dread creeping into his thoughts. "Estrith, Siged, Eohric—where are they?"

Qereth paused, his lips pressing tightly as he glanced back toward the tunnel entrance. Beowyn took a step closer, his eyes locked on the shadowed mouth of the passage as if sheer force of will could summon the figures he longed to see.

But the tunnel fell silent. No more footsteps echoed from within, no faint murmurs of voices. The oppressive quiet pressed down on Beowyn, and his chest tightened painfully.

"Where are they?" he demanded, his voice rising with a crack of desperation. He stepped closer to the tunnel's dark maw, peering into its depths as though he might glimpse the answers he sought.

But the darkness offered nothing.

Qereth stiffened, his head snapping toward the tunnel. The fatigue that had etched itself into his features moments before vanished, replaced by a sharp, volatile anger. His eyes blazed with disbelief and fury, the raw emotion cutting through his exhaustion. "They were supposed to follow," he growled, his tone clipped and hard. His voice wavered as the weight of reality bore down on him. He turned abruptly to the nearest soldier, his movements jerky with frustration. "Eohric was there! He met me at the tunnel!"

The soldier faltered, his gaze dropping to the ground as guilt darkened his expression. "He made me swear, my lord," the man stammered, his voice trembling. "He—he made me swear."

Before the man could finish, Qereth's fist lashed out, slamming into his jaw. The soldier crumpled to the ground with a groan as Qereth stood over him, his shoulders heaving with unspent rage.

Beowyn began to pace, his mind a whirlwind of panic. His heart pounded as the realization set in—Estrith, Siged, Eohric—they were still in the city. Every passing second drove a dagger deeper into his resolve.

"I'll go back for them!" Beowyn exclaimed, his voice tinged with desperation. He spun toward the tunnel, his steps frantic, but before he could get far, two of his men stepped forward, blocking his path.

"Your Grace," one of them said firmly, placing a hand on Beowyn's chest. "The enemy is already upon us. If you go back now, all will be lost."

"Move!" Beowyn roared, his voice cracking under the strain of his emotions. He shoved at the soldier, his fists trembling as his composure frayed. "They're my family! I will not leave them behind!"

Before he could push past, Qereth grabbed his arm, his voice cutting through Beowyn's fury. "Look!"

Beowyn's gaze followed Qereth's outstretched hand to the horizon. There, illuminated by the infernal glow of the siege fires, the dark, shifting shapes of Sidonis's forces emerged from the shadows. Their movements were deliberate, their numbers vast. They were closing in.

"We'll find another way," Qereth said, his voice uneven but urgent. "When Mistelfeld arrives, all will be well."

"They're not coming!" Beowyn shouted, the force of his words jolting Qereth.

Qereth's brow furrowed in confusion. "What are you saying?"

"Mistelfeld is fallen!" Beowyn spat, his voice hoarse with anger and despair. "Ceolfrid has taken the city. Helgisson is dead!"

The words hit Qereth like a hammer, leaving him momentarily stunned. His grip on Beowyn's armor slackened, and his expression crumbled into disbelief. He staggered back a step, dragging a hand through his hair as though trying to erase the weight of what he'd just heard. "They're alone in there," he muttered, the words almost inaudible.

"My lord," a soldier interjected cautiously, "we cannot linger here. If the tunnel is discovered, we'll lose everything."

Beowyn stood frozen, his fists clenched so tightly his nails bit into his palms. His shoulders sagged as the crushing weight of failure settled over him. For a moment, the two men stood in silence, their shared grief heavy in the air.

Finally, Beowyn stepped forward, his movements mechanical as he knelt before the tunnel's entrance. With a heavy heart, he reached for the stone slate and slid it back into place, sealing the dark passage as if burying a part of himself.

Around them, the refugees stirred uneasily. Whispers of panic rippled through the crowd as soldiers began organizing the retreat. Beowyn rose to his feet, his gaze lingering on the sealed tunnel. He glanced at Qereth, whose eyes remained fixed on the hidden entrance, as though hoping it would miraculously open again.

Placing a hand on Qereth's shoulder, Beowyn squeezed gently, anchoring them both in the grim reality of what had transpired. Without a word, they turned and began piling debris and foliage over the entrance, their movements slow and deliberate, as though delaying the inevitable.

The retreat was a blur of whispers and hurried steps as Beowyn and Qereth led the evacuees deeper into the forest. Behind them, Sidonis's forces advanced, their silhouettes growing sharper against the fiery backdrop of Elsterheim's burning walls.

Beowyn stole one final glance over his shoulder, his breath catching in his throat as he watched the flames devour the horizon. The walls of Elsterheim stood as a stark silhouette against the inferno, the city crumbling beneath the weight of the siege. The flames licked greedily at the night sky, their orange tongues reaching higher and higher, a cruel reminder of everything they had lost.

His steps faltered as the enormity of their failure pressed down on him, but there was no time to grieve. Somewhere in that burning city, Estrith and Siged still lived, and all he could do now was turn his back on them and lead what remained of his people to safety.

TWENTY FOUR

ELSTERHEIM, KINGDOM OF FAERMIRE

The dawn bled crimson across the horizon, its light a fragile promise against the turmoil of war. The relentless rumble of siege engines rolled like thunder, and each strike sent tremors through the fractured walls of Elsterheim. Once a bastion of strength, the palace now stood as a crumbling monument to its own grandeur, its halls echoing with the death knells of a kingdom on the brink.

Estrith sat beside Siged, her hands clasped tightly in her lap to steady their trembling. The air was cold, carrying the sharp bite of dust and smoke. She reached out to adjust the furs draped over her brother's frail form, her fingertips brushing his cheek. His skin was icy, a stark contrast to the firelight that flickered weakly against the chamber walls. The sight of him—so diminished, so helpless—clenched at her heart.

A low, resonant boom shook the palace, the earth groaning beneath the weight of another impact. Dust cascaded from the rafters, swirling in choking clouds that blurred the room in a haze of ash and shadow. Estrith flinched, instinctively shielding Siged as the walls shuddered around them. She bit down on the rising panic, forcing herself to stay composed.

The walls were falling. The walls of Elsterheim, which had withstood countless sieges, were crumbling at last.

She straightened her back, inhaling deeply to anchor herself. Fear would not serve her now. Her father's blood ran in her veins, and though her heart quaked beneath her ribs, she refused to let it consume her. She glanced toward the door, her ears straining against the muffled cacophony beyond—the shouts of men, the clash of swords, the distant screams of those who had already fallen. The invaders were closing in. It was only a matter of moments now.

The door slammed open with a deafening crash, striking the wall with enough force to shake loose more debris. Estrith shot to her feet, her pulse hammering in her ears as Eohric staggered into the room. His armor was streaked with blood—some his, some not—and soot clung to his sweat-slicked skin. His chest heaved as he struggled to catch his breath, and his eyes were alight with urgency.

"My lady," he gasped, his voice ragged. "The walls have fallen. They're inside."

Estrith's throat tightened. She swallowed against the dryness, her voice steady despite the terror clawing at her. "How much time?"

Eohric met her gaze, and the grimness in his expression was answer enough. "Not enough," he said softly.

Even as he spoke, the unmistakable sound of boots echoed down the corridor—a rhythmic clatter that sent shivers racing up her spine. Steel rang against steel, the clash of blades drawing closer with every heartbeat.

Eohric stepped forward, his broad frame blocking the doorway. He unsheathed his sword in one smooth motion, the blade gleaming like a shard of ice in the dim light. Firelight danced across the room, casting his shadow long and jagged against the stone walls.

"They're coming," he said, glancing back at her. "No matter what happens, you must—"

The door splintered under a brutal force, fragments of wood flying through the air as enemy soldiers burst into the room. Eohric's roar was thunderous, a defiant cry that seemed to shake the very foundation beneath them. He met the first attacker head-on, his sword slicing through the air with deadly precision. Steel clashed in a furious symphony, and sparks flew as blades collided in a desperate struggle for survival.

Estrith pressed herself against the wall, her arms wrapped tightly around Siged, as though her embrace alone could shield him from the chaos unraveling before her. Her mind raced, flitting between desperate thoughts and grim reality. She could see it—the inevitability, the hopelessness—etched in Eohric's every movement. He fought as though possessed, his sword an extension of his fury, but there was a desperation in the way he moved, a grim acceptance of the odds he faced.

The soldiers surged forward like a wave, their blades clashing against his with relentless ferocity. One found its mark, slicing through the fabric of his sleeve and carving a shallow wound along his arm. Blood welled and dripped, but Eohric did not falter. His grip on his sword remained firm, his stance unyielding as he pushed back against the tide.

But then another soldier lunged, his strike precise and unforgiving. Estrith could see it—could feel it—the inevitability of his collapse. It hung in the air like the crackling tension before a storm. She clenched her teeth, her heart twisting in her chest as she envisioned Eohric's body joining the others who had fallen, lifeless on the blood-slick floor.

"No!" Her voice tore through the clamor, sharp and commanding. "Stop! We will go."

The room stilled, the clang of swords falling silent as all eyes turned to her. Eohric froze mid-swing, his chest heaving with exertion, his face a mixture of disbelief and fury. His eyes burned as they met hers, a silent plea to reconsider. But Estrith stepped forward, her hands raised in surrender, her body trembling but her voice steady.

"Enough blood has been spilled," she said, forcing steel into her tone even as tears burned behind her eyes. "We will go. But only if you let him live."

The soldiers exchanged glances, their expressions hidden behind battered helmets and shadowed by the flickering firelight. One stepped forward, the fire glinting off the jagged edge of his blade. His eyes were cold, assessing, as they raked over Estrith. His presence was heavy, oppressive, and Estrith had to summon every ounce of resolve not to flinch beneath his gaze.

The soldier's eyes flicked to Eohric. He was breathing heavily, his sword still gripped tightly, but even he knew the fight was lost. The tense silence in the room was broken only by the soft crackle of the fire, its light dancing on the walls like specters of the fallen.

"Very well," the soldier said finally, his voice rough and impersonal, as though granting mercy was just another task in a day of bloodshed.

Estrith exhaled shakily, relief mingling with the cold dread that tightened around her chest. She turned to Eohric, who remained unmoving, his knuckles white on the hilt of his sword. His eyes burned with anguish, the weight of her decision pressing heavily on his shoulders.

"Eohric," she said softly, her voice trembling. "Please."

His gaze bore into hers for a long moment, searching for some way to defy the inevitable. But finally, with a slow, deliberate motion, he loosened his grip on the blade. It fell to the floor with a clang that echoed through the room, the sound final, like the closing of a door.

The soldiers wasted no time, swarming him with brutal efficiency. They shoved him back, forcing him to his knees, but his eyes remained fixed on Estrith, his expression a mixture of grief and resignation.

Two soldiers moved toward Estrith, their hands rough as they grabbed her arms and pulled her forward. She didn't resist, her focus snapping to Siged, who remained in his chair, oblivious to the chaos around him. His head lolled to the side, and his soft murmurs continued, untouched by the violence.

"He needs to be carried," she said sharply, her voice cutting through the tension. "He cannot make it down the steps on his own."

The lead soldier hesitated before nodding to Eohric. "You. Pick up the boy."

Eohric rose slowly, his movements stiff and deliberate, his shoulders hunched beneath the weight of more than just exhaustion. He crossed the room to Siged, his expression softening as he gently scooped the boy into his arms. Siged didn't protest, his murmurs continuing in a steady rhythm, as though the world around him didn't exist.

Estrith followed them as they were ushered out of the room, the soldiers' iron grip on her arms unrelenting. Her heart thundered in her chest, fear pounding through her veins with every step. She glanced back once, her eyes lingering on the room they were leaving behind—a sanctuary turned battleground, now littered with the debris of a shattered kingdom. Then the door closed behind them.

The courtyard of Elsterheim had become a grotesque tableau, a cruel theater of triumph and despair, bathed in the flickering glow of torches and the cold, ashen light of the rising sun. Blood pooled in the cracks of the cobblestones, its dark sheen catching the shifting firelight as though mocking the life it once carried. The jagged remnants of the palace gates framed the chaos, their splintered wood charred and crumbling. Cries of the defeated pierced the air, mingling with the relentless clang of steel and the guttural bark of orders from the invaders.

Estrith's heart clenched as she was forced into the chaos, her boots slipping on the blood-slicked ground. The metallic tang of spilled blood mixed with the acrid stench of smoke, filling her lungs with every trembling breath. Her gaze swept over the scene—the crumpled bodies of the fallen, the prisoners dragged forward with bound hands, their faces pale with terror. It was a portrait of annihilation, and she was caught at its center.

Behind her, Eohric followed, his movements heavy, his shoulders bowed as he cradled Siged in his arms. The boy's head lolled against his chest, his eyes half-closed, blissfully unaware of the nightmare engulfing them. Eohric's face was set, the weariness etched into every line of his features, but his grip on Siged was firm, a small act of defiance against the tide of despair.

A ripple passed through the throng of soldiers as a tall, dark figure appeared, framed by the fiery remnants of the gates. Sidonis. His silhouette loomed against the backdrop of ruin, his stride confident, almost leisurely, as if he were savoring his victory. The flames reflected in his dark eyes, which gleamed with predatory satisfaction. His armor, polished to a merciless sheen, bore little trace of the battle's grime, standing in stark contrast to the tattered remnants of Faermire's forces.

Estrith's breath hitched as he drew closer, his cruel smile deepening as his gaze swept over the scene. It was the first time she had seen him since his betrayal of their family, and the sight of him now—a conqueror basking in the ruins of her home—ignited a wave of fury and helplessness that threatened to overwhelm her.

"Well," Sidonis said, his voice smooth and unhurried, yet carrying easily over the din. "It seems we've reached the end of this little rebellion." His gaze settled on Estrith, and his smile widened with mockery. "And here you are. My dear niece, the last scion of Faermire, brought so very low."

Estrith forced herself to lift her chin, though her heart pounded like a war drum. She refused to let him see the fear coiled in her chest like a serpent. Behind her, she felt Eohric shift, his grip tightening protectively around Siged as if shielding the boy from Sidonis's gaze.

Sidonis's eyes flicked to Eohric, his expression hardening into a sneer. "And you," he said, his tone laced with disdain. "The loyal dog. Still standing, I see. Almost impressive."

Eohric said nothing, his silence a small act of defiance, though Estrith could see the tension in his jaw, the effort it took to hold back his fury.

"Enough, uncle," Estrith said, her voice steady despite the trembling in her hands. She kept her tone sharp, refusing to let him see the cracks in her armor.

Sidonis chuckled, the sound low and menacing, like a blade dragged against stone. "You always were my favorite," he said mockingly, his words dripping with venom. "But I suppose even favorites must learn the cruelties of fate." He gestured broadly to the courtyard, his smile widening. "On to other matters."

He turned, his gaze sweeping over a line of prisoners who had been dragged into the courtyard. Their faces were pale, their fine robes torn and smeared with dirt. Estrith's stomach twisted as she recognized them—nobles who had once pledged loyalty to her father, who had stood in the throne room and bowed before their king. Now they stood trembling, their dignity stripped away, their lives hanging by a thread.

Sidonis raised his hand, his voice turning sharp, each word cutting through the air like a lash. "These are the ones who dared to defy me, who chose the losing side of history." He paused, his gaze locking onto Estrith, his smile cruel and mocking. "And now, they will pay the price."

"No!" Estrith cried, her voice rising in despair. She surged forward, but the guards held her back, their iron grips biting into her arms. "They're innocent! They—"

"Innocent?" Sidonis cut her off, his voice dripping with disdain. "Spare me your pleas, niece. You should have expected this." He gestured again, and his guards moved forward, their swords glinting in the torchlight.

Estrith struggled against her captors, her cries echoing through the courtyard, but her protests were swallowed by the cold inevitability of her uncle's will. Around her, the chaos raged on, but for Estrith, the world had narrowed to the horror unfolding before her—a nightmare from which there would be no waking.

With a flick of his wrist, Sidonis sealed their fates. The first noble was dragged forward, his struggles futile against the iron grip of his captors. Estrith's breath caught in her throat as the executioner stepped forward, his axe glinting in the torchlight like a predator's fang. The noble's cries of defiance were silenced as the blade arced through the air and fell with a sickening thud. Blood sprayed in a macabre arc, splattering against the cobblestones.

Estrith wrenched her gaze away, her stomach churning as bile clawed its way up her throat. The metallic tang of blood thickened the air, mingling with the acrid stench of sweat and smoke. One by one, the nobles were forced to kneel before the executioner, their final moments swallowed by the cold efficiency of Sidonis's wrath. Each strike of the axe reverberated through the courtyard, a drumbeat of death that seemed to mock the silence of the fallen.

Her legs trembled beneath her, threatening to collapse entirely. When the guards seized Eohric and dragged him forward, her composure shattered.

"Eohric!" she screamed, her voice raw with desperation as she thrashed against the guards holding her. "No! Please, Uncle! Don't do this!"

Eohric turned his head, his gaze meeting hers. Despite the blood streaking his face, his expression was calm, almost serene, though his eyes flickered with a sorrow that cut deeper than any blade. "Be strong, my lady," he murmured softly, his voice steady. Then, almost as if in prayer, he began to murmur in his native tongue, the cadence a haunting melody amidst the chaos.

Sidonis didn't so much as flinch at her cries. He tilted his head slightly, savoring his dominance, before nodding toward the executioner.

"No! Stop!" Estrith's screams tore through the air, but they fell on deaf ears. The axe rose, gleaming in the cold light, and came down with brutal finality.

The world seemed to stop. Estrith's anguished cry ripped from her chest, shattering the brief silence that followed the execution. Her knees buckled, and she collapsed to the blood-slick stones, her body shaking with sobs as tears streamed down her face. Eohric's lifeless form crumpled before her, his sacrifice a stark testament to his loyalty. Her grief was all-consuming, a suffocating weight that pressed down on her chest and stole the air from her lungs.

Then, as if choreographed by some cruel god, the sound of approaching hoofbeats echoed through the courtyard, cutting through her despair. Estrith's tear-blurred vision lifted to see Elwin and his sons riding in, their banners snapping sharply in the morning breeze. The sigils of Valenmur stood stark against the crimson-streaked sky, a reminder of the power that had crushed Faermire.

Elwin dismounted with practiced ease, his sharp eyes surveying the scene. His sons followed, their expressions cold, their lips curled in faint smirks of satisfaction. Estrith's grief burned into fury at the sight of their smug faces, but her body was too weak, too broken, to summon more than a faint tremor of defiance.

"Sidonis," Elwin said coolly, his voice carrying an edge of disinterest. "Quite the spectacle you've orchestrated."

Sidonis turned, his cruel smile slipping into something more calculated. "Elwin," he replied, his tone steeped in false camaraderie.

Elwin's gaze swept the courtyard, lingering on the blood-stained cobblestones and the pile of bodies. His face betrayed no emotion, only cold indifference. "My men are due their spoils," he said simply, as though discussing the division of grain.

Sidonis waved a dismissive hand. "Take what you will."

Elwin inclined his head, signaling his soldiers. They wasted no time, fanning out across the palace grounds with predatory purpose. Estrith flinched at the distant screams of servants, their terror echoing through the halls as the looters descended. Laughter and shouted orders followed, a grotesque symphony to accompany the destruction of her home.

Elwin lingered with Ealric at his side, his presence a cold shadow against the chaos. Ealric, the man whose unsettling obsession with her had always carried a stern, unyielding intensity, stood silent, his gaze fixed on her with unnerving focus. Elwin's sharp eyes shifted intermittently between Sidonis and the unfolding carnage, his conversation with the victor an indistinct murmur drowned by the din of the courtyard. Yet, every so often, his attention returned to Estrith, a detached curiosity flickering in his expression.

For Estrith, their stares barely registered. Her world had shrunk to a singular, unbearable point: the lifeless form of Eohric sprawled before her. The weight of her loss pressed against her chest. Her body trembled with silent sobs, the grief tearing through her too vast for words. Strength had fled her entirely, leaving her a hollow shell, anchored only by the enormity of her sorrow.

Sidonis approached her, his boots clicking softly against the blood-slick stone. He crouched before her, tilting her chin upward with his gloved hand. His touch was icy, his grip firm but taunting. "Look at you," he said softly, his tone almost pitying. "A queen without a kingdom. A sister without a king." He leaned closer, his dark eyes gleaming with cruel amusement. "Tell me, niece, where is your brother? Where is Faermire's mighty savior?"

Estrith clenched her jaw, her voice trembling with fury and sorrow. "You'll never find him."

Sidonis chuckled, rising to his feet with infuriating ease. "Perhaps not," he mused. "But that's of little consequence to me now." His gaze shifted, settling on Siged, who stood apart from the scene, his frail form almost lost in the chaos.

Sidonis's brows lifted in mock surprise. "And what's this?" he said, his tone light with amusement. "The youngest heir to Faermire's throne—now crippled and dumb? How poetic."

Estrith's grief sparked into fury, but before she could speak, Sidonis silenced her with a raised hand. His expression darkened, his smile twisting into something far more sinister. "At least you have each other," he said, his voice a chilling whisper. "A sister and her broken prince."

He turned sharply, barking orders to his men. "And what of the boy's mother?" he asked, his voice cutting through the din. "Where is the lady of Faermire? Find her."

The guards emerged moments later as they escorted a woman between them. Richessa stumbled, her frail frame swaying with each step, yet she refused to fall. Her gown, once a symbol of her status, hung in tattered remnants, the delicate fabric caked with dirt and torn beyond recognition. Her hair clung to her face in matted strands streaked with filth, but it was her eyes—sharp and glittering—that held the courtyard captive. Amidst her gaunt and hollowed features, there burned a glimmer of something—triumph, defiance, or perhaps madness.

Estrith tensed as the group drew near, her breath catching in her throat. The air seemed to thicken around them, charged with a palpable animosity.

Richessa's gaze landed on Siged first, and her hardened expression softened, transforming in an instant. Her lips parted as a tremulous breath escaped her, and then, as though pulled by some unseen force, she stumbled forward. Her knees buckled beneath her, but she pressed on, breaking into a desperate, uneven run.

"Siged," she gasped, her voice raw and breaking with equal parts relief and sorrow. She collapsed before him, her knees striking the cobblestones as her trembling hands reached for his face. "My boy... my darling boy."

Siged stirred faintly, his lips parting in a ghost of movement, but no sound followed. Richessa pulled him into her embrace, cradling his frail body as if to shield him from the world around them. She rocked him gently, her voice a soothing murmur. "It's over now, my sweet. I'm here."

Estrith watched in silence, her emotions a tumult of anger and pity. The raw tenderness in Richessa's actions was undeniable, but it did little to soften

Estrith's view of the woman who had spent years twisting the lives of those around her.

Then, as if sensing Estrith's gaze, Richessa's head snapped up. The tenderness in her eyes vanished, replaced by a storm of fury that seemed to ignite her gaunt features. She released Siged, rising to her feet with a speed fueled by unbridled rage.

Estrith barely had time to process the shift before Richessa's hand struck her cheek with a resounding crack. The blow sent her reeling, her vision swimming with the sting of pain and shock. Her body wavered, but she forced herself upright, staring back at the woman with wide, tear-filled eyes.

"How I've waited for this moment," Richessa hissed, her voice trembling with both rage and triumph. Her words dripped with venom, cutting deeper than the slap.

Estrith opened her mouth to speak, but no words came. The weight of grief and exhaustion pressed down on her like a crushing tide, silencing whatever defiance she might have summoned.

From a short distance, Sidonis observed the exchange with a faint smirk, his dark eyes gleaming with amusement. "Richessa," he said smoothly, his tone a coaxing balm to the storm of her rage.

Richessa turned to him, her fury melting into something altogether different. Her gaze softened, a flicker of awe and longing coloring her expression as she stepped toward him. "Sidonis," she murmured, his name falling from her lips like a prayer.

For Richessa, he was salvation incarnate, the man who had rescued her from the dungeons and restored her place in the world. She reached for his hand, lifting it to her lips and pressing a reverent kiss to his gloved fingers. Sidonis responded with a faint smile, brushing his knuckles lightly against her cheek with a hint of affection.

"Get the queen something to eat," he commanded a nearby servant. "Tend to her every need."

The servant moved swiftly to obey, and with a final, searing glare at Estrith, Richessa allowed herself to be escorted toward the palace. Her tattered form vanished into the shadows, leaving Estrith standing alone in the wake of her fury.

Sidonis turned back to Estrith, his expression hardening. "Take them away," he ordered.

The guards moved without hesitation, their grip firm as they dragged Estrith to her feet. She stumbled, her body weak with grief, but her gaze lingered on Siged. She reached for him, her fingers trembling.

As the guards escorted her and Siged away, Estrith clung to her brother, her nails digging into the fabric of his tunic as though her grip alone could protect them from the horrors unfolding around them. Her frantic gaze roamed the chaos, searching for something—anything—that might anchor her amidst the despair.

Then her eyes found him.

Eohric's lifeless form lay crumpled on the blood-slicked stones, his once-proud armor dulled and battered, a cruel mockery of the man who had stood as her shield. Her chest tightened as a wave of desperation surged through her, clawing at her heart with a silent, anguished plea. *Get up. Please, get up.*

But there was no response. No flicker of movement, no reassuring voice to guide her. Only the cold finality of death greeted her cries, his body a haunting reminder of everything she had lost. The courtyard blurred as hot tears spilled down her cheeks, her knees threatening to buckle beneath her once more.

Still, the guards pressed forward, their iron grip unyielding as they wrenched her from the scene. Estrith's gaze lingered on Eohric until the growing distance consumed him, his form fading into the haze of smoke and shadows, leaving her with nothing but the hollow ache of her loss.

As they neared the edge of the courtyard, Estrith's eyes caught a movement—a presence that made her pause. Among the carnage, a figure emerged, half-obscured by a swirling, ethereal mist that danced unnaturally around it. A faint orange glow radiated from its form, casting a ghostly light that flickered against the bloodstained stones and the smoldering remains of the palace.

Wisps of dark hair floated weightlessly, as though caught in a phantom breeze, framing a face that seemed to blur the line between beauty and terror. Then the eyes—piercing, unearthly orange—locked onto hers with a force that froze her where she stood. The air seemed to thicken, pressing in on her chest, and for a moment, the cacophony of the courtyard fell away, replaced by a suffocating stillness. Time itself faltered, the figure's gaze anchoring her in a moment that stretched endlessly.

It was the same figure she had glimpsed before, standing silently in Siged's room. But here, amidst the ruin of the courtyard, it seemed even more vivid, more real.

Estrith's pulse thundered as questions churned in her mind. Was it watching her? Siged? Both of them? Her grief swirled with a new, unshakable fear that this figure wasn't just a figment of despair but a sign of something far worse.

Her grief and terror were momentarily eclipsed by a cold, unshakable dread. The figure's expression was unreadable, enigmatic—a presence that both lured and repelled, demanding her attention even as every instinct screamed to look away.

A sharp tug on her arm shattered the trance. The guards yanked her forward, their iron grips pulling her mercilessly toward the hazy passage ahead. She stumbled, craning her neck to see the figure again, but the mist dissolved into the chaos, leaving only empty space where it had stood.

Estrith's feet shuffled across the uneven ground, the courtyard fading into the distance, yet the image remained vivid, etched into her mind. The chaos, the suffocating grief, and now this—a specter, an omen, a harbinger of dread.

TWENTY FIVE

ELSTERHEIM, KINGDOM OF FAERMIRE

Richessa's hands moved with practiced elegance as she lifted the small silver spoon to Siged's lips. The boy sat motionless at the dining table, his fragile frame slouched as though the weight of his own existence was too much to bear. The pale morning light filtering through the arched windows fell softly upon him, tracing the soft contours of his face. He accepted the spoonful of porridge without resistance, his vacant gaze fixed on a distant point beyond the confines of the grand hall.

Richessa forced a serene smile, though her thoughts churned. Her hand, adorned with delicate rings that caught the light, brushed through Siged's unruly hair with a tenderness that felt foreign even to her. In his silence, she found a fragile illusion of peace, a desperate echo of the life she had once envisioned. Each small gesture—a gentle stroke of his hair, a soft murmur of reassurance—served as a fragile anchor, tethering her to the hope that this moment was real and not just a fleeting dream.

Her gown, a deep sapphire trimmed with silver embroidery, shimmered faintly as she moved. The garment was a deliberate choice. At her throat, a brooch of polished onyx and gold caught the sunlight, a symbol of the grandeur she still claimed as her right. She leaned closer to Siged, her voice a quiet lull. "Just a little more, my sweet boy. Then we'll rest. Everything will be all right."

The measured cadence of booted steps against polished stone broke the stillness. Richessa's heart lifted at the sound, a flutter of anticipation as Sidonis entered the hall. The air seemed to shift with his presence that both thrilled and unnerved her. He moved with the calculated authority of a conqueror, his dark, battle-worn leathers absorbing the morning light like a shadow given form.

Richessa rose at once, smoothing the folds of her gown as she motioned to the silent servants stationed along the edges of the room. "Tend to my son," she commanded, her tone brooking no argument. The servants moved swiftly, their steps as muted as their expressions, taking their places by Siged's side. Richessa stepped toward Sidonis, her chin held high, her smile warm and inviting.

"My lord," she greeted, her voice honeyed with warmth and renewed hope. "You're here at last."

Sidonis did not respond immediately. He strode to the head of the table with an air of deliberate indifference, his movements slow and purposeful. Taking the high-backed chair as though it were a throne, he settled into it, his sharp features unreadable. Richessa hesitated, her smile faltering for the briefest of moments before she followed him.

"You've done it," she said, admiration and gratitude mingling in her tone. "You've brought everything into balance again."

Reaching for the ornate decanter of wine resting on the table, she poured into a goblet with steady hands, her movements as graceful as they were practiced. Offering it to him with both hands, she tilted her head slightly, her eyes searching his face for any sign of affection or approval. He accepted the goblet without a word, his gaze flicking to hers for the briefest moment before returning to the plate before him.

Encouraged by his silence, Richessa approached, seating herself lightly on his lap as though their separation had not carved a canyon between them. Her hands rested delicately on his shoulders, her touch light but possessive. The moment stretched between them, laden with an unspoken history and an uneasy tension.

Her voice dropped to a murmur, intimate and soft. "How I've missed you," she said, her words heavy with longing.

Sidonis's response was not what she had hoped for. His body remained still beneath her, his gaze fixed ahead, and when he finally spoke, his words fell heavily in the quiet hall. "Things... cannot be as they were, Richessa."

Richessa froze, her composure slipping for an instant before she forced her features back into a mask of calm. "What are you saying?" she asked.

Sidonis's tone was cold and final. "You are owed fair treatment for your loyalty, Richessa. That much I can give. But no more."

The words landed like a slap, and Richessa flinched, her hand falling limply into her lap. "What are you saying?" she demanded, her voice tinged with desperation. "We had plans. We... I love you."

Sidonis reclined in his chair, his sharp features illuminated by the morning light. He regarded her with detached curiosity, as if she were an artifact of a life he'd already discarded. "Greater things are at play now," he said, his voice clinical, devoid of warmth. "Alliances have been forged. Paths have shifted. Those plans, unfortunately, no longer include you."

Her breath caught in her throat, and she struggled to form words. "No. No, you can't mean that." She leaned forward, her fingers clutching the edge of his tunic. "Sidonis, listen to me. You need me. We belong together."

"Need you?" Sidonis echoed, his voice steeped in cruel irony. He pried her hand from his tunic with deliberate care, his expression unyielding. "I spared you, Richessa, because of what we once shared. Out of respect. But your part in this is finished. You'll be taken to Valenmur with the others."

Her lips parted, but no sound escaped. A wave of panic surged through her, breaking past the carefully constructed composure she had clung to. Desperation gave her voice, and she blurted, "Siged is your son."

The room seemed to grow colder. Sidonis stilled, his eyes narrowing, his expression hardening into stone. For a brief moment, a flicker of something—doubt, curiosity, or irritation—passed across his face. Then it was gone, replaced by a disdainful sneer. "What nonsense is this?"

"It's true," she insisted, her voice trembling as she leaned closer. "He is yours, born of our love. You can't just cast us aside. We are bound by blood, Sidonis."

A bitter laugh escaped him as he leaned forward, his gaze boring into hers with icy contempt. "Whether he's mine or Ludica's, it doesn't matter. The boy is mute and crippled, one that can neither rule nor challenge me. He is of no consequence."

Richessa's face crumpled, the veneer of regal composure shattering. "You're wrong," she said, her voice quivering. "You're wrong."

Sidonis rose abruptly, lifted her from his lap, and set her aside with a detached air, as though she were no more than an inconvenience. "Guards," he called, his voice cutting through her protests like a blade. "Take her and the boy from my sight."

The heavy doors creaked open, and two armored soldiers entered the hall. Richessa's pleas turned frantic as they seized her by the arms. "You can't do this!" she shouted, her voice cracking under the weight of her despair. "I've given everything for you!"

Siged sat motionless, his vacant eyes fixed on the stone floor as the guards lifted him from his chair. He offered no resistance, his fragile frame a haunting contrast to his mother's frantic struggle. Richessa's sobs echoed through the hall as she was dragged toward the doors, her cries of anguish piercing the air.

Sidonis watched with detached indifference, his expression unreadable. As the doors slammed shut behind them, the echoes of Richessa's protests faded into silence. Sidonis adjusted his chair, the scrape of wood against stone breaking the stillness. He reached for his goblet, taking a measured sip before resuming his meal, the clatter of silverware filling the void left by her absence.

The faint murmur of Estrith's prayers wove through the cold, unyielding stone of the dungeon, soft as a breath against the silence. She sat curled in the shadowed corner of her cell, knees drawn tightly to her chest, her lips moving in whispers that seemed more plea than prayer. The chill was relentless, seeping into her bones, but she clung to the fragile thread of light piercing the gloom—a pale beam filtering through a high, narrow slit in the wall. It was little more than a crack, but it offered a glimmer of hope, a connection to the world beyond this suffocating dark.

Her eyes flickered to the light, the rhythm of her whispered prayers faltering as the sound of iron groaning against iron reached her ears. The jarring clang of a heavy door echoed through the stillness, each reverberation pulling her taut with tension. Footsteps followed, deliberate and slow, drawing nearer with every passing second. Estrith stiffened, her heart thundering in her chest as she scrambled to her feet, the faint, foolish hope of release igniting a fragile flame within her.

But the shadow arrived before the figure, stretching long and ominous across the cold stone floor. He emerged moments later, leaning casually against the iron bars of her cell with a smirk. Ealric.

A knot of dread coiled in her stomach, tightening as her memories betrayed her—his hand gripping her, his intent unmistakable, thwarted only by Eohric's timely intervention. The image rose unbidden, raw and unrelenting, and she pressed herself against the damp wall, recoiling instinctively.

"Lady Estrith," Ealric said, his voice was smooth and languid, his casual demeanor a deliberate mockery of her circumstances. "This is no place for the esteemed lady of Faermire."

Estrith said nothing. Her gaze darted between him and the cell door, her every muscle taut, her breath shallow. She could feel his eyes on her, sweeping over her with a predator's interest, and the weight of it made her skin crawl.

He chuckled, the sound low and cruel. "Come now, no need for such hostility. I've come to bring you news."

"Where is my brother?" she demanded, her voice sharper than she intended, though a tremor betrayed her fear. "What have you done with Siged?"

Ealric waved a hand dismissively, the motion as careless as his tone. "Your brother? He is of no concern to me. My interest lies solely with you." His eyes glinted with predatory delight as they bore into hers. "You, my dear, are my reward."

Estrith's chest tightened, her breath catching as his words sank in. "You're lying," she whispered, though the tremor in her voice betrayed the terror simmering beneath her defiance. "I will never belong to you. I'm promised to another."

Ealric's smirk widened, his satisfaction practically dripping from the curve of his lips. "Well then, this man of yours was a fool. For he should have claimed you long ago. Perhaps then you'd know the pleasures of his bed." He leaned closer, his voice dropping to a near-whisper, "But rest assured, mine shall suffice you well enough."

A surge of rage and desperation crashed over Estrith, drowning the fear that had threatened to paralyze her. Her fists clenched at her sides, her nails biting into her palms as she forced herself to stand taller, straighter. "I will fight you until my dying breath," she spat, her voice trembling but resolute. "By the gods, I swear it—I will never stop resisting you."

Ealric's smirk wavered, his expression hardening as a shadow of malice darkened his features. The mocking amusement that had played on his face vanished, leaving behind something far more sinister. His voice, once smooth and taunting, turned sharp and cruel. "Very well," he said. "But understand this—if you choose defiance, you will do so without the comfort of your brother."

He stepped closer, his looming figure casting a menacing shadow over her. His voice dropped to a venomous whisper, heavy with calculated cruelty. "I will ensure you never see him again. That is a promise. The choice is yours."

Estrith's chest tightened, her breath caught between defiance and despair. It was a cruelty beyond measure, forcing her into a choice where freedom came at the cost of another form of enslavement. She couldn't bear to look at him any longer—this man who embodied everything vile and detestable, who wrapped his threats in the guise of twisted mercy. Yet, to risk never seeing Siged again, to abandon the only family she had left, was an unbearable sacrifice.

Silence stretched between them, heavy and suffocating. Estrith lowered her gaze, her thoughts a tumult of fear, anger, and helplessness. Ealric, mistaking her silence for surrender, exhaled through his nose, his disappointment evident in the sharp tilt of his head.

"Very well," he said cooly, the faintest edge of disdain lacing his words. He turned on his heel, his boots echoing softly against the stone floor as he began to walk away.

The sound of his retreating footsteps struck something deep within Estrith—a desperate, primal urge that forced her lips to move before she could stop them.

"Wait," she called out, her voice cracking under the weight of her plea.

The oppressive dungeon air clung to Estrith as her captors led her from its dark, damp depths. Her legs trembled with weakness, her steps faltering on the uneven stone floor. Each movement felt as if it might betray her, but she gritted her teeth, forcing herself forward. Torchlight flickered along the walls, casting fleeting shadows over her anxious form. Loose strands of her hair clung to her damp skin, a testament to the suffocating chill she was leaving behind.

Behind her, muffled cries and whispers echoed, the hollow sounds of despair fading as the heavy iron door swung shut with a final, reverberating clang. The sound sent a shiver down her spine—a cruel punctuation to her departure from the prison's grip.

The cold air pricked her skin as they emerged into the open courtyard, but it was the sudden assault of daylight that made her recoil. After days in darkness, the brightness stung her eyes, forcing them to squint against the harsh glare. She blinked rapidly, her breath catching as the scene before her came into focus.

At the head of the courtyard stood Sidonis, his figure commanding and stark against the imposing palace gates behind him. He stood like a monolith, his presence cold and unyielding. To his side, Elwin loomed, his broad shoulders squared with authority. Yet, his narrowed eyes betrayed his growing impatience, his gloved fingers drumming against the hilt of his sword.

Flanking the two men were Alfric and Ealric. Estrith's stomach churned as her gaze fell on Ealric, his smug grin a sharp contrast to the frail boy standing silently at his side. His hand rested possessively on Siged's bony shoulder, a mockery of protection. Siged's head tilted downward, his slight frame trembling as if a gust of wind might topple him. The sight sent a sharp pang through Estrith's chest, a wave of helpless fury and despair crashing over her.

Her eyes swept across the courtyard, taking in the line of prisoners gathered there. Their faces bore the unmistakable marks of despair—hollow cheeks, downcast gazes, and the haunted expressions of people stripped of hope.

A sudden commotion broke the grim tableau, drawing Estrith's attention to the far end of the courtyard.

Richessa appeared, her once-impeccable regality reduced to shreds. Her red hair flew wildly as she struggled against the guards who flanked her. Despite the disheveled state of her gown, she clung fiercely to the last vestiges of her dignity, her movements defiant even in the face of her captors.

"Unhand me!" she shrieked, her voice cutting through the somber air like a jagged blade. She twisted in their grasp, her eyes blazing as she strained toward Sidonis. "Sidonis!" Her voice cracked, raw with desperation. "You promised me—us—a future! You swore we would rule together!"

Sidonis barely turned his head, his expression colder than the frost biting at the morning air. His disinterest was sharper than any verbal rebuke. With a single, dismissive gesture, he directed the guards to remove her.

Richessa's protests grew louder, her voice rising with each step the guards dragged her closer to the line of prisoners. "Sidonis! You swore—" Her cries faded into the background, drowned out by the quiet efficiency of soldiers carrying out their orders. Sidonis did not spare her a second glance.

The sound of approaching footsteps drew Estrith's gaze toward the palace gates. A procession of armored soldiers marched forward, their polished silver gleaming in the sunlight. At their center was a woman whose presence commanded immediate attention.

Tannica.

Draped in silken robes of deep blue, Tannica moved with an elegance that seemed at odds with the hardness in her eyes. The fabric of her gown flowed around her like water, shimmering faintly with each step. Her chin was held high, her posture regal, but there was a coldness to her that Estrith had not seen before—a stoicism forged in pain.

Estrith's heart sank as she watched Elwin approach Tannica with a calculated smile. He took her hand, guiding her toward Sidonis as if presenting her as a trophy. Sidonis bowed deeply, taking Tannica's hand in his own and pressing a courtly kiss to her knuckles.

"Lady Tannica," Sidonis said, his voice rich with practiced charm. "I had heard tales of your beauty, but even the most extravagant words fail to do you justice."

Tannica's expression remained unreadable, her eyes never meeting Estrith's. Yet the unspoken weight of the moment bore down on her like a collapsing sky. Tannica's presence was not one of rescue—it was of submission, of alliances made and futures exchanged. Estrith's chest tightened, a fissure of betrayal splintering through her resolve.

The courtyard was filled with movement, but for Estrith, time felt frozen.

Estrith watched as Tannica bowed, her movements deliberate but heavy with reluctance. The faint tension in her posture betrayed the forced nature of the act, though her expression remained composed, a mask of acceptance.

"Your bride," Elwin proclaimed, his voice ringing through the courtyard like a funeral bell. "The seal of peace between Faermire and Valenmur."

Estrith's world shifted, the solid ground beneath her seeming to give way as her vision blurred. The courtyard around her faded into an indistinct haze, the figures and sounds merging into a distant hum. Her lips parted to speak, but the words withered on her tongue. She stood frozen, her mind racing to bridge the chasm between the resolute figure before her and the friend she had come to cherish—a woman who had once loved her brother with a passion now seemingly extinguished.

Tannica's gaze flickered briefly toward Estrith, but it darted away just as quickly, as though the weight of meeting her eyes was unbearable. That fleeting glance, filled with unspoken emotion, twisted the knife in Estrith's chest.

"This is madness," Estrith whispered, her voice breaking on the words, though they barely carried over the heavy silence.

At her side, Richessa gasped, the sound raw and guttural, as if a part of her spirit had been ripped away. Her trembling hand gripped her disheveled dress, seeking an anchor amid the chaos.

If Tannica heard them, she gave no indication. She stepped forward to stand beside Sidonis, her silken gown flowing like water over stone. Sidonis placed a hand on the small of her back, the gesture one of ownership rather than affection. "With this union," he declared, his voice resonating with false conviction, "we will ensure a future of stability and prosperity."

Richessa's laughter shattered the stillness, sharp and venomous. "A union of stability?" she spat, her voice dripping with derision as she wrestled against her captors. "You replace me with her and call it peace? You're nothing but a—"

The crack of a guard's hand silenced her mid-sentence. The blow sent her head snapping to the side, her fiery hair spilling over her face as she recoiled in shock and pain. For a moment, her defiance faltered, her breath coming in ragged gasps.

Sidonis barely spared her a glance, his cold indifference cutting deeper than any blow. The other figures in the courtyard shifted uncomfortably but did not intervene. Richessa's dignity lay in tatters, and yet, in the trembling set of her jaw, a flicker of resistance still burned.

With their final matters settled, Elwin exhaled heavily, the sound weighted with impatience. His sharp gaze turned to the prisoners, sweeping over them with the detached scrutiny of a man assessing livestock. "Sort through them," he commanded, his tone cold and devoid of empathy. "Dispose of any too weak or feeble for the journey." His gloved hand rose, pointing with unyielding precision toward Siged. "Starting with that one."

Estrith's blood ran cold. Her brother, standing frail and silent beside Ealric, seemed even smaller under Elwin's scrutiny. Ealric hesitated, his hand tightening slightly on Siged's shoulder, his face flickering with a rare moment of uncertainty. But before he could speak, Estrith surged forward.

"No!" Her voice cut through the tension, trembling but resolute. Every eye in the courtyard turned to her, the weight of their stares pressing down like a physical force. Her hands balled into fists at her sides, her body taut with desperation. "He's cursed."

A murmur rippled through the assembled crowd, and Elwin turned to face her fully, his brow furrowing in annoyance. "Then all the more reason to rid ourselves of the burden," he replied coolly, his dismissive tone striking like a whip.

Estrith's heart pounded, but she held her ground. "If he dies," she said, her voice quaking, "the curse will fall upon you. I swear it."

The courtyard fell into a tense silence. Her words lingered in the air, like a challenge cast at their feet. Sidonis arched an eyebrow, his expression skeptically amused, but before anyone could voice dismissal, another voice broke the quiet.

"She speaks true," Tannica said, stepping forward. Her tone was steady, though her eyes betrayed a flicker of something—sympathy, or perhaps shame. "I've seen it myself, Father. His affliction... it's not natural. Ignoring her warning would be unwise."

Elwin's frown deepened, his lips pressing into a thin line as he considered her words. For a moment, the silence stretched unbearably, and then he waved a dismissive hand. "Fine. The boy lives—for now."

Estrith exhaled sharply, her knees nearly buckling under the weight of relief. She cast a fleeting glance toward Tannica, but her former friend refused to meet her gaze. In the hard set of her jaw, Estrith thought she glimpsed regret, but it vanished as quickly as it had appeared.

Beside her, Richessa sagged in the guards' grip, her relief audible in the trembling breath she released. But the moment of reprieve was short-lived as their captors began herding them into place for the march to Valenmur.

Estrith moved to Siged's side, her trembling hands gripping his thin arm as she helped lift him onto a wooden cart. The boy was silent as ever, his vacant eyes unfocused, but she leaned close, her voice a soft whisper meant only for him. "I will protect you. No matter what."

Before long, the order rang out, and the caravan lurched into motion, moving like a weary, segmented creature. Each step felt like another nail driven into the coffin of their fate, and Estrith fought to steady herself, clinging to the fragile threads of her composure.

The gates loomed ahead, and as they passed through, the vast expanse of Faermire unfolded before them—a land she had once cherished now blurred by sorrow. Behind them, the towering walls of Elsterheim stood silent and unyielding with the lingering echoes of defeat.

Estrith pulled her cloak tightly around her, seeking solace in its meager warmth as the weight of loss pressed heavier on her shoulders.

The sharp rattle of chains clashed against the quiet stillness of the morning, a cruel counterpoint to the faint rustle of the wind threading through the brittle branches of winter trees. Estrith trudged forward, her wrists encased in iron cuffs that bit cruelly into her skin with each step. Around her, the prisoners shuffled like a slow-moving tide of despair, their heads bowed low, their faces pale and etched with exhaustion.

At the head of the caravan, Elwin and Alfric rode astride their horses, their figures imposing as they guided the group through the narrow, frozen trail that wound through the forest. Behind them, Ealric lingered with calculated precision, his steady pace keeping him just ahead of the prisoners. Occasionally, his gaze flicked back, settling on Estrith. Whether his glance held malice, amusement, or some twisted form of guardianship, she couldn't say, but its presence was suffocating.

Richessa walked beside her, their chains binding them together in a grim mockery of unity. Despite the frayed and soiled state of her once-immaculate gown, Richessa held herself with an unbroken poise, her chin lifted in defiance of the humiliation thrust upon her. Even in chains, she wore the remnants of her regal pride like armor, though Estrith saw the cracks forming beneath the surface.

Estrith's stomach churned at their proximity. To be shackled to the very woman who despised her, and whom she equally loathed, was an irony too bitter to savor. Yet here they were, side by side, bound by circumstance and a shared fate, trudging toward a distant land that offered neither of them hope.

Siged sat atop a wagon laden with supplies, his frail frame wrapped tightly in a fur cloak that Estrith had begged from one of the guards. He remained silent and still, his vacant gaze fixed on nothing, a haunting portrait of fragility.

The caravan moved onward, the frozen ground crunching beneath their feet, the trail narrowing as the forest grew denser around them. The guards barked orders, their voices cutting through the cold air like whips, driving the prisoners forward with merciless efficiency. Estrith forced herself to keep moving, her breaths shallow and ragged as the chill seeped deeper into her bones.

As the sun climbed higher, pale beams of light pierced through the skeletal branches overhead, casting long, fragmented shadows across the group. Estrith kept her eyes forward, trying to focus on each step, each moment, as a means to block out the misery around her. But then, something shifted in her periphery.

At first, it was little more than a shadow, slipping in and out of sight at the edges of her vision. But as her eyes adjusted, the figure sharpened, its ethereal form flickering like a flame caught in the wind. Estrith's heart clenched as recognition struck her with a cold, unyielding force.

Eldra.

The spectral figure moved with an unnatural grace, gliding through the spaces between the prisoners and guards as though she existed in a realm just beyond their reality. Her translucent form shimmered faintly, and her hollow, orange eyes locked onto Estrith with an intensity that sent a shiver down her spine.

She faltered, her chains pulling taut as her knees threatened to buckle. Her breath hitched in her throat, the cold air now a dagger in her lungs. She blinked, hoping the apparition would vanish like a phantom conjured by her exhausted mind. But Eldra remained, her presence a chilling reminder of forces far beyond mortal comprehension.

Beside her, Richessa stiffened. Estrith turned her head slightly, enough to see the ashen pallor of her stepmother's face and the wide, terrified eyes fixed on the same spectral figure. Richessa's lips parted as if to speak, but no words came.

"You see her too," Estrith whispered, her voice barely audible over the clinking of chains. Her tone was a fragile thread of fear and desperation.

Richessa's gaze snapped toward her, the terror in her expression betraying her denial. "I see nothing," she replied sharply, though the tremor in her voice gave her away.

Estrith's stomach churned. "You do," she insisted, her voice trembling. "I can see it on your face, Richessa."

"Silence!" one of the guards barked, his sharp tone silencing any further exchange.

Estrith's protective instincts flared despite her restraints. She moved slightly closer to Siged's wagon, angling herself between the boy and the ghostly presence. Richessa, clutching her tattered cloak, cast furtive glances at the specter, her composure crumbling with every step.

The guards seemed oblivious to the spectral figure drifting just beyond their perception, their sharp voices and rigid movements incongruous with the silent, looming menace of Eldra. The specter paused ahead of them, her translucent form flickering like a dying ember. Her gaze lingered on Estrith and Richessa, unreadable but heavy with an otherworldly intensity.

And then, as suddenly as she had appeared, Eldra began to fade. Her form dissolved into the skeletal trees, leaving behind a void of unease that seemed to chill the air even further.

Estrith swallowed hard, her pulse thundering in her ears. Her steps grew heavier as the weight of Eldra's presence settled into her thoughts like a stone dropped into still water.

Richessa's regal facade shattered completely, her breaths shallow and uneven. She cast a fleeting glance at Estrith, and for the first time, there was no disdain or bitterness in her expression—only fear. In that moment, they shared an unspoken understanding.

The caravan pressed on, but the shadow of Eldra lingered, an unseen shroud over their journey into the unknown.

The ridge offered a solitary perch, a bleak vantage point where the wind howled with icy teeth, gnawing at Beowyn's face and cutting through the threadbare resolve he clung to. He stood motionless, his silhouette sharp against the pale hues of dawn, his gaze locked on the distant outline of Elsterheim. The city that had once been his home, his stronghold, now lay cloaked in a shroud of smoke, its proud towers reduced to shadowed remnants. Wisps of ash danced with the wind, carrying with them the bitter tang of loss and ruin.

The snow crunched faintly as Qereth approached, his steps measured, deliberate. He halted beside Beowyn, his breath escaping in visible plumes, his presence a quiet but steady reminder that even in the depths of despair, he was not alone. For a long moment, they stood in silence, the weight of unspoken grief stretching between them like an unbridgeable chasm.

"They're ready," Qereth said finally, his voice low and steady, as if afraid to disturb the fragile stillness of the morning.

Beowyn didn't answer right away. His jaw tightened, and his eyes remained fixed on the faint silhouette of Elsterheim against the horizon. Smoke curled upward in ghostly tendrils, mingling with the first light of dawn. The city, now little more than a distant memory, seemed to mock him—a reminder of what he had failed to protect.

"Where are we to go, Qereth?" Beowyn's voice broke the silence, rough and laden with weariness. "There is no one left to help us. We've become fugitives in our own lands."

Qereth's sharp blue eyes swept across the landscape, his expression unreadable but resolute. "We'll head south," he said firmly, his words carrying the weight of a man determined to carve hope out of despair. "To a place where your face won't be recognized. We'll gather strength, rebuild, and, after a time, we will return to reclaim what is rightfully ours."

Beowyn turned to face him, doubt flickering in his eyes. "I cannot leave them," he said, his voice barely above a whisper. Estrith and Siged's faces loomed in his mind, fragile and vulnerable, trapped behind those distant walls. The ache in his chest deepened, a heavy thrum of guilt and helplessness. "I cannot abandon them."

Qereth stepped closer, placing a hand on Beowyn's shoulder, his grip firm and grounding. "We will return," he said, his voice unyielding. "For them. For all of them. I swear it."

For a long moment, Beowyn stood frozen, the words echoing in his mind like a faint bell in the fog. He tightened his grip on the hilt of his sword, the cold steel grounding him as his thoughts churned in restless turmoil. Slowly, reluctantly, he nodded, though the gesture was burdened with quiet resignation.

"Elsterheim..." he murmured, the name barely audible, a vow wrapped in grief.

The cold wind at his back urged him forward as he turned and followed Qereth toward the gathered survivors. They huddled together in clusters, their faces pale and gaunt, etched with exhaustion and fear. Their eyes, hollow but searching, flicked toward him as he approached. Beowyn's heart clenched. These were his people—broken, scattered, but alive. And he owed them more than he could ever repay.

The faint clatter of movement and muted murmurs filled the still morning air as the survivors prepared to leave the ridge. Beowyn walked among them, his steps heavy but deliberate. They were fractured remnants of a kingdom, but they were still his to protect.

As they began their retreat, Beowyn cast one final glance over his shoulder. Elsterheim's outline loomed in the distance, its smoldering ruin a grim silhouette against the pale dawn. The ridge grew quieter, the echoes of their footsteps faded into the trees. But within Beowyn's chest, something stirred—a spark, small but fierce, igniting in the ashes of defeat.

This was not the end.

He turned his face southward, his steps purposeful as the caravan moved forward. Though the shadow of loss lingered behind them, Beowyn's heart carried the embers of resolve that would one day blaze into the fire of reclamation.

THE PEOPLE OF AECORATH

A guide to the rulers, warriors, and spirits shaping the fate of Aecorath.

Kingdom of Faermire

Beowyn – King of Faermire, son of Ludica, struggling with his rule and haunted by past decisions.

Estrith – Twin sister of Beowyn, a sharp-minded strategist, determined to save their younger brother.

Siged – Their younger brother, afflicted with a supernatural ailment linked to dark forces.

Ludica – The former King of Faermire, slain in battle, his legacy casting a long shadow over his son.

Kingdom of Valenmur

Tannica – Daughter of Elwin, once betrothed to Beowyn, torn between love and loyalty to her father.

Elwin – King of Valenmur, a ruthless and calculating ruler with ambitions beyond his borders.

Alfric & Ealric – Tannica's brothers, loyal to their father and fierce warriors.

Kingdom of Mistelfeld

Gwenora – Queen of Mistelfeld, a formidable ruler and a key player in the kingdom's shifting power struggles.

Ordric – A staunch opponent of Gwenora's rule, challenging her authority in Mistelfeld.

Kingdom of Abensloh

Ceolfrid – King of Abensloh, a relentless force in war, seeking to expand his dominion.

Kingdom of Helmere

Nurrock – A towering giant, King of Helmere, and a fearsome warrior allied with Ceolfrid.

Allies and Advisors

Sgell – A trusted advisor from Aecorath, known for his wisdom and loyalty to Beowyn and Estrith.

Qereth – Close friend to Beowyn and Estrith, Emissary to Mistelfeld.

The Supernatural

Eldra (Zemrapha) – An ancient, malevolent entity that feeds on its host, threatening Siged's life.

Manoth – A god associated with fate and sacrifice, worshiped and feared in equal measure.

Other Notable Figures

Sidonis – Brother of Ludica, bound to supernatural forces, struggling between his own ambition and the will of the gods.

Richessa – The imprisoned former queen, mother of Siged, whose past betrayals continue to cast a shadow.

Haemund – A skeptical elder in Beowyn's court, wary of outside influence and political shifts.

Gorhan – A mysterious seer, serving dark forces and wielding ancient magic.

Helgisson – Leader of Graefeld and ally of Gwenora, a key political figure in Mistelfeld

ACKNOWLEDGEMENTS

A work such as this is never created in isolation. Along the way, many have helped shape its path—offering insight, challenges, and support in ways both great and small. Some provided direction when the road ahead was uncertain, while others gave quiet encouragement that carried further than they may ever know.

To those who contributed their thoughts, their time, and their keen eyes—your influence is woven into these pages. To those who offered guidance, whether through conversation, critique, or simply standing by when the weight of creation grew heavy, your support has made all the difference.

To my Wise Counselor—You are beyond words, wonderful in every way. In patience, You have walked beside me; in kindness, You have steadied my steps. When the path was uncertain, Your encouragement became my foundation, Your love my refuge.

Thank You for being my light in the darkness, for lifting me when no one else could, and for carrying me through when my strength was not enough. No words could ever capture the depth of my gratitude—for all You have done, for all You continue to do, and for the love that never fails.

There is no greater love than that which is given through Your presence, a love that sustains, strengthens, and restores.

And finally, to the readers—those who journey beyond these words and into the world within—this story is now yours. May it carry you to places unknown, as all the best stories do.

About the Author

Tabitha Min has always believed that stories—whether spoken or written—carry a magic all their own, one that lingers long after the final word is read.

What began as a single book and a small table at events has since grown into a thriving business, where she brings storytelling to life through handcrafted items and artwork. Her love of writing has expanded beyond the page, weaving itself into the curiosities she creates, each piece a testament to the worlds that inspire her.

When she's not caring for her young children or tending to the home, she can usually be found immersed in her business or lost in the next chapter of a new story.

But the journey is far from over. To discover more about her work, her creations, and the stories yet to come, visit www.tabithamin.com.

OTHER WORKS BY TABITHA MIN

DAWN OF AVARICE -Book 1 (2023)

Ludica, king of Faermire, has devoted years to building a powerful legacy for his three children. But when the sudden death of a rival king stirs whispers of conflict across the land, Ludica realizes that threats to his reign are closer than he imagined—both beyond his borders and within them.

As Gwenora, the widowed queen, offers Ludica a treaty to secure peace, they both recognize that such an alliance risk inciting rebellion among their own people.

Meanwhile, Ludica's eldest children, Beowyn and Estrith, uncover a plot involving their uncle and stepmother, aimed at seizing the throne. Yet, in bringing the truth to light, they face consequences that threaten to unravel the world around them.

With treasonous alliances, deadly conspiracies, and fractured loyalties at every turn, Ludica and his family must rely on each other to hold their places in the kingdom of Aecorath—or risk losing everything they hold dear.

Scan the QR code to step beyond the page and immerse yourself in the animated audiobook of *Dawn of Avarice*. Watch the story unfold with captivating narration, rich sound design, and stunning visuals that bring the world of Aecorath to life.

HARU'S WORLD – Children's book (2024)

Haru, a little toadstool mushroom, comes to life when a sprinkle of magical dust falls from an ancient oak tree. Awakened to a world of wonder, Haru embarks on a journey of discovery, seeing everything through new eyes and making delightful friends along the way.

Stay up to date with the latest projects, upcoming releases, and handcrafted creations. Whether it's new additions to the *Siege of Aecorath* series, exclusive artwork, or unique, story-inspired items from **The Curious Emporium**, there is always something new on the horizon. Explore current works, discover what's to come, and be the first to know about future adventures. Join the journey and step into a world where stories take shape beyond the page.

Books are available for purchase **directly through the website** or can be found on **Amazon.com**.

Visit **www.tabithamin.com** to learn more.